Outside-in

Mick Gallolgy

Published in Australia in 2017 by Michael English

Disclaimer
All characters and events in this publication, other than those clearly in the public domain, are fictitious and any resemblance to real persons, living or dead, is purely coincidental.

National Library of Australia Cataloguing-in-Publication entry:

Author:	Gallogly, Mick – author.
Title:	Outside-in.
ISBN:	9780987613905 (paperback)
Subjects:	Mentally ill – Fiction.
	People with mental disabilities – Fiction.
	Institutional care – Fiction.

For dads.

Children, do not judge fathers too harshly when they have gone. You alone will be able to measure the extent of their absence. Know this: they were never paranoid … everyone *was* out to get them!

Chapter One

If compelled to nominate a leader of our exclusive gang of inmates it would have to be *Brains*. His outside name is Greg, but as we have little occasion to fraternise when not inside, outside names are cast off as an irrelevance. While he might not be considered an alpha male in the real world, he's the closest to alpha we have. He's at least a beta. Among his many skills, Brains speaks several languages, including Klingon and American. He can only curse in most of them, but it still counts. During our regular get-togethers he proves himself pretty much the sharpest in the group. Most of the time.

Brains isn't bad looking, and he knows it. We notice he gets the odd interested look from some of the newer female inmates. He's tall, well built and otherwise unmarked. He's well aware that he tends towards the athletic which is why he often wears tee-shirts a size too small. We suspect that Brains uses the gym for its intended purpose, although he's never been caught. He was born and raised in Birkenhead. Anyone who alleged he was from nearby Liverpool got a ready-made and often repeated threatening lecture on the geography of the Wirral Peninsula. He describes his home as being on "the right side of the water". He then describes the right side of the water for Liverpudlians to be "under". Brains is one of the longer-serving inmates in our group. His combination of wit and longevity qualify him as the bestower of nicknames on those new arrivals considered worthy. For instance, when Eddy first arrived he was vetted for potential fellowship. As Eddy's probationary period drew to a satisfactory conclusion, Brains mentioned his bowed legs. Or as Brains, in fact, remarked, '*Baise-moi*; those legs couldn't stop a greasy pig in a narrow corridor!'

Thereafter, Eddy was called *Legs*. The award of a nickname isn't an insult; rather it is intended as a badge of acceptance by the group: a *nom de guerre*. Bestowing a pseudonym occurs once a probationary period has elapsed and a reasonable level of familiarity established. While not intended to give offence, there has been one notable exception to the rule. That exception is Ray – a barely-tolerated member of the gang, and I do mean *member*. Ray was christened *Knob*, not because he possesses a noteworthy appendage but because no-one likes him. He proves himself an obnoxious snitch and a *Topper*. No matter what anyone has done, seen or heard, he always relates a superior anecdote.

If half of his tales are a quarter true then this Nobel Prize rejecting, part-time assassin, full-time scourge of super models is at least 200 years old to have done everything he claims – he was the second gunman on the grassy knoll. Knob is also a sneaky bastard. Within the group he is more often called *Nobby*, particularly when within earshot of the general population. The facility staff discourages the use of profanity, claiming to protect the sensibilities of the more delicate inmates.

Nobby is flabby and of average height. He was raised on the central Wales coast. He wears thick-lensed, heavy-framed glasses which hide a sizeable portion of his face, for which we are grateful. On the occasions when he removes his glasses to wipe them with his grubby shirt, there will be a barrage of "requests" for him to replace them at once. He has the overall aspect of a wax figure that spends too much time in the sunlight. A wax figure that disregards sound advice to wear high SPF sunblock. The droopiness of his expression has the appearance of someone who has simultaneously suffered strokes to both sides of his face. While Brains looks nothing like the character of the same name from *Thunderbirds*, Nobby bears a striking resemblance to the character *Parker*. Perhaps Nobby looks less realistic. Nobby's heritage is often called into question. His outlandish claims relating to his genealogy do nothing to discourage the scepticism within the gang.

His family tree would have to be the most complex in history, with an infinite number of branches; greater than the most mighty and ancient oak. His claimed DNA consists of contributions from the very best and brightest the human race could offer. I remember well one of his early announcements. I had mentioned that I was a very distant relation to Winston Churchill. During a short lull in the subsequent name-dropping, Nobby announced, 'I'm a blood relative of Lawrence of Arabia.'

After a moment of stunned silence, Brains responded. '*Cojones* you are. You might be related to his camel!'

Legs agreed. 'Yeah, I've seen Nobby's birth certificate. In the section for father's name it says "Some zoo animals".'

'Well, you don't have to believe me if you don't want, but it's true.'

'Thank you so much for giving me permission to believe you're a lying bastard. So kind of you,' Brains said, heavy on the sarcasm. 'Anyway, aren't you from Aberystwyth?'

'Yeah, so what? Lawrence of Arabia was born in Wales.'

'But he's famous for his Arabian exploits. Maybe you should call yourself "Nobby of Aberystwyth"?'

'You're just jealous!' was Nobby's final word.

Nobby of Aberystwyth never took off. There were too many candidate names to choose from because of his regular claims of blood-relation to everyone from Albert Einstein to Alexander the Great ('so that makes you "Nobby the Crap"?'). They say blood is thicker than water; well, Nobby is thicker than both.

We'd been surprised to learn that Nobby was *not* a Manchester United supporter. It didn't earn him any points but if he *had* been a United supporter it would have been end-times for Nobby. Harbouring a United supporter is beyond the tolerance of the group. Nobby isn't the loudest or the sneakiest bastard in the gang. He isn't even the ugliest or the smelliest. There are other people who lay claim to those particular accolades. Nobby, however, is the second-loudest, second-sneakiest, second-ugliest and second-smelliest in the group. If the possession of undesirable characteristics had been a sport then Nobby wouldn't be a specialist, but he would be an Olympic gold-medal-winning decathlete. To be fair to the other speciality gold-medallists in the group, at least they have other redeeming features to sweeten the deal.

Nobby was only able to latch onto our gang in his own unique, parasitic manner due to a perfect storm of circumstances. Well, a light shower and a gentle breeze; it was two circumstances to be precise. Firstly, he shares a room with one of the foremost associates of the gang. Secondly, and of much more import, Nobby proved to have an admirable appreciation of one of the principal values of the gang. The fact that he revealed his single redeeming feature before his numerous repellent features became apparent didn't do him any harm either. It was all the fault of Felicity Kendal's Bottom.

* * * *

Most of the time there are six or seven of us in the gang, dependent upon who's outside on parole. While there's an informal selection process of sorts, there are no particular criteria or qualifications required for membership of the group. The fact that we're all residents of the facility provides us with one significant common factor. We gravitated together not so much because of things in common, but rather due to a lack of reasons to *not* drift together. In a place where we found ourselves because we have problems belonging on the outside, we're less fussy about finding reasons to belong on the inside. That being said, once Nobby had been able to attach himself to the group, we learnt some valuable lessons and were thereafter more conscientious about the vetting process.

Being residents of the facility doesn't mean that my fellow gang members and I are simple-minded. It could be argued that we are *like-minded* in that our minds are fucked. We're probably a representative cross-section of the average arseholes you might find on the street, particularly if you're inattentive. I believe our difficulties lie not in a lack of general knowledge or in a poor understanding of the world at large. I believe they lie in our inability to cope with life's unexpected challenges. Where others are able to deal with adversity when it calls, we are less well-equipped. In all fairness, some of us have been thrust into situations that would test the coping mechanisms of even the hardiest to their limits. If the rest of the gang were bothered to give the matter as much consideration as I have, I'm sure they'd agree.

Brains provides the intellectual mainstay of the gang, but as the thinker, I represent the philosophical and moral barometer. I am expected to judge if someone has *gone too far*. For this reason, and not because I resemble the Rodin sculpture, I was, for a short time, called *Penseur* by Brains. At the time he was trying a little too hard to inject a touch of the cosmopolitan. Fortunately, the name didn't take and Brains instead decided the moniker *Silent* was more fitting. The gang recognises that I am cautious about when I contribute verbally and when I do I'm economical with my words. I will speak when I have no other reasonable option available, such as shrugging, nodding or general grunting. I was judged as falling under the *strong but silent* category, with the emphasis on *silent*. I was without doubt the quiet one of what can be a somewhat loud bunch. I was comfortable with being the representative of *silent*. Being the representative of *strong* might be too much responsibility. I don't need the pressure.

Some topics are without exception taboo and there's an unspoken understanding to that effect. We don't discuss the details of what led to us ending up inside. Once inside, however, anything done or said within earshot of any gang member is fair game and open to "analysis". There have been times when what started as light-hearted banter morphed into something more serious. Physical confrontation is considered unacceptable behaviour, although threats of violence are treated with the disdain they deserve. Interestingly, the moral barometer is quite flexible. When the alleged offended party is Nobby, the barometer is set very high indeed. Nobody objects, other than Nobby.

All of the gang are aged in their twenties, so we're of a comparable generation. Having been raised in the same part of the world, we've also had similar cultural exposure during our formative years. Something else we share is an appreciation of the culture of years gone by, in particular the music and television shows of decades ago. One particular example is the sitcom *The Good Life* from the mid-seventies. The show had not come to our attention through the classic sitcom graveyard of late-night television re-runs. Rather, it had been discovered as a box set of videos among the eclectic selection of videos available inside.

After a few episodes there was one aspect of the show that held us captivated. Of most important note was Felicity Kendal's Bottom, or FKB as it became known. The deserved legendary status of Felicity's 1981 Rear-of-the-year was something the entire group agreed upon without dissent. FKB was something more than simply an idol. It represented an aspiration that we all shared. The idea that unofficial wet-blanket-of-every-year Richard Briers, who played Tom, could marry Felicity Kendal's Barbara and her bottom made us feel that even the most ambitious dream was attainable. We didn't let the fact that they were characters from a sitcom, and not real life, lessen our wonder at the possibilities of our existence.

One evening, not long after Nobby attached himself to the gang, we took over the TV lounge, as we were inclined to do, and settled in for some therapeutic viewing of *The Good Life*. We watched the familiar goings-on between the characters unfold; the innocent mis-understandings and the understated sexual tension between Tom and his neighbour Margo. We often remarked in disbelief that Tom could even feign the potential for unfaithfulness to FKB. We all agreed the writers contemplated an altogether implausible situation suggesting Tom would look elsewhere than FKB, even if momentarily and in jest. As we watched one scene develop, Barbara entered stage left and bent to remove her freshly baked bread from their rustic range. It was at this point that Nobby felt obliged to comment.

'That's Felicity Kendal, isn't it? Didn't her bum win some contest?'

Nobody spoke; nobody moved. Time stood still. The sudden tension in the room was palpable. The next words from Nobby's mouth had to be heard unambiguously by all. His fate was now in his own hands. We all waited with bated breath to hear what would originate from Nobby with tainted breath.

'Yeah, I can see why she won. Her bottom is kind of ... *perfect*,' Nobby said as a look of awe crossed his face. He had passed through the valley of shadow uninjured. He had, consciously or not, chosen his words with care and had spoken righteously. While he wasn't *in*, he wasn't *out* either. Now he could be *tolerated*.

I suppose we all like to think it's possible for us to one day share life with an FKB of our own. In fact, I would consider being able to spoon Felicity's perfect botty every night as not *The Good Life* but *The Bloody Great Life*. I could never dream of violating such a venerable icon through physical possession or by giving way to other vulgar urges. I would gladly spend my entire life nurturing, protecting and worshipping my charge. But it would be a constant struggle to avoid staring overlong, as would be the most overwhelming temptation. The brilliance of FKB would fill me with fear of being stricken blind, like staring too long at the sun. Oh, but what a way to lose sight; with a final vision of FKB forever trapped behind ruined eyes to illuminate the perpetual darkness.

During my frequent and extensive musings regarding FKB, I never contemplated that any offensive sound or smell could emanate from such a wonderful corporeal vessel. It's implausible that FKB could be capable of any vulgar function associated with the common-or-garden bottom. Indeed, if this Holy Grail of body parts was capable of such function then I imagine the sound would be that of an angel serenading and soothing the most troubled soul. It would be a beacon call to any lost soul searching for aural sanctuary. Any aroma emitted could only be rivalled by the most fragrant perfume, hinting at the most wondrous scents that nature could produce. A suggestion of the first flowers of spring or the hint of rain at the end of a long, hot summer's day. FKB was indeed a bottom for all seasons. A panacea for the masses.

It wasn't simply a common appreciation of the bodily parts of sitcom actresses that brought us together. We all have a finer appreciation of the culture of decades past than we do for the present day. One possible explanation of why we appreciate the popular culture of years gone by is that we want to believe a time existed when we *could* have

7

fitted in. That there was a time when the culture was tailored for our enjoyment. The notion gives me some consolation. If I believe that my troubles are all about timing, then I feel better about not fitting in with the present. I was in the right place, I'd simply arrived too late. In fact, I was so late that the fat lady had not only sung but she had performed a couple of encores to rapturous applause, removed her make-up, got changed and had a few drinkies at the after-performance party. She had also been felt up by the art director in the back of the taxi on the way to the hotel, had finished off both Toblerones in the bar fridge, brushed her teeth, flossed, gargled and was now fast asleep in bed. That's how late I had arrived.

Chapter Two

I was born into humble beginnings, the only child of a father who worked in an auto-parts factory and a mother that I never knew. I was marked at birth by a physical uniqueness brought about through a myostatin deficiency. This very particular deficiency led to a considerable overdevelopment of the musculature of my back. At birth the midwife knew something was not right with me, a reaction I have had to deal with all my life. My lot is such that my back possesses over twice the muscle mass of the average male, giving me a somewhat incongruous appearance. I am a sheep in wolf's clothing.

I am a reflective person and I expend much mental energy analysing common sayings or phrases. One saying I find most relevant is "Don't judge a book by its cover". The saying must have transpired because it's what people tend to do when they encounter someone new. It provides a simple but perhaps erroneous approach. To be fair, you'd have to read the whole book before being able to say with conviction, "Well, that cover is unrepresentative of what the discerning reader could expect to find within". The particular and very personal issue I have with this saying is that my front cover and back cover do not match. They're not even close. From the front I am a book of average appearance; a not too demanding read. Light fare suited to a day at the beach. From the back, however, I am a nightmare-inspired Gothic horror from Lovecraft or Poe. My cover has the appearance of a mix-up at the printers on a bad day; maybe a Friday afternoon after a long liquid lunch.

Mick Gallogly

For as long as I can remember I have endured the puzzled looks of passers-by. These looks are from those people that approach me from behind then wanting to see how I appear from the front. They see the overly muscular back being carried about on average-looking legs that appear thinner than they are when compared to the bulk they carry. So many times I see the expression of open surprise when they realise my monstrous back is not coupled to a monstrous front. From time to time I detect a hint of disappointment in their expression. Perhaps if I was *monstrous* instead of *odd* their sighting would make a more interesting tale that night in the pub. My posture has been shaped by how I believe others perceive me. I have affected a stance I believe presents a frame as close to normal as I can accomplish. I assume a somewhat stooped bearing with shoulders pushed back in an attempt to conceal my bulk. It's the best I can do, but I know it's not near enough to normal to go unnoticed. At best the net result is that passers-by don't stare as long as they might.

I was born in an industrial city in the midlands of England but relocated to Wales with Dad before I was old enough to "appreciate" my birthplace. According to Dad, my hometown benefited from major renovation work, funded under the urban renewal programme. It was at this point that it was upgraded to a "dump". He told me stories of how the locals were able to recognise the classier residents. These privileged few were identified by their correctly spelled facial tattoos and by the wearing of matching slippers to the pub. The criteria for men was different though, also involving the number and condition of teeth owned. It was a place where men were men, women were men and the dogs fought with broken bottles.

My mother passed away before we moved to Wales. I have no memories of her, as she died before I was a year old. I often wonder if my abnormality took too much out of her during childbirth. I wonder if she had been unable to recover from the struggle of bringing me into the world. I try not to think about how she may have struggled *keeping* me in the world, my abnormality being too much for her to bear. My father never reminisced about my mother; neither her life nor death were the subject of discussion. I never forced the matter. I knew there was a chance my father may slip and I would hear something I didn't want to hear. I was resigned to the assumption that Dad was protecting my feelings. Assumption being preferable to confirmation. If the truth hurts then comfort me with lies and omission.

Until the age of four I was cared for during the day by an elderly neighbour, Mrs Reilly, while Dad worked his factory job. Mrs Reilly provided my first maternal role model and treated me well enough, from what I can recall. My most vivid memories are in fact quite hazy as Mrs Reilly chain-smoked Benson and Hedges. I never got a clear look at her as she walked around in her own personal haze but I never noticed any tattoos. I'm sure if Mrs Reilly ever got ink done then it would be correctly spelled; she was one of the classier neighbours. She never minded the second-hand smoke coming my way. I'd estimate it was worth ten cigarettes a week. I promised myself that if I ever saw her down the pub, in her matching slippers, I'd buy her a pint by way of compensation.

It would be unfair to belittle Mrs Reilly; she was kind and always ensured I was fed and clean by the time Dad returned from work, as long as it didn't clash with her TV viewing schedule. The favourite delicacy she served was strawberry jam sandwiches, with an occasional sprinkling of cigarette ash by way of garnish. Dad's arrival home coincided with a break between Australian soap operas, so Mrs Reilly was able to rush next door before she missed any of her vicarious antipodean adventures. Given our humble background and the limited choice of childcare options available to Dad, I guess I didn't do too badly having Mrs Reilly as my protector. She was reliable; she was predictable; she was there. Dad must have been fond of her. Even when he found cigarette burns on the furniture he still described her as, 'That unbelievable bloody woman!'

Dad was of average height and slender. When I started school he told me how to respond to classmates claiming their dad was bigger than mine. 'Tell them your dad can run faster than their dad, so it doesn't matter how big they are!' Dad appeared almost emaciated when compared to the local men who nursed their beer bellies with pride and dedication. Dad wasn't much of a drinker, which was not typical for an adult male in the area, or for a large proportion of teenaged boys. Rather than following the native custom of spending the hours between work and bedtime growing beer bellies at one of the many local pubs, Dad spent most of his free time with me. He entertained and educated me whenever he could. He ensured my upbringing wasn't over-protective by modifying traditional children's stories to reflect reality.

'Jack and Jill went up the hill to fetch a pail of water,

Jack fell down and broke his crown and lapsed into a coma.'

According to Dad the sequel involved Jill contacting Jack's insurance company to submit a claim for loss of income due to permanent and total disability. However, Jill was less than pleased to discover that the policy didn't cover Jack for injuries sustained as a result of hill-climbing activities. Jill argued that Jack had not technically been climbing, as he was descending when the accident occurred. The insurance company refused to budge and rejected the claim. However, on closer inspection Jill discovered the policy provided a tidy payout in the event of Jack's accidental death. Unfortunately, and without warning, Jack succumbed to his injuries and tragically passed away. Despite scurrilous rumours that Jill may have been complicit in his passing, the coroner found no evidence of foul play. Jill received a handsome payout and she lived quite comfortably. In fact, she lived happily ever after. Jack's grave remains neglected.

At weekends we took a drive to escape from the neighbourhood and into the countryside. Dad was the fount of all knowledge. He knew the name of every bird we spotted.

'See the big black bird over there? His name is Horace. Hey, Horace, how you doing?'

He also knew the variety of every tree we came across.

'That tree is a chicken pot noodle tree, but it's not in season at the moment. Wait until summer, there'll be pots everywhere!'

We were able to afford an ancient Ford panel van that had seen better days. It was so dilapidated it was the sole vehicle in the area that had sympathy cards left under the wipers by the local "car demolition experts". It was so crappy we called it *Vandalised* as it possessed the *post-abused* appearance that was the goal of ambitious car vandals everywhere.

We kept that van for years and Dad compensated for the lack of vehicular diversity by carrying out "non-dealer-approved budget modifications". His special alterations enabled us to adopt new technology way ahead of the rest of the neighbourhood. Sort of. When airbags were first publicised Dad blew up a couple of balloons and put them in the glovebox. It was exactly like real airbags, in that we knew they were there but hoped we'd never have the need to test their effectiveness. We never did; the van was incapable of achieving a speed where an airbag, real or artificial, would deploy.

Everything changed, however, when I was four years old. Dad won big on the lottery. There was nothing subtle about our change in circumstances. It seemed that one day we lived in a place where you had to be unemployed to be considered working class and the next day we lived in a modest detached house in rural Wales. A few intermediate steps were necessary before the move took place but none of them required the approval or even attention of a four-year-old.

The win enabled Dad to retire at a young age. He was not the recipient of many well wishes from his co-workers at the factory when he resigned. My father asked to remain anonymous, as he wanted to avoid unnecessary attention. However, local gossip, although as a rule slow off the mark, for once was able to put two and two together with commendable accuracy. Speculation was rife in the neighbourhood. When people suspected about his lottery win, he received a huge number of letters. The letters consisted of two varieties, about equal in number. The first variety was of a begging nature, regaling him with tales of hardship and need that could only be alleviated by my father's anticipated generosity. Many were poorly spelled. It may have been that the writer used the local tattoos as a form of portable dictionary. The begging letters were expected.

What was unexpected was the second variety of letter. These were of a threatening nature. Many people considered my father had stolen the winnings from them. It was as if he had broken into their homes, swapped lottery tickets and misappropriated the money directly from them. I can almost understand their motivation to blame others for their disappointment, even if I don't agree with it. When I buy a lottery ticket, for the days up until announcement of the winning numbers, in my mind I am a potential multi-millionaire. I protect my ticket as if it was worth millions. The astronomical odds of this eventuating is irrelevant at the time. I dream of everything I will do and everything I will buy. My mind-millionaire is even quite generous, dispersing tidy sums to needy charities everywhere. When the winning numbers are announced and my multi-million pound ticket turns into scrap paper I am of course disappointed, but not for long. I move on and won't buy another ticket until the desire to resurrect my mind-millionaire has to be satisfied. What I don't do is write poison-pen letters to the winners or send begging letters. Indeed, I have yet to send a congratulatory note.

Dad didn't bother contacting the local police to complain about the abuse and the veiled threats of harm. He didn't bear the writers any particular ill-will and knew the local police were already overwhelmed with the numerous burglaries and assaults and in trying to combat the activities of destructive youths in the area. On closer inspection of the handwritten letters, Dad was convinced that a significant number of the writers were having an each-way bet, having both begged and threatened. While he remained cautious, this made him doubt the veracity of their intentions.

We didn't hang around for long once the winnings cleared and Dad put the initial financial management in place. We ended up in Wales through the recommendation of a close friend of Dad's. Dad had kept in touch over the years with a school pal of his who had made good. When Dad left school he and his classmates had few options available to them as school leavers. The option my father and many of his friends took was to find work in the car industry, most often as semi-skilled labour. Dad considered this his sole realistic option, the other options being army, dole or jail. Had we stayed in the area my options on leaving school would have been identical to his, albeit with far less opportunities in the declining auto industry.

However, Dad's long-time friend, Doctor Jeffries, proved to be the exception. Doctor Jeffries moved out of the area to complete a medical degree and set up his own practice in Wales. It was he who convinced Dad that this locale provided a suitable environment for the recently retired and their soon to be school-age son. I suspect Dad didn't need much convincing; his reflections of his hometown were unflattering. He said its one positive was the many roads leading away from it. Now we had taken advantage of this fact and were a world apart.

Despite our change in fortune, Dad never took our new situation for granted. He always acknowledged that it was sheer chance that led to our much improved financial position. He said we shouldn't think of ourselves as rich people, but as "cashed up poor folk". He never forgot where we came from and the idea of returning to our hometown was unpalatable to him. Dad proved to be a wise investor. He took great care financially. It would be years before I learnt how cautious he had been.

* * * *

Dad and I were always close. Our domestic situation dictated that he would be the most significant person in my life. Mrs Reilly once dropped in to visit us in Wales. She filled the house with her B&H fall-out and regaled Dad with tales of the "old country". Tales of ill-health, misfortune and the recently released that further reinforced the veracity of his decision to move far away. We were relieved to note that Mrs Reilly hadn't acquired any visible tattoos since our last meeting and that she wore matching shoes, albeit a little scuffed.

I have many fond memories of time spent with my father. I know that Dad valued our time together. I don't recall a single instance where cross words were exchanged. Our financial situation was such that we didn't need to worry about much. They say money can't buy happiness but from my experience it takes the misery out of being poor. We enjoyed a life of comfort in our modest home; we wanted for nothing. We had a housekeeper, Mrs Montgomery, who graced us with her domestic services. She had been recommended by Doctor

Jeffries which was indeed a seal of approval. She was immaculately presented and everything about her matched, including her polished footwear. She favoured designer clothing and accessories. Her spotless apron was an advert for Laura Ashley at her finest. We had swapped the pall of B&H for the more delicate air of Chanel.

In addition to providing cleaning and laundry services, Mrs Montgomery *prepared nutritious meals*. She didn't *cook*. We enjoyed gourmet sandwiches for lunch and a variety of hot meals for dinner. The delicious smell of her casseroles, pasta bakes, roasts and, my favourite, her shepherd's pie would pervade our home. So much so that our stomachs counted down the seconds to when Mrs Montgomery announced, 'Dinner is served'. While Mrs Montgomery was never moody she possessed an air of competency that suggested "Don't disturb me unless it's a matter of life or death!" I don't believe Dad was intimidated but he always maintained a respectful distance when Mrs Montgomery was serving our best interests.

We enjoyed a refined relationship with Mrs M over the years. After a while, when the formalities of the domestic arrangements had been established and found agreeable by all, Mrs M let her guard down a little. We always referred to Mrs M as 'Mrs Montgomery' and she greeted us on arrival with, 'How are my gentlemen today?' We responded with, 'Very well, thank you, Mrs Montgomery. How are you?' and then Dad received his instructions. Mrs M referred to me as her "young gentleman" although I never heard her refer to Dad as her "old gentleman". The first task for Dad would be to unload the groceries from Mrs M's immaculate, bright red Mini 1275GT. It seemed too sporty for someone as staid as Mrs M. Even so, I could imagine Mrs M tearing her way to the shops while everyone on the road parted way to allow her through, not daring to delay her. I even pictured the rain parting around the shining red bodywork with the black go-fast stripe down each side for fear of suffering the displeasure of Mrs M for blemishing her car.

The kitchen was her sole domain during her visitations. We learnt that if we didn't want to be chewing at our arms with hunger before the official meal times, we had to organise our snacking pre-arrival of Mrs M. Dad had a study that Mrs M would deprive of any dirt or dust that dared accumulate since her last visit, but would otherwise leave undisturbed. This enabled us to use a number of handy places to store our snacks. In the best interest of the household, Dad and I stayed out of the way of the unstoppable force of Mrs M. The sound of the approaching vacuum cleaner provided us with an indication of the path of least resistance to Mrs M's flightpath.

When the weather was pleasant we took ourselves outside as soon as the perfunctory pleasantries had been shared and Dad received his orders of the day. I never discovered Mrs M's first name. Dad may have known but didn't share with me. For all I knew Mrs M was a domestic rock star and required just a single name by which to be known. Dad perhaps protected me from the potential faux pas of calling Mrs M by her first name. That would never have happened though; even thinking of her as *Mrs M* seemed indelicate.

With much gratitude, we accepted the nutritious meals served by Mrs M which she accompanied with a brief description of the culinary treat in store. Up until the age of ten I had no idea of the existence of fats, carbohydrates or proteins. My dietary knowledge was such that I believed the three major food groups were potato, chocolate and cake. Because Dad provided the meals between Mrs M's visits these food groups were our interim dietary staple and further increased our appreciation of Mrs M's culinary offerings.

While the quality of food varied somewhat, it was always plentiful, and despite Dad's cooking skills being basic, at best, I had no dietary complaints. I even enjoyed helping Dad when possible, although I was limited to tasks suitable for one so young. My coordination has always left something to be desired, usually by me, and to entrust me with anything sharp could have had serious consequences for all involved. This meant my contributions were restricted to the finding and unwrapping of processed foods and subsequent disposal of packaging. I knew of two sources of food: Mrs M and cardboard boxes.

Dad regularly read to me, although he didn't always stick to the script. He revised the stories to give them his own unique perspective. It came as a great surprise to me to discover that Sleeping Beauty did not suffer from narcolepsy or that Goldilocks was never arrested for vagrancy. I was also disappointed to learn that if it hadn't been for the third little pig the *Three Little Pigs Construction Company* would not have gone into receivership after all. My favourite stories, however, were pirate adventures. I devoured the tales of exploits on the high seas, where the anti-hero pirate fights with cunning against the odds. I was fond of the notion that guile was as important as bravery, if not more so. I always took the side of the pirate, in particular against the callous authorities, often led by the corrupt captain who had lost out in some way to the main character.

I suppose I had some affinity with the characters who were flawed. Sometimes the shortcoming was subtle and revealed as the story progressed. Most of the time the flaw was physical and obvious from the start; perhaps the loss of a limb or an eye. Typically, the imperfection didn't relate to something extra like my back. I also hold pirate stories as being responsible for my lifelong association of value with shininess. Whenever the treasure was uncovered the finder would be greeted by shimmering golden objects and sparkling jewels. It therefore held that the shinier the object the more valuable it was. Dad encouraged this conviction and would often present me with shiny coins, claiming they came from casual pirate acquaintances of his. However, he never revealed the location of the recently discovered treasure trove, as he was sworn to secrecy. He did not, however, encourage my early career aspiration to run away to sea and become a pirate. I was told I would not qualify as the Somalians had the piracy industry sewn up.

I remember one particular night. I awoke feeling thirsty and decided to slip downstairs to the kitchen to grab a drink. As I neared the foot of the stairs I noticed the kitchen light was on. Dad sat at the kitchen table. He didn't see me as his back was to the stairs. He hummed along to music on the radio. Or he tried. Dad couldn't hold a tune at the best of times so any correct notes would have been coincidental. I couldn't see what he was doing, as he was hunched over. I saw that he was absorbed with whatever occupied him and I could see his arm moving. Unsure what to do, I did nothing, simply stood silent on the stairs as the scene unfolded.

And then I saw Dad lift his hand up to examine what he held. He was inspecting a coin. The mystery of the source of the pirate booty had been solved. He had been polishing old coins before handing them over to me as shiny plunder. I moved back upstairs, trying to make no sound, not wishing to disturb Dad. Not wishing to spoil our special thing.

The following night when Dad removed the shiny coins from his authentic-looking faux-leather pirate coin pouch, I put them into my piggy bank with the rest of the spoils. I never let slip that I knew where the pieces of eight and gold doubloons came from. I knew how hard it was to acquire treasure in those days.

Chapter Three

When faced with the prospect of adversity, of the two options available to the human physiology, *fight* or *flight*, I prefer option three; *sit tight*. That is, do nothing until more information becomes available. It may well be that when the information becomes available, and is duly processed, I do choose fight. However, flight is the more likely outcome. There's no shame in running away, only in being caught. The universe provides me with countless opportunities to test my judgement, so I feel obliged to gather as much data as possible before making a decision, hasty or otherwise. In fact, the universe provides me with so many "opportunities" that I can state, after much deliberation, and with a high degree of confidence, that I suffer from *Questionable Judgement*.

I came to this considered conclusion over a number of years and, of more importance, through the impartial and thorough analysis of the more significant universe-provided incidents. I don't believe I gratuitously flatter myself when I claim to have developed certain skills relating to the analysis of stuff that has happened to me. I am, after all, in exceptional position to know the prevailing conditions and the whys and wherefores of what has led to stuff happening to me. Indeed, as a coroner of stuff that has happened to me I am uniquely qualified. Through harsh experience I acquired the skills to slice and weigh and view the microscopic details of the diseased organs of stuff that has happened to me, until I can give an unequivocal determination of the precise nature and timing of death.

Yet, despite being a first-class coroner of stuff, my insightful analysis occurs post-mortem, so as a doctor of stuff I am poorly qualified. That is, I have the ability to posthumously understand what has happened to me. However, I don't understand what is happening to me at the time. I am unable to stop stuff happening to me; most often it is stuff that I don't want to happen to me. Symptomatic of my *Questionable Judgement.*

By way of providing full disclosure, or perhaps partial, I should explain that my current situation allows me the luxury of having the time and resources to be able to conduct comprehensive analyses of stuff that has happened to me.

* * * *

For part of my adult life and a lesser part of my youth, I have been a resident of the Glyndwr Mental Health Facility, one of the larger and more modern facilities located in Wales. The facility is also referred to as a psychiatric hospital. Old-fashioned terminology such as Nut House or Funny Farm is considered unacceptable. These references are incorrect, politically and literally. There is a distinct lack of the nutty and it's not a suitable location for seekers of fun. Some of my fellow inmates and I use the term *Inside* to describe the facility and this term is selectively used by the chosen few when not *Outside*.

Many people believe a mental health facility resembles the lunatic asylums portrayed in old movies. A place where mindless patients stagger around oppressive-looking ascetic wards. Where the inmates practise violent self-abuse or bash their heads against padded walls while severe, angular nurses look on with a large, punitive needle at the ready. Where scenes of writhing bodies straining under the load of 50,000 volts beneath the watchful eye of vengeful doctors and sadistic porters are the norm. Where the treatment of mental illness is to punish this intolerable affliction through sedation and shock and by obliteration of the spirit.

The Glyndwr Mental Health Facility harbours no shades of *Bedlam*. In my time here I have yet to see a single individual sporting a straitjacket. No heads bash against walls. If they did, they would just do it once; there is no rubber wallpaper here. As for self-abuse, be it violent or of a more tender nature, it's not an activity tolerated by the general populace. What goes on in the privacy of a patient's room, however, is the concern of the occupant. There are timing issues to consider. A number of nursing assistants are engaged to take rollcall throughout the day and night. Every sixty minutes (sometimes even hourly) smiling attendants can be seen with clipboard in hand, ensuring everyone is indeed where they're supposed to be.

At night the hourly head-count should still provide an ample window of opportunity for those inclined to get in a bout of undisturbed self-abuse. The psychopharmaceutic medications typically do not encourage haste. They tend to prolong or even prevent achieving the onanistic goal. I learnt early on during my first confinement to leave the door ajar in order to minimise the disturbance caused by the night-time checking of patients. A closed door invites having your rest disturbed by the sound of the door opening and by the corridor light piercing the darkness of the room.

As a further complication to the determined onanist, most patients share a double room which provides further complexity to the pre-existing logistical considerations. These other considerations affect all room sharers, even those indifferent to self-abuse. When constructing the stately home 150 years ago the architect would not have possessed the clairvoyant powers necessary to predict the eventual function of the property. As such the configuration of the bedrooms provides hierarchical issues. All rooms have a single window. One bed is adjacent to the window, the other closer to the door. The window-side bed is considered the dominant position; the reason being that the occupier of the door-side bed should have no recourse to travel to the window-side of the room. Therefore any incursions are treated as hostile or at the very least, suspicious. For the window-side occupier, however, if found on the door-side of the room they have the *just passing through* justification. I know for a fact this particular defence has never been challenged with success.

Once the lines are drawn, sometimes literally, and the occupants of a shared room have time to settle into the arrangement, there are potential benefits to be had. On rare occasions, a friendship of sorts is struck up and roommate harmony ensues. Perhaps one percent of the time, roommate harmony results from resourceful patient allocation or perhaps plain luck. The remaining ninety-nine percent of the time, roommate harmony results from a couple of patients getting their heads together and petitioning management to re-allocate rooms so they can share. One hundred percent of the time, these appeals are a result of the petitioning patients despising their current room-mates. Management goes to great pains to ensure the re-allocation of patients to rooms is taken most seriously and a thorough review must be carried out.

I suspect many of the affirmative decisions are made on the basis that sixty minutes gives the determined resident ample night-time opportunity to resolve any ongoing issues they have with their annoy-ing roommate. It takes less than five minutes to suffocate someone. That would leave the suffocator fifty-five minutes to deal with the suffocatee. In the event that the suffocator retained the energy and inclination, they would have to work around their self-abuse schedule, of course.

At the start of my first stay I shared a room with an unfortunate who suffered with night terrors. It would be more accurate to say he *shared* the suffering rather than suffering alone with his most vocal and noisy disturbances. As the newer arrival I was allocated the door-side bed and, on that never-ending first night of oft-disturbed sleep, I was glad of the nearness of the door. The roommate bed hierarchy held no concern for me. The following morning I was quick to point out the shortcomings of the situation to management.

My petition for a change of room was heard with much sympa-thy. My case was given due consideration. My request was rejected. I was asked to endure for a few more nights after which the situation would be reviewed. Having little choice, I relented. Two days later I was asked if anything had changed, to which I replied, 'Yes. Now I haven't slept for three nights.'

It was about this time that I began to appreciate *the power of the almighty dollar*, or the more relevant, and therefore more powerful, pound. My financial situation for most of my life has been fortunate. I have access to a trust fund set up by my father. It was with this knowledge that management lobbied the trust on my behalf, stating that it would optimise the effectiveness of my treatment by occupying my own room. Although this privilege comes at a premium, management was quite adamant that the benefits more than outweighed the cost. A cynical bastard might say that management was financially motivated when determining exactly what my best interests were. I am that cynical bastard. However, I can live with the notion of a non-altruistic-driven decision. After all, I now have my own room where any night terrors are of my own making.

During my first stay I didn't mix much with the other patients unless it was unavoidable. There was some acknowledgement of familiar faces during meal times in the cafeteria where all meals were taken, but this was a formality of recognition. General greetings were shared but little else. We never questioned about others' current status of health. Most people were comfortable keeping to themselves within the boundaries of their own muggy inner world.

During group sessions – and I was obliged to attend the non-voluntary sessions (the use of the word "compulsory" being discouraged) – I would participate when no other option was available. I tried the classic "Ignore it and it'll go away" approach, but this proved unsuccessful. I even tried the "smile politely and look directly at the questioner" bluff but this too provided no escape. Being a quieter attendee I was doomed to be singled out. It was about this time that I started perfecting my neutral façade. I wished to remain anonymous. To present a blank canvas to the world inside that said, "Don't bother me; just move on. Nothing to see here".

This was only a concern for me inside. Outside, despite my efforts to the contrary, I was already a blank canvas, perceived as unworthy of acknowledgement.

* * * *

Through an exhaustive process of trial and error and through no mean personal sacrifice, the gang has made some pioneering findings relating to mental health care. We have developed a tailor-made system of group therapy, called *Casual Therapy*. A three-pillar approach to Casual Therapy was established as leading practice. The first pillar is, of course, Felicity Kendal's Bottom. This pillar provides us with a constant point of focus to help negotiate the vicissitudes of life. As long as there is FKB we are able to convince ourselves that the world *could* be a beautiful place, however unlikely. FKB provides us with *possibility* in a world of *no certainty*. Whenever and wherever our thoughts wander, in particular when struggling through the darker places, FKB is the light that guides us back to a better destination. The first pillar provides us with a mental anchor.

The second pillar is *controlled self-medication*. This particular pillar has been subject to comprehensive and wide-ranging research and is considered a work in progress. We believe that it's impossible to spend too much time tweaking the formulae in the pursuit of optimum effectiveness. The medications involved come in plastic bags and are of a nature that sends airport sniffer dogs into fits of leg-humping ecstasy. We do not, however, ingest Ecstasy, party drugs being unworthy of consideration. As we believe hospital management wouldn't officially condone our selfless work on pillar two, we don't seek approval, on the basis that refusal would be counterproductive to achieving the big-picture goals of Casual Therapy. Unofficially, the involvement of a lower level of hospital hierarchy is necessary to practise pillar number two. There exists an understanding between the gang and specific members of staff to the effect that, as long as we *purchase* the product on-site, we can *use* the product on-site. The message is "buy local".

Caution was paramount when establishing the necessary logistics for practising pillar two. While it's less complex for an individual to organise solo "practice sessions" we have to be wary of the hourly head-count. The solution was elegant in that we incorporated the rollcall into our therapeutic processes. The completion of the rollcall and subsequent retreat of the clipboard and attached staff member marks a point of process change. The issue of supply has never been challenging, given that certain elements within the hospital staff not only condone but actively encourage our endeavours. The gist of the second pillar is to facilitate mental relaxation and preparedness. It enables our mental readiness for pillar three.

The third pillar is the collective appreciation of popular culture, in particular music. Agreeing on the music that could be mutually appreciated didn't involve as many discussions, or take as long, as could be expected. Other than music the gang brought to the hospital, we had access to only a few collections. The first, and lesser, of the collections consists of the cast-offs from patients and staff alike. This collection accumulated over the years and so we have a cross-section of music embracing many genres. It also covers a wide period that reflects the operational lifespan of the hospital. The collection ranges from offerings from the Kinks of the 1960s to more recent years. We are able to find the occasional musical gem among the hand-me-downs. We have ample time and resources to carry out regular and thorough searches. However, the second collection to which we have access provides us with the greatest yield. This collection belongs to the Chief of Psychiatry. He was "absolutely delighted" that we took an interest in his music collection and that we seemed to approve of his tastes. The third pillar is designed to be a source of controlled mental stimulation.

Over time the group developed great reliance upon the three pillars of Casual Therapy. However, we had to concede that CT was combined with the more conventional and sanctioned methods of psychotherapy practised at the hospital. As standard, when these types of studies are conducted, there is a control group by which the test results are verified. In our case the control group is Nobby, as he abstains from joining us in our ground-breaking efforts associated with pillar two. In addition, his commitment to pillar three has been called into question on numerous occasions. He is the least enthusiastic about demonstrating appreciation of the sanctioned music. The boy has no rhythm and is tone deaf. This could be a symptom of his abstinence from the practice of pillar two, which is designed to promote willingness to loosen up. However, his commitment to pillar number one has never been called into question; his dedication has been established beyond doubt. It is this fact alone that persuaded us to adopt him as the control group. Despite our findings demonstrating, with a high degree of confidence, that the test group consistently exhibits favourable results when compared to the control group, aka Nobby, we do not yet feel ready to publish our findings to the world. We unanimously resolved that additional work is required before we could publish our results to what will be critical acclaim. We confirmed our commitment and willingness to sacrifice our personal time and resources for the greater good. A more dedicated band of scientists would be hard to find. Would "band of heroes" be overstating our contributions to the world of psychotherapy? Only history will tell.

* * * *

Our musical benefactor, Doctor Fenty, is the Chief of Psychiatry. We call him *Doc Friendly,* due to his unshakeably agreeable disposition. No matter the circumstances or the subject matter being discussed, Doc Friendly can be relied upon to listen with attention and consideration; his expression composed around a sympathetic smile. As the Chief of Psychiatry Doc Friendly has a degree of flexibility relating to his duties and how he carries them out. Doc Friendly adopts a hands-on approach. He has a number of professional staff, comprising psychologists and psychiatrists, that report to him and who work under his direction. Even so, the doc enjoys getting his hands dirty. He organises his days so that, in addition to the day-to-day management of the professional staff, he spends time in one-on-one therapy sessions with select patients. One job for which Doc Friendly does not care, and which he avoids, is conducting group therapy sessions. His position allows him to allocate these sessions to other members of staff. It's possible he feels his style of personal empathy might be strained by application to a larger crowd.

Every few weeks he holds introductory sessions with new arrivals, to introduce them to the key members of staff and to the hospital amenities. I recall my introductory session with Doc Friendly. I'd been resident for a week and there were three other recent arrivals yet to benefit from the doc's welcome talk. We were called to the day room to be greeted by a tallish, trim man, wearing a retro-looking Triumph motorcycle jacket. He appeared quite candid in his unashamed attempt to affect a cool, approachable demeanour. The Doc is in his fifties, but looks weeks younger. He gives the impression of being someone who would be offended if you guessed their age as being older than forty. He hasn't asked me the question yet, but I have my response prepared. 'Somewhere about sixty?' designed to test his perpetual friendly smile.

His manner of speech makes me think he is *from* the fifties. He avoids using slang or any modern idiom. He favours words such as "frightful" and "jolly" and refers to the men and women as "lads" and "lasses". With his old-fashioned leather motorcycle jacket, trim figure and antiquated turn of phrase he reminds me of a World War II fighter pilot. The doctor has more than a hint of the "what-ho" about him. Towards the end of his address he leant casually against the wall of the day room and having had no response to his 'Any questions?' he made what was intended as his parting comment. 'You're all welcome to pop in and see me in my office, even without an appointment. Don't forget, my door is always open.'

'You should get the lock fixed!' somebody on the sidelines responded.

I would discover later that the somebody on the sidelines was Brains. The doc maintained his composure, however, refusing to acknowledge the comment, despite the fact that the response still echoed across the room. His second and actual parting comment was, 'Jolly good', affable smile in place.

We take the opportunity of hanging around on the periphery when the doc gives his welcome talk in order to inspect the latest arrivals. It isn't so much to scrutinise the rookies for any prospective gang members as to check for potential usurpers. The successful conduct of Casual Therapy demands that particular sections of the hospital must be devoted to our sole custodianship at particular times. We look out for any individuals having the appearances of a regular gym user. This is because a significant component of Casual Therapy is conducted in the hospital gym, namely activities associated with the practice of pillars two and three. This particular location possesses certain characteristics that are absent elsewhere. The gym is situated as an annexe to the main hospital building. We speculated it had been a conservatory when the building was a stately home, in its previous incarnation.

Whatever function the gym once fulfilled, the pertinent factor in its favour is the lack of direct access to the gym from the main building. Anyone wishing to visit the gymnasium is required to walk from the main building, under the watchful eyes of whoever is occupying the gym at the time. Also, and most important when partaking in self-medication, the outer walls of the gymnasium are constructed of glass, a significant proportion of which are windows. Therefore, with the posting of a lookout there is enough time to detect any potential party-poopers heading our way from the main building and to then dispose of any evidence of non-sanctioned activities. In addition, the surplus of windows ensures the room has ample ventilation to remove traces of suspect odours. Taking everything into account, the gym provides us with an ideal environment for practising self-medication while minimising the potential for awkward situations.

If any new arrivals labour under the illusion that we use the gym for its intended purpose, we also have recourse to other measures to circumvent potential incursion. While the gymnasium is not extensive, there are numerous items of equipment scattered around the room. It has the aspect of an ergonomically designed torture chamber; the pads, cables and weights organised in a scientifically proven arrangement to provide the greatest amount of pain to body. The layout is such that it's possible for six or seven individuals to arrange themselves in such a way that the entire room appears occupied. Fortunately, this lends itself to our practice of spreading ourselves around the room to prevent the build-up of any concentration of self-medication by-product. We have to consider the potential effects of second-hand smoke that could distort vital scientific data.

In the case of emergency we have Nobby to fall back upon. Nobby has been allocated a position close to the entrance so that he is the first person seen by anyone attempting to stage an invasion. It also means he is equidistant from everyone, so that we have equal share of his pestilence, and so are more able to withstand the burden. If Nobby possesses a super power it is his ability to repel anyone entering a space in which he is already present. Nobby could enter an empty room and it would remain empty, not counting Nobby, which we don't. The sole way that Nobby ended up in a room with others was if they were already there when he arrived, with no option for a quick exit. If the sight of Nobby alone was inadequate to deter the more determined gym goer then his breath provides a much stronger challenge. His infamous halitosis is such that if anyone has the misfortune of being in close quarters when he exhales they do not forget the experience. It is such as you might experience if you were slapped in the face with a large, putrid fish that has been turned inside-out. That is a good day. On a bad day the smell is indescribable. Survivors would wonder if death would not have been a more favourable outcome. Nobby is indeed our most effective gatekeeper, although he proved to be a less than reliable lookout.

Chapter Four

During the development of Casual Therapy, had we consulted Doc Friendly, our initiatives would not have gained his full and unconditional support. He may have approved of pillar number three, recognising that we rely upon his personal music catalogue. Even without insider knowledge of the significance of FKB, I suspect he would have grudgingly accepted there is some logic, however tenuous, to support the first pillar. He may find *The Good Life* and Ms Kendal somewhat contemporary for his tastes. He might prefer to substitute FKB with Marilyn Monroe's boobs (MMB?) but I hope he would at least admit to the fundamental theory supporting pillar number one. However, I have no doubt that he would not support, or even acknowledge, any theory or logic behind the practice of pillar number two. There is one subject where Doc Friendly turns into Doc Resolute: psychopharmacology. Psychopharmacology is his considered area of expertise and he monitors with dedication the efficacy of prescribed medications on both the patients whom he treats himself and patients of the professional staff under his control.

If my experience is typical then the prescription of medication as part of the psychotherapy process is more art than science. What works today may not work in the same way, or at all, tomorrow. There are similarities between the effects of prescribed drugs and that most common of drugs, alcohol. Both are designed and manufactured in such a way to alter the chemical make-up of an individual. The time frame for feeling the effects and for monitoring the success of the respective drugs are quite dissimilar, however. While the short-term effects of alcohol are apparent, and pretty much anticipated, there can also be long-term effects that accumulate over time. These can be less easy to recognise and are unwelcome, assuming the individual is still capable of caring about their health at that stage of their addiction. The typical alcohol user is looking for the perceived short-term benefits while accepting, or more often ignoring, the potential long-term harm. The alcohol user also has to consider the possibility that the more immediate effects may not be as beneficial as envisioned. This can be the realisation once the more immediate effects start to wear off and vague memories of inappropriate behaviour resurrect themselves the following day. The short-term pain can of course be alleviated through the consumption of yet more alcohol to give temporary respite from the offending memories. This particular approach is called *alcoholism*.

The more significant concern with prescribed drugs is that there may be adverse short-term effects. This is assessed against the anticipated long-term benefits. The first few weeks of any new drug regimen is most closely monitored as, more often than not, this is when the unwelcome side-effects will emerge. The undesirable indications are often associated with the digestive system. They appear determined to take all pleasure out of eating, while simultaneously making the disposal of the by-products as uncomfortable as possible. It starts at the point of entry with dry mouth, bleeding or tender gums, bad breath and mouth ulcers all being potential symptoms to which you can look forward. The side-effects then work their way from the raw and battered mouth through the tender and bloated stomach and intestines all the way to the rectum. And it doesn't stop at this fundamental exit. Here you can look forward to possible bleeding and burning sensations, exacerbated by potential diarrhoea.

The drug manufacturers have an each-way bet when publishing the mandatory prescription information. For every attack of diarrhoea there is a bout of constipation to redress the balance. For loss of appetite, increased appetite appears and difficulties sleeping are balanced with difficulties staying awake. All the excess of prescription information that has been, is being, and ever will be published by the pharmaceutical industry can be summed up in a few short statements: "This medication may work as intended. This medication may not work as intended. This medication may not work at all". Publishing of potential side-effects should be outlawed. This would force the pharmaceutical companies to expend more effort into making a drug *without* the nasty side-effects in the first place. The established approach of attaching an exhaustive list of sometimes conflicting potential side-effects to cover themselves in the event of pretty much any eventuality is pure indolence. Imagine the scenario: "Hello, Mr Pharmaceutical Executive? One of my patients took your drug and his head exploded. What's that? The tendency for head explosion is listed as a possible side-effect? Oh, righty-ho then, that's okay. I shall inform my patient … through a fucking medium!"

In addition, removal of the exhaustive list of potential side-effects is in the best interests of patients that are of a more suggestible nature. I refer to those patients that pore over the prescription information and take every word as gospel and then settle in to await the onset of symptoms. I refer to myself. When Doc Friendly asks how I am faring with new medication I have to resist the impulse to tell him about my tender, enlarged breasts, increased period pain and other less than manly symptoms. The doc used to ask about specific side-effects but he realised he was enabling me by putting ideas into my head. For example, the first time he asked if I was sleeping okay, I paused for thought. 'Now that you mention it, I have been a bit restless lately,' and I meant it. I just hadn't realised I was enduring sleepless nights until the doc raised it.

I must confess I am more than a little impressionable. I've been told this on numerous occasions, but I've never disagreed. In any case, the impacts of any medication I take, whether they are good or bad, appear to be short-lived. The effects settle down over a couple of weeks until I reach a kind of placebo-addled state. I often wonder if my biological chemistry is abnormal, so that what works for the majority is wasted upon me. Trying to gauge the effectiveness of any medication is complicated by its very nature. It's similar to how the effects of alcohol can vary. Some people have a high tolerance and appear to drink without end with little effect, while all around them stagger and fall. At the other end of the spectrum are the one-pint tragics, also known as the *cheap date*. They are those that stagger and fall while all around them look on unimpressed. I fall somewhere between the two, metaphorically. I tend more towards the high tolerance end of the scale. This could be attributed to my gender and age. While I may not enjoy the hollow legs of the mythical Irish Catholic priest, I cannot discount that my tolerance is influenced by having room to spare elsewhere in my bulk.

There are some basic imperatives, however, applying to all recipients of medication. Any drug regimen must consider a number of elements which can be varied from time to time as the efficacy is monitored. The type or class of medication is prescribed based on which chemical imbalance is considered to be the leading suspect contributor to our troubles. For the inhabitants of the hospital, that means they'll be either anti-depressants or anti-anxiety meds. Within the gang we don't often discuss details of our meds and *never* what they are trying to fix. Most of these meds are available in a variety of strengths. The lower dose is taken as the starting point. Once the patient's reactions have been monitored over a few weeks, or months, the next step may be to increase the strength. The process of administering meds is also further complicated by the patient building up a tolerance to the drug over time. The patient might even develop a sensitivity and present with signs of the adverse symptoms, even though absent earlier in the course of treatment. In my case it's less to do with developing a sensitivity and more to do with discovering the list of side-effects.

What this means is that dispensing medication is a long and complicated process, requiring commitment and effort from both patient and doctor. The ultimate aim of all this hard work is to discover and maintain a chemical balance that can be endured by the patient. But it's not like changing the oil in a car. That's simply replacing all the corrupted gunk with fresh, predictable lubricant to ease operations.

Dispensing drugs as part of psychotherapy is about altering existing chemistry, not about replacing it. Everyone's chemistry differs and everyone's chemistry reacts differently to change which means the road ahead is long and meandering. And that's great news for the pharmaceutical corporations.

I have to take special care during the first few weeks after changing meds. I'm not at my sharpest during this time. My thoughts exist in a mental fog. I find it harder to focus on what is happening. My perception and my reactions are on a delay. I see something or hear something and it takes a few seconds to process what it is. It then takes another few seconds to determine how to react and then to act upon that determination. It therefore requires more effort for me to recognise what is transpiring. I can only focus on what is close and right in front of me. Everything else is too remote and indistinct. This can be a big problem when I have therapy sessions with Doc Friendly, as he's quick to recognise when I'm at my most submissive. The doc is always keen to explore certain aspects of my life and I try to resist revealing too much information. I'm not trying to spite him. I respect his position and his professionalism. I simply don't want to discuss certain matters. Rod Stewart hit the nail on the head when he sang in his gravelly Scottish drawl: 'I don't wanna talk about it'. I say, 'Sing it how it is, Rodney!'

I don't want to think about my past. I know Doc Friendly is trying to help; it's his calling and what he's getting paid for, after all. I'm not trying to be ungrateful; it just seems to come naturally. The doc does provide me with food for thought, sometimes. His probing leads me to question some of the stuff that's happened to me. My thoughts then tend to revisit old reflections, but I nonetheless take the opportunity to confirm nothing has changed that might alter my view in a material way.

Throughout our many sessions we have developed a contest-like relationship. The doc encourages me to spill the beans about all the dramas of my life and I withstand his sorties. There are a few psychotherapy rules to which Doc Friendly must adhere. I have uncovered these over time and I use this knowledge to my advantage. It may be over-dramatising the situation, but our sessions can take on the aspect of a game of chess. A game of chess in which my strategy consists entirely of blocking moves. Thus far, my resistance to the doc's efforts to dredge up my past have been successful to a certain extent. My sole lapses have resulted from my lack of caution when burdened by the mental fog of changed meds. He asks one of his standard leading questions about some aspect of my life and, in my time-delayed state, I respond before I realise I have spoken. These occasional morsels are then used to kick off sessions for weeks, or even months, after the initial indiscretion. However, once the doc realises my resistance has returned to its former level he will yield that particular line of questioning.

Now and again, Doc Friendly raises what he perceives to be my unhelpful reticence. He suggests that it may be in my best interests to address the stuff that is so difficult to discuss and just as difficult to consider. 'Well, Alan, do you not think it might be good for you to discuss some of these things that have happened to you? The things you may find quite upsetting?' the doc asked, approachable smile front and centre.

'What, you mean the upsetting things I don't want to think about because they are done and are in the past and that's where I want to leave them?'

'Is that what you think, Alan? Are you worried that if you recall some of these things they may upset you again?'

'Something like that. I don't know.'

'Don't you think it might help to discuss these things and get a fresh perspective? Sometimes talking about a painful subject helps the process of understanding and accepting what has happened. It helps you come to terms with it, Alan.'

'And maybe it's like picking at an old wound that's nearly healed. Maybe it's best to leave it alone and let it heal.'

'Do you think that's what will happen if you leave these things unresolved, Alan? Do you think these issues should be swept under the carpet?'

'No, Doctor, I don't think they should be swept under the carpet.'

'That's good, Alan. Do you want to tell me why you think that?' The doc sensed a breakthrough. Big smile now.

'Well, to sweep something under the carpet is a pain in the arse. You'd have to pull the carpet up from the edges of the room. You could end up damaging the skirting board. Then you'd have to decide whether you're going to sweep the stuff underneath or on top of the overlay. Even then, once you'd got the carpet up and swept the stuff under it you'd have to fix it back down again. Seems like a lot of effort to me.'

'I can see what you've done there, Alan. You've taken what I've said quite literally. Perhaps I should have asked if you thought the issues should be swept under the *rug* then.'

'Are you talking about a free-standing, not-attached-to-anything, sitting-on-the-floor type rug?'

'I suppose I am Alan, for the purposes of our discussion'

'Oh well, that's different. In that case, yes, you should definitely sweep stuff under the rug. I mean, what's it there for if not to sweep stuff under?'

'Well, Alan, I think they're designed to do more than have things swept under them. Decoration, for one thing.' The doc tried speaking my language now.

'Yeah, but they're still useful for sweeping stuff under, aren't they? Are they there just to keep your feet warm? I don't think so. Why are you able to lift them or roll them up if not to hide stuff under? I'll bet there isn't a single rug in the whole world that doesn't have something swept under it sometimes.'

'Well, Alan, do you think that might be a short-term solution?'

'The thing is, Doc, you focus on "short-term" whereas I focus on "solution".'

'Quite. Jolly good,' he concluded, default smile in place.

Psychotherapy rule number one is: *Never tell the patient they are wrong.* Of course this doesn't mean the patient is always right, or even sometimes right. The gist of the rule is that Doc Friendly can never unequivocally accuse me of talking shit. Not even when I *know* I'm talking shit and I do enjoy talking shit from time to time. The doc has a strategy in place should this particular rule impede his progress. I'm certain he's had plenty of practice perfecting the technique, in particular with me. What he does is to get me to ask myself the same question but in a different way. Well, Doc, I see your *never accuse the patient of being wrong* rule and raise you my *take what he says literally* tactic.

Doc Friendly tries to open doors to my past to revisit the life-defining painful events and incidents of questionable behaviour. He invites me to step through those doorways to re-examine what happened. What he cannot do, is shove me through the doorway against my will. For Doc Friendly, it is all about the carrot and not the stick. In essence, I don't want to relive the past, above all the bad stuff, and there's been a fair amount of bad stuff for me to ignore. I'm not being lazy; ignoring stuff is a full-time job, requiring a lot of effort. I don't want to dredge up the past. I prefer to let the troubling thoughts settle like silt in my life's river and sit forever undisturbed. Neither do I want to think about the future too much. There are so many variables it makes my brain hurt figuring out all the potential pathways. I want to live in a sort of timeless state where I can focus on the now, and even then, only when I must.

At the end of one of our more challenging engagements, Doc Friendly, smiling of course, told me that he thought I was "like an onion". He didn't mean it in the sense that he thinks I'm complicated, with many layers that need to be carefully removed. He meant it in the sense that I sometimes made him want to cry.

* * * *

I enjoyed an idyllic existence at home in rural Wales with Dad and Mrs M. Doctor Jeffries was a regular visitor to our home. We had been in Wales for a year when Dad decided we needed to expand our household. We got a dog. Dad discussed it with me first, before making a decision. He asked how I felt about bringing a "hound into the manor". I was very excited, as any five-year-old should be. I held visions of a huge, terrifying beast that would obey Dad and me alone; the mere idea of which would scare all the natives and be the subject of local mythology. We got a Jack Russell terrier. After securing my endorsement, Dad discussed getting a dog with Mrs M. He told her we were both keen. He wanted to ensure Mrs M was agreeable and, if so, identify any conditions upon which she insisted to cement the new arrangement. Not only did Mrs M unequivocally agree to the canine addition to the household, she even helped procure the beast. One week after the initial discussion with Dad, Mrs M arrived in her shiny red car to deliver our newest housemate. He was eight weeks old and looked impossibly tiny, even when being off-loaded from a Mini.

Any concerns about how Mrs M would interact with our new addition were soon appeased. While Dad had chosen the particular dog, Mrs M had advised Dad where suitable candidates could be found. Therefore, Mrs M had given pre-approval of the stock. It wasn't long before she also approved of the individual. The hound was a quick learner. It took a few short months for him to understand his position which he demonstrated whenever Mrs M arrived. He would wait patiently while Mrs M greeted Dad and me, and only then would he approach Mrs M. She would crouch down, in a ladylike manner, and ruffle the top of the dog's head while advising him that he was a "good boy". Mrs M would then wash her hands before commencing her domestic duties. No-one took it personally, not even the dog; it was a matter of hygiene after all. The dog then returned to whatever occupied him prior to the arrival of Mrs M. Like Dad and me, he kept out of the way, using acoustic clues such as the sound of an approaching vacuum cleaner. His canine nature meant he also possessed a keen sense of smell. I am convinced he used his ability to detect the hint of Mrs M's Chanel that preceded her arrival as an early warning system from which we all benefited.

Dad and I walked him around the neighbourhood during the week and further afield at the weekend when time allowed. Often we were accompanied by Doctor Jeffries. Despite not owning a dog, he had extensive knowledge of the best walks in the area. I learnt from Dad that Doctor Jeffries was a widower, his wife having died many years back. Doctor Jeffries had no family of his own. The couple had been childless and he had not remarried. Dad hinted there had been an element of tragedy in the doctor's life, but he was friendly and happy at all times in our company. And always welcome.

Our puppy suffered from small dog syndrome as soon as he was old enough to be walked on a leash. He would square off to dogs that happened to pass within range of his rather sensitive radar. He liked to confront those dogs that were bigger than him, which were many. He ignored those that were of a similar stature, which were few. Often we caught a sympathetic smile from the owner of something resembling a well-fed wolf as our diminutive beast yapped enthusiastically at the perceived adversary. There were some advantages to owning such a small dog. It was hardly an effort to hold him back when he did square off. To say he strained at the leash would be flattering him. Most of the time the other dog took one look at our yapping bundle and ignored him, sensing no threat. After one such incident Dad asked, 'Would you have preferred a bigger dog?'

'No, he's great. I'm really glad we got him,' I said, and I meant it.

'Are you sure? He's more dangerous than he looks.'

'How dangerous is he?'

'Well, one of those big dogs could choke on him, so he's a potential killer!' Dad said, with a big smile.

At that, the dog gave a short yelp, pricked up his ears and gave Dad a look, as if to say *"Oi!"* Typical Jack Russell terrier; can't take a joke.

After much deliberation, and a few weeks of referring to him as "the hound", Dad named him *Gelert* after a renowned Welsh dog. I discovered that Gelert was famous for being unjustly slain by his owner for a crime he didn't commit. Indeed, rather than being the villain of the story, Gelert was the hero. I adored the dog and thought the name suited his character when he was first christened. Although I didn't care for the history behind the name, by the time I became aware of its origin it was too late. He was, and always would be, Gelert.

Much of the time we don't get to pick the names by which we are called. I have had the misfortune to learn that, in many cases, any objection to a nickname is taken as encouragement rather than deterrent to further use. You just can't win.

* * * *

About a year after starting school, the name calling started in earnest. The first few years of school life are spent benchmarking what is normal or acceptable. Because of this, children are more forgiving of what has yet to be acknowledged as abnormal or unacceptable. The values of the greater collective need to be established and understood before they can be used as a weapon against those that don't fit.

During my first few years of school I learnt about being different. The school uniform didn't flatter my shape. It seemed to be designed to draw attention to my overdeveloped back. I was forced to wear shirts and jumpers that were intended for much older children. While the clothes were snug at the back they hung loose and baggy at the front. No amount of tucking in to my shorts could hide the excess material. During the first few weeks of school a couple of classmates asked, 'What's wrong with you?'

I didn't know how to answer; all I could say was, 'Nothing'. Of course I knew I was different. I knew how but I couldn't explain why. I ignored the question and hoped they would lose interest. They didn't. Another boy in my class called Gary attracted almost as much curiosity as me. He was ginger. Our unusual appearances drew us together and Gary was my best friend in primary school for a while. By the end of the first year my classmates realised Gary's gingerness wasn't so unusual, the gingers being represented elsewhere. And so he became acceptable to a larger group of potential friends.

However, my classmates became aware of how unusual my own uniqueness was. Halfway through the second year I became known as *Alan the Alien*; then simply *Alien*. I attended a private school as Dad wanted to ensure I benefited from a decent education. While Dad was careful with money, he considered my education to be an investment in my future, so it was an allowed luxury. The school had been recommended by Doctor Jeffries. Children at the school tended to be from professional families, with parents who were lawyers or doctors or the like. My having a sole, retired parent did nothing to further my membership of the various cliques that were formed. Neither did my appearance promote an image of affluence. From the front my clothes appeared too big and so I looked like someone who had to make a single uniform last over several years. From the back, my clothes appeared too small. I appeared to be someone who had outgrown his clothes but couldn't afford newer, better-fitting uniforms. With the double whammy of my appearance and my humble background I felt about as welcome as a pig in a Gestapo uniform trying to gain entry to a synagogue.

Gary was the sole person in my class who didn't call me Alien. Despite having other friends, he remained a friend to me during the first year. The rest of the class left me to my own devices. While Gary never discouraged the name calling, he did not encourage it. I thought Gary felt sorry for me and even though I considered him my best friend I knew I wasn't his. I was okay with that. Even at such a tender age I got used to the notion that it can be unrealistic to hope someone is on your side. I was coming round to the idea that not having someone against you is a positive. That notion is most evident when that someone proves to be against you after all.

By the end of the second year my classmates started wearying of calling me Alien. I hoped they could look past my abnormality and ditch the nickname. I hoped this was the first indication that I was no longer an outsider. It would be a sign that I was being accepted at last. This did not prove to be the case. They tired of calling me Alien, but instead found other names to add to their repertoire. At that time there was a popular cartoon on television which inspired a new source of spiteful ammunition to be fired in my direction. To my great detriment *Teenage Mutant Ninja Turtles* was all the rage. My uniform comprised a bottle-green jumper, similar in shade to the carapace of the cartoon characters. With the shell-like shape of my back, it was too good an opportunity to miss. I was too young to be labelled *Teenage,* and *Ninja* could be considered complimentary. So, at first I was branded with *Mutant* and then *Turtle.* In time, one genius put the names together and I became *Mutant Turtle.* In the end they settled on *Mutant,* with the occasional *Alien* thrown in for the sake of nostalgia.

I had many nicknames at school. Most were ingenious and all were effective. When they began calling me Alien I made the mistake of complaining; telling them it wasn't clever and they were being stupid. My complaints served to fuel the name calling. They then went out of their way to provoke me. I sat in class, listening to the teacher and I would hear it start in the background. 'Alien,' someone behind me would say, just loud enough for me to hear but not so loud to attract the teacher's attention. Someone else would then take up the call – 'Alien'. They carried this on until the teacher turned around, suspicions aroused. I tried to block it out by focusing on my lessons but found the effort of ignoring the taunting required all of my concentration, causing my schoolwork to suffer. To my credit, I never snitched on anyone, not even to Dad. No-one made me cry, or at least not at school. I saved the tears for when I was in bed at night with the lights out and the door closed. It happened a lot when I started school, but by the end of the second year I had developed a measure of resilience and the name calling would not cause me to cry again.

Between the end of the second year and the beginning of the third year I decided to adopt a new approach. I dreaded the start of the new school year but I hoped the long break would provide me with some respite before the taunting started in earnest. I hoped my classmates would grow out of it. I had tried protesting and that had inspired escalation. I tried ignoring it and that made no difference. So I determined to brave it all with a non-committal smile. I would show them that they wasted their time; that I could take it. It worked for a while, up to a point.

Towards the end of the first week, I heard the call-to-arms sounding behind me. 'Alien.'

I turned and said, 'Yes?' in the direction of the offending voice. I failed to get a response but neither did the initiator of the chant; it was not taken up. I didn't turn around until the teacher asked what I was doing. 'Nothing,' I replied. There was another attempt the following week, but I repeated my approach, with the same results. This ended the class-time taunting.

During the breaks in lessons I sat on the periphery of the groups of playing boys, always hopeful but never expecting that I might be invited to join in the games. At the start of the first year, I had been called upon to join a game of football. However, armed with my clumsiness, I was destined to end my days on the sidelines. Once my skill level was established, I was demoted to goalie a few times, but my lack of coordination let me down. On the rare occasion that I managed to stop the ball I would then miss my mark and throw the ball straight back to the opposition. If I felt adventurous, wishing to display my complete range of ineptitude, I would even throw the ball into my own goal. The others soon grew tired of my repeated demonstrations of incompetence and by the middle of the first year I wasn't picked again. Not even as lucky last.

I learnt to keep myself occupied during breaks while the rest of the class played together. I started carrying comics in my bag to enable me to escape into the various cartoon kingdoms. The fantasy of the wonderful sci-fi-derived worlds provided me with respite from the reality of school life. My isolation was not absolute though; I met with fellow outsiders from other classes. Like me they were ungainly and deemed unworthy of joining in games with their respective classmates. I was alone in not wearing spectacles. I shuddered to think how much worse my hand–eye coordination could be if I had also been blessed with poor eyesight. There were four of us who swapped comics and discussed the heroes and their relative merits. We spent more time reading than talking, but if they were like me they were at least glad to have the facility to sound off to someone else; to speak and be heard.

I didn't consider myself an outcast; that would suggest I had been cast out from something of which I had never been a part in the first place. Neither did I consider myself a loner, as that would suggest there was a conscious decision made to exclude myself. I was on the outside looking in. The choice of not belonging was not mine, but I was able to settle in to a reluctant resignation. School life became tolerable.

By the start of the third year I suspected Gary, who had become popular and was now the *Ginger Ninja*, was encouraging the rest of the class to call me by whatever my latest alias happened to be. He no longer spent time with me and I noticed the others would call me Alien and Mutant even when Gary was listening. Even so, over time, and with the constant name calling, I had built up a resistance. I found it easier every passing day to withdraw into my own shell, like the mutant turtle I was supposed to be. The irony didn't escape me, although there was one major point of differentiation. The shell of a turtle acts as a shield, protecting its vital organs against attack. Its shell acts as a deterrent to convince a predator to look for sustenance elsewhere. However, my "shell" didn't offer me protection then and it doesn't now. In fact, my shell *defines* my point of weakness. It provides the bullseye on a target for which the insults and hurt are aimed.

While I kept to myself on the outskirts, I was never unfriendly towards my classmates. I didn't want to provide reason for their animosity, to change the passive hostility into something more active. I hoped there would come a time when some unusual set of circumstances led to me finding favour with the others. I didn't know how or when that something might occur but I didn't want to discount the possibility. One day at lunch I thought to have made a breakthrough when Gary called me over as I was leaving the classroom, last one out as usual. Not only was it uncommon for someone to call me but he had called me *Alan*. This was unprecedented when beyond earshot of the teachers. I wandered over, remaining as nonchalant as I could, but nervous inside. 'Hey, Alan. What was the comic you were reading earlier? Was it *The Incredible Hulk*? Des reckons it wasn't.'

'Yeah, *The Incredible Hulk*. The one where he meets Thor for the first time,' I said.

Then Des moved forward to speak. 'No, it wasn't. You were reading *Teenage Mutant Ninja Turtles* so you can look at yourself!' As he said the last word he shoved me violently in the chest. I fell backwards over another boy who had crouched, unnoticed, behind me. I landed hard on my back.

'What did you do that for, Des? You know a turtle can't roll over when it lands on its back. He'll be stuck now,' Gary said.

I was winded for a second. At first, I didn't know what to do. I decided to play along and waggled my arms and legs in the air, squirming on my back, in imitation of a stranded turtle. I did this for a few seconds while the others laughed. I didn't discourage them. Then Des piped up, 'Jesus Christ, Alien, you're rolling in shit, you dirty bastard!'

I jumped up to discover I had been rolling in dog shit. It must have been their plan all along. Gary must have orchestrated the whole thing. I turned and ran to the amenities block, their cruel laughter chasing after me as I fled.

When I got to the toilet I locked myself in a cubicle. I stripped off my jumper and shirt. My jumper was soiled through. I tossed it in the bin. I knew Dad would ask where the missing jumper was, but I would endure his disappointment and tell him I had lost it. What I wasn't prepared to explain was the real reason for my misplaced jumper. That would require an answer I wasn't capable of giving. My shirt appeared unmarked so I put it back on. For the rest of the day, and even in the following weeks, I could not rid myself of the suggestion of ordure. The incident marked a change in my school life. It was the first time that I made a major deposit to the Bank of Self-loathing. I hated myself for debasing myself in front of the class; for trying to curry favour. I copped abuse about it for months afterwards, but I ignored it all. Nothing they would say to me would provoke any response from me ever again. I accepted my lot.

What did they see when they looked at me? Did they see something less than I was; as if they looked the wrong way through a telescope? Whatever I was, whatever I thought I was, be it misfit, outsider or reject, the end result was the same – I didn't belong.

The incident of the dog shit taught me about the value of patience. I ignored the taunting but I didn't forget, even when they grew tired of resurrecting the incident. I waited for three months, until the school year was nearly over. By then, the abuse had returned to a background level. The occasional Alien or Mutant would be called to me across the playground; always heard but never acknowledged. I didn't actively seek revenge, or feel a burning need for retribution. However, I never ignore an opportunity, should it present itself, and what I did would have to be categorised as opportunistic.

During the last break in the day at mid-afternoon, my classmates went to the far field to play football. As Gary passed me with the other boys he could not resist taunting me. 'Hi, Alien. With all your mates as usual?' drawing laughter from the group as they moved away. Face reddened, I assumed my usual position, now and always, away from the crowd since the dog shit incident, comic in hand, when I felt nature calling. It was going to be a quite substantial number two. I started out towards the toilet but halfway there decided that my waste didn't need to be wasted. I looked around to confirm I was quite alone. I made my way to the cloakroom where we left our coats and sundries that weren't needed in class. It was Friday and we'd had sports class that morning, so everyone's kit bags were stored in the cloakroom. I located and opened Gary's bag. It was a distinctive red like the stupid hair on his stupid head. I grabbed some tissues from my bag, took one last look around, dropped my shorts and underpants and began my movement. My nervousness worked in my favour and I made my deposit with haste. They say that "revenge is a dish best served cold", but I say shit is best delivered at body temperature.

It was all I could do to contain myself for the remainder of the day. The last few hours dragged as I tried to control my nervousness. At the end of class, I filed into the cloakroom to pick up my stuff. I saw Gary heading out, kit bag over his shoulder. My curious expression must have suggested that something was awry. He gave a questioning look when he passed me, but I turned, unable to meet his gaze.

I was nervous throughout the entire weekend. I was driven to distraction right up to Monday morning. I had no idea what the consequences of my actions would be. My mind was muddled with all the potential scenarios. I decided I wouldn't actively avoid Gary, which might arouse suspicion. I also decided to avoid putting myself in a position where it would be easy for him to confront me. I was going for a business-as-usual approach. I caught sight of Gary in the playground before first class. From his expression it was evident he had been eyeballing me with anger for some time before I noticed. I dragged my gaze away and affected the look of pure innocence that I had been perfecting all weekend. That was as close to confrontation as it got.

He never did say anything to me about it. I don't think he told anyone at school about the "present" that was left for him in his kit bag. His mum must have known, though. The next Friday Gary wore a spotless, brand-new games kit which he carried in a brand-new kit bag. I wasn't bothered that I was never formally unmasked as the "donor". I knew, and Gary suspected the truth of the matter and that's what counted. Still, it might have been nice to have had the effort acknowledged. After all, I hadn't simply used dog shit. It had been all mine. It's what I called "the personal touch".

Chapter Five

One of the longer-standing members of the group is Carl, but we call him *Bomber* due to his unfortunate case of Irritable Bowel Syndrome. As Brains remarks when Bomber releases his deadly cargo, '*Ficken*, Bomber! That's what I call an irritable bowel. It irritates the fuck out of me!' His emissions kill canaries within a one-mile radius and their destructive powers are such that he has his own personal hole in the ozone layer attributed to his anal efforts. His gaseous releases are subject to frequent, comprehensive speculation by the gang. We "suggest" that they consist of varying combinations of mustard gas, napalm and tear gas.

Bomber isn't thoughtless though. He provides us with notice of his intention to detonate, with a warning call of, 'Bombs away!' On hearing the call go out, we have learned to hold our breath until the heaviest concentrate dissipates. The half-life of the deadlier concentrations is in the range of thirty to sixty seconds. However, he keeps us on our toes by throwing in the occasional "lingerer". When we occupy the gymnasium we sit in our reserved place each time. This is less to do with tradition and more to do with self-preservation, having determined through trial and error how long it takes for Bomber's emissions to reach our position. Hence, we time our breath-holding to optimum effect. Failure to calculate the timing with precision can lead to injury. This ranges from mere dizziness to sustaining burns to the lining of the lung.

Bomber – *Weapon of Ass Destruction* that he is – has the dubious pleasure of being roommate to Nobby. Given that it is a rare occurrence for residents to possess asbestos lungs and to possess no sense of smell, this particular roommate arrangement was destined. It is common knowledge that before entering the room, members of staff draw straws, toss coins or take part in other games of chance in order to avoid having to take the plunge. It is less common knowledge that the staff have petitioned management to have the window nailed permanently open to provide some semblance of ventilation. The cleaners are paid danger money, but it would never be sufficient. Residents give their room a wide berth, although that is more to do with wanting to avoid Nobby. However, the addition of the toxic environment of their room reinforces their resolve to steer clear. You would not have to be bloodhound-of-the-year material to track down their room. Indeed, even the most robust bloodhound would find that particular assignment to be fatal; death by overload.

As the senior roommate, both in terms of time served and level of esteem, Bomber took the prime bed location next to the window. Had I been Nobby, and I often praised various deities that I was not, I would be satisfied with the arrangement. The smells that emanate from Nobby are continuous. He emits a background stench all of the time. That's not to say that Nobby is powerless. If he makes the effort to brush his teeth, take a shower and put on deodorant and clean clothes, he can smell almost human. Perhaps a decomposing human at best, but close enough. It seems that the effort needed to take adequate care of his personal hygiene is beyond Nobby's capability or desire.

The smells from Bomber however are deadlier in nature and can be more potent than anything produced by Nobby. Bomber's saving grace, allowing him to be survivable, is that his deadliest smells are not continuous. One day, Brains was obliged to summarise. Nobby complained about his situation and, unusually for Nobby, Bomber was present at the time. Nobby tended to complain about someone when they weren't around to defend themselves, or offer counter-argument. The counter-argument consisted of throwing a few choice expletives at Nobby. While Nobby doesn't hold back from complaining (it's kind of what he does), the rest of us are more restrained. To complain about something or, even worse, about someone, involves taking a big risk; like tap dancing in a mine field. A complaint can be, and often is, seen as a sign of weakness, providing the gang with a wealth of ammunition to be fired in the complainant's direction. Bear in mind that we are, to all intents and purposes, a small, captive audience with little else to do. Sniping is kind of what *we* do.

Nobby complained that we victimised him. He pointed out the perceived disparity in our respective treatment towards him and Bomber, regarding our reaction to the generation of unpleasant odours. Or as Nobby paraphrased, 'It's not fair. You're always picking on me and never Bomber!' He was of course correct. We do pick on him, and so in this he was stating the obvious. His specific grievance, on this occasion, was that we more often, and with much fervour, complained about his bad breath and body odour. 'What about Bomber? He stinks worse than me!'

'That's debatable,' said Brains. 'Anyway, what you're failing to consider is the relative degree of exposure.'

'The what of what?'

'The relative degree of exposure, *tu culo*! Let me articulate for you. While Bomber produces a more toxic emission, he only stinks *some* of the time, whereas you, Nobby, stink *all* of the time.'

'Yeah but Bomber *really* stinks when he lets rip. He kills entire flocks of birds, for Christ's sake!'

'Ah, ah,' Brains said. He pointed toward Bomber, '*Some* of the time.' He pointed at Nobby, '*All* of the time.' Brains had expressed the gang's collective view most eloquently.

Nobby isn't the sole member of the group to be targeted. He is the easiest and by far the most deserving though. It also isn't as if Bomber's uninvited donations to the group go without comment. During one session our scientific endeavours were interrupted by the warning call, 'Bombs away!' We were on our second spliff of the self-medicating session and well on the way to reaching our Happy Places. Jimmy Cliff performed 'The harder they come' to assist our journey.

Bomber's contribution to the soundtrack was both unwarranted and unhelpful. His variation upon a theme went, '... the harder they PPPPAAAAARRRPPPP!' This particular payload from Bomber was especially potent and of a longer than normal half-life, so the usual precautions proved to be ineffective.

After regaining consciousness and enjoying a spell of spluttering and eye-watering, I was just able to speak. 'Your arsehole could make you a fortune, Bomber.'

'Is that right, how so?'

'Think about all the toxic emissions that have passed through it.'

'Okay?'

'Well, your arsehole still works like it's supposed to, doesn't it? You have control of your sphincter. You don't shit yourself, do you?'

'Not since I was a baby.'

'Well, if your arsehole has survived, undamaged, after all those seriously caustic farts, it must be, more or less, indestructible.'

'Point taken, but how does that earn me a fortune?'

'You should contact NASA. Tell them you have an indestructible arsehole, or better still *asshole*. Let them test it, then they could reproduce something of the same indestructible quality. They could use it to coat the space shuttle or make bomb-proof vehicles and shelters and stuff.'

'Oh, what a great idea, Silent. I'll contact NASA to book myself in for some anal probing as soon as possible. I'm sure they've had plenty of practice watching aliens. And don't worry, I'll make sure you get a share of the profits. In fact, here's your commission right now. Bombs away!'

I would have preferred cash.

* * * *

My school life didn't improve as I moved through the latter years of primary school. I remained distant from my classmates. I tried feigning indifference to the name calling that was still being directed at me. To some extent, I learnt to accept how things stood, although I had no choice. It still hurt when I heard Alien or Mutant. Every incidence chipped away at my self-esteem. I learnt it was possible to minimise my exposure to the verbal abuse if I was careful. I noticed the boys only called me names when they were in a group and out of hearing range of the teachers. They never taunted me when they were alone. In fact, when alone they tended to steer clear of me, as if I made them uncomfortable. It was as if the name calling was driven by some kind of pack mentality. *Stupidity in numbers.* The unpleasantness enabled me to develop at least one virtue: patience. I withstood the ostracism with the hope that secondary school would *have* to be better.

Despite the secondary school being part of the same institute, it was housed in separate grounds. The class intake came from a much broader area than just our adjoining primary school. This meant I would have some, if not all, different classmates, so I hoped for somewhat of a fresh start. And there would be girls, but one challenge at a time. The primary school years were not all bad though; I enjoyed a contented home life.

Every afternoon, as soon as I arrived home from school I was greeted by Gelert who reacted as if I'd been away for years. He may have been small, with a stubby tail, but he compensated by wagging his entire body. On first greeting me he jumped up while performing a full body-wag which invariably resulted in him going arse-over-tit. He then shook himself off, regained his composure and approached me in a more dignified manner. I rewarded him with some heavy-duty scratching behind the ears and generalised doggy talk. Next in line was Dad, who would ask how my day had been. I always offered the standard response of, 'Same old, same old.'

When I first started having problems at school, I mentioned it to Dad. I never identified the tormentors. He asked if I wanted him to come to school to speak to the teacher. I told him it wasn't that bad and that I could handle it. I wasn't being bullied physically; the individual boys were wary of me because of my bulk. I refrained from sharing those particular suspicions with Dad. I knew Dad worried and he made me promise to tell him if it got worse or if I changed my mind about him coming to school. Knowing he cared was a comfort but it upset me to see him worry. And so, 'Same old, same old,' became the compromise. If I told Dad everything was great I knew it would arouse his suspicions, so I began practising my tendency towards verbal restraint at an early age.

While I adapted with reluctant resignation to my school life, I nevertheless attempted to join in where I could. When I started secondary school, Dad suggested I look into extracurricular activities, where I would be away from my usual classmates. When I asked my form teacher he talked me through what the school had to offer by way of after-hours activities. I tried to learn who in my class was taking part, so I could avoid specific individuals or groups that caused me grief. I reassured myself that if it was only a few of my old classmates, chances were that they wouldn't think it worthwhile to restore the unpleasantness. That would require a conscious effort to reinstate the animosity and surely they needed a break. As it transpired, there wasn't too much available that suited someone of my exceptional clumsiness. However, there was one activity that I thought might favour my overdeveloped physique: *rowing*. Our school was close to the River Alyn, and so one Friday afternoon I met with the rowing coach and the student rowers to make our way to the school equipment sheds at water's edge.

The coach viewed me with an approving expression, perhaps hoping that I was as powerful as I appeared. What ensued proved he may have underestimated the extent of my strength. Unfortunately, what ensued also proved I had underestimated the extent of my clumsiness. After giving me the once over, the coach suggested I might be suited to the *coxless fours* crew. Straightaway, I proved my worth by not sniggering. The arrangement was such that four rowers sat in the boat, all facing the same way, each possessed of a single oar. Two rowers have their oars on the stroke side of the boat and two have their oars on the bow side. The boat is steered by way of a cable which, at one end, is attached to the toe of one rower and, at the other end, to the rudder. The theory is that the rudder is only needed to make minor adjustments to the course of the vessel. As a first-timer, I was positioned at *number two*. Again, my silence demonstrated great restraint. The theory of how the craft is propelled dictates that the rowers row in unison. They pull together both in terms of timing of the stroke and in the magnitude of energy that is transferred to the boat via the pull on the oar.

While I understood the theory, I did not possess the means by which to put it into practice. The end result was not pretty. I comforted myself retrospectively that no-one was killed or seriously injured. The sole injury sustained was the sprained toe of the boy who tried to steer the boat with increasing desperation. It would have been better if the other three rowers had been rowing on the opposite side of the boat to me, thus leaving me to provide an equal force on my own. Perhaps then the boat wouldn't have sunk which was the result of adopting the traditional arrangement of rowers.

Some of my strokes found air and I had been warned this is a common occurrence for the novice. What I wasn't told was that as a consequence of missing an entire river full of water, I would then fall violently backwards. After the first few misses I panicked. I tried to make up for my lack of input with yet more effort when I did find water. A few strokes merely skimmed the surface. I might have found the resulting waves to be quite spectacular, if I hadn't been the originator of those surf-worthy breakers. When I got a good hit in the water, the nose of the boat surged towards the opposite side of the boat. Any stroke that happened to be in time with the other rowers was coincidental. There were not many.

It all came to a chaotic, watery end when I made an almighty effort to find my stroke. The stroke proved beyond the capacity of the boat to endure. I should have confirmed the other boys could swim before setting off. Perhaps I should also have confirmed that they'd seen the movie *Titanic* which could have provided some aquatic disaster survival techniques. The net result of my efforts was similar to the end of the movie but, thankfully, it ended a lot quicker. Silver linings.

That was my single attempt to row as part of a team. The coach wasn't too enthusiastic about exposing more of the expensive equipment to my destructive powers. He may have also been worried about the welfare of the other students. His expression as we emerged from the water spoke of, "Oh, the humanity!" Had I attempted team rowing again, the costs of the measures necessary to protect the safety of the crew would prove prohibitive. The lifeboat wouldn't have done much for the dynamics of the boat either. I had tried enthusiastically. I had failed spectacularly.

However, I refused to abandon hope. I wouldn't let the risk to the welfare of others hinder my pursuit of sporting greatness. And so, after a week during which vessels were salvaged, students were dried out and toes un-sprained, I once again turned up for the rowing club. This time I took the opportunity to learn from my previous aquatic adventures. I determined that kayaking was a more suitable pursuit. Previous experience had demonstrated that there were aspects to team rowing to which I was violently ill-suited. There was the issue of synchronisation; being able to time my strokes with that of the other rowers was beyond my awkward skill-set. In addition, there was the matter of control; I was unable to measure the strength of my stroke. It was either at zero percent, where I carved air, or at one hundred percent, which was so much more than the one hundred percent of which the other rowers were capable. By resorting to kayaking, where I was the sole occupant of my own vessel, I removed these quite considerable barriers to my watery pursuits.

The coach took my intention to kayak quite well. He wasn't exactly relieved when I made the suggestion but he looked less terrified when he realised I had given up on team rowing. My reasoning was undeniable and my resolve unquestionable as I sat myself into the oldest, dirtiest and saddest-looking kayak that ever sat upon water. It also appeared to have spent some time *under* water. I wasn't offended by the miserable vessel that had been made available to me. I understood the coach had also taken the opportunity to learn from my previous efforts.

As it turned out, our respective lessons learnt didn't provide an adequate education. Five brave kayakers started the first practice race, but three despondent kayakers finished. The two kayakers adjacent to my – what proved to be quite arbitrarily assigned – lane suffered from a severe case of *wrong place, wrong time.*

Once again, I competed with enthusiasm. Had I been capable of maintaining my vessel in a straight line I would have finished the race well ahead of the pack. But a straight line was not in my destiny. I zigged and zagged to an Olympic slalom standard. Try as I might, each stroke of the paddle set the nose of my kayak to a brand new course. The unfortunates to either side of me suffered the consequences of my inability to keep to my own lane, despite it being a standard width. A width that was more than sufficient for everyone else but inadequate to accommodate my sideways-directed travels. What had appeared to be a most flimsy vessel in fact proved to be quite sturdy. I first struck and toppled the kayaker to my left and then, having satisfied myself of the effectiveness of my scuppering technique, I repeated the manoeuvre to the kayaker on my right.

I finished at the same time as the two remaining shell-shocked survivors who had been too far away to suffer from the case of *wrong place, wrong time* that sank their two companions. Despite having travelled twice as fast as them, I'd also travelled twice the distance, favouring a more scenic route. In theory, my performance had improved. I had only almost drowned two students this time compared to four on my previous attempt. I resolved to hang up the paddle and retire from all rowing-related activities. The coach didn't beg me to reconsider, nor did he complain. His sleep quality would've improved somewhat knowing my destructive forces would seek less fluid outlets. However, I suspect the memory of my two chaotic tryouts would've still troubled his slumbers for some time. In any case, he knows how to contact me. I'm sure if rowing ever becomes a full-contact sport, where the victor is determined simply by being the last man afloat, I will be the first person he thinks of.

* * * *

I stand alone in a hotel lobby. I must get to a particular room. The reason escapes me, but I am driven by the sense of urgency. I look for the lifts. Now the lobby is full of meandering patrons and staff. They are determined to impede my progress at every turn, putting body and luggage in my path. I see the lifts. They are odd, lattice-fronted devices giving access to indeterminate floors. I make my way with difficulty through the growing throng. I struggle to open the lift door sufficiently to squeeze inside. The sense of urgency increases. I enter the lift. There is a cage inside, taking up most of the interior space. It is another lift within this lift. I don't know the floor I need, only that I must get to the other side of the lift where the doors are now located. I wriggle between the wall of the lift and the cage. It's hard to breathe. My progress is slow. Panic rises as I struggle to reach the doors in time to exit before it is too late. I stretch out my arm, struggling to reach the control panel. I hit a button at random. The lift stops. The doors open with ease this time.

I emerge into the roof space of a large complex of empty factories. The lift has vanished. I look behind me to see a suburban landscape. There are rooftops and roads and offices and shops, punctuated by the occasional tree. The clear sky is a brilliant blue. I am on the outside of a massive building. I am surrounded by a framework of metal girders. I need to get to a particular house, situated in the town below. The purpose escapes me but I am driven by the need. The external access stairs that must take me to ground level are close by. Unstable handrails obstruct my path. I climb over them to the stairs. I begin my descent. The handrail has gone. I press up against the outside of the building, away from the drop. The stairway ends before reaching the ground. I jump into the branches of a tree close to the bottom of the stairway. The branches snap as I struggle to descend. I fall to the ground.

I make my way to the nearest road. I don't know my destination, only the course which I must follow. I run down a street, on the bearing I have to take. The once straight road now bends away from the direction I need. I take a side street to correct my course. The daylight at the end of the side street is replaced by a large, high, impenetrable brick wall. I take an alleyway to the right. Clouds loom claustrophobically overhead in the once-clear sky. The sense of urgency is overtaken by an overwhelming sensation of panic. I am in a maze. I am hopelessly lost ...

I awaken, perspiring and exhausted. The sense of frustration that plagued my dream follows me into the waking world.

* * * *

One morning, sitting on my bed, reading a textbook on Celtic mythology, I heard the familiar voice of Doc Friendly. 'Knock, knock.'

I looked up from my book and straight at the doc who stood in the doorway. 'Who's there?'

'What's that? Oh no, terribly sorry, I don't have any knock-knock jokes to hand. Just making sure you hadn't forgotten our appointment. What's that book you're reading? Celtic mythology?' he said, answering his own question. 'Enjoying it?'

'I've laughed, I've cried, it's changed my life! It's okay. You're not going to give away the ending, are you?'

'No, of course not. Our appointment is in thirty minutes' time. But you can make it half an hour, if that's easier.' The doc sniggered at his witticism. There was more. 'Well, try not to dilly-dally, we don't want to be late. Tell you what, you can dilly a bit as long as you promise not to dally!' By now the doc was guffawing at his comic genius.

I offered no such promise. I nodded and smiled and the doc went on his way. In the end, after a decent spell of dillying, followed by an unauthorised spell of dallying, I turned up fifteen minutes late. Or was I quarter of an hour late? As usual, I maintained my reluctance to discuss the stuff I wanted to forget. That's not to say I won't engage the doc from time to time in alternate, meaningful discussion. I ask questions along the way. The doc will start our sessions by asking, 'How are you feeling today, Alan?' He wants me to gauge what my all-encompassing, self-adjudged state of being is.

I responded in a generic fashion. 'Okay, I guess.' During an early session I almost answered, 'Same old, same old,' but I managed to check myself.

Having established that he needed to expend more effort before I shared the goods, he then asked a more specific question. 'And how are you eating?' I invariably resisted the urge to tell him I adopt the traditional approach of putting food in my mouth, chewing it and following up with a bout of swallowing.

'Good as always, Doc. No problems with the appetite.' This is very true. The food in the hospital is nutritious, delicious and, most important, plentiful. There was one period in my life when eating was too much of a chore. A period of time which belongs with the stuff I don't want to think or talk about.

Once the doc confirmed my dietary fortitude was intact, his next question attempted to establish if I rested well. 'How are you sleeping, Alan; are you getting enough rest?'

It may have been the higher-strength meds I started a week earlier, but my auto-response mode disengaged and I thought a moment before answering. 'Now that you ask, Doc, I haven't been sleeping too great. I have dreams that wake me. Then I can't get back to sleep. Not easily, anyway.'

'Is that so?'

No, I just thought I'd say the words outside of my head to see how they sound, for fuck's sake! I thought. 'Yes, I get them quite often,' is what I said.

'And what are these dreams about, Alan? Do you always have the same dream?'

'It's not the same each time. I can't remember the details, but they follow a theme. In the dream, I have to get somewhere or do something, but no matter what I do, or where I go, I never get any closer to my goal.'

'That's interesting. What stops you getting where you want to go, Alan?'

'Lots of obstacles. It can be people or objects or animals or the landscape. Everything in the dream seems determined to frustrate me. What does it all mean, Doc?'

'What do *you* think it means, Alan?' the doc said, confirming that his auto-response mode *was* engaged.

Bloody stronger meds! I'd forgotten all about psychotherapy rule number two: *Never give the patient a straightforward answer.* The doctor echoes the question back at the patient. This is also known as the "answer a question with a question" strategy. To be fair, it's also one of my favourite strategies, but I'm not so bloody obvious about it. Once again, I found myself biting my tongue and resisting the urge to ask the doc what *he* thinks *I* think it means. It could be the session without end if we go down that path. I'm sure the doc universally employs this strategy. I'm not arrogant enough to think he saves it solely for me. I once overheard him talking to a nurse. She asked him what the time was. 'What time do *you* think it is?' he answered. Bloody auto-response mode. I suppose it's reasonable that the doc would answer my question with a question now and again. I often stonewall the doc, so he has to gain traction somehow. I think our sessions resemble a challenging game that, more often than not, ends in stalemate. Having said that, I suspect there are times when Doc Friendly thinks he engages me in a game of chess, not realising I am playing draughts.

Chapter Six

I experienced some improvement at secondary school. However, the presence of at least one former classmate in every lesson meant I could not altogether dissociate myself from my unpleasant past. There was no return to the veiled taunting during lessons and there was very little name calling outside classes. Secondary school years are those in which to develop social skills. Children learn how to communicate and become engaged with the larger world. It's a time when perception expands to take in and appreciate the opportunities the world has to offer after school. My marginalisation left me socially inept, outside my domestic existence. My experiences were such that I didn't foresee opportunity in later life, only the potential for more animosity. I exhibited poor communication skills and sometimes, when unwelcome memories of my school days sneak up on me in times of lassitude, I believe my reticence was always destined.

My journey into social exclusion was a long and painful one. I told myself that even though I had been driven onto that path, I consciously took the last small step myself. One day I might believe that. It failed to lessen my sense of not belonging. I endured primary school by hoping that secondary school would be an improvement. Now, I endured secondary school, by hoping that university or work would be better. While my social skills were deficient, my powers of perseverance developed in compensation. I spent most of the time on my own during breaks, but graduated from comics to reading books. I still enjoyed tales of adventure, but I also developed an appreciation of Westerns. The characteristic of Westerns I enjoyed, in particular, was how the story is always resolved by the end of the book. There was no room for ambivalence; no permitted loose ends. There was only absolute resolution. The inevitable final showdown between goody and baddy always provided a definitive ending. The white-hatted goody triumphed over the black-hatted baddy.

As I entered adolescence I filled out physically. I added height to my stature and my back became larger and more muscular in sympathy, straining beneath the unflattering uniform. The transitionary muscles in my neck and upper arms also started to thicken. Not as overdeveloped as my back, they were still weightier than average. Their proximity to my back camouflaged their size to some extent, and they were easier to conceal within long sleeves and shirt collars. One side-effect of my thicker neck muscles was a susceptibility to severe tension headaches. At least they were infrequent and alleviated by the simple expedient of lying down and resting. Not wanting to feel neglected, my upper legs became somewhat thicker than normal; doubtless a symptom of the burden of carrying my bulky torso around. While I never entirely grew out of my clumsiness, I avoided those tasks that proved challenging to my questionable coordination. I didn't further my pursuit of a suitable after-school activity on the well-proven basis of "if at first you don't succeed, give up!"

There was one sport in which participation was compulsory. A sport at which I proved to be not so bad. It was the sport of *rugby*. Because decent coordination wasn't vital for all rugby positions, I became competent at the less complex aspects of the game. Indeed, being able to use my bulk and physical strength was most advantageous. The rugby toolbox is incomplete without its hammer and my approach to the game was very hammer-like indeed. My tackling method lent itself to the style of *crouch down and wait for them to trip over you*. It was at least more effective than the boys who employed the *run out of the way* approach. In a ruck, where the players are on their feet and battling for possession of the ball, I was particularly suited. No-one kept the ball from me once I laid my hands upon it. My grip and pulling strength proved too much for opponents, no matter how big or how many tried to keep hold of the ball. I even ripped the ball from my own teammates' grasp from time to time, but never on purpose. It was a manifestation of my over-eagerness to show good at something at which I excelled. I was a claw hammer in the rugby toolbox, designed for extraction.

Despite being unfamiliar with the collaboration that is intrinsic to being part of a team, I still considered myself a team player. Many boys on my team hadn't been in my class at primary school, so while they weren't overly friendly, neither were they hostile. There was one notable occasion when I made the choice to act against one of my team. Phil had been in my class for the last year of primary school. Although he hadn't been one of the active tormentors he was nevertheless tainted by association. When playing rugby, Phil would declare himself vice-captain, which was meaningless in the context of the class. He was without exception the most vocal player on the pitch. His supposed commands took the form of delayed commentary. His typical approach was to direct his teammates to do something they had just done. Mark passes the ball to Simon. 'That's it, Mark. Pass it to Simon. Catch the ball, Simon,' Phil would say, pointlessly confirming the transaction. He was never helpful, but there was one instance when he was less helpful than usual.

I was keen to expand my limited but effective repertoire of rugby tricks. I was determined to attempt to pass the ball. As expected, I won the ball from a ruck and I experienced a sudden rush of blood to the head. I resolved that now was the time for me to attempt *the pass* to one of my teammates. Some people are born into greatness, theirs the destiny of kings and emperors. Some people have greatness thrust upon them and they embrace it without hesitation. Then there are those people that stumble upon the possibility of greatness and in attempting to grasp it with both hands, they completely miss. Unrewarded they are and destined not even for a footnote in the history books, but they are fearless, nevertheless. They care not for what others think of their actions. At least we tried!

In my excitement I forgot the full extent of my questionable coordination. I threw the ball true and straight. It truly went straight out of bounds. While my attempt at *the pass* had gone nowhere near the player for whom I aimed, I consoled myself that at least I hadn't given the ball to the opposition. Phil, however, failed to see the silver lining that had presented itself to me. Phil deviated from his usual practice of running away from play to provide remote commentary. Instead, he determined to provide criticism. 'What the hell was that, *Alien*? Is that how they play rugby on your planet, 'cos that's not how we do it here?' My *flabber* was *gasted*. I hadn't heard that word in an age and never while playing rugby. Phil dispelled any doubts about his intent, as from that point on he riled me with, 'Planet Earth to Alien,' at every available opportunity. He looked to the other boys as he spoke, grinning as though perfecting a new trick of his own and seeking their approval.

I waited with unerring patience for opportunity to call, my sporting goals different to those possessed earlier in the game. During the second half I spotted an opening and pounced. Phil was too slow getting out of the way of play and he ended up in a ruck. Seeing my chance I dived straight into the melee, as was my usual practice. However, rather than go for the ball, I went straight for Phil's head. I grabbed him securely by his ears and extracted him from the ruck through a combination of twisting and pulling. Once extracted, I threw him to the ground where he rolled around, clutching his ears and moaning. He looked up at me with a pained and confused expression. 'What the hell are you doing … *Alien*?' My *flabber* was further *gasted*. How did he know that I hadn't seen him getting trapped in a ruck with all those rough boys and had risked my own physical wellbeing to extricate him? I found it implausible that he had misunderstood the most obvious message he'd been given. In fact, I was so confused and distracted by his reaction that I accidentally stood on his groin as I ran to rejoin play. Perhaps my coordination wasn't so bad after all.

This unfortunate accident corrected his perception. He never again called me Alien. Indeed, the little he said during the remainder of the game, and for the next few days, seemed to be pitched a little higher than usual. He may have lost his place as a baritone in the school choir but at least he could've tried out as a sopranist. He should've been grateful that he hadn't joined the *castrato*. While I hadn't been able to master the art of *the pass*, I nonetheless added another trick to my rugby repertoire.

My advancement to secondary school didn't provide the improvements for which I wished. I hoped as I matured physically I would be afforded the opportunity to mature socially. An ambition that should have flourished in an environment where all were expected to mature emotionally. We entered secondary school as children, but exited as young adults. I was still unable to escape the animosity of my past. I remained on the outside, looking in. My aspirations were all superficial, centred on my appearance. I was convinced my abnormal shape was at the root of all my problems. I hoped that, like the ugly duckling of fairy tales, time would transform me into something wonderful. I hoped that I would at least look less anomalous as I grew older. The problem, I discovered, is that an ugly duckling only matures into a beautiful swan in fairy tales.

In real life, ugly ducklings grow up to be ugly ducks.

* * * *

My introduction to the gang was innocuous. It started with a nod. It happened early in my on-again off-again relationship with the facility. Now and again I would see a few of the guys hanging out in the rec room, sitting around, watching movies. I remembered Brains from the introductory session with Doc Friendly, suggesting the doc get his lock fixed. I thought at the time, *I like this guy's style*. Brains sat in front of the TV, the remote control close at hand. There was a hint of something whiffy in the air, a half-smell of something almost forgotten. Bomber sat to Brains' left, in his own armchair, close to an open window. There was another viewer who sat to Brains' right. His back was to me as I entered. He turned to see who had arrived and the sight I beheld is something I will never forget, no matter how I try. Had I enlisted Doc Friendly's dedicated assistance, not even he would have proven up to the task of ridding me of the memory.

The turnarounder was Mike who, I later discovered, was better known as *Face*. His self-description was: 'There's ugly, fucking ugly, freak-show ugly, and then there's me.' I discovered that, rather than be self-conscious about his appearance, he wore his unique looks with a measure of pride. During one later session, the guys had loosened up and were engaging in pseudo-friendly banter. Legs and Face disagreed on some important trivia. Legs vocalised his irritation. 'What will you do for a face when the pig wants his arsehole back?'

'Oi!' Face said, acting offended.

'What's up, do you like pigs?' Legs said, surprised at the reaction.

'Yeah, bacon, ham, sausages ...'

I was unprepared for the vision that greeted me when Face turned. I was so startled that I jumped several feet; some vertically but mostly backwards in the general direction of away-from-Face. It was obvious that Face was no stranger to my reaction and, rather than be offended, he offered what may have been intended as a friendly smile. It was difficult to tell for what he was aiming. His change in expression did nothing to lessen the shock. Being better prepared, I didn't jump but I flinched, nevertheless. It wasn't simply that his individual features were unattractive. It was exacerbated by their peculiar arrangement on what could only charitably be described as his face. Face turned back to the TV and I stood, somewhat shaken, with my composure returning. Brains looked over towards me with a big grin and nodded. 'You okay?'

'Yes, thanks,' I lied and took a few steps into the room.

Brains sat up and introduced the group. 'I'm Greg, that's Carl and the good-looking geezer is Mike.'

'Hi, I'm Alan.' They threw a 'Hi' or two in my direction which I took as permission to join them. The chat was frequent and inconsequential and the one other memorable event paled in comparison to my first sighting of Face. A member of staff entered the room for rollcall. She was a rather pretty nursing assistant that I spied now and again around the facility. She entered the rec room smiling, perhaps intending to say, 'Hi' or 'Hello'. I never discovered what she did intend to say. All we heard was, 'H ...' as she spotted Bomber, at which point she held her breath. She looked around with haste, counted the bodies, and darted out of the room.

I was baffled by her odd behaviour but the guys grinned knowingly, sharing a laugh or two. I smiled in a token sympathetic display, having no idea what the source of mirth was, but not wishing to appear standoffish. Knowing now what I do, I can state without doubt that Bomber was on his best behaviour and demonstrating superior sphincter control. With hindsight, the clues were there; the remnants of the dead animal smell as I entered the room and Bomber seated next to an open window despite the coolness of the room. I know now that Bomber saves his legendary rectal performances for the "benefit" of the gang and, at that time, I had been an unknown quantity. His restraint could not have been easy and his discomfort must have been considerable by the end of the evening.

I seem to recall, later that night, wondering if I sensed indistinct rumblings as I drifted off to sleep. At one point, the window gently rattled in its frame. I suppose Bomber couldn't hold it in forever. I was glad I hadn't had a proper introduction to Bomber's talents that night. I'd already had enough of a shock to my system. I never thanked him for that.

* * * *

The success of the self-medicating endeavours of the gang relies upon a certain level of cooperation on the part of hospital management. I'd never tried recreational drugs on the outside; I was never offered them. This was yet another manifestation of my social exclusion; one that I wasn't aware of until I ended up inside. It was my second internment at the facility when I was close to 21 years old that I was, at last, offered the opportunity to "partake". I was in my room, putting away freshly laundered clothes, when I heard a knock at my door. I turned to see that the supplier of knocks was Jeff, one of the orderlies who wandered the corridors, keeping things in order that were deserving of it. 'Hey, Alan, how goes it?'

'Fine, thanks,' I said. After an uncomfortable pause I added, 'I'm putting my clothes away,' breaking the silence, by way of stating the obvious.

'I wanted to let you know about some things that don't make it to the official welcome pack.' He stood in the doorway and after glancing up and down the corridor, he entered the room. 'I wanted to let you know that if you're in the market for something a bit more ... *recreational* I might be able to help you out,' he said.

I had no idea what he was talking about. Was he trying to sell me ping-pong balls; perhaps they were the local currency here, like "snout" is in gaol? He saw from my blank stare that he hadn't got through. I needed clues.

'Nothing too heavy. Maybe a little, you know, "Kate Bush".' I didn't know. Was he selling bootleg CDs? He wasn't giving up. 'You know, "Mary Jane".' Nope, that wasn't any clearer, although I now wondered if he was a pimp. He was getting impatient. 'You must know. *"Laughing Grass, Jolly Green, Weed, Ganja"*!' Ah, knowledge dawned; starting to understand, but not confident enough to commit to a response. 'I'm talking about cannabis, man. Hashish. All the good shit!' he said, in a final fit of desperation.

Yep, message received and understood. 'Oh, ah, I don't know about that. I'm not sure. I'll have to think about it.' I tried to stall, exposing myself as the man of the world that I wasn't.

'Cool, man. Let me know if you need anything; we can work something out. Catch you whenever,' he said, full of cheer. And so he departed.

My heart beat quicker at the thought of my first run-in with a drug dealer. It wasn't in the same league as a briefcase full of non-sequential cash for several kilos of white powder, hand poised above firearm, in case shit hits fan, but it was technically *illicit* nevertheless. Of most importance, someone thought I was worldly enough to be worth approaching.

I thought of little else over the next few days. Had he selected me for some specific reason? Had I met some minimum criteria to be considered a potential partaker? Or was his offer part of the unofficial welcome for all new residents? I wondered what the outcome would be if I took him up on his proposal. How much does it cost? Would I get a fair deal? How would I know if the "shit" was indeed "good"? How would I ingest the illicit substance? All these thoughts, and more, whirled around my brain until two days later, when they were all silenced with extreme prejudice.

I sat in my room, just after lunchtime, reading as I often did, letting the digestive process do its thing. The head orderly, Dai, strode into my room unannounced and slid the door closed. Dai was a tall, heavily-built individual and the light from the window reflected off his shaved scalp. I looked up in surprise; I was used to people giving warning and asking for permission before entering. I wasn't used to someone barging in and closing the door behind them, all without consent. He walked towards me. 'Alan, I need to ask you something serious now. I want you to be honest with me.'

'Okay,' I said, puzzled.

'Has Jeff offered to sell you drugs?' he asked.

'What? I don't know what you mean. No, of course he hasn't,' I lied. I wondered how the hell Dai had found out. I hadn't discussed it with anyone and Jeff seemed pretty careful at ensuring no-one over-heard. Then I remembered it took him a while to get through, during which time someone could have approached the door. Shit! What if Jeff blames me for taking longer than he thought it would to deliver his sales pitch? Double shit! What if he thinks I was the one who grassed him up? I didn't want to wake up one morning to find a horse's head in my bed, although it would more likely be a sheep's head in Wales. No matter; the only animal parts that interest me are selected parts of selected animals on a plate covered by a delicious sauce, accompanied by freshly cooked vegetables, and never in my bed.

'Are you sure, Alan? You can tell me. There won't be any hassle.' Dai persisted, wanting confirmation.

'Yes, of course I'm sure. Christ, I'd remember something like that,' I lied again, getting better.

'Good. 'Cos if you want that sort of thing, you come straight to me.' He made to leave the room. As he got to the door he turned, tapped the side of his nose and winked. 'Don't forget, straight to me.' He left me alone with many questions. It appeared that there was an unofficial hierarchy within the official hospital hierarchy that had to be respected. I wondered what other "unofficial services" I might be unaware of. What sort of a place was this?

* * * *

My education in the workings of the hospital accelerated when I accepted an invitation to the gym from Brains. I hung around with the guys in the evening for a while, building my stake as a potential associate. I proved, beyond doubt, my commitment to the worship of FKB which improved my social capital to the point where I was entrusted with an invite to join in the more covert activities of the gang. By now I had been introduced to another member of the elite who hadn't been around when I met the others. Vic was known as *Voice* due to his tendency towards inadvertent and deafening verbal assault. He wasn't deliberately loud, he would simply forget that his "normal" voice was equivalent to a lung-bursting scream of the average punter. When he forgot to reign in his stentorian voice, it was such that he believed himself miles away from you on a windy day, when in fact he stood right next to you.

Voice was short and of solid build. He embodied *stocky*. He possessed the lungs and vocal chords of someone much larger. Perhaps a much larger creature, such as a disoriented elephant or a pissed-off lion. He was raised in Aberdeen but moved around much in his later years. We thought he possessed a decent Scottish accent but he noisily assured us that his accent was so mild it was, 'Almost not there'. His laugh had much of the orgasming donkey about it. Attempting to preserve the integrity of my eardrums, I was forced to develop an essential skill. It was simple; most brilliant ideas are. When Voice talked loudly, I would simply listen quietly. I'd adopted a similar trick in order to survive Face. When faced with facing Face I prepared my eyes for what they were about to see, so that the shock would not prove overwhelming. With Voice I prepared my eardrums for the aural assault that might be on the way.

Both Face and Voice sometimes caught me unawares. Either assault, whether visual or auditory, caused me to jump. The effect of Face always threatened my backwards long jump record, as I attempted to move in the general direction of away-from-Face. Voice edged Face in the high jump stakes, though. Voice was a huge fan of reggae. He could often be heard, all the way to town and beyond, singing along to the classics, such as Gregory Isaacs, Jimmy Cliff or Bob Marley. His rendition of "I shot the sheriff" was inspiring, once we were well into a spell of self-medication and loosened up. Voice would unearth his Scottish heritage, singing, 'Ah shoat the sheruff, but I didnae shoat they deputy,' at which point we joined in his subsequent ad-lib, 'Ya lyin' basturt!' He sang in the style of Scottish Reggae sensation *Rab McMarley*.

As I wandered into the gym with Brains to experience my first formal session, he reassured me there would be no need to demonstrate any feats of strength. '*Non preoccuparti*, Alan. You won't need to break a sweat today, unless you are so inclined. You'll find we have a relaxed attitude to exercising, with the focus on "relaxed".'

I held no concerns relating to feats of strength, other than issues regarding my questionable control, so his assurance was redundant. He had, however, intrigued me with his comments. I was uncertain what I would find. When we walked into the well-lit room the others were already there, evenly scattered around the space. The presence of Dai near the doorway did nothing to diminish the sense of intrigue. I nodded to the others and distributed a 'Hi' or two in various directions as I followed Brains.

He indicated a vacant spot, close to a window and equidistant from the others in the room. 'Take a pew.' He wandered over to the sound system that spewed music via several speakers situated in various spots around the room. I remember the first track playing – "Rudy got soul" by Desmond Dekker, an unhurried and not unpleasant ska track. It seemed an incongruous choice, inappropriate for a place of exercise. I'd expected something livelier that would inspire activity. That confusion, and a number of other questions, were resolved when the boys removed their spliffs and lit up. I didn't know if they smoked

Kate Bush, Mary Jane, Laughing Grass, Jolly Green, Weed or Ganja. But thanks to Jeff, it was all "the good shit" to me.

Brains walked up to where I sat as he made his way from the sound system to his seat. 'So Alan, would you care to join? The first one is on the house,' he said, offering me a tailor-made. I had spent considerable time wondering about the sales pitches I'd received from Jeff and Dai. I'd wondered how the logistical challenges to "partaking" could be surmounted, should I accept Dai's offer. The decision to discount the offer from Jeff, despite his earlier and lengthier sales pitch, was automatic once Dai clarified the unofficial hierarchy. The remaining challenges to how, where and what to do to avoid detection were now answered.

I held out my hand to accept the offered product. 'Sure, thanks,' I said. I risked a quick glance towards Dai to see if he witnessed the transaction. He glanced towards me. I was relieved to see him purse his lips and give a small nod of his head. Approved.

'Need a light?' Brains said.

'Sure, thanks.'

I placed the spliff in my mouth. Brains applied the flame, and I inhaled. Other than the second-hand smoke from Mrs Reilly, I had never smoked in my life. My reaction did nothing to conceal that fact. In desperation, I tried to contain the inhalation; my cheeks bulged and my eyes watered. My efforts were to no avail. The smoke exploded out of all available orifices to the accompaniment of a cacophony of coughing.

'Smooth, isn't it?' Voice yelled at me from across the room, causing the smoke to dispel somewhat. 'Don't worry about it. We've all been there,' he reassured me.

I knew little about the anticipated effects of absorbing cannabis but I was certain that bringing up a lung wouldn't be on the "desired" list. Bloody side-effects! I waited until a semblance of lung function returned. I tried again, with extreme caution. This time I took time to inhale less than half the volume of my previous effort. It proved to be my first successful drag. I held the smoke for a few seconds before exhaling leisurely, without displacing any internal organs. The desired effects were not immediate. There was no definitive point at which I thought, *hey, this is working,* although halfway through the spliff I began to feel *something.*

I felt relaxed and a little light-headed; nothing severe, but enough that I had to make an effort to focus on the discussion.

'You know *cage fighting*? Well, I reckon I could do that,' Face said.

'I didn't think you're into fisticuffs or "footicuffs". I couldn't see you having a go,' Voice shouted.

'Are you after some cheap, although somewhat arbitrary, alternative to cosmetic surgery?' Brains said.

'Yer arse!' Face said. 'Well, I mean how hard could it be to fight a cage? A cage can't move and it can't hit back. That's got to be an advantage to the novice cage fighter! All you'd have to do is be careful not to hurt yourself when you hit it.'

'Yeah, that's true,' Voice shouted. 'And you could start out with something easy, like a hamster or a mouse cage.'

I thought to contribute. 'Yeah, but I'll bet the champions have to tackle something serious, like a lion cage. That'd be the real deal.'

Everyone nodded in agreement. We all inhaled by way of intermission. By now, my partaking technique was somewhat improved and I felt less self-conscious of the occasional small cough that escaped from me. I was pleased that I'd been able to follow the conversation. Indeed, I knew exactly where the boys were coming from.

I still thought we were talking a complete load of bollocks. I simply no longer cared.

* * * *

When I was fifteen Dad took me for the Christmas break to the Glenshee ski resort in Scotland. We were unable to sample any of the more exotic European resorts, because that would have required air travel. Dad wasn't keen on flying. He had a number of explanations in support of his misgivings; his favourite excuse being that he was worried the plane could run out of fuel during the flight and we could be "stuck up there for ages!" So we left Gelert with Doctor Jeffries for a week and, through a combination of taxi, trains and coaches, we made our way to Glenshee. We found accommodation in a cosy hotel, a short bus ride to the main resort. It was a boutique hotel which I thought sounded poncy; overtones of hairdressers. There was no salon, but there were numerous open fires, pine furniture and timber-covered walls and floors. It was like staying in a large, well-appointed IKEA sauna, but with less humidity.

The resort was busy and recent snowfall accommodated the visiting skiers. Being novices, Dad and I took skiing lessons during the first couple of days. The instructor told us not to worry about falling over. 'That's why snow is soft,' he said. He also advised that if we weren't falling over then we weren't trying hard enough. I began with much enthusiasm. I tried to move in a ski-like manner; I fell over, I dusted myself off, I picked myself up and repeated the process. I consoled myself, knowing that every time I fell it was evidence of my "trying hard". I tried *too* hard. I suspect my unusual physique didn't help, the activity being designed for punters of a more traditional physique. At least the overweight profit from having a lower centre of gravity. With my physique, my centre of gravity was neither low nor high. It was simply wrong.

However, without even trying, I became a proficient, if unconventional, tobogganist. Despite becoming quite adept at skiing on my arse and even my face, I couldn't perfect the *skiing-on-the-skis* technique adopted by traditionalists. To further complicate matters, the size and shape of my back was conducive to sledding type activities. It was as though I carried my own personal bobsled on my back. Unfortunately for the surrounding skiers I was incapable of steering, and when on my face incapable of seeing. All I could do was offer a warning shout of, 'Watch out!' and then brace for impact before sliding into some unfortunate punter. At one point, my passage downslope resembled that of a ten pin bowling ball as I slid into a large group of waiting innocents, skittling them in random directions. As I skidded to a halt I heard someone calling out, 'Strike!'

Dad didn't share my shortcomings. He was able to pick up the techniques with relative ease and by the end of the week he was negotiating the intermediate slopes while I languished on the beginner slopes. Nevertheless, the week was enjoyable and I hold fond memories of the snow and the cold and the open fires. I had yet more fond memories of time with Dad; joking and swapping war stories.

By the end of the holiday, my scorecard for the week was one broken arm and two broken legs. None of them were mine.

Chapter Seven

My predictable domestic existence was the one constant onto which I held. The sun rose in the morning, Dad distracted me with his funny tales, Mrs M radiated her competent presence, Gelert went arse-over-tit when I returned from school and the sun set at night. Doctor Jeffries was also part of the domestic picture. He demonstrated that decent, caring people existed in the big, wide world. He visited most weekends, carrying a sample of the latest batch of home brew for Dad's appraisal. He often accompanied us when the dog took us for walks. The four of us made a happy, chatty, barky group as we explored the local countryside.

After returning from our skiing holiday, I realised we hadn't seen Doctor Jeffries for almost a month. His non-appearance could be explained by his being a practising GP and an active member of the community. His eventual visit one Saturday night was notably unusual. In all the years we'd been in Wales, the doctor only called during the day. When Dad opened the door I wandered out to the hallway to say hello. Most unusual was Doctor Jeffries expression; he appeared worried, almost to the point of distraction. As Doctor Jeffries walked in, it took him a few moments to realise I was there. His look of worry changed to an expression I didn't recognise at the time. Now I believe it may have been something akin to pity. He was quick to regain his composure. 'Hello, Alan. How are you?'

'Fine, thank you, Doctor Jeffries. How are you?'

He hesitated. 'Well, yes. I'm well, thank you.'

'Okay, Alan, you need to get to bed now,' Dad said. His face was flushed and his voice a little slurred. He had been drinking quite heavily, something I had not witnessed before. Dad would sometimes have a few drinks with a meal but I'd never seen him "under the influence". He never allowed alcohol to affect his behaviour.

'Already? But it's not even eight thirty.'

Dad seemed irritated. 'Just … please. Be a good boy and head up now.' His shoulders drooped, as if fatigued. 'Read for a while and I'll come up to you later. Doctor Jeffries and I have some things to discuss.'

'Okay,' I said, heading for the stairs.

The doctor called after me, 'Goodnight, Alan.'

I responded with a perfunctory goodnight, reaching the top of the stairs.

I waited until I heard the study door close. I crept down a few steps until their voices were clear. I felt scared and guilty. Scared that I might get caught if they left the study without warning. Guilty that I eavesdropped. It would disappoint Dad if I was discovered. But I had to uncover what troubled Doctor Jeffries and Dad.

I crept down the stairs, straining to hear the conversation. 'You don't have to do this, John,' Doctor Jeffries said.

'Well, I think I do. It's the right thing to do, Barry.'

'But it will change everything. What about the boy? How is he going to take it?'

'He'll be fine. Alan will understand.'

'Will he understand *everything* though?'

'Alan doesn't need to know *everything*. He only needs to know the essentials. I'll not have him being upset!'

'I understand, but what if he finds out the rest?'

'How? Are you going to tell him?'

'No, of course not. I would never do that to him. Or to you.'

'Well, like I said; it's the right thing to do.'

'But is now the right time to start "doing the right thing"?'

'What the fuck is that supposed to mean?' Hearing Dad swear was like a slap to the face. Once he'd hit his thumb with a hammer and blurted out, 'Bastard!' before he could restrain himself. He followed that up with ten minutes of apologies and lectures about the use of "grown-up words".

'You know I didn't mean it like that, John. I'm only saying you need to consider that you may be doing the wrong thing for the right reasons.'

'Barry, you offered to help when this came up. I am trying to take you up on your offer. If you don't want to help, that's fine. I understand. But you must understand that I'm going to do this.' Dad sounded calmer. And determined.

'Okay, John. I said I'll help and I will. I just hope I'm wrong,' the doctor said.

I heard footsteps. I leapt up the stairs where I could remain hidden. I heard the study door open, followed by clearer footsteps and then the sound of the front door opening. 'I'll see you soon John. Maybe once you've slept on it you might see things differently.'

'I won't, Barry. See you soon ... and thanks.' Dad sounded sober.

'Take care, John,' the doctor said, and he left. I timed my movements so the sound of the front door closing masked any noise my bedroom door made, as I tiptoed into the room.

Dad didn't say goodnight later. He returned to his study, I suspect to rid himself of his short-lived sobriety.

Countless thoughts hounded my attempts to sleep. I couldn't make sense of what I'd overheard. I didn't understand the implications of their discussion. Not then anyway. I would soon learn. It wasn't long before everything changed.

* * * *

It didn't take me long to learn the ways of the underbelly of the hospital. In fact, that's glamorising the situation; it was more of a side-belly. Both metaphorically and literally, we existed off to the side of the sanctioned affairs of the facility. Dai proved to be a central resource to the successful practice of our unsanctioned self-medication. Dai supplied the product and also provided supervision of the use of said product. Through supreme effort, I conducted myself capably during my introduction to the group's unauthorised activities, discounting the initial displacement of a lung. Neither did I find my introduction to the world of recreational drugs harmful to my sleep which may have been a symptom of using the product. Perhaps it was a result of a number of related questions that had once troubled my sleep being unequivocally answered, but I slept well. The following day, after enjoying a substantial breakfast, I repaired to my room where I prepared myself for the day ahead.

Dai confirmed he was not a knocker when, once again, he entered my room unheralded, closing the door behind him. 'Hey, Alan. How are you shaping up?'

'Oh yeah, not so bad.' I felt a bit more worldly than during our first meeting.

'So, what do you think of the lads? Not a bad bunch, eh?'

'Yeah, they seem like a decent gang.' I had yet to meet Nobby.

'So, you'll want to join in the activities? You seemed to enjoy yourself. The get-togethers are two or three times a week, depending on who's about and other stuff.'

'Sure, that's sounds like something I'd be interested in,' I said, sounding keener than I wanted.

'No problems. Look, me and the guys work out details on an individual basis, if that's okay.'

'Sure, whatever's easiest,' I said, not having a bloody clue how else to progress.

'Most of the guys get resin from me. The usual portion lasts about a week or so.'

'Okay, let's try that and see how it goes.' Like I had a choice.

'Forty quid a pop and no credit facilities is the usual arrangement.'

'Fine, I'll grab the cash,' I said as Dai's hand disappeared within his shirt. I gave him the cash and he handed me a greenish brown ball about the size of an impoverished sprout. It was heavier than I expected. I could feel my heart pounding as I took my first delivery of illicit drugs. I was now a *player*.

'There you go. Glyndwr's finest. All the way from a little place, starting with "C".'

'What, Columbia?' I said, unable to contain my awe.

'No. *Cardiff*! How far do you think I travel? I don't have a private jet,' he said. I was less impressed but thankful, assuming travel costs would be incorporated into the going rate.

'If you like, I can show you how to get the product into a useable form,' he said.

'Huh?'

'Do you need some tips on how to roll a spliff?' he clarified. I further appreciated how Dai was the supplier of choice. In addition to being the more senior member of staff, he straightaway recognised my level of ignorance. Jeff would still be throwing random words in my direction, hoping something would stick.

'Oh yeah. That would be a big help.' There was little point in denying the obvious.

'Okay. Let's meet back here at 2 pm. Then we don't need to rush,' he said, recognising me for the beginner I was. With that, he left, lighter for product but heavier for cash.

As it transpired, I became a gifted producer of the spliff. Later, Dai demonstrated with the product I purchased, of course, which motivated me to comprehensively learn my lessons. Dai's advice proved invaluable. As well as providing practical guidance to promote effective use of the product, he offered insight into the general ways of the gang. He advised that the group would "burn a couple" during a standard gathering. He demonstrated how to distribute the product within the contents of a roll-your-own cigarette for optimal effect. He cautioned against rolling too many before they were needed in the heat of battle. They would be harder to conceal and the product would dry out to suboptimal moisture content if not consumed soon after spliff-construction. When Dai tried to explain the mechanisms behind spliff degradation in technical terms, I responded with 'Huh?'

He summarised for my benefit. 'All you need to remember is make them on the day. Easier to conceal and makes for better quality control.' When Dai left, I felt as prepared as I thought possible. At the next session I wouldn't make the mistake of turning up with an amateur-looking "here's one I made earlier". No, I would assume my place as *one of the lads* and demonstrate my doobie-developing dexterity.

Within two weeks I had established myself as a member of the gang, in time earning my nickname, *Silent*. During my probationary fortnight I learnt the pseudonyms of the other associates and a little of how they acquired those names. Of course, Face needed no explanation and Bomber soon made it clear how he acquired his *nom de guerre*. That first fortnight allowed me to learn a good deal about what was considered acceptable subject matter for discussion when in session. I was relieved to discover that the specifics that led to our becoming inmates of the facility were off-limits. This policy complemented my personal practice of ignoring those very specifics.

It wasn't long before I actively contributed to the group. It would be towards the latter half of the session before I'd loosened up enough to find my voice. I had an alias to protect, after all. In addition to my selective offerings to the discussion, I demonstrated an ability to innovate by introducing some rigour to the practice of pillar number two. While Dai's supervision provided protection against discovery of our unsanctioned activities, his protection wasn't absolute. We were obliged to remain vigilant against the chance someone might wander in and interrupt our important work. The nature and location of the room provided us with ample warning of potential incursions, if we were attentive. Dai also acted in the capacity of early warning system. He wasn't in the habit of partaking, having more to lose should our activities be exposed. He worked on the basis of "Don't defecate where you devour".

We didn't always have the benefit of Dai's supervision. This would depend upon his allocated shifts. His availability was subject to change at short notice as the result of variations to his workload. On those occasions, when lacking official supervision, we had to be extra vigilant. We didn't only have to worry about unexpected interlopers wandering into the gym, under the illusion it was being used for its intended purpose. We also had to take into account the hourly roll-call. The timing between head counts was between fifty and seventy minutes, depending on the clipboard bearer. Once we knew the identity of the clip-boarder, we estimated an earliest time of arrival and tailored our sessions to suit. It was my bright idea to make better use of the music that was played to accompany us to our Happy Places. We synchronised our activities to match the rhythm of the music. We would allow ourselves to be lulled by the distinctive, smooth beat of assorted reggae. The combination of the effects of self-medication and the tempo of the music led to a perilous lethargy overcoming the group, leading to a less-than-meerkat level of awareness. This in itself presented a problem if we got carried away in our scientific endeavours.

I hatched a scheme to punctuate the reggae with an astutely placed punk track. I discovered that Doc Friendly had provided many useful examples of the genre. At first I was surprised at his choice of music, but not at the implied nostalgia. The distinct change in music acted as clear warning of an imminent head-count and roused us from any potentially dangerous lethargy. My inspiration not yet exhausted, I further suggested that the punk track be considered the "roll-them-up" track. The typical punk track duration of a few minutes provided an appropriate interval for production of the spliff. In essence, it was an indicator to re-set the process of pillar number two. We chatted about nothing in particular while awaiting the clip-boarder to put in an appearance. Once this occurred, we were equipped to dive straight back into our scientific work. The process was such that the punk music provided our "rolling soundtrack" while the reggae music provided our "relaxing soundtrack".

On those few occasions when interlopers loomed, the sheer number of eyes in the room meant that someone almost always spotted the potential intruder and raised the alarm. We had one exceptionally close call from which we all learnt some lessons. At the time of the closest call, Nobby had latched onto the group. He was standing at the entrance of the gym, acting as our last-ditch deterrent.

Nobby had already established he was not going to join us in the commissioning of pillar two. Or as Nobby phrased it, 'I refuse to smoke dope!' When we quite reasonably asked him to explain his position he said he had concerns about potential side-effects. He claimed to have reviewed several, indisputable reports proving beyond doubt that smoking dope led to the development of schizophrenia.

However, Face wouldn't let this explanation pass untested. 'Schizophrenia, isn't that where you have multiple personalities?'

'Yeah, that's right,' Nobby said.

'Fuck me, Nobby! Any alternative personality has got to be an improvement on what passes for your personality right now. If I were you I'd be smoking shit non-stop!'

It was at this point we determined to make Nobby the control group. It was an innovative compromise; he remained part of the group, despite not joining in the full spectrum of activities. Just as important, being the sole inhabitant of the control group he could still be excluded even when he was technically included. We were also influenced by the uncomfortable need to trust Nobby. We worked on the basis that Nobby would have more to lose than to gain by grassing us up. No-one believed Nobby had the backbone to squeal, but we still felt a little safer having him where we could unfortunately see him. His attendance was considered a necessary evil. There was no need for threats, implied or otherwise. Nobody would ever put a horse's head in Nobby's bed. Even if someone was capable of girding their loins to the extent that they could brave an incursion into the charnel pit that was Nobby and Bomber's room, there were the feelings of the horse to consider. Putting a horse's head in Nobby's bed would be tantamount to animal cruelty, disregarding the horse's decapitated state. I would feel sorry for the horse's head.

The closest we came to being exposed was the product of a combination of circumstances and process failures. Bloody Nobby! Bloody Duracell! And by way of full disclosure, bloody me! For the purposes of timekeeping, we relied upon an impressive-looking wall clock, positioned on the back wall of the gym. Most important, it was visible to everyone in the group when positioned at our customary spots. On the day in question a full complement of members was present as all were incarcerated at the time. Dai was unavailable to provide supervision and so Nobby was the session lookout. The head nurse, Ms Hughes, possessed the clipboard and was a most predictable pollster. Resembling Mrs Montgomery, Nurse Hughes possessed an aura of strict competence and no-nonsense. The rest of the staff afforded her the deference due to someone of her exalted rank. I noticed even Dai would smarten himself up when she was near.

We sat at our customary positions, talking our usual load of bollocks. We had already finished our first spliff of the session, had our first head-count and were now well into spliff number two. Bob Marley and the Wailers were promoting the relaxation phase of the process with "Three little birds". The Cockney Rejects were ready with "Flares and Slippers" to alert us of a change in process. Our official timepiece indicated we had ten minutes before needing to conceal our nefarious activities in time for the next rollcall. We were a little distracted at the time. As usual, our watchman Nobby was making valuable use of his time by searching for something buried deep within his frontal sinuses. Brains noticed Nobby struggling to remove the stubborn matter from his nose. 'Oi, Nobby, *Sie schmutzig bastard*. It's "roll, flick, goal!"' Brains said.

'What are you talking about?'

'You appear to be stuck on the "pick" stage of the "pick, roll, flick, goal" procedure.'

'Yeah, it's disgusting. Stop picking your nose,' Legs said.

'Whose nose should I pick then?'

'How about using a hanky, you dirty bastard?' Voice yelled. 'Better still, how about you fuck off and take your nose, and whatever is stuck up it, with you?'

Face contributed. 'How do you break Nobby's finger?'

'Punch him in the nose!' Voice correctly answered.

Brains, satisfied that the gang had taken up his initial sortie into Nobby's questionable hygiene, turned his attention towards me. 'Hey, Silent, any chance I can bum a stick off you? I'll see you right next time.'

I have a policy that I assiduously observe with regards to the borrower-versus-lender minefield. I lend a single time until the agreed debt is repaid. Should the debt remain outstanding then I shall lend no more to the defaulter. I always repay a debt at the earliest convenience, as I hold my reputation as a man of my word in high regard. I expect my policy of courtesy to be reciprocated. I checked my mental accounts to confirm that Brains had no outstanding debts. I replied accordingly. 'Sure thing, Brains. I have a "here's-one-I-made-earlier" available to be despatched on the next departing flight.' I retrieved the aforementioned HOIME, lined up Brains and prepared for launch. The same qualities that made my spliffs so smoke-worthy also lent themselves to the facilitation of aerial delivery. Their tightly packed density and torpedo shape made them most aerodynamic. Being a full spliff into the session I was loosened up. In my non-loosened state I would never dare to attempt an across-the-room pilot-less flight. In general, when playing darts in my default condition the safest place to stand is right in front of the dartboard.

I was in the zone. I was relaxed. I was confident. I was mistaken. I held the request with care and drew my hand back to fuel its flight. Bringing my hand swiftly forward, I released the missile with confidence. I watched, mesmerised, as it described a perfect arc across the room, as if borne on the wing of cherubim and seraphim. Unfortunately these baby angels were not equipped with GPS. I watched the missile descend from the zenith of its flight and make good its escape, via a small open window just out of Brains' reach. It would have been an astonishing feat had I been trying to make the shot. It sailed straight out of the tiny opening, not even touching the window frame. 'Balls!' I said and stood, preparing to recapture the escapee. I took but one step, freezing as I spotted Nurse Hughes, clipboard in hand, bearing down upon the gym. Ten minutes early.

'Oh fuck!' I declared, realising I could not reach the wayward spliff before the nurse. My profanity wasn't wasted on the gang. With commendable reactions they comprehended my motivation. We had perfunctorily discussed the need for an emergency procedure should the ensuing event appear imminent. We decided that with the measures we had in place an emergency procedure was unnecessary. We were mistaken.

With the notable exception of our commitment to the furthering of the psychopharmaceutic field, our group does not consist of the courageous. Should someone roll a live hand grenade into the room, there would be no volunteer willing to make the ultimate sacrifice and throw themselves upon the grenade. A more likely scenario would be a volunteer willing to throw Nobby on the grenade. Not so much "I am Spartacus" and more "Nobby is Spartacus". To give the guys credit, they did at least react with speed when adversity approached. We all sat on, or adjacent to, an item of exercise equipment. While I froze with cold indecision, the rest of the lads positioned themselves on the nearest piece of equipment, in a mockery of gym users.

Brains took it further, deciding to reinforce the illusion by shouting out encouragement. 'C'mon, guys! Max it to the extreme! Resistance training is useless training!' A couple of the guys were sitting on the machine when they should have been lying down. Some were pulling when they should have pushed. Face was standing on his head. I noticed that his inverted features were still fucking ugly. I assumed they were going for an *overall* illusion, hoping the need for detail was superfluous. I had decided that Nurse Hughes belonged to the Tyrannosaurus family and would be unable to see me if I remained motionless. The rest of the gang were able to hide their evidence, whereas I had thrown mine straight in the path of the approaching nurse. I saw her look intently at her clipboard, as she approached the gym. I told myself there was no way she would notice the evidence; uh-uh, ain't gonna happen.

As she stooped to pick up the fugitive contraband, time stood still. The last thump of my heart resounded with finality in my chest. Nobody moved. Even Nobby curtailed his nasal excavations as we waited for *the reaction*. Nurse Hughes didn't appear shocked in the slightest. She had what could be described as a *hello, what's this then?* expression as she picked up the wandering weed. She placed it underneath her nose and inhaled. I wondered if she was a weed connoisseur that, like a wine buff, could place the product by the bouquet alone. Was she thinking, *ah, Cardiff?* The nurse held it to her ear and rolled it with care between fingers and thumb. She gave a small nod, dropped the spliff into her breast pocket, turned, and retreated to the main building. It appeared that the consequences of my poor throwing skills had been mitigated by my superior rolling skills.

Later, the gang would discuss at length the implications of the nurse's reaction without reaching a satisfactory conclusion. At the time, all we cared was that we had dodged what could have been a very significant bullet.

As the nurse returned to the main building, life returned to the gang, 'When you have a heart attack, do you always shit yourself?' I said.

'No, I don't think so,' Brains said.

'Thank Christ. At least that's some good news; it might not be a heart attack then,' I said, calming down to a panic.

'Silver linings, Silent,' Brains said. 'Oh, by the way, that didn't count, did it?'

'What do you mean?'

'I assume that, as your tailor-made never reached me, the agreed transaction hasn't been completed to the satisfaction of both parties. To be specific, you have yet to deliver the goods. Or are you going to ask Nurse Hughes, "Please miss, can I have my spliff back?"'

'No, I'll get you another. I'll put that last one down to wastage.'

Nobody had noticed that the wall clock, upon which the timing of our activities relied, had failed. On closer inspection, the fancy-looking clock was not quite as fancy as we believed. Like many things in the hospital, the exterior hid the reality of what lurked beneath. It was a simple mechanism, powered by a single battery. In fact, it was powered by a *charged* battery. For the sake of a single AA battery our scientific endeavours could have been compromised with extreme prejudice.

It was a day of edification for all. We had learnt not to rely upon the wall clock for such an important aspect as timekeeping. Also, each of us confirmed how the adjacent exercise equipment was intended to be operated. Not simply for the sake of authenticity in the event of an emergency but also to avoid the risk of injury. In addition, the incident confirmed what an altogether shit lookout Nobby was, and we told him so. Repeatedly. An additional, personal lesson for me was; ensure you always know where the nearest set of clean underpants are. Oh, and allow for wastage.

It wasn't all bad though. At least Nobby took his finger out of his nose for a while.

* * * *

Dad was unusually withdrawn following the Saturday night visit by Doctor Jeffries. In hindsight, that visit marked a permanent change in Dad. While he never neglected me, our relationship became more passive. I was preoccupied with the argument that I'd overheard. Even my usual frustrations at school were relegated to school hours alone. I spent increasing time alone on a platform that Dad and I had built a few years earlier, in a large oak tree that lived in the back garden. The configuration of the branches dictated that anything more substantial than a simple platform would require prohibitive removal of limbs. We had needed a ladder to get access to a group of branches that seemed destined to accommodate a reasonably sized landing. My contribution to the construction was limited to unskilled-labour. I held the *idiot's end* of the tape when Dad measured up and then I held the timber as he cut it to size. Once the platform was almost completed Dad insisted I nail the final boards in place which I was able to do without damage to property or person. The platform went from concept to completion in a single weekend. We were proud of our achievement; it was something permanent and useful that existed because we had built it together.

It hadn't been all easy; we had to brainstorm potential solutions to the challenge of reaching the platform. The branches of the tree didn't lend themselves to ease of access, so we created an elegant solution. A knotted rope was suspended from the edge of the platform and we nailed some short boards to the trunk of the tree. Using the rope to pull myself up, the boards gave my feet purchase as I climbed onto the platform.

Dad said the platform was all mine and that I was responsible for its upkeep. Dad was capable of reaching it, using both rope and boards, but I knew I would still be undisturbed when in residence. The rope snapped when I was descending one day. Being close to the ground I suffered nothing worse than a bruised backside. I never replaced the rope. By then my grip was such that I could ascend and descend using the boards alone. I knew then it was in truth my private place; only someone with my attributes could now reach it. When the changes began, I would lie on the platform, picturing myself at sea. Sometimes I would pretend that I was the sole survivor of a scuppered pirate galleon. After Dad broke the big news, I would look over the rooftops, imagining I was drifting without aim, while everyone around me sailed towards happiness. I wondered if I was alone or if there was an entire ocean of castaways, set adrift in our own lives. But the thought was fleeting. I was being pathetic and dramatic. I was being "pathmatic".

When Dad made the big announcement he didn't say that everything would change for the worse; he didn't need to. I was eating breakfast in the kitchen while Mrs M banished the dirty dishes to the dishwasher. Her method was, of course, most effective, giving the dishes a decent wipe down before placing them in the machine. 'It's a dishwasher, not a waste disposal,' Mrs M explained. In a similar fashion, Dad and I would tidy up before Mrs M arrived; we didn't want her to feel that we took her for granted. This respect also extended to the sharing of important news that impacted the household.

When Dad said, 'Excuse me, Mrs Montgomery; Alan, can I have a moment of your time? I have something to tell you,' I knew we were about to hear something significant.

He took a deep, uncomfortable breath. 'I'll get right to the point; I'm getting married next month. Of course, that means there will be some changes, but nothing insurmountable,' he said. 'I very much hope you will stay with us, Mrs Montgomery. If you need extra to allow for there being more people in the house, I'm sure we can come to some arrangement. I'm sure Alan would agree we couldn't cope without you.' I nodded my head, in the early stage of shock.

If Mrs M was surprised by the news she didn't show it. She preserved her dignified composure. 'I should think we can carry on under the current arrangements. But let's see how we go for a while,' she said.

It was difficult keeping hold of any one thought. I had a host of questions about the bombshell. I would have a stepmother! Then there was the prospect of Mrs M finding the new arrangements untenable and leaving. While I tried to come to terms with these questions the memory of the argument between Dad and Doctor Jeffries pushed them from my thoughts. This must have been what they were talking about. It seemed to explain some of the pieces of the puzzle. Perhaps not all.

* * * *

When I met Dad's intended two days later, the questions that drove me to distraction weren't resolved; if anything they *evolved*. There had been no suggestion of Dad's intention to remarry; he'd never discussed such an eventuality. I thought I had Dad's unreserved trust. I believed I was old enough at fifteen for my feelings to be considered. Among all the questions that troubled me, greatest was the reason why Dad had neglected to consult me before taking this huge step. A step that altered all our lives on such a fundamental level. I began to wonder how well I knew Dad; something I had never questioned before.

We met Ruth on Sunday for lunch at a country pub. The pub was a thirty-minute drive from our home. There was none of our usual light-hearted banter during the drive. The awkward silence drew the journey out so that the relief was palpable when we arrived at the faux-rural tavern. Everything about it appeared disingenuous. A copious number of plastic-looking horse brasses adorned the interior in an apparent attempt to distract from the fading and peeling paintwork. Yet more plastic was found covering the uncomfortable chairs scattered around tired-looking tables. We joined Ruth who was already waiting for us inside, an empty wine glass in her hand. Dad made the introductions. 'Ruth this is Alan. Alan this is Ruth.' He was ill at ease.

'Hello,' Ruth said.

'Hello, nice to meet you,' I said. I wondered if she knew more about me than I did about her; she couldn't know less. Instinctively, I concealed my bulk, remaining face-on to her as I sat. Dad went to the bar to get drinks. Ruth and I sat in silence until he returned. I attempted a friendly demeanour by smiling but conversation was not forthcoming. I spent the time discreetly checking her out. She looked quite plain and there was no obvious evidence to suggest she had gone to great effort to prepare for the meeting. She appeared a little overweight and her Sunday-best would not have won prizes. I knew she would be wondering about my appearance, unavoidable when first setting eyes on me. The most overpowering impression I had of Ruth was one of weariness. So much so that it was difficult to put an age to her, but she looked to be younger than Dad.

We were both relieved when Dad returned with our drinks. His arrival provided a welcome respite from the silence. Once we worked our way through "here you go" and "thank you" the conversation stalled. There was general chat about the tavern. Ruth thought it 'Okay, but looks better from the outside'. Once meals were ordered, we settled into an unsettled silence. It wasn't long before the meals arrived and I was thankful to find my steak and kidney pie was delicious. If the policy of the tavern was to save money on fixtures and fittings, in order to focus on the quality of the food, then I concurred. I left a clean plate but Dad lost his appetite halfway through his meal. Ruth picked at her already small portion. She spread the food around her plate in such a way that it appeared she returned more food than had been delivered to the table. Ruth appeared focused on drinking wine, her dining efforts tending more towards the liquid.

During the meal I observed no evidence of intimacy between Dad and Ruth. There was no hand-holding or physical contact, even discounting potential concerns about my discomfort. Their conversation was perfunctory at best. There was no mention of "the big day". When it came time to leave, I shook hands with an indifferent Ruth and we swapped goodbyes. Dad pecked her on the cheek, the sole contact between them that day. 'I'll call later.'

Ruth replied without enthusiasm. 'Fine, speak to you then.' The last I saw of her, she lifted the glass of wine to her mouth in a well-practised manner.

Dad and I returned unspeaking to the car. It was many miles before Dad broke the silence. I expected him to ask what I thought of Ruth, or maybe offer some reason for her lethargy. All he said was, 'Don't worry, Alan. Things won't change between us,' attempting to reassure me.

'Okay,' I said, but I knew what he'd said was untrue. I sensed a newly formed distance between us. It was a distance that became more difficult to span as time passed. Dad had never lied to me like that before.

He should have told me, 'Nothing changes until it does.'

Chapter Eight

It was near Christmas and a light fall of snow blanketed the hospital grounds, illuminating the interior of the gym with a white glow. As we sat in our usual positions, conducting our scientific research with much courage, the discussion turned to all things Christmassy. Bomber had started the conversation with a familiar call of, 'Bombs away!' We were listening to "Get up, stand up" by Bob Marley at the time and Bomber timed his detonation so what we heard was, 'Get up, Paaaarrrpppp!'

'*Foda-me!*' Brains said. 'Hark, the fucking herald angels sing!'

'Christ, if that was the angels then they all have really bad halitosis!' Face said. 'There was nothing angelic about that. That was demonic.'

'Yeah. There was something of sulphur and brimstone about it,' Brains said. 'Hey, Silent. What's your favourite Christmas carol? It's got to be "Silent night", hasn't it?'

'No. My favourite Christmas carol is "Happy birthday to you".'

'What the *fanculo* are you talking about? "Happy birthday to you" isn't a Christmas carol.'

'Yes, it is.' I demonstrated. '*Happy birthday to you, happy birthday to you, happy birthday dear Jesus, happy birthday to you.*' Brains, however, pointed out a flaw in my choice.

'Did you know that academics believe Christ was born in the middle of the year? "Christmas" is a pagan festival that the Christians misappropriated. All the stuff about holly and ivy and yuletide is pagan in origin.'

'Does Jesus have two birthdays, like the Queen? You know, an official one and a proper one?' Legs said.

Brains simply shrugged, our lesson completed.

'So are you a pagan then?' I said to Brains.

'No, I'm a born-again-atheist. What about you?'

'I don't believe in atheism.'

'What do you believe in then?'

'I believe in doubt. Bollocks to faith, hope and charity. Doubt, despair and parsimony is more like it nowadays!'

'What about you, Bomber? Do you have a favourite Christmas carol that you fart along to?' Voice shouted.

'I don't celebrate Christmas. I'm Jewish.'

'Seriously?' Face said.

Bomber hooked his thumb into the waist of his trousers, pulled it out and looked down. 'Yep, I'm sure.'

Face was yet to be convinced. 'Well, are you a practising Jew?'

'No, I'm not practising.'

'Why? Have you perfected being Jewish or did your mum get fed up picking you up from training?'

'No, I didn't get round to perfecting it. Once I left home it started being a pain in the arse; too complicated.'

'What, you mean like all the rules for what you can and can't eat?'

'Well, it's kind of difficult ...'

'What, the rules?'

'No, the rules are clear. It's just too difficult to abide by them.'

Voice then posed a loud conundrum. 'What would you do if someone offered you free bacon?'

'Yeah,' Face said. 'What would you do if faced with the Jewish "Sophie's Choice"? Do you take the free bacon or not?'

'No, I don't take the free bacon,' Bomber said straightaway.

'Why not?'

'I don't like bacon.'

'You could always take it and then sell it to someone else who *does* like bacon,' Face said.

'What, and *I'm* Jewish?'

Bomber didn't take what he called "the whole Jewish thing" too seriously. He admitted he hadn't been to a synagogue for years and only went for family occasions, when expected of him. One time he asked us, 'You know how the Jews wandered the desert for forty years?'

'Yeah, I think I've heard about that,' Voice shouted.

'But do you know why?'

'No.'

'They were avoiding having to pay a restaurant bill; someone had ordered pork chops!'

As the day and the session progressed, more snow fell, adding to the thin layer already grounded. The temperature in the gym dropped. Although the room temperature was controlled by a thermostat, our practice of leaving windows open to provide ventilation in essence made the system redundant. Yet another example of the sacrifices the gang was prepared to make for the greater good. Voice summarised at volume, 'We're cool on the outside and on the inside.'

It may have been the uncharacteristic ambient temperature, or the fact that by this time we had burnt a couple, but the conversation started to get heavy. This was unusual for the group. Even if someone brought up what might be considered serious we wouldn't allow ourselves to stray from the trivial. Earlier that week, for example, we had discussed politics. We didn't discuss the relative merits of the policies of the major parties or how we felt they performed. We talked about more important matters, such as which party leader would win a foot race, or who would prevail in a fist fight. It had proved difficult to gain consensus; most of us didn't even know who the party leaders were.

On this particular day, having already broached the subject of religion, we talked about Judgement Day and where we thought we'd end up. Perhaps Face felt the cold and wanted to think about warm places, as it was he that started the conversation. The topic hadn't followed on from the subject matter we were discussing. It wasn't a problem though, going off at a tangent was never considered disadvantageous. It's kind of what we did. 'You know Judgement Day? How do you reckon you'll shape up?' Face asked no-one in particular. 'I mean, do you think you'll spend eternity "upstairs" or "downstairs"? Of course, I'm not talking about you Nobby. You'll end up in Limbo.'

'Why do you say that?'

'Well, no-one is going to want you. It'll be "you have him. No, you have him!" and you'll not get in anywhere.'

'Well, Face. I have an alternative proposition to put to you.'

'Oh yeah, what's that?'

'Get fucked!'

'Tell that to Saint Peter!'

Having determined Nobby's eternal fate, it was now my turn. 'What about you, Silent? "Upstairs" or "downstairs"?'

It didn't need much consideration. This was a subject to which I had already given frequent and serious thought. 'I'll be heading "downstairs".'

'Whoa, bit of a dark horse are you, Silent?'

I simply shrugged. There was inadequate time and inclination in the room to justify a comprehensive answer. Some of the guys said they too would be heading downstairs. I wasn't alone in failing to provide justification of the self-assessment. I didn't know why the others believed they're destined for the fiery abyss. There was one thing of which I was sure; they hadn't reached their conclusion by the same reasoning as me. You see, I don't believe that the moral résumé of my mortal life will be a significant consideration for determining my eternal destination. I don't subscribe to the traditional views of what form God takes. I think the versions of God inferred by mainstream religions are too self-serving. Their Gods are constantly subject to convenient change. Indeed, I don't believe in a loving God. Neither do I believe in a vengeful God. I believe in an *incompetent* God.

Come Judgement Day, I'll demand to see God's job description. I won't be God's first choice to appraise his performance but that is indeed what I mean to do. I shall insist. I have more than a few questions for which I will demand answers. It won't be questions that

God might expect. I won't ask 'How could you let all the bad stuff happen?' No, I'm sure God will be prepared for those old clichés. I expect the Creator will choose the lazy option and will frequently and arbitrarily employ his 'It's all to do with free will,' get-out-of-jail card. I will demand to know why life is so *inconsistent*. Half the world starves while the other half gorges itself into a diabetic frenzy. People die of thirst in ever-expanding deserts while others drown in flash floods. More than anything, I will demand an explanation for the unforgiveable *waste*.

My God is not a courageous God. Insurance policies are a dead giveaway. Imagine the scene: you're sitting in your car at the local shopping centre minding your own business when all of a sudden – *BAM!* Someone reverses into you. You get out of your car to inspect the damage and the other driver gets out of his vehicle and approaches. It's God. 'Hey, pal, where the hell were you looking?' He looks sheepish. You exchange details. His are – Name: God; Address: Heaven; Date of Birth: On the First Day. You contact your insurance company to be told in no uncertain terms that you aren't covered. 'Why not?' you ask reasonably.

'You're not covered for an *Act of God*.' See, no courage.

Come Judgement Day, when God sees me approaching, the curtains will be drawn tight, the television will be turned down and everyone will be told to *shush* when I come a-knocking. God will crouch behind the sofa, praying to self for me to push off. I have no doubt I'll get the Jehovah's Witnesses' treatment. I could try subterfuge. I could knock on and say 'Hi, is your son in? Can Jesus come out to play?' but I don't think God would fall for it. My God is inept, not stupid. Though I suspect God will hide from me, I won't make the mistake of engaging God in a game of hide and seek. It's not that I'm lazy. If I thought there was any chance of locating God I would make the effort. You see, I wouldn't trouble myself on the basis that God is *omnipresent*. My God can't just hide *anywhere*; my God can hide *everywhere*. Cheating bastard!

I expect when Judgement Day arrives, I'll be found sitting down in a nice comfy chair alongside Satan, enjoying a refreshing drink in front of what I'm sure will be a quite substantial fire. We'll engage in a bitch session about how it all could have been so much better under different management. Chances are Satan will be more welcoming than my God. I suspect Satan and I will empathise on a few matters. My feelings about God won't be as strong as those of Satan. Their relationship has spanned a very long time and they were once pals. Some of God's efforts were tailored very specifically against Satan. Their issues would have to be more personal. While I sometimes want to protest against God, I don't consider myself a *creator hater*. My feelings towards God tend more towards disappointment.

Satan has had plenty of bad press through the ages. I think I know how he must feel. History is written by the victor, after all. We've all heard how Satan expressed his displeasure at how God was running things. God was unimpressed with his challenge and they had a falling-out. God, having no capacity for dissent, cast out the one-time angel and resumed the old ways. Is might always right or did the bully prevail? What would the outcome have been if Satan had held his tongue and tried a different approach? How would life be if Satan had stayed around to keep an eye on the big G? Perhaps he would have kept the bastard honest; it couldn't have made things worse. But, in the end, it was a case of "to the conqueror goes the spoils". I wouldn't put it past God to big himself up by failing to correct those that make the devil out to be more of a bad boy than he really is. *'Satan? You should have seen the size of him! Huge; and ripped too, not an ounce of flab on him. Talk about a temper!'* God would simply shrug his shoulders, denying nothing.

There is a consistent theme throughout many forms of mythology relating to the never-ending struggle between light and darkness. The theme is often expressed as day versus night, or summer versus winter. While the common theme takes many forms one thing is clear; you cannot have light without darkness. In fact, darkness and light define each other. Who wants to live in a world of endless day, with no respite from the light? Day needs night for balance, as well as to give it meaning, just as God needs Satan. If only my God had contained his insecurities and kept Satan closer. My God erred in casting Satan out with such finality.

History hasn't been flattering to Satan, either in terms of character or appearance. Most of the time he's deemed to err towards the wicked. A red-skinned demon sporting horns and hooves. I think he'll be more of a "Stan" than a "Satan": a pipe and slippers kind of guy. I'll bet he doesn't even support United.

Even if I'm wrong and the traditional view of the hereafter is correct, it won't make any difference to my final destination. No matter what, I'll be spending the afterlife sipping iced tea with Satan. If my eternal fate will indeed be determined by the history of my moral performance, well, I'll still end up "downstairs". I have killed someone after all.

* * * *

One month after meeting Ruth at the sad excuse for a tavern, I attended the ceremony that joined her and Dad in matrimony. It was a small, private affair, held at the local council chambers. The ceremony was conducted by the registrar and the wedding party consisted of a few, select guests. In addition to myself, Doctor Jeffries and Mrs Montgomery attended on Dad's side. Mrs Montgomery was accompanied by her husband. When introduced to him, he told me to call him 'Mister Montgomery'. Concealing first names must have been a family convention. Perhaps they were of a culture where to know someone's full name is to exert power over them. On the surface, he was a male version of Mrs M; immaculately dressed in a formal suit, his face adorned with the neatest moustache I had ever seen and a pair of tasteful designer glasses.

We had been saddened to discover the passing of Mrs Reilly a few months beforehand. Dad's lack of contact with his old life meant he didn't find out about her death until he attempted to invite her to the wedding. We had not been surprised to discover that she had succumbed to a smoking-related disease. I wondered how B&H shares had fared and immediately felt contrite for such improper thoughts.

Mrs Reilly had been attentive and kind. She was someone upon whom Dad had relied. I made a deposit into my self-loathing account.

We met Ruth's best friend, Louise. A bottle-blonde, she was the antithesis of Ruth, talking at volume and exploding in raucous laughter at the slightest provocation. Friends since school, they were of the same vintage and appeared to embrace a similar attitude towards alcohol. Indeed, Ruth and Louise seemed engaged in a contest to deplete the reception of its stock of wine. Ruth's sister, Janice, and her husband, Tony, were the other guests attending on the bride's side. And so this small group was easily accommodated at the reception held at our home following the ceremony. Dad seemed awkward during the ceremony and appeared relieved when it concluded and we returned home. Again, I noted the lack of intimacy between Ruth and Dad. Even the officiated kiss at the end of the ceremony had been wooden and uncomfortable. I knew little of relationships between man and woman, but even I knew there should be some level of familiarity between them that was noticeably absent. Ruth did not relieve herself of the lethargy that had affected her during our first meeting. She had been tired and disinterested in the proceedings. I'd noticed Doctor Jeffries had been very quiet throughout and didn't stay long at the reception.

The doctor sought me out before leaving. If he had waited for me to be free of company he didn't wait long. When around strangers I habitually endeavour to keep out of their line of sight, attempting to conceal my bulk. When there are a few strangers around whom I must navigate, as was the case at the reception, I was in the habit of resorting to blatant concealment. During the course of the ceremony and the reception I had spoken to most guests and so considered my duties fulfilled, which as the groom's son were vague at best. Doctor Jeffries tracked me down to where I semi-hid and shook my hand. 'Your father is a good man, Alan. Never forget that. He would never do anything to upset you,' he said in a low voice.

'Of course. I know that, Doctor Jeffries,' I said, confused. My thoughts returned to their argument. I knew it was related; I just didn't know how.

'Well, yes. I'm sure you do. Please remember, I'm always here for you. And for your father, too. I … I hope it all works out for you all. Yes, I'm sure everything will work out.' He nodded as he spoke; he seemed to be trying to convince himself. He was lost in thought. We stood in silence until the doctor regained his composure. 'Well, Alan, I'll say goodbye now. I'll see you soon. Take care.'

'I will, Doctor. You take care, too. See you soon.' But it would be some time before I saw the doctor again. I'd seen him and Dad speaking earlier, but I hadn't seen Doctor Jeffries speak to Ruth during the proceedings. I didn't think much of it at the time. Ruth was absorbed with ridding the reception of its stock of white wine. She and Louise sat at the garden table, outside the French windows. Ruth only made such necessary small talk as could be accommodated around her wine-drinking activities. She only strayed from her position to collect more liquid provisions and was disturbed by Dad now and again when he asked after her condition. I noticed Dad was also drinking what was, for him, a lot of whiskey. But he at least worked the room, mingling throughout the small group. Dad and I didn't speak much during the reception. I was tired by the time the last guest left at 10 pm. Relieved, I retired to my room.

Everything had changed and it wasn't long before everything changed again.

* * * *

When Ruth moved in the household's atmosphere was subjected to a form of inertia. Her presence extracted all energy from Dad. I knew no different to Ruth's constant weariness, but I wasn't equipped to deal with how she affected Dad. There were unsubtle changes to the household routine. When I awakened in the morning, I descended the stairs with my appetite demanding satisfaction. Before Ruth's arrival, Dad had always been in the kitchen to greet me. My breakfast awaited me on the table; freshly made toast, a bowl of cereal and a glass of orange juice. Dad and I would shoot the breeze, talking about television, books and sometimes about school. When it came time for me to leave and catch the bus I would say goodbye to Gelert, who would relish the attention. Dad would then hug me, wish me a good day and I departed, knowing that, whatever the day held, I would return to my caring home.

The arrival of Ruth marked a change in the routine so that I descended the stairs to an empty kitchen. There was no breakfast on the table but there was a cardboard box by the bin that reflected the previous night's activities. There would be empty white wine bottles in evidence and the occasional empty whiskey bottle. Ruth was nothing if not consistent as she maintained her weary wine-drinking ways. Even three months into the marriage I still hadn't observed any suggestion of intimacy between Ruth and Dad. They existed in their own private worlds, only interacting when those worlds were forced to drift together.

Returning from school in the afternoon, I would still be on the receiving end of an animated welcome from an excited Gelert. He remained the dedicated hound, who still squared up to large dogs, just to keep in practice. When Ruth arrived he attempted to befriend her but his attempts proved unsuccessful. Ruth dismissed his friendly overtures with indifference. Soon Gelert dismissed her dismissals, ignoring Ruth altogether. For Gelert alone nothing had changed.

I seldom saw Dad upon my return from school. He was either locked in his study or, more often, was away from the house, not returning until dinner time. Ruth sat at the kitchen table without fail, reading a magazine and working on reducing the volume of wine in the glass she held. When the weather was mild, she sat outside at the garden table reading and drinking. Different location; same occupation. We never talked, other than a perfunctory exchange of greetings. Sometimes I attempted to engage Ruth in conversation, but my lack of confidence was such that I conceded defeat almost at once. Ruth was not interested and even her conversations with Dad were restricted to what was for dinner and what television programmes were on offer that evening.

One particular morning as I descended the stairs, I noticed the door to Dad's study was ajar and he was nowhere to be seen. This in itself was surprising as he always locked the study door overnight.

More unexpected was the sight of rumpled bedclothes and a pillow on the sofa that was the major fixture of the study. There were more obvious signs that Dad was treating his study as a full-time refuge. A half-empty whiskey bottle stood on the desk next to dirty dishes. My immediate thought was, *what would Mrs M think?* I suspected Dad kept the study door locked to keep it off Mrs M's radar. If not, he must have cleaned the room before her arrival. I couldn't contemplate the notion that he would expose Mrs M to the mess.

We all had our private sanctuaries. Dad had his study and I was spending even more time alone on my platform reading and ruminating. Ruth's sanctuary was the bottom of a wine glass.

Four months after the wedding I arrived home from school to find Ruth and Dad awaiting my return. I exchanged the usual pleasantries with a somersaulting Gelert on my arrival and walked into the kitchen expecting to see Ruth at the table, alone but for her wine glass. Ruth was unusually wine-free. Dad stood at her side, his hand on her shoulder in an unfamiliar tactile display. 'Alan, we have something to tell you. You see, Ruth has a son from a previous relationship. His name is Kevin and he's a little younger than you. We have discussed this at length and we have decided he should come and live with us here. That would be nice for you, don't you think?' he said. I sensed pleading in his voice.

The shock of seeing Ruth without a drink paled in comparison to what I'd heard. I thought back to six months ago when it was only me, Dad, Mrs M and Gelert. Now I had to face the prospect of another stranger occupying our home. I couldn't speak. I had no idea what to say; this was too much information to process. Dad and Ruth waited patiently for my response. I contemplated the domestic situation that existed right then. It was no longer the once happy household. The protracted silences that littered the house were punctuated by the regular *clink* of bottle against glass alone.

Perhaps Ruth would shed her weariness when her son came to live with us. If Kevin was a little younger than me, perhaps he and I could become friends; maybe even to the extent of brotherliness.

'Yeah, okay. Sounds good,' I said. Dad looked relieved and Ruth preserved her indifference.

Kevin was due to arrive the following week. I spent the interval in a state of expectation. He would have the spare bedroom, so I still had my own space. Once he settled in, I could re-install the rope to the platform and he could join me if he wished. Having so recently felt I was losing the emotional anchor of Dad's affection, I may have been desperate to form a new connection. I considered the notion of a stepbrother as a potential boon. I still hoped that Dad would resurface and that the new domestic arrangements would facilitate that hope. Once again, I learnt my expectations could not be endured. The domestic situation did not improve; it deteriorated. It worsened to such an extent that on a couple of occasions I almost called Doctor Jeffries to enlist his help. I never did make the calls; I told myself not to be pathmatic. It wasn't the single factor that deterred me from calling the doctor; he hadn't visited since Dad remarried. Our weekend walks had once provided a figurative and literal breath of fresh air to the household, and they were sorely missed.

I thought it had been far too long since we had seen Doctor Jeffries. We desperately needed a regular dose of his invigorating influence. As it transpired, the next time I saw Doctor Jeffries was far too soon. I wouldn't see him again until death brought him back to our door.

* * * *

We had survived the winter snow and our resolve to continue with our vital psychotherapeutic research had, if anything, strengthened. Our first session in the New Year did nothing to ring in the changes; it was business as usual. The lads discussed how they had indulged over the holidays and this, for once, led to conversational continuity. The subject of diet was then furthered. Most of the gang, myself included, had been resident at the hospital for the duration of the holiday. For myself, this meant I'd eaten my usual amount, with due deference to my healthy appetite. The sole difference was a greater choice of meals. I found no cause for complaint. Brains had returned from a week's parole with his family. Voice shouted about the food and drink he'd consumed over the last week. His account resembled the inventory of a cruise ship about to set sail on a two-week voyage with three hundred passengers on board. Brains, being the fit bastard that he was, took umbrage at the extent of Voice's gluttony. It was low-fat umbrage, of course.

'*Que Coño*! You should take better care of yourself, Voice. That is not demonstrating healthy behaviour.'

'Well, it's tradition, isn't it? Eat and drink as much as you can, put on heaps of weight and then make a New Year resolution to lose weight. One decent shit later and it's job done!'

'That's a very poor attitude. Look at me; I'm the same weight now as I was at nineteen,' a smug Brains said.

'So am I. I've always been a fat bastard!'

I was holder of the music system remote control and was focused on my task of delivering an appropriate soundtrack. "Rat race" by the Specials was up next, which was fine as rolling music but was too lively to be suitable relaxing music. As we were in relaxing mode I skipped forward to "Do nothing". My responsibilities met, I thought to contribute. 'Brains is dead right. I've put on a bit of weight. I used to be 8lbs 2oz.' *Hello Happy Place.*

Brains wasn't finished. 'How many of you have had your three serves of fruit?'

'What, this week?' Legs said.

'No, today. You should have three serves of fruit every *day*.'

'Bugger off, I'm no fruit bat!'

Voice looked puzzled. 'Is an apple Pop-Tart a serve of fruit?'

'No it isn't, Voice. If there's one guarantee, it's that an apple Pop-Tart is a completely apple-free zone.'

Voice continued. 'What about …'

'No, Voice,' Brains interrupted. 'A strawberry Pop-Tart isn't a serve of fruit either.'

'Well, I'm screwed then.'

'That's kind of my point. You should watch what you eat.'

'I do,' Voice shouted. 'I like watching my food. I just find burgers and kebabs to be easier on the eye than fruit and muesli.'

My unique physique is such that it's difficult to determine if I'm overweight. There's no benchmark for someone of my size and shape. Nevertheless, I pride myself in being reasonably trim. I possess but a single chin and there's no belly-overspill challenging my belt. Nobby, however, had chins aplenty and his belt strained to the challenge of restraining his paunch. He wasn't hugely fat; he merely looked extremely unfit, like someone who doesn't care *about* his appearance. Everyone else didn't care *for* his appearance. Legs didn't want to exclude Nobby from the conversation. 'Hey, Nobby. You know that saying "you are what you eat"?'

'Yeah.'

'Exactly how much shit *do* you eat then?'

'Yeah well, at least I can eat vegetables. I know you can't,' Nobby said.

'Oh yeah? Why's that?'

'That would be cannibalism,' a smug Nobby answered. He was on form. New meds, anyone?

'Touché, Nobby. Well played, sir,' Legs said, a note of restrained respect in his voice. 'You smelly, obnoxious twat!' And there it went; bye-bye restraint, bye-bye respect.

'Well, my doctor told me that I have "the body of an Olympic athlete",' Bomber said.

I attempted to find an elegant way in which to express my disbelief. 'Bullshit!' I said.

'It's true. Although, he was talking about the body that is currently accommodating the Peruvian speed-walker who finished dead last in the 1924 Paris Olympics,' Bomber said.

'I thought he was disqualified,' Brains said.

'Why was that?'

'Well, he competed in two Games *running*.' Brains smiled to himself. I was the only one to get it. Eventually.

'Has anyone ever tried that gluten-free stuff? That's healthy, isn't it?' Face said.

'I don't know about healthy, but it's bloody disgusting!' I said. 'I tried gluten-free snack bars once. I ate the cardboard box they came in 'cos it had more flavour.'

'So, not a fan then?'

'No way. Ever since then I've been on the lookout for food with *extra* gluten.'

In fact, I'd once tried a gluten-free cake. It hadn't gone well; it had been bland and indigestible. I've never tried eating a mouthful of sawdust, but if I do, I expect the experience would be similar. I didn't mention this occasion to the guys. At the time of the assault on my taste buds and digestive system, I'd been so upset by the incident, I'd shed a tear. It had been a crime against confectionery; a cake crime!

Chapter Nine

Ruth's sister Janice, with her husband Tony, dropped Kevin off without ceremony late on Sunday morning. Dad and I waited to the side as Ruth received Kevin. It wasn't a warm reception. Their embrace was perfunctory and then Ruth was engaged in conversation by her sister. Janice did most of the talking, bringing Ruth up to date with her son's welfare, as Kevin had lived with his aunt. I wondered why Kevin hadn't attended the wedding ceremony. Perhaps Kevin was unable or unwilling to attend. Whatever the arrangements that were made for Kevin's upbringing, they must have already been complicated. It was apparent by the tangible awkwardness that there was a level of discomfort relating to the new arrangements. They marked a considerable change for our household, and for Janice's. On seeing Ruth and Janice absorbed in their discussion, Dad approached Tony to chat with him. I remembered Tony from the wedding; he was a short, stocky man about the same age as Dad. I recalled he'd been quiet, but friendly when we talked.

Kevin stood in silence, no doubt assessing his new home as he scanned the layout of the house. He was a little shorter than me but not as heavy. I saw traces of Ruth in him, but that may have simply been his disinterested demeanour. He was strangely familiar in other ways that I couldn't pin down. I wandered over to introduce myself, dog at my heel. Gelert conducted himself with commendable behaviour around all the visitors. When he saw the strange car pull up his auto-pilot had engaged and he moved to inspect the new arrivals. I called him to heel and since then he was a coiled spring, waiting at my feet to be released. We walked to where Kevin stood. 'Hi, I'm Alan and this is Gelert.' Kevin gave me the familiar "what's wrong with him?" expression. Finding nothing to challenge his disinterest, he then scrutinised Gelert. He seemed unimpressed. Even when Gelert pricked up his ears and gave Kevin his most endearing look, Kevin remained unmoved.

'Yeah, I'm Kevin,' he said after a few seconds and continued looking over his new home. I supposed the new arrangements were more demanding of him than for anyone else. At least I was in my own home, or a pale version of it, anyway.

'Do you want to see your bedroom? It's upstairs, you have your own room.'

'Oh great,' he said, with sarcasm. 'I suppose I'd better put my bag away,' and he grabbed his suitcase that had been deposited by the front door. 'Better show me the way.'

Gelert took the hint from Kevin and wandered over to where Dad and Tony talked. His advances to Tony met with success, and so Gelert was content. I spotted Dad looking across to where Kevin and I talked. He nodded to me approvingly and I smiled to him. I was heartened when he returned the smile; he hadn't smiled much in recent times. I led Kevin upstairs and pointed out the other rooms in the house as we passed them. 'That's the bathroom and that's my bedroom. Yours is across the hall from mine.' We reached his bedroom and I opened the door. 'Here it is. Let me know if you need anything.'

'No, this is fine. It's got a door,' and in saying so, he stepped into the room, closing the door behind him. He seemed even more like Ruth than I had first thought. I returned to the gathering downstairs. Perhaps Kevin was tired; it had been a long drive from Manchester where his aunt lived. I expected he would have been restless too with all the imminent changes.

Dad was on the lookout for us. As soon as I reached the bottom of the stairs he approached me. 'Is everything okay? Where's Kevin?'

'He's in his room. I think he's tired.'

'Is he? Okay, we'll let him rest then.'

It was then that Janice and Tony announced they were leaving. 'We'd best be off; we have a fair way to travel. Sunday drivers and all that,' Tony said.

'Yes, well, thanks again. Lovely to see you and you must drop in whenever you can,' Dad said. As he shook their hands, he looked towards Ruth, prompting her to contribute.

'Yeah, thanks. See you soon,' Ruth said. She shook Tony's hand but Janice insisted on an embrace.

'You take care. Promise me that you'll get in touch if you have any … problems, okay?' Janice said in a low voice.

'Yes, sure. Everything will be fine; don't fuss.'

Before Janice left she gave both Dad and me a hug for good measure. We waved to them as they drove away. Ruth stood by, a model of indifference. When we returned to the house Dad spoke to Ruth. 'Kevin's in his room. He's resting, so maybe we should leave him for now. What say you fetch him in an hour or so for lunch?'

'Yeah, fine,' Ruth said as she headed for the kitchen. It was but a matter of moments before she held her familiar glass of white wine and was reading a magazine at the garden table. The lightening of Dad's mood that I'd detected earlier evaporated. He turned and walked into his study, closing the door behind him.

Kevin's arrival had not yet marked the significant changes I'd expected. Dad was in his study, Ruth was drinking wine and I headed for a spot of rumination on my platform before lunch. In fact, I detected only one obvious change; we no longer had a spare room. In time I would wish that had been the solitary change.

* * * *

The encounter with Kevin on his arrival proved to be indicative of his character. He was a reticent individual and while he didn't display blatant hostility, he didn't feign friendliness. It was obvious that he and Ruth didn't enjoy a close relationship. There was no familiarity between them. Both Dad and Ruth endeavoured to relate to him. During meals they attempted to involve him in the conversation which tended toward domestic matters or how he found his new school. I also tried to encourage his participation by raising current issues at school, but he wasn't interested. Ruth made some effort to make her son feel welcome. She even stopped drinking during meals and became more animated for a while. During the first few weeks she asked Kevin questions about life with his aunt and uncle. Perhaps she was trying to uncover aspects of his previous domestic life that might inspire his interest. Kevin remained indifferent to the numerous conversational forays and would provide sharp responses where a gesture was insufficient. I felt positively garrulous compared to Kevin. At first, we adopted the guise of a functional family. We ate our meals together, the sound of cutlery on crockery punctuating the occasional failed attempt at dialogue. In the evenings we watched television or videos together, Gelert at my feet. Kevin didn't like Westerns. He never did bother to share what genre of movies he liked.

After four weeks Ruth gave up. We still ate together on occasion but her faithful glass of white wine was restored to her grasp, whether at meals or not. Dad and I still tried to involve Ruth and Kevin in our discussions but, more often than not, we ended up in our own personal exchange. It was a few weeks after Ruth yielded that Dad also capitulated. He fell back to his old ways, withdrawing to his study, the sound of classical music masking the tell-tale noise of whiskey bottle on glass. Kevin never took to Gelert. The sentiment was reciprocated. I never saw or heard Kevin abusing him but whenever Gelert saw Kevin approaching, he gave him a wide berth, head cocked to the side, keeping Kevin in his line of sight. When we arrived home from school, Gelert watched from a safe distance until Kevin left my side before welcoming me home. Kevin spent most of his time at home either in his room or watching television alone. I still tried to engage with Kevin, even to the extent that I was willing to expose my clumsiness, asking if he wanted to kick a ball about in the garden. He never accepted. At best I got a pointed 'No,' for my effort. I lasted longest of all; I didn't surrender until a further two weeks after Dad relented.

Kevin was ten months younger than me and was enrolled in the year below me at school. I'd hoped he wouldn't be exposed to any collateral damage from the animosity that followed me throughout my school tenure. Kevin suffered by association, but not in the manner I expected. Rather than tar Kevin with the same cruel brush that was used without restraint on myself, he was pitied for having to share a home with me. Three weeks after Kevin commenced school, I heard a voice behind me as I walked to the bus. 'Look, Kev. Isn't that your *Bro?*'

'He's no brother of mine!' Kevin said.

It wasn't long before Kevin gravitated towards the *Bad Lads*. These boys were from the upper years, a year or two older than me. It was therefore unusual for them to adopt Kevin despite his being the junior of the group by some years. I always considered Kevin as older than his years. There was little of the child about him and the Bad Lads must have realised this; recognising his potential. I counted myself fortunate that there were no Bad Lads in my class. No doubt, I would have been considered worthy of more personal attention if my first-hand history had been available to them. As it was, while I was on the receiving end of the occasional insult thrown my way; I was just one of their many targets. Once again, it was doubtless my bulky shape that saved me from any physical abuse by the gang. Even lone Bad Lads were wary around me.

The Bad Lads were led by the Cavanagh twins, Peter and Roger. They were known as "Pete and Re-Pete" by the other Bad Lads. To the rest of the school they were "The Cavanagh Boys", or "Sirs" to the more persecuted. I always thought there was supposed to be a good twin and an evil twin. Neither of them tended towards the good, even on a well-behaved day. Perhaps the good-to-evil ratio applied to all multiple births. If so, the Cavanaghs must have been the evil quadruplets, the good quadruplets having perhaps been despatched. It was a theory I kept to myself. Kevin started spending time with the twins and other Bad Lads after school. I was given the task of notifying Ruth and Dad that Kevin would be returning home late. Kevin would waylay me on my way to the bus at the end of the day. 'Oi, tell them I've got something on but I'll be home for tea.' Then he took off to where the twins awaited him. When I arrived home I passed the message on but neither Ruth nor Dad asked for details, which was just as well, as Kevin had not provided any. Gelert didn't miss Kevin either. After confirming I was indeed alone, Gelert would bestow upon me his usual enthusiastic welcome.

Life carried on much in this manner and while not agreeable, it was tolerable. My studies progressed well; a symptom of my isolation being I could concentrate on my academic efforts. I spent increasing time in the school library during breaks, either completing homework or reading textbooks that interested me. Kevin's membership of the Bad Lads didn't seem to influence their attentions in any noticeable way. There was no obvious escalation in hostilities. More than anything, I began to feel I could *cope* with life. I should have known it couldn't last. I should have known that my modest expectations still could not be endured.

* * * *

When I turned sixteen years old Dad made an effort to celebrate the occasion. He bought me a bicycle upon which I would explore the countryside at weekends. He also organised a party which was attended by our "faux-family". I had hoped that Doctor Jeffries might attend but he was a no-show. Mrs Montgomery baked a cake and delivered it to the table at the appointed time. When the cake was placed at the centre of the table and the candles lit, Dad set off singing "Happy birthday". His sole accompaniment was that of Mrs M. I heard Ruth mumble a few words in her time-worn way and Kevin looked bored. Mrs M wished me a happy birthday, hoping I would enjoy the cake. I knew there was no danger of me finding it anything less than delicious.

My seventeenth year turned out to be a most formative year. It wasn't long before the first defining event would come to pass.

We played rugby for half the school year and, despite never mastering *the pass*, I enjoyed participating. During the other months the class was afflicted with athletics. When the weather was unfavourable, activities were restricted to a large sports hall. It was three weeks after my sixteenth birthday and the weather was such that any outdoor athletic endeavours would have required the use of SCUBA. Our sports teacher, Mr Evans, therefore determined the class would instead suffer a series of physical challenges. He attempted to make the session more palatable through supposed encouragement. 'Come on, boys. This is how they train the SAS,' perhaps working on the basis that all teenage boys aspired to become super soldiers. I didn't. My aspirations tended towards the mundane. While other boys dreamt of the life extraordinary, I dreamt of the life most ordinary. Other boys wanted to be *someone*: a rock-god or a football star. I wanted to be *anyone*; anyone but me. Maybe a different version of me.

The sports hall was filled with an abundance of equipment designed to test the physical aptitude of the school child. After coaxing us through a number of what Mr Evans euphemistically termed warm-up exercises, we were then subjected to a number of physical trials to test our limitations. We were split into several groups, all the members of which would complete one specific exercise before moving on to the next. A record was kept of each participant's performance; the intention being that the best performer in each exercise would be announced at the end of the session. There was little doubt in the class about who the best performer would be. That accolade fell to Tom Jones. Not *the* Tom Jones, and no relation. Tom was the fastest, strongest and possessed the best coordination of anyone in our entire year. He was tall, athletic and good-looking in an obvious way. All the boys were jealous of his made-to-be-envied traits and all the girls loved him. None, however, loved him more than he did himself. I did not waste envious energy on him; I already envied those that envied *him*.

The physical trials consisted of a number of exercises that the class suffered through from time to time. While I was average at certain exercises, such as push-ups, there were other movements where my bulk proved most disadvantageous. The sit-up, for me, was a most taxing and elusive action. But there were other exercises for which I was better suited. The rope climb was an effortless activity. I knew, should I wish, I could climb the rope like a squirrel on speed using the strength in my back and arms. I repressed any pretensions to sporting greatness that I had. I needed only to consider the new names that would be generated should I reveal my peculiar powers. It wasn't worth the risk and so I curtailed my efforts. In the allotted time of thirty seconds, Tom scaled and descended the rope three times. Myself, and a couple of the other boys managed the feat two and a bit times. We were closest to Tom's performance. Mr Evans enthused about my efforts. Like a fool, I allowed the unfamiliar praise to take root.

The last activity was the pull-up. The object of the exercise was to complete as many repetitions as possible in sixty seconds. This was an activity I knew was accommodated without effort by my physique. I determined a plan of action; I would wait until Tom had his turn and then I would put in a performance that fell just short of his effort. I waited until Tom was up. Under the watchful eye of Mr Evans and the rest of the class Tom completed twenty-seven pull-ups in the allocated time. As he strained to complete the last few, the class shouted encouragement. His descent back to Earth was greeted by a round of applause. A few turns later and I was up. I turned to face the class before starting. Not because I wanted to see their expressions; I knew it was the best of the bad options available. I had seen how the muscles in the other boys' backs had bunched up as they strained to complete the exercise. That was not a vision I wished to expose.

I jumped and gripped the horizontal bar in both hands. Taking my time, I completed my repetitions, waiting until I got to twenty before feigning fatigue. I'd taken note of how the other boys faded as they had reached their limits. I used this knowledge to mimic exhaustion. When I reached the end of my performance the official count was twenty-five. Mr Evans shouted encouragement, telling me I was so close to the best score. I didn't get the applause that had met Tom when he'd finished but I merited a small ripple. I knew my performance of restraint deserved better, but I'd finished second, the only other boy to exceed twenty repetitions. It was on this note that one of my more memorable classes at school concluded. It also preceded one of my more memorable afternoons.

As I left the changing rooms, feeling upbeat for once, I heard a voice behind me. 'Alan, wait up.' It was Tom. I waited for him to catch up. 'Hey, Man. Good effort. For a moment there I thought you would beat me at the chin-ups.' *Praise indeed*, I thought.

'Yeah, I ran out of steam at the end; it's harder than it looks,' I lied.

'You looked pretty strong in there. Have you thought about trying out for a school team?'

I suppressed a shudder as I recalled my rowing endeavours. 'No, I haven't thought about it.' I assumed Tom hadn't tried rowing. With his natural abilities he would have been a certainty for the team.

'You should try out for the rugby team. I've seen you play; you're not bad.' Of course, Tom was the captain of the rugby team and as such his endorsement would be considered sacred.

'You think so? Maybe I'll give it a go.' I was in uncharted waters. Did someone want *me* on their team? And not just any someone: this was the mighty Tom Jones.

'Yeah, for sure. Come along to the next practice. See how you go.'

'Okay. Yeah, I'll do that then,' I said, equal parts nervous and excited.

'Come on; I'll introduce you to some of the lads,' he said, as he moved towards a group of boys gathered by the playing fields.

As I walked alongside Tom, my head was awash with unparalleled thoughts. Was this the moment for which I had waited; the moment when I would be accepted? I tried hard to contain my anticipation. No matter how foreign it felt, I must project an air of self-assurance. *Be cool,* I told myself.

'Hey, guys. Alan here is thinking of trying out for the rugby team,' Tom said.

'Yeah, you were looking good in there,' Derek said. He was one of the two boys who matched my pseudo-performance on the rope climb.

'At some of the stuff anyway,' Terry said. I didn't like Terry. In the last years of primary school we had been in the same class. He had been one of the more active tormentors.

'Play nice, Tel,' Tom said and Terry's comment, thankfully, was not pursued.

I loitered on the sidelines as the boys occupied themselves with idle chit-chat. They started discussing girls. 'It's a shame the girls weren't with us in the gym. They could have watched us. They would have been well impressed with your chin-ups, Al,' Derek said.

'I don't know about that,' I said. He had called me "Al". *I could get used to that.* It was without doubt an improvement on the names to date.

'I would have preferred to watch the girls do the exercises,' Terry said, grabbing at his crotch. 'Imagine *Double D* doing star-jumps; she'd have two black eyes!'

The other boys laughed but I merely smiled, the familiar feeling of discomfort creeping up on me. Terry referred to Cathy Davies, a girl in our year. There was another Cathy in the class, so the teachers referred to her as "Cathy D". Over the last year Cathy had blossomed. The most noticeable symptom of this blossoming was her impressive bosom. She had been christened *Double D* by the boys, in homage to her most striking feature. I was sure none of the boys used this tribute to her face. I was also sure that word of her nickname would have reached her through other means. Having been on the receiving end of unwanted nicknames, I was reluctant to laugh when Terry mentioned *Double D*. Cathy's situation was different to mine. The pseudonym that was bestowed upon her by the boys was arguably complimentary. All my nicknames were created solely to cause offence and they had, for the most part, been effective. Of course, Cathy may not find the name complimentary; her perception alone determined the offensiveness of the nickname. *Offensiveness is in the ear of the beholder.* I had no doubt some of the less well-developed girls in our form would have been delighted to have such a name bestowed upon them. However, no-one would ever want my labels.

But the group hadn't finished admiring Cathy. She appeared to be the subject of regular discussion. As soon as Terry spoke the words *Double D* all the boys started making the universally recognised big boobs sign. They cupped their hands in front of their chests as if cradling a large pair of breasts and danced around, singing, "Titty Titty Wank Wank" to the tune of "Chitty Chitty Bang Bang". I doubted that any of them – with the notable exception of Tom – would have cradled a breast of any size. Rumour had it that Tom had already gone all the way, although the name of the accommodating partner varied depending on the originator of the tale. They were quick to end the dancing. Terry took exception to my reluctance to join their ritual. 'What's the matter, Lavelle? You not a tit-man then?' he said. 'You're not a poof, are you?'

'No, of course not. I like boobs,' I said, my wariness growing.

'But do you like big ones?' Terry asked, cupping his hands in front of himself. No dancing this time though.

'Yeah, sure.'

'Show me how big you like them,' Terry demanded.

All eyes were on me. I feebly held my hands out in front of me, cradling what was supposed to be my representation of perfect boobs. I stood there, feeling like a fool, when Terry passed judgement. 'Oh yeah. Those are some big boobies!'

'Nice one, Al,' Derek said. Then they started singing "Titty Titty Wank Wank" again. I took that as my cue. I began dancing, with less animation than they had, but enough that at least they knew I understood the form now. Perhaps this was an initiation ceremony of sorts, my invisible boobs having met the approval of the group. I got caught up in my thoughts. For some reason, I wondered what the offspring of Cathy and me would look like. If the result of our coupling possessed my back and Cathy's front then our progeny would be almost perfectly spherical in shape. I knew the chance of ever testing this hypothesis was remote in the extreme. And then the chance became less than zero.

Over the laughter of the other boys, I heard Terry calling out. 'Hey, Cathy, do you want to see Lavelle's impersonation of you?' I turned to where they looked to see Cathy watching my performance. Her expression was one of pure contempt and I shrivelled under her glare. The blood rushed to my face and I could feel my heart thump.

I barely heard Tom speak. 'Oops, I think she's already seen it,' and he turned, laughing, to the other boys.

Cathy took one last, disgusted look at me before walking towards her friends. '*Creep!*' she shouted. I retreated, covered in humiliation. Another name to add to my repertoire.

I never discovered if Tom's offer to join the rugby team had been genuine. My humiliation made the sincerity of his intentions irrelevant. I remained outside where I belonged.

I stayed in the library for the remainder of the break and returned to the classroom barely in time for the last lesson. I wanted to disappear. I wished I'd never talked to Tom or his teammates. Most of all, I wished I hadn't been so weak and foolish. I made another significant deposit to the Bank of Self-loathing, a deposit so substantial that the bank surely must have reached capacity. The last class dragged. I couldn't focus on the lesson. My prime concern was that I still had to navigate the journey home when I might bump into Tom and his gang. I didn't want to contemplate the notion of bumping into Cathy. I suspected she would give me a wide berth henceforth. I hoped she wouldn't shit in my bag. When the final bell sounded I already had my bag packed in accordance with my plan. I would seek sanctuary in the sports hall until I was confident I could escape unobserved. For once, I was first out of the classroom. I ran to the hall. I kept my head down, not caring what I could see other than the path in front of me. I gained the hall and checked inside to confirm it was empty.

I walked into the empty hall, feeling heavy as I sat on a pile of mats, dropping my bag to the floor. I told myself I could face the consequences tomorrow, but not today. I had been feeble and incautious, and it would take a night to achieve partial restoration of self. I just wanted the day to be over. The hall was quiet and I shed a little of the unease that weighed upon me. I looked over to where the ropes hung from the high ceiling. I walked over to them and took hold. I steadily climbed the rope using only my hands, letting my legs dangle. I remained motionless at the top for a few moments before lowering myself to the ground. I walked over to the chin-up bar, the scene of my recent success. I felt stupid and slimy and creepy; guilty of trying to impress the boys with my restraint. I jumped and gripped the bar in both hands. I moved up and down, slowly at first but increasing the speed as the count rose. I was a piston in an engine, tireless and efficient. When the count got to fifty I stopped at the top of the movement, the bar below my chin. I held that position for a while before dropping to the ground, bored, not fatigued.

It was then that I noticed the figure standing in the doorway. 'Lavelle?' Mr Evans said. We looked at each other for seconds that dragged out to ages. He shook his head, with an expression of contempt, before turning to leave. Twice in one day. This time the contempt had been a product of disappointment rather than disgust.

I had been wrong earlier; the Bank of Self-loathing had not been filled to capacity. Now it was.

* * * *

I was sitting on my bed, book in hand, waiting for Dai. My room, 2 pm on Wednesday was the arranged time and place for delivery of those goods necessary for the pursuit of the second pillar of CT. As usual, Dai was punctual and let himself into my room, surprisingly quiet for a big geezer. He slid the door closed behind him. 'Hey, Man, how goes it?'

'Oh yeah, not so bad. And you?'

'Good as gold, my man. Look, I need to tell you straight up. My usual supplier let me down so I've had to source the goods from a different guy. It's cost a bit more so I'm gonna' need forty-five quid a pop.'

'Oh, okay I guess. How good is the new stuff; where's it from?'

'Don't worry about the quality; you'll get more bang for your buck. It's well worth the extra fiver. I needed to spread the net wider for this stuff; all the way from a little place that starts with "M".'

'What, *Mexico?*'

'No, *Merthyr Tydfil!* I thought we'd done this before!'

'Yeah, but *Merthyr Tydfil!* That's nearer than Cardiff.'

'Yeah, but bloody *Mexico!* Is that the closest you could think of? Anyway, you up for it?'

'Yeah, go on then. I shall assume you aren't taking advantage of my good nature.'

'Would I do that?' he said with a look that suggested, *Yes, I would!*

I got the extra fiver out of my wallet, already having the forty pounds ready for our usual transaction. Dai handed over the product which looked darker than usual but otherwise seemed no different. Later in the week, the "performance" of the gang appeared to support Dai's contention that the quality was of a higher standard. We did indeed get more "bang for our buck".

* * * *

We took a well-earned *intermezzo* from our endeavours relating to pillar two. As was our custom, we repaired to the rec room. It was here we watched videos or television programmes while we descended from the heights of our gym-based scientific researches. Our discussions, however, did not elevate as our mental state descended. We felt the trivia was too important to dismiss. All but one of the gang attended. Nobody knew where Nobby was. Nobody asked where Nobby was. Nobody cared where Nobby was. As such, our prime deterrent was absent. Therefore, we relied upon our own initiative as an interloper opened the rec room door, as a precursor to joining us. Perceiving the threat, Legs stood up and said at a Voice-rivalling volume, 'This might sound funny but ... bollocks, bollocks, bollocks, bollocks, BOLLOCKS!' His voice reached a crescendo as he arrived at his final bollocks. The intruder, appreciating Legs' performance, turned and departed. They may have retreated to the other rec room, located in an adjacent wing, to try their luck. They may have even retreated to their own room, perhaps deciding they needed increased security from Legs' *bollocks*. It mattered not; the space was ours again. We could now pursue the remaining pillars of Casual Therapy unhindered.

Brains checked the television guide and proposed we watch a scheduled programme rather than resort to a video. 'What do you reckon, guys? It's a Bob Marley documentary. They'll have to play heaps of his music.' His suggestion met with general assent and so Brains switched channels to the documentary. As Brains surmised, the programme in most part concerned itself with the performance of Bob's music and a little on his background. As we watched and listened, in silence for once, I realised I still felt light-headed from our earlier session in the gym. The feeling may have been aggravated by Bob's "relaxing music". There was some important scientific data to be collected from this experience but I'd worry about that later. Usually by this time, hours later, I was well into the descent, if not landed and taxying the runway. It seemed I wasn't the only one still circling the airport.

'Is this live?' Legs said.

'*Du Fotze*! Of course it's not live. He's been dead for years!' Brains replied.

'Are you sure he's dead?' Legs was unconvinced.

'He had better be; they buried him in 1981,' Bomber said.

'Well, if he wasn't dead before they buried him, he would be by now,' Face said.

'No, what I mean is: was it live when they recorded it?' Legs "clarified".

'You fucking what? Well, let's see at the end when it was recorded and if it was 1981 or earlier then he recorded it before he died,' Brains replied from the land of the sarcastic.

'Fair enough,' Legs said as the sarcasm bounced off him, across the room and out of the window.

I consider sarcasm to be like poison. It doesn't matter how much is administered, if the intended recipient doesn't swallow, it ain't gonna work. Legs often got confused. His coping mechanism involved trying to confuse everyone else. Even when his methods proved successful I expect he didn't end up any less confused, but he would at least have company. To be fair to Legs, we had been discussing zombies earlier. When you combine that fact with the consumption of stronger weed, his increased confusion was inevitable. It was a practical certainty when considering his pre-existing *intellectual peculiarities.*

Earlier, mid-session in the gym, Bomber had raised the subject of a zombie apocalypse. The incident of the wandering weed and Nurse Hughes had taught us a valuable lesson about being prepared. We therefore considered being prepared for a zombie apocalypse was a matter of utmost importance, meriting our undivided attention. We unequivocally agreed that it was a matter of *when* and not *if. Zombies are inevitable,* was the consensus. 'What do you reckon, guys? Zombie apocalypse: ready or not?' Bomber asked.

'How much notice would we get?' Nobby said.

'How much notice do *you* think you'd get?' *Recent session with Doc Friendly, Bomber?*

'Well, I don't reckon it would happen overnight. There would have to be some sort of warning,' Face said.

'Yeah, but you'd rely on the authorities to contain an outbreak. They'd have to keep quiet about it to stop people panicking,' Voice shouted.

'What about that programme we saw last week? That was the problem; the authorities didn't tell anyone and then when they couldn't contain the outbreak, no-one was ready.'

'You do know we were watching a zombie *movie*, Bomber, not a zombie *documentary?*' Brains said.

'Yeah, but in the absence of any historical precedents, other than the spread of the plague or Ebola and the like, the film is a reasonable preliminary reference,' Bomber said in a most Brains-like way. *New meds, Bomber?*

'But how would you know when it's started?' I said. 'You can't simply assume every time you see someone staggering around that they're part of the first zombie wave and start hacking away at their spinal cord.'

'That's true, especially around here. Imagine; you'd be chopping up half the residents,' Voice shouted. I allowed myself a smile as I visualised decapitating Nobby. If, or should that be when, it occurs, Nobby would fare well in the zombie apocalypse; he'd be their king. He already looked and smelled like a zombie.

'Do you reckon you'd survive then, Silent?' Bomber said.

'Yeah, no sweat. Piece of cake. Get shelter; get food; get water; get armed; get going! We've plenty of experience with the zombies around here.' At once, I regretted saying that. I made another deposit to the Bank of SL. I had occupied the zombie state myself more than once. I was no better than the other poor sods around here. Where I was different to the other poor sods however, was that I would be in my element in a zombie-plagued world. It would be a world in which I could better cope. I had difficulties *living* in this world; it was too unpredictable. Surviving in a zombie-beleaguered land would be somewhat simpler. The issues would be all about life or death. I would find it easier just *staying alive*. I don't tell the lads this, of course. They would consider it dramatic; and quite right too. I'm sure if I introduced them to the concept of *pathmatic* they would've employed the term.

What I also don't tell them is that I would be on the side of the zombies. I would cheer them on as they gave the remnant of mankind the payback it so richly deserved.

Chapter Ten

Several months passed at home in which we each settled into our separate existences. When not at meals, Dad spent most of his time in his study, the sound of classical music drifting beneath the closed door. He distanced himself not only from me but from the world at large. Other than mealtimes, we spent little time together. I discovered that during the day, when Kevin and I were at school, Dad walked into town rather than linger in the house. Ruth remained dedicated to reducing the world's stock of white wine. Her short interlude of animation when Kevin first arrived was a dim memory. Ruth never demonstrated any interest in my welfare and, at best, displayed a passing interest in the welfare of her own son. The world weariness that possessed Ruth infected the entire household.

I noted that their one-year wedding anniversary came and went without acknowledgement; an ominous portent. There was no attempt to celebrate that which it seemed did not merit celebration. It was clear that the single year had aged my father. He had lost much of his vitality that was once such an important part of his character. A year ago the grey highlights at his temples served to give him a somewhat distinguished look. Now, his hair was altogether grey, ageing him beyond his years. His face had become more lined and he wore a weary expression. He was slower too, as if his bearing was subjected to a greater gravitational force than a year ago. Dad looked more tired than ill; the lack of contact between us serving to accentuate the changes of a year. I considered contacting Doctor Jeffries but once again I prevaricated. To make the call would have seemed like betrayal and I didn't want to upset Dad. However, one evening after a typically quiet dinner, I was determined to reconnect. 'Hey, Dad, there's a good movie on later. Do you want to watch it with me?'

'Is there? We'll see; maybe if I have time.'

'Okay. I think you'd like it. Orson Welles is in it.' Dad liked Orson's work. I did not. I could never tell him that I thought *Citizen Kane* was overrated.

'I might be busy. What about Kevin, maybe he'd like to watch it?'

'Kevin's gone out,' I said. He was spending all his free time with the Bad Lads. 'Hey, when was the last time you saw Doctor Jeffries? I haven't seen him in ages.' I chanced a different approach.

'Doctor Jeffries?' Dad looked thoughtful. 'The last time I saw Barry was a couple of weeks ago. I see him in town sometimes.' I derived some comfort knowing he kept in touch with the doctor.

'So, the movie starts at seven.'

'Maybe next time,' Dad said. He turned to take the familiar path to his study.

'Dad?' I said, louder than intended.

He turned to face me. 'Yes?'

'Is everything … I mean … Are you okay?' I asked the question out loud, at long last.

He looked at me with weary, ancient eyes. '*Same old, same old …*' He turned from me, walked into his study, struggling against the weight of movement, and closed the door behind him. I stood in silence for a few moments. The sound of bottle against glass brought me back from my thoughts.

I never watched the movie. I retrieved Stevenson's *Kidnapped* from my room and made straight for sanctuary. It was a matter of moments for me to achieve the platform, gripping the boards, hand over hand. I sat there for a long time. I didn't descend until it had been dark for some time. I didn't need to see to be able to descend. My frequent retreats to the platform afforded me a familiarity with all the contours of the tree.

It wasn't night that forced me to stop reading; the tears saw to that long before the dark.

* * * *

I often wonder if it was the question I had longed to ask that prompted Dad to action. Perhaps when he reflected upon his answer Dad resolved to remedy the domestic situation. It could be no coincidence that the arguing started not long after I'd talked to Dad. I arrived home from school one afternoon to be greeted by the sound of quarrelling. Gelert was there to greet me but was more restrained than usual. He seemed relieved to see me. As I approached the study, the source of the argument, the noise clarified into words. 'You can't simply sit there all day drinking wine and reading magazines.' Dad sounded frustrated. I stood at the foot of the stairs where I could eavesdrop and be ready to beat a retreat if necessary. They wouldn't have noticed me arriving over their noise and with Gelert making less of a disturbance than usual.

'Well, I don't have my own study, do I?' Ruth said.

'You should make more of an effort. In fact, just make any bloody effort!'

'I've told you; he's not my son!'

'So you insist on saying. But he is *my* son! No-one is asking you to mother Alan. Mrs Montgomery looks after the domestic stuff and Alan is old enough to take care of himself.'

'Then what *are* you asking?'

'I … I don't know. I want you to be happier … be happy.'

'Look who's talking. You're not exactly Mr Sunshine, are you?'

'No, I'm not,' Dad said. 'We all need to work together. At least I'm willing to make an effort. For the boys. Can't you?'

'I don't even know where Kevin is half the time.' Ruth sounded jaded.

'That's my point. We need to show the boys we care; that they have something worth coming home to.' Dad was being diplomatic. He hadn't singled Kevin out. I wasn't offended. He was trying.

'We'll see.' Ruth seemed unconvinced. She wouldn't agree, but she was less hostile. I retreated to my room. It was dinner time when I next descended the stairs. Kevin had returned. His school bag and jacket hung from the back of his chair. I was the last to sit. Dad had heated the hot-pot that Mrs M had prepared earlier that day. He put the casserole dish in the centre of the table and waited for Ruth to serve herself first. As Ruth prevaricated over the offering, Dad spoke. 'I thought we might go for a drive in the country this weekend. We haven't done that for a while. It should be nice.' In fact, we had only once taken a drive at the weekend, six months earlier. It had rained and everything we'd seen, apart from the wipers, had been a vague blur. The café we'd visited had been full and we'd returned home wet and hungry. No-one had complained of course, that would have required conversation. Dad had turned the radio on to provide a soundtrack to accompany the solitary noise of the wipers.

I waited for Ruth to respond but she said nothing. 'Yeah, that sounds good,' I said to break the silence. Kevin looked at me and scoffed.

That got Dad's attention. 'That sounds okay, doesn't it, Kevin? The weather is forecast to be fine.'

'Yeah, sure,' Kevin said.

'There we go, dear. It's all settled. A nice drive in the country-side this weekend,' Dad said to Ruth. She looked at him and nodded without enthusiasm. It had needed the lengthiest conversation we'd had in a long time, but it was agreed.

We headed out for our drive that Sunday. Dad drove, with Ruth in the front passenger seat. Kevin and I sat in the back, both of us squeezed up against the doors, maximising the distance between us. Dad had purchased a new medium-sized sedan. While it was a modest vehicle compared to some flashy cars that were available, it possessed most of the mod cons. This car had real airbags; not balloons in the glovebox. He had kept Vandalised, which was now stored under wraps in the garage. Dad planned to get Vandalised restored to its former glory for my eighteenth birthday and so it sat in the garage awaiting its rebirth.

The weather was clear and sunny – perfect driving conditions. Dad was determined to visit somewhere that would minimise the potential for complaint. As we set out, Dad advised we were heading to Betws-y-Coed. Ruth became surprisingly vocal when she learnt of our destination. 'Betws-y-Coed? Why are we going there?' she unsurprisingly protested.

'There was an article in the paper. The local council spent a lot of money tidying it up. There are heaps of places to eat and lots of picturesque little shops. It's supposed to be a great place to visit.'

'Is that it, then?'

'No, there's other stuff as well. There are some nice walks,' Dad said.

Gelert had stayed at home; the drive was long and he wouldn't have wanted to sit in a car with Kevin. He was also pulling guard duty. 'Don't forget, kill all intruders on sight! Take no prisoners!' had been my final instruction to Gelert before we left.

Despite the car having most of the safety features available at the time, there was no satnav installed. Dad claimed it would insult his sense of direction. However, there was a map book in the car; a concession to some navigational limitations. After an hour of driving through identical-looking countryside, it seemed we were adrift. 'You don't know where we are, do you?' Ruth accused Dad.

'I know exactly where we are. We're lost. Time to get the map book out, Alan.'

'I thought you knew where you're going,' Ruth said.

'So did I for a while,' Dad said.

'Okay, Dad. Got the book. So where are we?' I needed a starting point.

'Ah, there lies the question. I don't know. Let's keep going down this road until we see an intersection.'

'Don't you have satnav?' Ruth said.

'Nope, and neither does the car.'

'You have an answer for everything, don't you?' she said. I saw a twinkle in Dad's eyes, the first in forever, as he declined to respond. 'Ugh!' Ruth said, irritated. Another couple of minutes passed without sign of an intersection or any useful landmark. Perhaps Ruth's wine content dipped towards critical level and she worried about how long before her liquid lunch would be available. 'Oh, we're never going to get there!'

I don't know if Dad was trying to relieve the tension or if he was truly irritated but he stopped the car by a gate leading into a large pasture. 'Okay, tell you what. Let's ask one of the locals,' he said. A horse was in the field with its head extended over the gate to eat the adjacent bushes. Dad slid his window down. 'Excuse me, old boy, but could you point me in the direction of Betws-y-Coed? I'd be most grateful.' The horse looked on unmoved and chewed at whatever managed to find its way into its mouth. Kevin shook his head and Ruth turned to look out of her window, trying to ignore Dad. 'Perhaps that was too difficult a request. Okay, can you tell me where we are then?' Dad said. This time he got a response. The horse turned side on and rid itself of a load of horse-apples that made a dull thump as they landed. 'I say, that's rude!' Dad said and I laughed. This was the most animated he'd been in months. It didn't last. Ruth turned towards Dad as he made his last remark to the "rude" horse. She stared at him for a second before turning to look at me in much the same dismissive manner.

Looking at the horse, she said, 'Do I detect a family resemblance?' Kevin laughed and I felt blood flow to my face. I don't know if Dad's face reddened. He put the car in gear and we continued on our journey. We arrived at our destination after a while; we had been closer than we had suspected. There was a signpost at the next intersection, telling how far and in which direction we should travel. We arrived at a picturesque and tidy town. The local council had spent well. We stayed long enough to find a quiet pub where we ate lunch. While Kevin and I ate, Ruth worked on restoring her white wine content. Dad, map book to hand, plotted our silent route home.

The journey home was much quicker and less animated than the trip there. Nobody spoke. Dad didn't even bother turning the radio on to break the silence. On arriving home, we exited the car in haste. I sought out Gelert. He waited for Kevin to leave before running to me to make his report. There was a complete lack of dismembered burglars around the place, so the report was brief. Gelert was a pretty good ratter, a common trait of terriers. He caught and dispatched vermin now and again but once alone brought his trophy into the house. On that occasion, he'd trotted into the house, dead rat gripped between his teeth, and deposited it with pride at the feet of Mrs M, the first person he'd seen. Perhaps Mrs M might have reacted differently had the rat possessed a semblance of life but she did not flinch when confronted with Gelert's gift.

Mrs M, sang-froid intact, went to a drawer and withdrew a plastic bag. She picked up the dead rodent and exited the house by the kitchen door, calling Gelert after her. When Mrs M was well into the garden she dropped the rat on the ground and stooped to address Gelert. I couldn't hear what Mrs M said, or how she said it, but Gelert sat at her side hanging on her every word, ears cocked to attention. Whatever the message was, it was successful. Gelert never brought another dead trophy into the house. Instead he would deposit them in the exact same spot he had received his pep-talk from Mrs M. What a team they were. If only the rest of the household could have existed in such harmony.

* * * *

I retired to my room at the hospital, searching for peace and quiet. Over lunch I'd felt a tension headache building. By the time I'd finished eating, a throbbing ache filled my head. I made my way to my room, keeping as motionless as possible; each movement sending a stabbing pain through my head. I drew the blinds and slid the door almost closed. I left enough gap for the nurse on duty to confirm I was in my room for the head-count. I adjusted the pillows on my bed and lay down, taking the weight off my head and shoulders. That simple expedient afforded me instant respite and the headache receded. I closed my eyes and focused on my breathing – deep inhalations and slow exhalations. After a few still minutes I felt much improved but not quite ready to abandon my comfortable post.

I heard an unwelcome voice at the doorway, the owner oblivious to my need for privacy. The sight of the almost-closed door, drawn blinds and motionless, closed-eyed occupant was little deterrent to someone as thoughtless as Nobby. Perhaps he'd sensed my pain levels diminish and came to restore them. 'Hey, Silent. Can I come in?' he said, quietly for him. I felt the headache reviving and I didn't respond. I hoped he would think I was asleep. I also hoped that, by some miracle, Nobby had learnt the art of consideration. Unfortunately, the major improvements to Nobby's personality that were necessary for him to bugger off had not occurred. He slid the door open and entered. 'Can I have a word?' the request for entry now redundant. I resolved to adopt the *ignore him and he'll go away* approach. It had never worked before but there was a first time for everything.

Nobby elected to ignore my attentive ignorance and wandered closer to the bed, sighing in a feeble attempt to attract my attention. My focus went from ignoring Nobby to surviving Nobby. I was too busy trying not to inhale any fumes he was exuding to be interested in his amateur dramatics. His BO wasn't as potent as usual; perhaps a sign that he'd just had a session with Doc Friendly. The doc isn't only concerned about a patient's appetite and sleep patterns but also their personal hygiene. Hygiene is considered an important indicator of a person's willingness to take care of themselves. In Nobby's case his poor hygiene was simply an indication of him being a lazy bastard. Nobby had perhaps applied deodorant before his session, as a pre-emptive measure. He may have even applied the deodorant after the session, if the doc had raised the issue. I'm sure the doc would have broached the subject with the appropriate level of sensitivity. I'm also sure the doc wouldn't have objected if Nobby had applied deodorant *during* the session, out of sight, of course.

After loitering at the foot of my bed, encouraging a resurgence in my headache, he spoke again. 'You know something, Silent, you're my only friend.'

I kept my eyes closed. I might have been compelled to listen to him, but I didn't have to look at him too. 'Don't say that, Nobby. You know that's not true.'

'Well, who else is my friend?'

'No, you misunderstand. I mean, I'm not your friend.'

This misconception of Nobby's was something I endeavoured to discourage. It was bad enough that Nobby accused me of such a transgression to my face but he also shared this delusion with others. Doc Friendly once raised the issue. 'I understand that Ray says you are his only friend. Is that true, Alan?'

'Yes it is,' I said. 'He has been saying that.'

Nobby persisted. 'But everyone picks on me, apart from you.'

I don't pick on you because you're not worth the effort! I thought. He also wasn't worth the effort of an explanation. 'Look, Nobby, do me a massive favour and bugger off. I'm trying to rest.'

'Okay. Well, I'll see you later then,' he said and left the room, neglecting to replace the door in its pre-Nobby position. *Yes, you probably bloody well will,* I thought.

The Nobby-effect overwhelmed me to such an extent that I was unable to regain the relaxed state I had achieved before the disturbance. There was little recourse available to me. It was time for a spot of solo self-medication. I sat up with care and unlocked the drawer containing my kit and other small valuables. I retrieved my vintage tobacco tin that protected both tobacco and other, arguably healthier but ironically more illicit, products. I locked the drawer and headed for the gardens.

The hospital had been the stately home of aristocrats in a previous life. As such, the grounds were extensive. There were a number of newish concrete seats, impersonating Roman marble, dotted around the gardens. I often strolled alone around the well-appointed gardens to relax, take in the view and smell the flowers. In my wanderings I had discovered a few spots that were conducive to the sort of relaxation I was now seeking. My throbbing head was grateful to discover that the nearest suitable spot was vacant. I sat on the stone bench with a sense of relief. It was at this juncture that I would embrace mindfulness; actively committing to the here and now. I would scan the garden with care, selecting a specific plant for close inspection. I would trace the colours and lines of the petals, the leaves and the stem, noting how the flower fitted together; how the stem merged with the greater plant. I immersed myself in the mechanics of nature. I then focused on the sounds and smells surrounding me; enriching my meditation. Today the subject matter of my mindfulness, while still natural in origin, focused more on plant life that had been some-what processed for further appreciation.

I took a quick look around to confirm I wouldn't be disturbed and removed the tin from my pocket. I removed two rolling papers first, overlapped them and placed them on the bench next to me. I then removed a measure of tobacco, distributing it evenly across the paper. I took another look around to confirm the area remained secure and removed the resin from where it was concealed within the tobacco.

I unwrapped the enclosing cling-film, used to retain moisture. I pinched a practised measure of product from the greater lump and placed it with care next to the spliff-in-waiting. I then replaced the remaining product in the cling-film, re-moulding it to a sphere without compromising the integrity of the seal. Rather than apply a flame, I chose the more artisan approach of rolling the product between finger and thumb until it reached the perfect consistency for crumbling into the spliff. This I then did, leaving the first half-inch free of product where I would hold it in my mouth, to minimise wastage. That left the sealing of the spliff to be carried out. I licked the paper and rolled the spliff to completion, pinching it at the ends to enclose the contents. I looked at the completed work of art and rolled it between fingers to confirm it was of optimum consistency. Nurse Hughes would have judged it a thing of beauty.

I had constructed it with love and care and now came the time to deconstruct it as it realised its destiny. I sat on the bench, inhaling deeply and letting the external and internal atmosphere do its thing to rid me of my headache and of Nobby side-effects. It wasn't long before the headache receded and I felt less murderous towards Nobby. I remained seated after I'd finished smoking, looking across the garden, appreciating the stillness and natural beauty. I took a moment to watch a butterfly flutter by. I was better prepared for the rest of the day and had needed the unscheduled dose of self-medication. There hadn't been any sanctioned research carried out that day pertaining to pillar two. There was only a cultural alignment session scheduled for later to be held in the rec room. Management had taken delivery of new material, quite a few CDs and a few videos. We needed to collectively assess their potential value to the group's important works.

Being five minutes late, I was last to arrive at the recreation room. That wasn't necessarily a bad thing. There was no reserved seating, as was the case in the gym, and so we worked on a first-in, first-served basis. While the prime locations were taken, I could position myself to achieve the greatest distance from Nobby. My earlier encounter had been ample exposure for one day. It was unlikely that Nobby would claim my friendship in front of the gang. It would be asking for trouble, even for him. He may have believed that he was already victimised but it could have been much worse should he make such spurious claims public. He'd be wasting his time anyway; no-one would believe him. Not only because the notion of Nobby having a friend was implausible but because nobody believed anything he said, on principle.

Voice was the nominated reviewer. He was representative of the musical tastes of the greater group and we would have no problems hearing his commentary. Voice rummaged through the large cardboard box full of CDs and videos. The music was first up for assessment. 'Christ, how old is this one?' Voice yelled. 'The Best of Louis Armstrong.'

'Wasn't he the first man to play the trumpet on the moon?' Legs said.

'Yeah, I think so,' a distracted Face said. Perhaps I hadn't been the only one to partake in extracurricular self-medication.

'Hold on. How the fuck could he play the trumpet when he's wearing that bloody big goldfish bowl on his head?' Bomber said. Brains suppressed a laugh.

'Well ... he would have played it in the module of course.'

'Oh yeah, I suppose that would work.'

Wherever and however Louis played the trumpet, he didn't make the cut. He was relegated to the reject pile without further discussion. While we didn't disparage his musical talents, his was not the sound for which we searched. We sought a soundtrack that didn't necessarily consist of "serious" music but could still be taken seriously for the purposes of our vital endeavours. The gang liked music that could be considered a little serious or a little trivial; sometimes simultaneously. That very specific criteria led us to develop a fondness for punk, ska and reggae. We all jumped as Voice discovered a potential nugget. My vertical leap record was sorely tested. 'Hoy, hoy, guys! I think we've struck gold here: "The Selecter, Greatest Hits". What do you reckon; is it one for the "yes" pile?'

'Does the Pope shit in the woods?' Face said.

'The saying is either "Does a *bear* shit in the woods?" or "Is the Pope a *Catholic*?" It's a rhetorical question,' Brains said.

'Well, now you've asked the question, Face, it needs to be answered. I'd imagine the Pope shits wherever he wants,' Voice offered. 'I also reckon if the Pope wanted to shit in the woods, there would be some special arrangements made to accommodate such a yearning.'

'What, you mean like the Pope Mobile?'

'More like a *Poop* Mobile. It would be a mobile-golden-throne-studded-with-precious-stones kind of affair. No squatting behind a tree to squeeze one out for the *Popester*!'

'I never understood why the Pope Mobile has bulletproof glass. I mean, who the fuck is the Pope going to shoot?' Legs' comment went unanswered.

'They should save his poop. They could sell it as a religious artefact,' Brains said.

'What, would *you* buy pope poop?' Bomber said.

'I might be tempted at the right price. It would depend on the marketing. I'd want to see promotion of all the special abilities afforded by possession of pope poop.'

'What sort of abilities would you be after?'

'Oh, the usual sort of thing. You know; bring the dead back to life and time travel. Maybe help Chelsea get a win.'

'Come on, be realistic, Brains. Chelsea win a game; there's miracles and then there's kidding yourself! Chelsea are crap!' Face said.

'Well, I don't agree.'

'Why, are you a Chelsea supporter?'

'No; you should have said Chelsea *is* crap, not Chelsea *are* crap!'

Irrespective of the Holy Father's toilet practices, "The Selecter" made the cut even if we took the scenic route to get there. As the evening progressed and the discussions deteriorated, I began to suspect that more than a few of the gang had also indulged in solo self-medication that day.

Holy shit, indeed.

* * * *

The disastrous day trip to Betws-y-Coed marked another turning point in the devices of the household. Dad's discontent became less passive and more active. Whenever he and Ruth were together they argued. As far as I knew Dad still spent time away from the house during the day which meant they reserved their disagreements for when I was at home. I found it ironic that Ruth, who had once been so fatigued, discovered energy enough to engage my father in argument. Indeed, at the cessation of a bout of hostilities, Ruth appeared to be reinvigorated whereas Dad was exhausted. It was as if she used the hostile medium to drain him of his life-force. The situation deteriorated so badly that I found myself longing for the silences that had once been so familiar.

Much of their arguing related to Ruth's apparent unhappiness and the unnamed solutions. Dad sounded increasingly frustrated at Ruth's inability or unwillingness to reveal what might remedy her discontent. She would not disclose what might enable her happiness but was more than capable of voicing that which drove her dissatisfaction. Often, I heard Ruth employ the phrase 'He's not my son!' At first, Dad vigorously defended me, telling her 'Well, he is *my* son!' No matter how he responded or how often he responded, Ruth remained oblivious to all contention. I retreated to my platform even more often. It became my fortress of solitude. From there I couldn't hear them and I couldn't see them. No-one could get to me. I sat on my platform, brooding in silence, looking out over the town and nurturing my sense of envy. Dad became most jaded when the sense of hopelessness became overwhelming. Six weeks after the excursion, Dad gave up.

The confrontational atmosphere yielded other outcomes. Mrs Montgomery resigned from her position. Dad attempted to curb hostilities when Mrs M was present, but Ruth refused to cooperate. The antagonism was palpable and someone of Mrs M's astuteness couldn't fail to sense that the situation was dire. There were other indicators. The box full of empty bottles that met me each morning increased in size. I noted with concern that the empty whiskey bottles became more frequent. Whereas there used to be a single whiskey bottle to every four bottles of wine, the ratio was down to one in two. I wasn't present for the final discussion between Dad and Mrs M. I expect Mrs M would have been calm and logical; her usual competent self. I expect Dad would have yielded without argument, possessing no energy for conflict.

I knew something was amiss when I returned from school one afternoon and saw Mrs M's red Mini in the driveway. I would only see Mrs M on Saturday morning. Her other visits occurred on weekdays when Mrs M would appear, competently carry out her domestic duties and then disappear, all while I was at school. On this particular day Mrs M sat at the kitchen table, it seemed awaiting my arrival. As I walked into the house Mrs M stood and walked towards me. I could not have been more stunned when Mrs M enveloped me in her arms, hugging me for an age. 'Do take care, Alan. I shall miss you,' she said. She stood back and looked at me with moist eyes. Her parting words were, 'And do look after your father, dear.' Mrs M walked to the front door, put on her jacket and stopped to say goodbye to Gelert before climbing into her car and leaving the Lavelle household.

I was unable to process the fact of her departure until later. At that moment, I was overwhelmed by the manner of her departure. Mrs M had displayed emotions of which I had thought her incapable. I watched the car driving out of the driveway and out of our lives, not yet appreciating the implications. Ruth sat outside at the garden table, assuming her normal position; wine glass in hand, scanning a magazine.

I sought out Dad. I heard classical music coming from his study. I knocked at the door. 'Dad, are you there?' There was no response and so I knocked louder. 'Dad, what's going on? What happened with Mrs Montgomery?' This time Dad did respond; the music became louder. I tried the handle but the room was locked. I walked away, out of the house and retired to my sanctuary. I was angry and felt altogether alone; a degree of isolation to which I had not even descended at school.

I remained on my platform for hours, not returning to the house until dark. I waited until dinner time had passed. I didn't want to see anyone, let alone sit down to eat with them. When I got to the kitchen it was empty. I saw Ruth, seated outside at the garden table, reading and drinking beneath the light of a lamp. I crossed to the kitchen table where there was something covered by a tea towel. When I removed the towel I was greeted by the sight of Mrs M's shepherd's pie. I took in the warm, delicious smell of the dish. Then I began to understand the loss.

* * * *

Life at secondary school persisted. The incident with Cathy D hadn't been excessively publicised outside of the immediate rugby team. For that I was grateful. I was still unable to look at or be anywhere near Cathy or her friends but avoiding them wasn't a difficult task. We didn't mix in the same circles. My circle consisted of the few nerds that frequented the library during breaks. Without doubt, Cathy would not forget the incident. I know I hadn't. I'd learnt some hard-won lessons from my transgression, related to withholding trust. In many ways the incident served to reinforce already held convictions. Life went on. It was a large school and there were always new events that dominated and diluted older incidents.

Now and again, tales of various deeds attributed to the Bad Lads were brought to my attention. One tale in particular that persevered related to the abuse of small animals. The gang was accredited with responsibility for the disappearance of a number of animals in the area. Rumour was the Bad Lads enticed and captured any cat that had the misfortune to cross their path. While the ultimate fate of the poor creatures was not known, it was assumed that they met with a wretched end. It may have been coincidence, but these rumours didn't start circulating until Kevin enlisted with the gang. Gelert disliked Kevin, but I related that to the lack of affection afforded by Kevin rather than through fear. In any case, Gelert was secured at home. He only left the property when he took me for a walk. In addition, I knew he would be a much tougher quarry than a cat. None of the local moggies dared set paw near our house more than once; Gelert saw them off with extreme prejudice. There may have been other reasons for their caution.

My seventeenth birthday passed without celebration, there being a general lack of interest, myself included. There had been a celebration of sorts for Kevin's sixteenth birthday, two months previous. His get-together had been much the same perfunctory celebration as that for my sixteenth. The cake was shop-bought rather than homemade and the rendition of "Happy Birthday" had been a little more vocal, but just as uninspiring. I didn't feel like celebrating my birthday; I still harboured anger towards Dad. I was angry because he gave up. He gave up on life, he gave up on me and, most inexcusable, he gave up on himself. When I did spend any time with him, I could observe the apathy that ruled his existence. He had become more world-weary than Ruth. At least Ruth atrophied in the open; Dad hid in his study. He seemed subjected to an unendurable gravitational force. I didn't realise at the time exactly how eroded he'd become.

* * * *

It was mid-afternoon. We were halfway through an English literature class – my favourite subject. The teacher, Miss Jennings, was pleasant and approachable. I always enjoyed the work and this was reflected in my respectable grades. There was a tap at the door and we looked up to see Mr Williams, our Head of Year. 'Sorry to interrupt, Miss Jennings, but I need to take Alan Lavelle from you.' He looked in my direction. 'You need to pack your bag please, Alan.' He wore a strange expression such that I had no idea to what the summons related. I felt sure I wasn't in trouble; I hadn't taken a shit in anyone's bag in years. It was in this state of confusion that I walked in silence with Mr Williams as he accompanied me to the headmaster's office. He knocked on the door and opened it with care. 'I have Alan Lavelle here for you, Headmaster.' He stepped aside and guided me into the room.

The headmaster, Mr Damon, sat behind his large wooden desk, a look of grave concern on his face. My sense of confusion was seasoned with apprehension. I noticed Kevin already sat in front of the headmaster. He wore an expression I did not recognise. It was then that I perceived Doctor Jeffries, standing at the back of the room. His expression was easier to decipher. His eyes were red and moist and his brow was furrowed. He was distraught. It was then that I was struck by the cold realisation of why I had been summoned. I knew something had happened to Dad.

'I'm so sorry, Alan,' Doctor Jeffries said, voice quivering. 'Your father ... he's ... he's dead.' He stifled a sob.

The whole world collapsed into me. I couldn't stand. I sat down hard on the floor, my bag breaking the fall only a little. My senses were overwhelmed. I was unable to process what I'd heard. There was too much; I was engulfed in a sensory avalanche. Everything was cold and white and close.

I turned and looked towards Kevin and, right then, I knew with absolute certainty what his expression revealed. It was a look of *triumph*.

Chapter Eleven

I stand in a large expanse. The sky is white. The ground is grey and hard. I am surrounded by people. Their expressions are indecipherable. They are oblivious to all but their own individual journey. They walk with purpose. Each moves at a steady pace. They do not deviate from their path. Their movements are synchronised. Their paths cross but they do not slow; neither do they collide. I turn, searching for a destination.

I sense an anomaly. Through the moving multitudes I see a huge tiger. It flashes in and out of view among the masses. The tiger moves closer as it stalks towards me. I move away from the approaching danger. I stagger through the crowd, knowing touch is not permitted. My movements are awkward as people impede me. I search for the beast. Fear rises as I realise I can no longer see it. There is a flash of orange through the crowd. The tiger moves towards me without pause. It moves in a straight line, in perfect harmony with the others. Why am I alone in seeing the approaching danger?

Through the crowds, I perceive the vague outline of a building. I experience hope and head towards potential sanctuary. I reach the building and search for an entryway. I see a door nearby. I glance back to see the tiger moving closer. I step through the doorway. The building is massive; the ceiling lost to view. I see another doorway in the opposite wall. There are more people milling around inside the building. I take care not to touch them, as I move across the room. I dare not run for fear of drawing attention to my flight. My progress is slow. I arrive at the other doorway and look behind me. The tiger pursues me, still. It is so close now.

I enter the room with haste. My loud heart thumps. The beast must hear it. The room is small. By the time realisation hits it is too late. I have not discovered a means of escape; I am trapped. The tiger stands in the doorway. There is a single chair positioned in the centre of the room. I sit in the chair. I remain motionless and silent. The tiger is still. It looks at me with huge, dark, bottomless eyes. The tiger is impossibly large; impossibly beautiful. The orange and white and black pelt is stunning. The magnificent, massive head is now inches from me. The tiger takes an age to open its jaws. How can they be so huge? I am being enveloped in the maws; they are everything. I am perplexed. Why does the tiger pursue me? Why does it ignore the other people through which it flows? Why ME? Then darkness.

It is not fear that awakens me; it is anger.

* * * *

During an early session with Doc Friendly, he wanted to consider anger. This was before the days of my selfless commitment to self-medication and the other pillars of Casual Therapy. We had passed through the preliminaries and so had established the status of my appetite and energy levels. 'You seem a little perturbed, Alan. Is something bothering you?'

No, I thought, *everything is fucking super; that's why I'm in the fucking nut house!* 'I'm okay, I guess. Maybe just feeling a bit out of sorts.' In fact, I was highly irritated and not concealing the fact very well. This sense of irritation pervaded my mood sometimes. It stole up on me in such a way that I wanted to withdraw from interacting with others. I was unable to cope with the emotion that infected me and so I put myself into social quarantine. I never could pin down the exact reason for it. This fact in itself served to further feed my irritation. It was as if the irritation built up over a matter of time, sometimes months, with no specific trigger. The only way I could control the feeling was to capitulate and give it free rein. It was not the most elegant solution, nor would I consider it overly effective, but it was available.

'*A bit out of sorts?* Oh dear, Alan, that's not good.'

You don't fucking say? I thought but said nothing. He hadn't asked a direct question and he knew the rule; no question means no answer. Though we had not played the game for long that condition had already been established.

'If you don't mind me saying, Alan, you seem a little angry. Has something happened to upset you?'

His question increased my irritation to such an extent that I relented. 'I'm sick of all the shit that happens to me. I want a break.'

'What has brought this on, Alan? Is it something specific?'

'No. Nothing specific. Lots of little things. It all adds up.'

'I see, Alan. Do you think then, that you are due some good luck? That it's about time good things happened to you?'

'I'm not saying that; not at all. I don't need good things to happen to me. I just want the bad things to *stop* happening!' I said, irritation peaking.

'Well, have you heard the expression "All things happen for a reason", Alan?'

'Yes, I have. It's a lazy way of expressing Newton's laws of motion. Either lazy or stupid!' I said, giving him an idea of with whom he was dealing.

'I see, Alan, perhaps it's not intended to be taken quite so literally.' The doc was not yet familiar with what would become one of my preferred strategies.

I employed another favourite tactic: *diversion.* 'You said I was angry and I'm neither confirming nor denying. But isn't there another expression about "Depression is anger turned inwards"?'

'Well, Alan, I wasn't suggesting you're angry. You appeared to display some possible signs and I was merely asking if that was the case. As for the expression about anger turned inwards causing depression, that's no longer the current thinking. It's not a philosophy that I advocate to my patients, or my colleagues. Not in and of itself, at least,' the doc said, giving me an idea of with whom *I* was dealing. *Balls!* I thought. I had all sorts of arguments prepared for why I believe the expression is a load of cobblers. It's tantamount to suggesting if you turn your anger outwards, you will rid yourself of depression. Complete bollocks; that would make me feel worse. Anger is a symptom, not a cause. And so on …

That made the score one-all. We had both proffered what was supposed to be a pertinent expression which had been rejected by the other party. It was a position with which I was comfortable, both then and in future sessions. A score-draw was fine with me. We were still establishing the finer rules of the game at that stage, as well as sounding out our opponent. Having reached stalemate quite early on in the session, Doc Friendly resorted to Psychotherapy Rule number three: *If the wheels start spinning, bring out the games.* This is a first resort rather than a last resort. If there's little progress being made towards the end of a session, then finish early; everyone wins. If there's little progress being made, and time allows, introduce fresh stimulus. For Doc Friendly, the sole games to which we have ever resorted have been the Rorschach test, or ink blots, and word association. On the few occasions that we had fallen back on these tests I had been doubtful to their real value to the psychotherapeutic process. The Rorschach test, in particular, I suspect is of questionable value. How often would a patient look at the dark, amorphous splodge and exclaim, 'That looks like my mother and Santa shagging on my bed during the Queen's speech in 1982'? Not often, I say.

Doc Friendly brought out the ink blots twice in total. Rorschach and his work do not inspire my imagination. On my first exposure to the blots I thought they looked like mangled moths or battered butterflies. These were the sole responses I offered. Some months later, when the wheels started spinning and the doc got the ink blots out again, I thought to humour him. After I offered commentary on a couple of mutilated Lepidoptera, the doc asked with less enthusiasm than usual, 'And does this next picture bring anything to mind, Alan?'

'Let's see … that one sort of looks like … an Eskimo in boxing gloves, tuning a harpsichord.'

'Is that so, Alan?' The doc got excited.

'Nah. Squashed moth.' We never bothered with the blots again.

However, word association is still brought out from the games cupboard now and again, as was the case in this particular session.

'Okay, Alan. I'm going to say a word and I want you to respond with the first word you think of. Okay?'

'Yes,' I said with purpose.

'What's that? Oh, I see, we haven't started yet, Alan,' the doc said, still smiling.

'No,' I declared, but he wasn't taking the bait. 'Sure. Ready when you are.'

'Okay. Cat,' he said.

'Kit Kat,' I said.

'Dog,' he said.

'Hot dog,' I said.

'Cow.' Him.

'Beef burger.' Me.

'Pig.' Him.

'Sausages.' Me.

The doc paused for a moment, taking a different tack. 'Comforting.' Him.

'Chocolate.' Me.

'Complicated.' Him.

'Curly Wurly.' Me.

'Rich.' Him.

'Terry's chocolate orange.' Me.

'Sad.' Him.

'Hungry.' Me.

'Happy.' Him.

'Fed.' Me.

The doc put down his notepad. He looked at me over the top of his glasses 'Are you perhaps hungry, Alan?' His permanent smile hadn't left his expression all session. Perhaps it now looked a little strained.

'Well, now that you mention it, I am feeling peckish.'

147

'I suppose we can call a halt if you're finding it hard to focus. It is almost lunchtime. You can head off now then, Alan.' He sounded unimpressed.

I couldn't understand why he was upset. It wasn't my fault; he was the one who started talking about food.

* * * *

After my summons to the headmaster's office, Doctor Jeffries drove Kevin and me home. My memories are vague; I was incapable of processing the bombshell. I still felt the sensory overload as an inescapable avalanche; the suffocating cold and brightness was unrelenting. Doctor Jeffries assisted me in the headmaster's office, picking me up from the floor and sitting me on a seat. I was offered water but couldn't drink. The doctor took me by the arm and led me to his car where he put me in the front passenger seat. Kevin fell in behind, sitting in the rear of the car, appearing unaffected. I didn't recall the drive home. It seemed that, no sooner had I sat in the doctor's car, I was being encouraged to exit. Kevin beat me into the house and retired directly to his room. Gelert, sensing something amiss, was restrained. I was incapable of demonstrating any affection towards him.

As I walked into the kitchen, Doctor Jeffries behind me, I saw Ruth at the table, divesting a wine glass of its contents. We were silent as we looked at each other. Ruth seemed to make an effort to focus on me. 'You've heard the news then?' she said. I said nothing; I simply studied her. She was the picture of a newly widowed woman. Too shocked to yet grieve. Stoically fighting the desire to capitulate to her insufferable reality. And yet, she proffered a sight that I'd witnessed so many times before. The eyes were a little more red and glazed than usual, but the air of weariness was so very familiar. She had been rehearsing for this moment ever since she arrived.

The doctor took me by the elbow. 'Come along, Alan. Let's get you settled.' He had composed himself and had control of his expression. Even so, he looked ambivalent as he regarded Ruth. 'Let's get you to your room. You need rest,' he said and we withdrew. 'I'm going to prescribe something to help you rest. You're going to need to take this for a week or two before things … well, before they settle.' He opened the bottle and handed me two small, beige tablets. Undetected, the doctor had acquired a glass of water. My body was there but my mind was elsewhere. I put the tablets in my mouth and swallowed them with the water. I lay back on my bed.

'That's right, try and get some rest. And don't worry about the … arrangements. I'll discuss everything with Ruth. Your father had certain measures in place so I know what he wanted.'

He made to leave but at the doorway he turned. 'I'll pop in later to see how you're getting on. And Alan, your father … was a good man, don't ever doubt that.' Emotion constricted his throat. The last thing he'd said confused me. I tried to fathom his meaning. But those thoughts were absorbed by the sense of devastation. The turmoil in my head didn't diminish but the drugs made it less distinct; things became vaguer. I was grateful for the numbing sensation and I fell into an uneasy sleep.

When I awoke, confused and groggy, it was difficult to hold on to any thought. I felt as if I were waking from a bad dream until I saw the bottle of tablets. The sight brought me crashing back to reality; to the unbearable knowledge of Dad's death. I sat motionless on my bed, intending to never leave. I was unable and unwilling to reconcile my loss. As the sensation of grogginess abated, I detected another emotion combine with the shock. I was angry. Angry at fate for dumping this on me. Angry at Ruth for her disingenuous displays and for being a shit wife. But most of all, angry with Dad. How could he have done this to me? The details of his death were irrelevant, only the fact of his passing. As far as I was concerned, Dad must have made a conscious decision to stop living, which was tantamount to making a decision to start dying. As it transpired, I didn't need to seek out the details of his death, they sought me out.

My father's death was noteworthy to the extent that it made the local newspaper. I was searching the paper for the announcement placed by Doctor Jeffries under "obituaries" when instead I found the glaring headline, "Local Man Found Dead in Town Library". The article served to fill in the gaps from Doctor Jeffries' simple explanation that Dad had suffered a heart attack in town. The article provided a most dramatic account, but the basic facts were indisputable. Dad had been discovered slumped over a desk at the local library. The reporter had interviewed the librarian who confirmed that Dad was a regular patron. He attended most week days and kept to himself. On the day of his death the librarian had noted that Dad sat at his usual, secluded desk. He had no reading material of any description with him. Even later in the day, when she'd noticed that Dad was resting his head on the table she didn't think anything untoward. She said he would often sit with his eyes closed for long periods, perhaps resting or lost in thought. After a few hours the librarian had begun to worry. She'd approached my father with the intention of waking him. She discovered he was cold, grey and unresponsive. He was quite dead. The paramedics that arrived not long after they'd been contacted by the shaken librarian confirmed he'd been dead for hours.

The official cause of death was heart failure, but I knew that wasn't what had killed him. Heart failure was merely a symptom of his true killer. I'd witnessed over time how he'd succumbed to an increasing lassitude. It was obvious he'd been worn down, although I had not appreciated how terminal his situation had been. Reading the article didn't help me understand his death, it served to fuel my anger. I wasn't concerned with how other people reacted to the nature of his death. My lifelong association with animosity and rejection had taught me painful lessons to disregard the opinion of others. I was angry because he hadn't cared how *I* might react. He appeared to have collapsed under the weight of his life; a victim of his own entropy. He'd made a decision to not fight. He'd been killed by his own capitulation.

On the morning of his funeral, I experienced an epiphany. Dad's soul, his life-essence, had been dead for many months. His demise had started some time after the overheard argument with Doctor Jeffries, ages ago. It had been drawn out but he'd expired spiritually some time ago, nonetheless.

I understood how Dad had chosen to respond. His essence departed, he had sat in the library, day after day, waiting for his body to catch up to his spirit until the inevitable had come to pass and he had suffered physical death.

* * * *

Doctor Jeffries was true to his word and organised the service and cremation in accordance with my father's wishes. The group of mourners was almost identical to the small group that had attended the wedding ceremony, less than two years ago. Mrs Montgomery, accompanied by her husband, mingled respectfully with Tony and Janice who'd travelled from Manchester to attend. I wondered if I should consider Dad as being present. Technically, his body was with us. Then again, had he even been present at his wedding? Certainly more than now. One addition was Kevin. He sat alone, brooding on whatever occupied his thoughts those days. Since Dad's death he affected a cockiness that he flaunted at home for the benefit of me and Ruth. When in mixed company he made an effort to disguise this newfound arrogance. On the day of Dad's funeral, he was without doubt behaving, while he assumed the role of the sulking, teenaged stepson.

My thoughts were becoming less muddled. While the sedatives Doctor Jeffries had prescribed took the edge off reality, they at least afforded me some relief. As I studied the gathering I recognised something familiar. The women were somberly dressed, as the occasion demanded, with the exception of Louise, who wore a brightly coloured dress. Without exception, the men were dressed in the same suits they had worn to the wedding. I supposed the intervening period between wedding and funeral was not enough to warrant a change. There hadn't been enough time for the men to materially alter their size, or for men's fashion to change. Mr Montgomery still looked stylish in his designer suit and glasses. The most obvious change occupied the coffin at the front of the room.

The short, non-denominational service was held in the crematorium, the facility designed for such ceremony. Our local councillor joined us for the short period between service and cremation. I assumed he attended out of a sense of civic duty, as Dad had expired on council property. His civic duty extended to almost twenty minutes. After offering condolences to each individual mourner, he spent a few moments talking with Doctor Jeffries. While I waited for the system to be primed in order to accept and process my father's remains, I looked to where Ruth sat, between Louise and Janice. Ruth put in a stellar performance as the textbook grieving widow, facing the future in a husbandless world with bravery.

It seemed the most considerate thing that Dad ever did for their relationship was to expire. Perhaps Ruth relied upon the "Don't know what you've got until it's gone" approach. If so, she was unconvincing, attracting little sympathy.

The funeral director gave a small cough to gain our attention. He spoke in solemn tones. 'Ladies and gentlemen, we have come to that time in the proceedings where the remains of Mr Lavelle will be withdrawn for cremation. With respect, I request that everyone remain silent for a few minutes. You may wish to take this time to offer up thoughts and prayers on behalf of the departed. Thank you.' In saying this, he subtly began the process through some mechanism hidden from sight. The red velvet curtains positioned behind the coffin slowly opened. The curtains came to rest and I watched as the coffin containing my father's body withdrew. As the coffin disappeared behind the curtains I thought, *Fifty-three years of life. Two years of death. Fifty minutes to reduce it all to ash.* It was then that the finality struck me. It was as if my anger retreated with the coffin on its final journey to the flames. The sight of Dad's receding remains was the catalyst I'd needed to finally understand that Dad had gone. I would never see him again. I would never hear him again.

I remained seated even after the director announced that the meditative period had elapsed. Doctor Jeffries approached me and I stood to receive him. I studied him closely. He looked uncomfortable and tired. 'Well, Alan. That was a simple affair, as your father wished. I'll collect your father … his ashes later and bring them to you.'

'Thank you, Doctor Jeffries. For everything.' I looked over towards Ruth who stood beside Kevin, her performance unappreciated by the other mourners. 'Thank you on behalf of the … household. We couldn't have managed without your help,' I said, aiming for some semblance of decorum.

'Of course. Anything to help. Your father had measures in place, just in case. There is a substantial trust fund in your name. He always wanted to ensure you would be looked after … no matter what the circumstances.'

'Thank you. That is a comfort,' I lied.

'He was a very dear friend to me, Alan. You can always rely on my support, no matter what. Please, do contact me if you have any difficulties at all. Your father would want that.' I nodded in appreciation, disinclined to speak. The doctor paused and looked uncertain. 'No matter what you may hear, or … No matter what, Alan … Remember; your father always had your best interests at heart. You were always his priority.' There it was again, assuring me of Dad's good intentions. Why did he feel the need to say that? I was confused and my thoughts returned to the argument between Dad and the doctor. My confusion turned to shock when the doctor hugged me. It wasn't a perfunctory embrace, but one of substance that persisted for what seemed an over long duration. When he released me I saw him look over my shoulder. Contempt passed over his expression. Shocked, I turned to see where he looked. There was no doubt; the doctor looked straight at Ruth where she sat next to Louise, their heads close together in deep discussion. Ruth appeared to have cast off her pretence of grief. Both she and Louise wore expressions of intense seriousness. Ruth clearly saw the doctor's unmistakeable expression but she looked away as if unaffected; unimpressed.

As the doctor made his way to organise the retrieval of Dad's ashes, I wondered again why he'd felt it necessary to reassure me that Dad cared about me. Had Dad raised doubts about my affections? Had Dad thought I didn't care about him; that I didn't love him? My anger had been a dense inescapable weight, but my remorse was denser still. As I entertained these thoughts, the guilt overwhelmed any anger I might have retained. Didn't Dad know how much he meant to me? He was everything; my whole world. He must have known it; he did know it!

Didn't he?

* * * *

The gang acquired a new member under unusual circumstances. This was despite having made an executive decision that any potential member must undergo an exhaustive vetting process and would be subject to a non-negotiable probationary period. This decision was reached after Nobby became attached to the gang. It was very much a case of "closing the stable door after the horse has bolted" but we all violently agreed that one Nobby in the group was two too many. Nobby's approval of the new regime was unnecessary.

The exception to what was intended to be a carved-in-stone rule was a tall, solid-looking individual who hailed from Dublin's fair city. He was christened Patrick Murphy but acquired the alias *Spud* and it was to this name alone that he would respond. In addition to arriving pre-nicknamed, he was also somewhat of a known entity. Some years ago Spud and Face had been roommates at university. As we later discovered, Face had forewarning of Spud's arrival through unusual channels. As an established patron of the facility, Face convinced management that it would serve everyone's best interests for him and Spud to share a room. His timing was impeccable. Face's previous roommate had just departed the facility, his re-alignment completed for now. Perhaps not fixed but without doubt sedated.

Face greeted his old friend and escorted him to their room. As Spud dropped his belongings on his bed, nearest the door as befitted his status, he turned to Face. 'You know what, Mike? This reminds me of our time at university. Without the drugs anyway.'

'Well, Spud, perhaps I can do something about that. Let me introduce you to the rest of the gang.'

Face introduced Spud to the gang in the rec room on his first evening and we took to him straightaway. It was clear that Face had spoken to Spud about the gang. The first comment Spud made was, 'That's Nobby? I thought you said he was built like a brick shithouse?'

'No. I said he *smells* like a brick shithouse.'

'You're not fucking wrong!' Spud said. Yes, we would get along fine. Nobby said nothing. He simply stared at Spud with an expression that said, 'Great; another one!' Spud proved to be interesting. He was the only one among us that had been committed for psychiatric assessment. Face had been alerted to Spud's imminent arrival through a newspaper article covering the incident that had led to Spud's committal. 'Hey, Spud, tell the guys why you're here. I read the newspaper article and when I saw the name and what happened, I knew it was you,' Face said with a note of admiration. This was new territory for the group; the motives behind our incarceration remaining unexplored for good reason.

'You want to hear about *that*?' Spud said. A couple of the guys confirmed they did but I remained silent. I was going for *indifferent*; I wanted to project an air of cool. But I too was curious. There was plenty of time for him to discover the real me. 'Okay, if you want to know. But be warned; it's not for the squeamish and you'll need the extra large popcorn to make it all the way to the end.'

He related his tale.

'One day I'm driving along, when this arsehole cut me up. I leant on the horn to let him know I was there. You know how it is; that's what the horn is for, isn't it? Anyway, Mr Sensitive got offside 'cos I'd questioned his driving skills, so he slammed the anchors on. That's when I had to test the brakes! Tyres squealing and smoke everywhere. Anyway, the fuckwit got right out of his pram. He was straight out of his car, calling me out. He left me no option. So I got out of my car and at first the geezer seemed a bit spooked.'

I could imagine the other guy, red mist descending, jumping out of his car, ready to shape up and then being greeted by the sight of an imposing Spud emerging from his vehicle. That would take the wind out of his sails. He'd have been spooked all right.

Spud continued. 'So then Einstein pulled out this knife and said "You want a piece of me?" I thought he'd said "Do you want a piece of *meat*?" like he's some sort of fucked-up mobile butcher. So I said "Got any pork chops?" Then he got confused and he flipped me the bird. Well, no bastard gives *me* the finger! Use *two* fingers. It's not fucking America! He stood there, one finger in one hand and a knife in the other. So I walked over to him, took the knife off him and knocked him to the ground. Then I decided I shouldn't be rude. Well, he had given me the finger and it would've been impolite to refuse … I cut his finger off,' Spud said, matter of fact. This was greeted with stunned silence. I thought, *High four, anyone?* but the time wasn't right to share.

'Anyhow,' Spud went on, 'I grabbed the finger and said "Cheers pal!" I got in my car and drove off. Long story short, some bastard saw me deprive your man of a digit. Bastard also took down my rego and grassed me up which I found out about later when the coppers came calling.'

'Seriously?' Voice shouted.

'As a heart attack!' Face said. 'I read all about it in the paper. I knew it was you, Spud. You always get shitty when someone gives you the finger. So what happened with plod?'

'I'm being done for GBH. But the Beak wants to see a psychological report before he gives a ruling.'

'I don't suppose you could get convicted of theft. He did *give* you the finger, after all. What did you do with it?' Brains said.

'The finger? Well, when the coppers turned up I was in the kitchen. My flatmate answered the door and the finger was still in my pocket so I didn't have much time to hide it. Where I did put it was really funny, though.' Spud paused for effect. 'I stuck it in a box of fish fingers.'

'*Boludeces*, you're kidding!'

'I am not. I heard from my flatmate yesterday. He said he got stoned a couple of weeks ago and got hungry. He's a lazy bastard and hates going shopping so there probably wasn't much food in the house. He must have had a serious case of the munchies 'cos he's not partial to fish fingers. Anyway, if he hated them before, he *fucking* hates them now because he emptied the packet out under the grill and cooked them up. So there he is, stoned out of his head, chomping away at these fish fingers when all of a sudden he gets to a tough one.

He told me he knew something was up straightaway because it tasted of fish!'

'So what did he do?'

'That's why he contacted me. He sent a letter of complaint to Birds Eye. He even enclosed the finger. And get this; yesterday he gets a letter back from them. They've sent him a ten-pound voucher by way of compensation. Plus, he said it came with a standard letter of apology. Must happen regularly.'

'Perhaps the chance loss of a digit during the working day is something the workers accept as the price of being part of the Birds Eye family?' Brains said.

I suspected the veracity of the tale and even later, when more familiar with Spud, I still had doubts. What was certain, though, was that he was special; he had been committed.

'So what's this Doctor Fenty like? He's supposed to do my psych evaluation.'

'Doc Friendly? He's okay. You'll know him when you see him. He has more than a little of *Biggles* about him,' Face said.

'Oh, great!' Spud said.

The gang must have taken to him because just then Bomber honoured him with, 'Bombs away!' followed by a resounding *PPPAAARRRRPPP*!

'What the fuck was that?' a startled Spud said. Then the smell hit him. 'Jesus Christ! And what the fuck is that? It smells like a skunk has crawled up another skunk's arse and died and then that skunk has crawled up *your* arse and died!'

Yes, Spud would be fine.

Chapter Twelve

The atmosphere in the household deteriorated further following Dad's funeral. It was still bound together by silence but it became clear that Dad's presence had been more influential than I'd appreciated; the effect not apparent until he'd gone. Kevin, in particular, viewed the change as an opportunity to cast off any pretence of self-restraint. His covert activities with the Bad Lads became overt. The stories I heard at school, once committed by anonymous miscreants, were now attributed to Kevin. He didn't care that he was named as the perpetrator. Indeed, if anything, he seemed proud of the fact. Kevin spent increasingly more time with the Bad Lads. Every afternoon without fail, he would head off with the twins and the rest of his cohorts. When even that exposure proved insufficient, he began skipping lessons. It got to the stage where Kevin spent more time in the office of the Head of Year than the HoY himself. I have no doubt Kevin was afforded extreme leniency; his stepfather had recently passed away, after all.

I, however, did not benefit from any special treatment, nor did I wish to. I had four weeks off school while I attempted to recover. Kevin enjoyed a similar sabbatical, during which time he maintained an active membership of the Bad Lads outside of school hours. When I eventually returned to school, people ignored me, as always; perhaps now with a trace of morbid curiosity, more so after the article in the newspaper was published. I didn't care, I wanted to be left alone. I didn't want to discuss it or think about it. Doctor Jeffries called at the house during my time off school, checking on my welfare. I swapped the pair of beige tablets for a single, larger white tablet, and I still benefited from the effects of the medication.

Ruth persevered in her pursuit of ridding the world of white wine. Following Dad's death the empty bottle count steadily climbed. She got through at least three bottles a day according to my early morning inventories. Ruth's behaviour was at least consistent. She sat either in the kitchen or outside at the garden table, glass in hand and magazine opened before her. It was here that I would find her when I returned from school or after lunch on weekends, once she'd bothered to get out of bed. Ruth favoured only a few magazines. This led me to question the seriousness of her study of the lives of the rich and famous, or to the low-fat recipes that populated the pages. Perhaps she used the magazine as a preventative to succumbing to what had incapacitated Dad. He'd had no reading material when he expired. Her alcoholic existence was more likely intended to preserve her life-force rather than extinguish it.

Once more Mrs Montgomery was engaged to provide us with the benefit of her domestic services. Doctor Jeffries had persuaded Mrs M to attend the household every Saturday morning. All details of the conditions of service, including financial matters, were handled by the doctor. He told me he'd consulted Ruth, but I suspected the consultation was rather a direction by the doctor. Not so much "What do you want?" and more "This is what you'll get". Mrs M had never taken to Ruth. It wasn't that Mrs M openly displayed any animosity towards Ruth; that impropriety was unthinkable. But she would only interact with her when unavoidable. With the arrangements put in place after Dad died, their interaction was minimal. I didn't think it coincidental that Mrs M attended on Saturday morning, when I was at home and Ruth still in bed.

Arriving home from the funeral, I was weighed down by the guilt that had assailed me as Dad's remains were removed for cremation. The burden was such that, at first, I didn't notice what had happened to his ashes. After wishing Doctor Jeffries goodbye, I'd retreated to my room with the start of a tension headache. It was not until the following day, when I descended for breakfast, that I noticed the urn in which Dad's ashes rested. The urn was placed on the large, wooden dresser that dominated one side of the kitchen. The smooth, brass urn looked incongruous among the old-style crockery, purchased to compliment the olde-worlde cabinet. Seeing where the urn was positioned did nothing to assuage my guilt. I knew it wasn't him, the ashes merely a remnant, a symbol, but they were a symbol of Dad, nevertheless. I didn't want his remains to bear witness to Ruth's continuing licentiousness. I determined to find a more fitting resting place. But not yet; I was tired and heavy. Nowhere obvious suggested itself.

Six weeks later, I knew where his ashes should rest.

* * * *

We were learning about National Parks in geography when I realised where Dad's ashes should be relocated. The teacher could see that I was distracted. 'Are you okay, Alan?' she said, with kindness.

I thought for a second and said, 'Yes, I'm fine, thank you,' and I was, for the first time in forever.

I was reminded of the time Dad took me to Snowdon. I was seven years old, the name calling at school had begun in earnest and I'd discovered Gary was no friend of mine. I arrived home one afternoon, reflecting on the unpleasantness I had endured at school. As usual, Dad met me on arrival. He didn't ask how my day had been which was not usual. 'Hey, Alan. Would you like to go somewhere interesting this weekend?'

'Sure, that would be great, Dad. Will Doctor Jeffries be coming too?'

'No, not this time, Sport. He'll be looking after Gelert for us. It'll only be the two of us. That's okay, isn't it? Surely you don't mind spending some time with your old dad?' he said, adopting his "innocent and sad" face.

'Course not … and don't call me *Shirley*.' I laughed at the line from one of our favourite movies. And so, early on Saturday morning we set off on our quest. Dad encouraged me to attempt map reading.

He knew the route we would take, but he wanted me to feel more involved in the adventure. He often reminded me of the importance of cartography to the successful pirate; you can't find treasure if you can't decipher the treasure map. As we travelled closer to our destination, I found areas of the map where Dad had added personalised notes. Many areas of land were barren and boring, so Dad had noted, "Here be dragons", variously along the route. I knew we were getting close to our final destination when I saw his last note. In Lake *Llyn Llydaw,* which lay within sight of Snowdon, he noted, "Here be serpents". Alongside his note, he'd drawn the happiest-looking serpent that ever swam. A less monstrous cousin of Nessie. We arrived after a drive of ninety minutes. The car park was situated at the bottom of a popular path that led to the summit of Snowdon. There were a few other cars dotted around the car park but it wasn't anywhere close to capacity.

'Looks quiet. We should have some of the mountain to ourselves,' Dad said. 'It might be because of the weather forecast; it's supposed to rain.'

'What will happen if it rains?'

'Well, I suppose we'll get wet.'

Dad collected his rucksack containing our provisions, locked the car and we set off up the mountain.

I thought we would never reach the top; everything looked so big. The path was delineated and well worn. I discovered later that it's possible to take a bus, or even a train to the summit, weather permitting. Even so, in my mind we were scaling K2 in mid-winter. I was Sherpa Tenzing to Dad's Edmund Hillary. Although when the café at the top of the mountain serves tea and scones rather than dispensing oxygen or frostbite remedies, there should be no illusion of mountaineering greatness. It was a hard walk, nevertheless, and Dad had insisted I wear my proper walking boots – the comfy boots I wore when we took our walks at the weekend with Gelert and the doctor.

A slave to clumsiness, I stumbled often along the way. Dad was always there, assisting me with a steady hand. He was as solid and dependable as the rock that we were scaling. We stopped now and again for refreshment, Dad allowing me some rest and telling me about the wildlife with whom he was personally acquainted. We steadily climbed and while I felt the effort of climbing, I wasn't overtaxed. As we neared the summit we saw dark, heavy rain clouds closing in, as forecast. We were quite by ourselves. Dad had taken us off the beaten track. He wanted the last part of our climb to be ours alone to enjoy. When I saw the rain clouds approaching, I thought we would have to find cover but Dad had other ideas. 'Hey, let's do something cool.' I nodded assent. He picked me up and put me on his shoulders.

'What are we doing, Dad?'

He looked up at me, head tilted to the side, his expression composed around a huge grin. 'When the rain gets here, you will be the first person in the whole world that it will touch.' I sat on his shoulders, full of wonder as I watched the clouds getting nearer. I waited to become the rain's first patron.

'How's the weather up there, Alan? Let me know when the rain starts.' I waited attentively, not wanting to miss the first drops. When the rain arrived, it was sudden and heavy.

I turned my face to the downpour, mouth wide open, 'It's raining, Dad!' I exclaimed and spread my arms wide.

'Is it? I can't feel anything. Are you sure?' Dad put a hand out, palm up, waiting for a sign. After a while he said, 'Wait a moment. Oh yeah, now I can feel it. Hey, why didn't you tell me it's cold? And wet! You thirsty, are you? I'm going to have a drink too.'

We remained like that, mouths and arms open wide, until the shower was spent. The rain was as quick to stop as it had been to start and we were both soaking wet by the time it passed. As I had climbed Snowdon alongside Dad, the climb seemed to never end. I'd felt clumsy and small. But now Dad made me feel big. I was Atlas, shouldering the sky. He lowered me to the ground and took my hand so I wouldn't slip on the saturated, rocky surface. We walked with care to a secluded spot where we could sit and eat. It was getting late; we had taken a while to reach our goal.

We sat alone at the top of the world, watching the light filtering red through a thin layer of cloud as the huge sun took its time to drift towards the horizon. The shower had passed, unable to prevent the sun from setting the sky on fire. We looked out over that wide, green world, taking in the majestic countryside as we ate. The air was so clear that it possessed a surreal quality. For a moment I believed the landscape was a picture, so close that I could reach out and touch it. The walk hadn't been overtaxing. We had been able to exchange idle chat on the way up. But now we sat in silence, as I leant over and rested my head on Dad. He put his arm around my shoulder, and we watched the sun go down together. There was no-one else in the world; it was our private sunset. No-one had ever seen a sunset the way that we were seeing it, nor would they. I felt as close to Dad at that moment as I ever would.

I would find that place and I would scatter Dad's ashes there. I knew I could never recapture that moment, but I could at least commemorate it.

* * * *

The Saturday after resolving to re-settle Dad's ashes, I arose early. I took the urn from the kitchen dresser, wrapped it with care in a towel and placed it in my backpack. The resulting gap on the dresser was as conspicuous as the copper urn had been. I left a note for Mrs M so she would know I had gone out for the day. I grabbed some food and a bottle of water and put them in the backpack, extending the straps to their full extent to accommodate my physique. Before I left I had one more thing to do. I grabbed the car keys and retrieved the map book in order to plot my course to the mountain. I returned the keys and left the house, closing the back door in silence so not to disturb Kevin or Ruth. I had checked the bike's tyres and chain the previous evening and was ready to leave. I studied the first map to start me on my journey. I'd decided to approach the route in stages, to avoid becoming overwhelmed by excessive directions, adopting a one-step-at-a-time approach.

My chosen method proved effective and I was up to the task of negotiating all the "dragons" and "serpents" en route. Even so, with occasional breaks for rest, it took six hours to reach my destination. It was early afternoon when I arrived and my legs confirmed the effort to which they had been subjected. I found a secure spot for my bike, locked it and, after resting, started up the delineated track that Dad and I had taken ten years ago. I determined to pace myself, attempting to conserve energy. Although I spent many weekends riding, the latter part of the ride had been all uphill. At least this time I had better control of my clumsiness and my stride was lengthier. As I ascended the mountain I looked for any familiar landmarks or features that could help me retrace our previous route. I recognised nothing, the mountain was still huge and the increased number of people climbing did nothing to reduce the scale. I resolved to continue my climb until I either located the place for which I was searching or I found an alternative appropriate site.

I had been climbing steadily for two hours with no familiar sights. Had I been naïve to think I could retrace our previous expedition after all these years? I didn't lose hope, however; I remained confident that I would find a fitting location. As I watched the other climbers, I decided to take the path less travelled. Instead of being deterred by warning signs that dotted the mountainside, I used them as a guide to a route not yet taken. I kept going until I left the warning signs well behind; until I was comfortable I'd chosen a path that had not been, and would not be, undertaken by others. As I climbed higher, skirting an escarpment that defined one edge of the mountain, I saw the shadow of Snowdon. The dark ghost of the mountain was cast far into the distance across fields and hills and rivers and lakes and roads and towns. Across everything. I thought how Dad had and always would influence me, even in death. I wanted to make him proud.

By now I was convinced that I was on a different part of Snowdon to that where Dad and I watched our sunset. This section of the mountain appeared to be as elevated as any other and I decided to look for somewhere secluded where Dad's ashes could rest. As I climbed higher something stirred in my peripheral vision, high up in the direction in which I travelled. I navigated with caution towards the place where I'd seen movement, advancing towards a massive column of rock, standing overt and high above the surrounding area. I could perceive a shelf in the column, hidden in afternoon shade. When I arrived at the bottom of the rock-face, I saw the shelf, some fifty feet above where I stood. The rock-face was almost sheer, the surface appeared rough and I had to assess if there was sufficient purchase by which I might scale it. The area of the mountain upon which the column sat would soon be in shadow and so I determined to trust in my climbing abilities. Evidence of the questionable integrity of the rock-face lay strewn at my feet, the scree loose underfoot. I stood back to plot an overall route to the shelf and, stepping up to the rock-face, commenced my ascent. Only once did the face crumble beneath my grip and I hung by a single hand until I regained purchase to continue the climb. Otherwise, the rock proved unyielding. I took comfort in the knowledge that only someone with my unique strengths was capable of reaching the shelf.

By the time I attained the ledge my hands, arms and back ached. I rolled away from the edge, relieved and tired. It was almost dark and I absently wished I had remembered to bring the fridge; that was where I had left the torch. There was insufficient light to appraise the suitability of the shelf for my purposes. I wouldn't chance a descent in the dark, having just reached my goal, and so I resolved to spend the night upon my temporary refuge. The shelf proved to be about eight feet deep at its widest point and so I lay against the rock-face with my backpack between me and the fifty foot drop. I lay in the dark, feeling the urn in the backpack resting against me and I experienced a sense of accomplishment. It had been an arduous journey, which had taken all the light the day provided. I rode for six hours and walked and climbed for three hours. For the first time in forever, I felt I had *done something;* that I had earned my rest. It didn't take long to fall asleep, beneath a clear night sky, full of glimmering stars. I wondered dreamily if I had discovered a fitting place to expire when that day came. I smiled at my "pathmaticism" and slept.

I awoke at daybreak, the light of the rising sun illuminating my face. I rubbed the sleep from my eyes and it took a moment to recall where I was. As I sat up, squinting against the light of the new day,

I realised I had company. I froze as I detected the silhouette of a large bird of prey against the rising sun as it too awoke to the day. The bird sat a few short feet away from my boots. It took a moment for my eyes to adjust to the glare. The bird casually studied me, altogether unconcerned. It made no attempt to fly away; to escape me. As the breaking sun rose behind the bird, it spread its wings and they took on the appearance of fire. The massive wings were at once everything. Impossibly wide, impossibly bright; giant wings of flame. The bird froze for long moments, wings fully extended and then took off, unencumbered by gravity, lighter than the wind. As I continued staring, my eyes watered against the glare of the sun. I watched the bird ascend, getting higher and smaller as it flew beyond where I could follow.

And then I wept. The tears flooded my eyes and streamed down my face. It was only then that I was able to mourn for my father. I wrapped my arms around myself, the harsh sobs wracking my body as I knelt on the ledge. I wasn't holding anything in; I was squeezing everything out. I leant forward, unbreathing, until my head rested on the rough surface.

I thought about my father, not the man of recent times whose body had expired but the man I truly knew as *Dad*. As the sun climbed higher, light returned to the world. I rose up tired, but I sensed this was a tiredness that could be endured and remedied. Not the inescapable fatigue that had plagued me since Dad's death. I sat on the ledge looking out across the world and it wasn't long before an energy suffused me.

I left the urn nestled securely in a natural nook, set back on the ledge, embraced by Snowdon. I knew I had discovered a most fitting last resting place for Dad's remains. I thought that Dad was freer than he had been in years. It was an act of contrition for my doubt and my anger. I felt better. Not better *fixed*, but better *improved*. It was a start. I chose to remember Dad for all his strengths; not for his few weaknesses. I knew Dad was defined by who he was; not who he became. And then, as I prepared to descend, I was certain. He had known; he *knew*, what he meant to me.

I took one last look at the urn before lowering myself with care over the edge. The descent was easier than the ascent; the morning light exposed abundant handholds to assist the return. I reached the ground without incident and took a quick look around to confirm I was still alone and isolated. I left the foot of the rock-face and wondered if Dad knew the genus of the bird. Maybe he even knew its name. As I hiked back to where I'd secured my bike, I knew Dad had all the time he'd need to acquaint himself intimately with his avian neighbour.

I hoped the bird approved. I knew Dad would.

* * * *

Spud settled in with ease despite his claims that as an Irishman he was obliged to reserve an inherent disrespect for all things English. I suspected this claim was purely symbolic. His taste in music did not stray far from that favoured by the majority of the gang, much of which was of an English disposition. Indeed, he proved to be a most enthusiastic fellow worshipper of our most exalted icon, Felicity's extremely English bottom. Fortunately for Spud, he would not allow hundreds of years of English subjugation to stand in his way of appreciating that which merited appreciation. One evening when we had gravitated to the rec room, preparatory to a session of video dissection, Voice loudly asked the question that had been troubling nobody but himself. 'Hey, Spud, how did you end up with your nickname?'

'It's a law or something,' Spud said. 'You see, the Normans invaded Ireland in the late twelfth century. Strangely enough, we took exception and so the Irish and the Normans ended up kicking the shit out of each other. After a while the Normans tried to reduce the massive losses being suffered by drawing up a treaty. Anyway, it didn't last long and most of the terms were doomed to failure. With the exception of one, solitary condition.' He paused for effect.

'What was that?' Voice conveniently shouted.

'The one term that has endured for over eight hundred years of Irish struggle and hardship is this: "Any and all that are named Patrick

Murphy shall henceforth, and into perpetuity, be known as *Spud*, for this name shall be easier to recall when mead hath taken hold. Let it be known that any that shall forsake this law shall have their genitalia exposed to mockery by the village idiot. Amen",' a sombre Spud said.

'So, were you called Spud at school then?'

'I was called "Spud Two".'

'So there were two of you called Patrick Murphy in your class then?'

'No. There were three of us.'

I again suspected the veracity of his tale but it sounded somewhat plausible. *Near enough,* I thought. I was a little distracted anyway; it was my turn to select the movie. This was not a responsibility to be taken lightly. The movie itself was not alone in being subjected to scorn and criticism but so was the movie-chooser. Even Brains was not immune; he was still living down his selection of *Midnight Cowboy*. Three months later and his assertion that "It won the Oscar for best film!" served as fuel for the dissent rather than as suppressant. I had already mentally selected the movie; it was one I'd supplied myself. Even so, I went through the motions of carefully studying the available offerings before picking my movie out and shrugging my shoulders as if to say, "Oh well, this will have to do". I was confident my selection would meet with approval. Eventually. Nevertheless, I prepared myself for the obligatory complaints that were voiced as part of the process. It's kind of what we did.

'Okay, guys. Tonight we will be viewing the Sergio Leone classic *For a Few Dollars More,*' I said.

'Sergio who?' Face said. *Bloody Philistine!*

'That's "Mr Leone" to you, Face. It stars Clint Eastwood and Lee Van Cleef.'

'Oh Christ, not another bloody cowboy film!' Legs whined, the shades of *Midnight Cowboy* tainting my choice.

'No, it's not another "bloody cowboy film". It's a Western.'

'What's the bloody difference?'

'Why don't you shut your bloody yap, watch the bloody film and find out for your bloody self?'

'Yeah, okay. Only asking.'

Having dispensed with the initial whingeing, we settled in to watch. The viewing was sporadically interrupted by our inane observations, which is also kind of what we did. On occasion, an issue was broached that merited further discussion. Bomber raised an interesting point when the two main characters were revealed as bounty hunters. 'So they're bounty hunters, are they?' There being no takers, he continued. 'How hard is that job? I mean, everyone knows you can find them right next to the Kit Kats!' Not content to merely irritate me, he also had to make me hungry.

As it eventuated, my selection was well received, even earning a 'That was pretty good. Liked the ending,' from Legs. Praise indeed; a possible convert to the Western, if not the cowboy movie. In my estimation one of, if not the most important criterion for a movie to be considered "good" is that it *must* have a sound ending. The beginning can be brilliant, followed by an even better middle but if the ending is unsound then under no circumstances can the movie be considered "good". *FAFDM* concludes in excellent fashion. The goodies best the baddies, as is always the case, but motivations and tensions build all the way to the fulfilling conclusion.

While it is my favourite Western, there is one aspect that I find less than gratifying. One of the characters in the film is a hunchback and I acknowledge that my own peculiar physique may influence my sympathies. He is a baddy, of course, but to really hammer home the notion that the character is an outsider, he is also a clean-shaven, blond-haired German. He could not look more out of place among the dark-complexioned, sombrero-wearing, bearded Mexican banditos if he wore a tutu and rode in on a unicycle.

The hunchback ends up being the first baddy dispatched by the goodies. He has a run-in with Colonel Mortimer, one of the bounty hunters, in a saloon when the colonel humiliates him. The hunchback is restrained by one of his swarthy companions as they are casing the joint and mustn't blow their cover. Later on, however, after the heist has been successfully concluded, they meet again in yet another saloon. This time there is no reason to curtail hostilities and so the colonel and the hunchback square off in typical shootout fashion. As they face each other across the grubby tavern I was hoping the hunchback would prevail, or at least wing the colonel. But, unsurprisingly, it was not to be. The hunchback ends up dead, on the filthy floor of the cheap Mexican saloon. To further the insult, his fellow banditos end up welcoming Colonel Mortimer into the gang over the lifeless, perforated body of the hunchback.

The fact that the colonel had to cheat to get the drop on the hunchback by resorting to the use of a small pistol hidden in his coat sleeve provided no consolation to my sensibilities. He didn't give him a fighting chance. However, I derived some comfort, later in the film, when Colonel Mortimer gets a decent hiding from the gang when they discover his traitorous intentions. Despite that, by the end of the film the colonel still ends up riding off into the sunset, after taking long-awaited revenge on the head bandito who was responsible for the death of his sister. Even then, at that late stage, I still hoped the colonel might at least fall off his horse, but it was not meant to be.

My solitary thought as he rode off into the sunset was, *Cheating bastard!*

Chapter Thirteen

It was late Sunday afternoon by the time I returned home from relocating Dad's remains. The return journey wasn't as tasking as the outward trip. Gravity was most obliging at the outset, during the hike back down the mountain and when riding, until I found myself beyond the geophysical influence of Snowdon. I felt lighter too; not only by the weight of the urn entrusted to Snowdon but by the lifting of my guilt. My adventure had required my absence from the house for nearly two days, but by all appearances I had not been missed. I rode into the driveway, fatigued but retaining a sense of achievement. When I walked into the kitchen I met with the familiar sight of Ruth, sitting at the table, glass in hand. I looked at the conspicuous gap on the dresser where the urn once stood, and I felt content. Ruth had not noticed, nor had cared, about my absence and the same appeared to be the case concerning Dad's ashes.

I went upstairs to freshen up and get changed before returning to the kitchen. I felt hungrier than I had for ages and I was overjoyed to find Mrs M's unmolested casserole awaiting me in the refrigerator. I thought to engage with Ruth. 'Hi, Ruth. I'm going to heat up some casserole. Do you want some?' Ruth looked up from the magazine. She seemed to look through me but then focused on where the query originated. She shook her head before dropping her gaze back to the magazine. I retrieved a decent portion from the dish and placed it in the microwave. The sound of the oven heating the meal disturbed

Ruth and she left the kitchen to sit outside. I returned the remnants of the casserole to the refrigerator and sat alone at the kitchen table where I demolished the heated portion. That night I felt emotionally and physically restored and slept as soundly as I had for a long time.

Life continued in a manageable fashion for a time. I listened to the radio in the mornings as I prepared for the school day. Kevin rarely woke before I left and so I was free to select the listening experience. After hearing a number of tracks from one particular CD, I decided to purchase the disc. That weekend I opened my money box to withdraw the necessary funds. I emptied the contents on my bed and beheld all the shiny "pirate treasure" that Dad had collected for me over the years. It was nostalgia, not remorse that convinced me to return the booty to the money box. I counted the residual to find I had insufficient funds for the CD, but that was okay; it could wait. I was content to be reminded of the times of wonder, when pirates had roamed the seven seas and had shared the fruits of their exploits with Dad, who'd shared them with me.

* * * *

Three months after my mission to Snowdon, Gelert went missing. I returned home from school one Friday without receiving my usual welcome. This happened from time to time. He could be occupied seeing off intruding fauna from the property. Sometimes I'd find him doing some landscaping in the garden, burying whatever Jack Russells are inclined to bury. I called his name and waited for a responding bark, but all was silent. I wandered out to the back garden, expecting to find him with his head down a hole, inspecting his handiwork. He was nowhere to be seen, even when I did a full sweep of the gardens. The gate was closed when I'd arrived and so I expected to find him somewhere on the property. I went indoors, thinking perhaps he was trapped inside. I walked into the house, calling his name and waiting for his response. Only my call, echoing through the house, was audible.

The fact I asked Ruth if she knew where Gelert was reflected my level of concern. 'Hi, Ruth. Have you seen Gelert? He was here when I left for school and the gate was closed when I got home.'

Ruth looked up with a blank expression. 'What, the dog? No, I haven't seen him,' she said, uncaring.

'Is Kevin home?' I knew chances were he was with the Bad Lads.

'Don't know. Haven't seen him either.'

After checking the house and the gardens again, I decided to take a walk around the surrounding area in case Gelert had somehow escaped. I wandered the lanes, calling his name, becoming increasingly anxious as the light faded. On returning home I called to him again but received no response. 'Ruth, has Gelert come home yet?' I said as I entered the kitchen. She looked up from her magazine, took a sip of wine and shook her head. I went outside and walked to the roadside where I called his name at the top of my voice, hoping to find him returning from some adventure. The lone sound was the distant hum of traffic. I retired to my room to gather my thoughts, leaving the gate open, in case Gelert returned before morning.

As I tried to control the rising panic, I determined a course of action. I resolved to continue searching in the morning, as soon as it was light. I would ride around the area in search of the missing hound. While I was searching, I would post flyers, offering a reward for Gelert's return. I went downstairs to Dad's study where there was a computer and printer. There were a number of photographs of Gelert saved to the hard drive. I looked them over to find something representative. He was a blur in every single photograph, the camera shutter speed proving unequal to the task of capturing a distinct Gelert. I selected one of the lesser-blurred options, reassuring myself that he was just as blurred in real life as in the picture. I printed twenty copies, put them in my backpack and armed myself with enough tape to fix them to the available roadside fixtures in the neighbourhood. Rural areas afforded few promotional opportunities. I would have to rely upon trees and telegraph poles dotted around the area.

Satisfied I'd done everything possible until daybreak, I retired to my room. Gelert's disappearance was unprecedented, to such a degree that I questioned his ability to retrace whatever steps he'd taken to absent himself. When he took me for walks around the district, he was easily distracted. Sometimes he would walk past the house, appearing to be unaware of his surroundings. I was, however, convinced of his resilience; he was small but tough. I contemplated the longer-term issues. What if my initial campaign was unproductive? What were the available options in a case such as this? I figured I could place an ad under the "Lost" section of the local newspaper. That required money and so I grabbed my money box to empty it. As soon as I lifted the box, I knew something was wrong. When I tipped out the coins, there were only a few grubby coppers. All the shiny coins of higher denomination were missing. Bloody Kevin must have stolen my money. He had ample opportunity. Despite his spending little time at home, I often retired to my sanctuary, leaving my room unguarded.

I moved across the hall to his bedroom door and threw it open not knowing, or caring, if he was in residence. His room was unoccupied and disordered. So much so that by the time I'd finished searching his room, opening drawers and upending them on his bed, the already present clutter masked the signs of my rummaging. I walked downstairs and, barely containing my anger, I addressed Ruth. 'Do you know where Kevin is? When will he get home?'

She put down her glass and looked at me in disbelief. 'What did you say? Who the hell do you think you're talking to?'

'I want to know where he is!'

'I don't know where he is. Even if I did, I wouldn't tell you when you are being so rude. I'm not his keeper!'

'No, Ruth, that's exactly what you're supposed to be. You're supposed to be his keeper!' and I stormed out of the room.

I didn't sleep that night, my anger at the theft of the money receded as concern for Gelert's welfare took priority. Kevin didn't return that night. Chances were that he was up to no good with the Bad Lads.

It was a long night. I thought day would never break. I spent all day cycling around the area, frequently stopping to call for Gelert but never hearing a response. I put up the posters on my travels; running out of posts before I ran out of flyers. Whenever I saw someone walking their dog I stopped and asked if they had seen Gelert. I knew most of them in passing. All were approachable and sympathetic. Most recalled Gelert, in particular those that owned large dogs. As the day drew out I broadened the search as my desperation grew. The return trip was emotionally exhausting. I began to believe I would not find him intact. I started checking the roadside ditches, both wanting and not wanting to find him. When I arrived home, I hoped against all odds that he had somehow made his way back while I was searching. I didn't trouble Ruth who attended to the preservation of her alcohol content. I retired to my bedroom, tired and disheartened. I resolved to continue my search the following day and, if unsuccessful, I would advance the search with an advert in the newspaper. I called Doctor Jeffries to solicit his help, leaving a message for him to contact me as a matter of urgency.

The thoughts did not comfort me. I decided to withdraw to my sanctuary where I could see and hear over the neighbourhood before the light faded. As I climbed to the platform, I was distracted by my worries to such a degree that it took a moment to realise I was not alone. Kevin sat cross-legged against the bole of the tree, unmoving and silent. 'What are you doing here?' I said, off-guard.

'Why, I thought you were looking for me, *Brother*!' Kevin spat the last word. 'Have you any idea what a pain in the arse it was to get up here?' he said, revealing a hatchet in his hand. I looked to the rear of the platform where there was a rope hanging from a nearby branch. 'I had to cut back half the tree before I could even throw a rope up here. But don't worry; I've had a nice rest, waiting for you.'

'What do you want?'

'What, can't brothers get together for a nice chat every so often?' he said with sarcasm.

'You took my money!'

'Did I? Yes, I suppose I did appropriate your loose change. That's kind of why I want to chat; about money, that is. You see Mummy Dearest has been hitting the bottle even more than usual and she unburdened herself of a little secret. A *family* secret. Want to know what it is?' I refused to take the bait. 'Well, I'll tell you anyway. It seems we aren't stepbrothers after all. Or I should say, we're not *just* stepbrothers. You see, Alan my old chum, we are in fact *half-brothers!*' He paused to let it sink in. I processed what he'd said. 'That's right, we have different mummies but the same daddy. It seems our daddy got drunk and ended up in a one-night stand with my mummy. The union was blessed, as they say.'

'Bullshit! You're lying!' I said, trying, and failing, to disbelieve.

'Would I lie to you, *Brother?* You're worried about missing a few coins when our father didn't leave anything to me in his will. He didn't even acknowledge me; his own fucking son!' He snarled, stood up and waved the hatchet around. 'Even my own mother doesn't give a shit! All she's bothered about is that our father left everything to his beloved Alan. He only left her with enough to keep her in cheap plonk until her liver gives out. The house and all the other stuff is in a trust in your name. Did you know that, hmm?'

That must be the substantial trust fund Doctor Jeffries told me of at Dad's funeral. Suddenly, I recalled the argument I'd overheard years ago. I didn't want to believe it, but pieces fell into place; the things I didn't need to know; the things I might find out about. Secret things.

'So, Brother, I don't think you should resent me taking it upon myself to claim a tiny part of the inheritance that's owed me. Anyway, you said there's a reward.'

'What? What are you talking about?'

'The reward for information about the whereabouts of your little dog.'

'What do you know?' I was fully attentive.

'You really want to know?'

'What have you done; where is he?' I stepped closer.

'Well, I can't tell you his exact location but I can tell you he's at the bottom of the River Alyn,' he said, raising the hatchet.

'*What did you do?*' I screamed.

'Me and the twins wanted to play with your dog, Alan. When I went to pick him up, the little fucker bit me. I had to teach him a lesson; you understand, don't you? I couldn't let him get away with that. We managed to get him into a sack, after a big struggle, let me tell you. He wriggled like fuck right up to when we dropped him into the river. We wanted to see if he was part Houdini; see if he would escape. End result … he wasn't and he didn't.'

'*You bastard*!' I shouted, running towards him. I wanted to grab him and squeeze the truth out of him, make him admit that everything he'd said was a lie. But he was ready for my reaction and dodged to the side, shoving me hard in the back as I missed him.

Kevin had started with the upper-hand but he was on my territory. I knew every inch of the tree: every branch and twig. He followed up, expecting me to try and stop before the edge; but I didn't. I kept moving, picking up the pace until I reached the edge of the platform. Then I jumped. I grabbed at a branch above me with both hands. As I swung away, I let go with one hand so that I turned to face the platform on the downward swing. Kevin hadn't anticipated my agility and stood, uncomprehending near the centre of the platform. I let go of the branch and launched myself at him, knees up, striking him in the chest. He staggered backwards towards the edge of the platform.

I landed heavily, skidding to a halt as Kevin dropped the hatchet and stumbled over the brink. He reached out in desperation as he stepped over the side. He was able to grab my ankle with one hand, leaving himself hanging precariously. There was nothing by which he could gain purchase. The platform was smooth and featureless and the lower branches had been cut back for access. I was only a little better off. The tree offered no handholds and the friction of my bulk against the platform alone provided resistance to Kevin's mass. I felt him swinging his legs. At first I thought he was trying to regain the platform, but his efforts were hopeless. Even when he somehow managed to grab my ankle with his other hand he was still just head and shoulders above the platform with nothing below him to serve as a foothold.

It was then that I realised Kevin was not trying to save himself. He was trying to pull me down with him. His swinging became more animated as he kicked out, each jolt bringing me closer to the edge.

'You're not getting rid of me that easily, *Big Brother*!' I knew that once my foot was over the side there was nothing to stop us both plunging to the ground.

I had but one recourse. I shifted my weight, sitting up with care, which caused a sudden lurch closer to the edge. Kevin's death-grip was absolute. He held on fast to my ankle. I reached down to where his hands gripped me. I took hold of one wrist. Then I squeezed. Kevin cried out and released his grip so that he hung on with a single hand now. I steadied myself as I slipped closer still to the fall. As I reached down again, Kevin taunted me. 'What's this, have you grown some balls at last, Big Brother? You're still a fucking embarrassment!' I studied his expression; his face flushed from exertion and with something else I couldn't identify. Perhaps this was how evil looked; a complete absence of good. I took firm hold of his remaining wrist, causing another lurch towards the edge. Then I was balanced precariously. Kevin looked me in the eyes. 'Go on, I dare you. *Brother*!' And so, I removed his hand from my ankle.

I sat, teetering on the brink, watching Kevin as he seemed to hover for an instant as if his rage resisted gravity. Then he dropped in slow motion, acquiescing to the gravitational imperative. His fall was interrupted by a large branch. I heard a sickening crunch as his back took the full weight of the fall before he spun and hit the ground hard, face down. I looked below to where he lay at the foot of the tree, his posture somehow wrong; a symptom of something mortally broken. I rolled back onto my tainted sanctuary, hugging my knees, retreating inside my shell. My head a swirl of thoughts; the revelation of Dad's infidelity central to my mental maelstrom.

I was despondent. I grieved not for the loss of the brother I had cast out of my sanctuary, but for the corruption of my father's memory. I mourned too for the loss of my friend Gelert; distressed by thoughts of his wretched, terrifying last moments. I was unable to move; weighed down by the burden of fratricide.

My father had possessed feet of clay and genitals of flesh. He'd transgressed by being party to producing a child out of wedlock. But my transgression had eliminated that child. The sin of the son had erased the sin of the father.

* * * *

I walked into the gym to find Dai the sole attendee. Earlier, I'd strolled through the gardens, taking in the relaxing sights and smells offered by the well-maintained, extensive grounds. I had been distracted to such an extent that I almost missed the most unrelaxing sight and smell of Nobby approaching me. With complete disdain for my clumsiness, I darted behind a neatly trimmed bush and crouched so I would be hidden from all but the most observant. Through the bush, I could still spy Nobby, hands deep in pockets and head down, meandering past where I hid. The indignity of my position was irrelevant when faced with the prospect of twenty minutes of one-on-one Nobby-time before the appointed session in the gym. As his pace slowed, I exerted all my telekinetic powers in an attempt to drive him away. I even tried to will his spontaneous combustion but my mental powers were unequal to the task. When he'd sauntered out of sight, around the corner, I made for the refuge of the gym where I should be safe for twenty minutes, Nobby usually one of the last to arrive for sessions.

I found Dai messing about with the loose weights at the back of the room. He was surprised to see me but took on a welcoming aspect. 'Hey, Alan, you're early. I wasn't expecting anyone yet. I thought I'd get a few sets in.' I nodded in faux comprehension. Dai continued. 'While you're here, can you spot me?' *Wow*, I thought; *he's really shit at hide and seek.* Perhaps he'd bumped his head and was concussed. I thought to humour him.

'Yes, of course I can spot you, Dai.'

'Great.' Dai loaded up some serious-looking weights on a bar perched above the bench near him. I watched him as he lay on his back and grabbed the bar that now rested above his head. He paused and looked at me. 'What's up, Al? I thought you said you can spot me?'

'Oh, is it my turn to hide now?'

'What? No, when I say "spot me", I mean I want you to act as my spotter. You know, keep an eye on the weights in case I need help. You stand at the end of the bench and put your hands near the bar when I'm lifting. Don't touch it, just be ready to take the weight if I slip.' His detailed explanation was once again a reflection of his accurate assessment of my level of ignorance. It's kind of what he did.

'Oh right, "spot" you, of course.'

I did not enjoy the experience. As Dai strained against the weight of the laden bar, I couldn't help but notice the uncomfortable near-homoeroticism of the situation. Dai's exertions left him red-faced and grunting as he arched his back off the bench, his face barely eighteen inches from my genitals, separated from him by only two layers of cloth. I tried not to over-think the situation, but I do not possess that particular skill. I was at least grateful that it wasn't my face in the arrangement. After an endless set of straining and grunting, Dai sat up, it seemed satisfied. 'Thanks, Alan, I needed that. I can't do the proper heavy stuff unless I have a spotter. Hey, do you want a turn now?'

'No!' I said, rather too loud and abrupt. 'I'm here to relax, not to exert myself,' I added, in a vain attempt to extract some cool. I retreated to my reserved position and resolved to remain hidden behind the bush the next time Nobby threatened.

I was relieved when the boys started wandering in not long after my introduction to spotting. We had a number of rules relating to session commencement to which we assiduously adhered. The session couldn't start until there was a quorum of at least four active members. While Nobby was considered a "member", he wasn't considered active. Nobby was considered irrelevant. Activities were delayed or instigated irrespective of his attendance; he didn't "indulge" after all. In addition to delaying burning activities, neither would we start listening to music. Our methods proved too persuasive. After a few minutes of relaxing music we felt compelled to further our state of relaxation.

On this occasion, Face was the sole absentee when we formally continued our valiant labours. Sometimes the officially endorsed hospital activities disrupted our important work, but we endured, as heroes do. We were fifteen minutes into the session, still taking off and not yet at cruising altitude, when Face arrived. 'What-ho, Chaps. Permission to disembark? Terribly sorry for the late landing;

ETA kyboshed. Squadron Leader Biggles thought he spotted Jerry at nine o'clock. Wanted to see the kite go down in flames. Mission aborted. What-what? No time for tiffin, so here for the spliffin," Face said, waggling an invisible spliff, Groucho-style. Face was relating the reasons for his tardiness. Roughly translated: his session with Doc Friendly had gone beyond the allocated time. The doc thought he'd detected an issue that merited further investigation but his forays proved unsuccessful. Face had sacrificed sustenance in order to attend our valuable research.

He was also in such a rush to join us that he'd forgotten his product. He did this from time to time. It's kind of what he did – cheating bastard. 'Hey, Silent, I didn't have time to go to my room for my kit. Can I scrounge a spliff off you? I'll see you right next week.'

I checked my mental accounts to reveal he was already in arrears. 'No, you can't. That's what you said last week when you scrounged one and you still haven't paid it back.'

'Are you sure? I thought I'd repaid you,' he said. The lad was optimistic, if also forgetful.

'Yes, I'm positive. I have an excellent memory. It's so good that I can't remember the last time I forgot something.'

'Well, my memory is so bad I have to carry a notebook with me at all times to jot stuff down before I forget,' Face said.

'So you have it on you now?'

'No, I haven't.'

'Why not?'

'Forgot. Oh, tell you what. I've remembered something else I forgot; I know what's happened to Spud.' Spud had been discharged a month previously and in the intervening period, his case had been heard. Face shared what had happened since Spud's release.

It had taken three weeks for Doc Friendly to complete Spud's psychological assessment. According to Face, Spud had attained a clean bill of mental health and had been judged fit to be held responsible for his digit-severing activities. The implications of his assessment were not lost on me. Spud had fitted in most comfortably with the gang; he had been one of the lads. I entertained thoughts of classifying his assessment as yet another success story to be attributed to our heroic work relating to Casual Therapy. Indeed, I was unsure if we hadn't done Spud a disservice in promoting his sanity, or maybe lack of insanity. The magistrate may have tended more towards rehabilitation rather than the punitive had Spud been considered mentally negligent. However, as Doc Friendly had been the official bestower of sanity, I wasn't too remorseful. I refused to entertain the notion that anyone else in the group could be considered mentally competent by association with Spud.

Face knew all about it. 'Yeah, my cousin was involved in the case. He's a paralegal.'

'Oh shit, man! That's terrible,' Legs said, heavy with sympathy.

'What are you talking about?'

'Well, he's in a wheelchair, isn't he?'

'No, you stupid twat; he works for a legal firm. You're thinking of a *paraplegic*!' Face said. 'Anyway,' he continued, 'Spud was judged mentally fit and he ended up getting done for GBH. That's "grievous bodily harm", before you ask, Legs.'

'*Merda*! What did he end up getting?' Brains said.

'Eighteen months in Cardiff gaol. He should be out in six months with good behaviour.'

Oh well, I thought, *he'll be okay, as long as no-one gives him the finger.* Spud had the aspect of a chap that could look after himself. I was sure it wouldn't be lost on his fellow inmates. Maybe he would even find his way into a specialist group similar to ours. Cardiff was a *growing* area after all.

Then I considered how my association with Spud would affect my "street cred". I now knew a convicted felon and not merely a white collar criminal. No, Spud and his crime without doubt ranked towards the serious end of the criminal spectrum; a view his victim was bound to endorse. I calculated the improvement to my street cred capital. My association with Spud would add at least ten points to my rating. That would give me ... let's see ... a total of ... ten points. I was on my way.

* * * *

My recollection of the aftermath of Kevin's death was equivocal. I remained unmoving on the platform overnight, weighed down by the affliction of what I'd heard and what I'd done. By what I'd been *forced* to do. Kevin's body was discovered the next morning by Doctor Jeffries when he'd called to follow up on the message I'd left the previous day. He'd checked the body for signs of life but Kevin was clearly dead. He'd then called the emergency services before rousing Ruth. He'd searched the house for me, perhaps calling my name. Once again, the house had merely echoed to the name of the lost. By this time the ambulance had arrived to deal with Kevin and it was then that I was discovered. The local fire brigade was enlisted to retrieve me and I have vague memories of being recovered from the platform.

The incident was not altogether unquestioned. The death of a teenager was something that stirred the sensibilities of the local community. There was a formal inquest conducted, of which I played no part. I suspect Doctor Jeffries employed his not insignificant influence on the proceedings, thereby ensuring that the Lavelle family, already suffering much as a result of one recent tragedy, would not be exposed to further distress through unnecessary and cruel scrutiny of yet another.

It was at this time that I was first admitted as an in-patient of the Glyndwr Mental Health Facility. Too young to be considered an adult, I was not subjected to the ministrations of Doc Friendly. The youth psychiatrist to whom I was referred focused on treatment that was palliative in nature. My treatment addressed the short-term situational concerns and, to a lesser extent, the longer-term chronic issues that subsequently developed.

It was at this point that I started my relationship with psycho-pharmacology. Despite my unclear recollections, I do recall the intensity of the treatment. During the first four weeks of my incarceration, the fugue state, fuelled by drugs, was punctuated by daily sessions with the psychiatrist. By the time I left the facility, some six months after admittance, the sessions were less frequent. The female psychiatrist didn't share the same genial disposition as Doc Friendly, though at the time I could not appreciate the dissimilar approaches. She was not unsympathetic, but possessed a sense of something close to impatience that was wholly absent in Doc Friendly. The mental fog in which I existed became less dense as my visit advanced. Perhaps the strength of medication was reduced, as reward for my progress. It might even have been attributed to my becoming acclimatised to the pharmacological campaign.

When first admitted, I'd rarely spoken and not at all about the events that led to Kevin's death. My mental weakness and emotional fragility didn't permit me to even contemplate the incident. During the latter stage of my incarceration, while I'd conversed more, I'd remained reticent about the fatality. My restraint was driven by an inherent sense of self-preservation; a lesson well learnt and long held. I never disclosed to anyone what transpired with Kevin. I wouldn't even share what happened to Gelert. While I was never subjected to the formal dealings of the inquiry, I became aware of the findings. The inquiry found that Kevin's death resulted from injuries sustained as the consequence of an accidental fall. My involvement didn't provide a material part of the findings and I was not officially suspected of any wrongdoing. My admittance to a mental health facility was seen purely as a side effect of having witnessed the tragedy.

I never knew if the psychiatrist suspected me of wrongdoing. She never advised me of doctor–patient confidentiality. It may have been an oversight, as the doctor gave the impression she would rather be somewhere else when in session with me. She wasn't a resident so would have had to fit my burdensome workload into her regular assignments. I never felt inclined to apologise for the apparent inconvenience I'd caused her.

There was one thing though, that I regretted discussing with her. It was during our last session. I was due to leave the facility and return home that afternoon. My progress over the previous six months was such that a plan was devised and agreed upon. When discharged from the hospital, I would be under the stewardship of Doctor Jeffries, who would act as both family doctor and family friend. The psychiatrist provided me with a few parting thoughts. Things to consider on my release.

'You know, Alan, it's not necessarily about effecting change. No-one can alter the past. Sometimes the crux of the matter is about encouraging acceptance.'

Thoughts of my imminent departure made me imprudent. 'So, I have to learn to accept who I am?'

'Yes, that is one aspect of your recovery.'

'But how can I not hate myself?' I said, immediately ruing the slip.

She looked at me with an expression of curiosity, her first genuine reaction in six months. 'I didn't say you could do that. If you cannot change who you think you are, then you need to learn to accept who you think you are.'

It was to prove easier said than done.

Chapter Fourteen

I returned to school where I was now considered even more of an oddity. I was obliged to be held back a year, due to my extended stay in the mental health facility. While my new classmates were not as familiar with the animosity of my more distant school life, they were without doubt aware of my most recent and public history. I was the single surviving male of the Lavelle family since the others had expired under questionable circumstances. Having been ostracised for so many years, my newfound infamy was not apparent to me at first. I was still excluded from much of the school life but the exclusion was subtly changed. Whereas I had once been routinely ignored and avoided, it now became more obvious. People started noticing me; their expressions no longer blank or dismissive but now hesitant or cautious. Even the library nerds stopped approaching me at lunchtime, choosing to sit apart. Perhaps they thought I was cursed. Perhaps they were right.

I wasn't troubled by the attention that I both was, and was not, receiving. I had no desire to fraternise and was comfortable restricting my conversation to only that required as part of classroom activities. My isolation enabled me to quickly catch up on the schoolwork I had missed while an inmate of the hospital.

The Bad Lads were fewer in number. Not only by the loss of Kevin. A couple of the older associates had graduated from school. By then, there were two active members that still attended school. They would stop and glare at me whenever encountered. They may have had suspicions but I reassured myself knowing that putting two and two together was beyond their collective ability. Neither did I forget their involvement in Gelert's murder.

My home life changed. Again. I didn't experience Kevin's loss physically. After Dad's death – *our* dad's death – I had rarely seen Kevin around the house anyway. One significant change was that I never returned to the platform. The initial effects on Ruth proved more profound. While her reaction to Dad's death had been affected and unpersuasive, Kevin's death inspired a more genuine response. For a while she curtailed her alcoholic intake, needing only the tactile presence of the glass to fulfil her needs, as she sat holding the same empty glass for hours. She dispensed with the pretence of reading magazines and instead took to sitting in front of the television. The change in media failed to improve her level of awareness. She sat in front of the screen blankly staring at whatever happened to be showing. I would hear the sound of the television until the early hours of the morning, at which point Ruth must have grasped where she was. Ruth and I lived an awkward, isolated existence, or as isolated as two people could be while sharing the same house.

Ruth was beyond world-weary. She was physically present in that her body occupied a volume of space, but in a mental and emotional sense, she was altogether absent. I wondered if it was just a matter of time before her body caught up to her defeated soul, as had happened to Dad. Her lack of animosity surprised me. I'd been sure she would blame me for Kevin's death, despite her not knowing the full facts. There was one instance when I detected genuine hostility.

I'd been for a stroll around the neighbourhood and as I walked in through the front door on my return, I thought I heard a noise coming from Dad's study. I saw the door was ajar and so moved towards it and pushed it open. Ruth had her back to me. She was on the phone. I caught a snatch of the conversation.

'… It's not fair. There must be something I can do …'

'Sorry, Ruth. I didn't know you were in here,' I said.

Ruth turned, taken unawares, with an expression of undisguised malice. 'What the hell do you think you're doing? How dare you just walk in here!' she spat.

'I'm sorry,' I said and left the study, running upstairs to take cover in my bedroom.

Hours later when I returned downstairs I found Ruth assuming her usual position, sitting in front of the television, fatigued demeanour in place.

'I'm sorry about before. I didn't know you were in the study. I thought I heard the music system,' I said. Ruth turned towards me and looked straight through me as though the earlier incident had never happened. As if I was not there. As if Ruth was not there.

Perhaps Ruth was incapable of conjuring up the energy required to hate me. I felt pity towards her. The marriage to my father had been symbolic at best; even destructive. Certainly so for my father. It would have been so easy for me to blame Ruth for everything. For Dad's death and all that eventuated thereafter. I could have even blamed her for the death of her own son. That wouldn't have happened if Dad was alive. It wouldn't have happened if Ruth hadn't cared to share secrets with Kevin. But that was being indolent and unfair. Their marriage had been between two people. The household had comprised of four people and we had all shared a measure of responsibility for the prevailing atmosphere.

I tried to reach Ruth, even when the one-word answers diminished to no answer at all. I tidied up in the morning when I arose for school; removing the detritus of the previous day. In the evenings I asked her if she wanted something to eat but she failed to even acknowledge the question. Nevertheless, I would prepare food and place it on the table in the evening on the chance she wanted something more solid than her usual liquid fare. Most of the time the meals would be neglected, making their way intact from microwave to table and on to the bin. Mrs M had been retained as our part-time housekeeper, providing us with some semblance of domestic continuity. Doctor Jeffries visited more regularly, calling twice weekly to check how I was coping. He attempted to engage with Ruth, disbursing his responsibilities as the executor of Dad's will. There was no indication of the animosity I'd perceived at Dad's funeral. But by then the doctor would have had time to come to terms with the nature of Dad's passing. Kevin's death may have also tempered his attitude towards Ruth.

* * * *

I persevered, using my studies as an effective distraction. So much so that on graduation from secondary school my academic achievements afforded me a decent choice of post-school options. I was accepted to read a number of courses at several universities of dependable reputation. After much consideration, I chose to study engineering at Loughborough University. Both the course and the location were well suited to offer the greatest opportunities. The university was ninety minutes' drive from home; close enough to be convenient when necessary and far enough to be considered inconvenient if necessary. In addition, Doctor Jeffries advised that the family trust included a portfolio of properties; one of which was a two-bedroomed flat, not too far from the university.

At the tender age of nineteen and a half, I disembarked from a restored Vandalised and set foot in a new land, equipped to begin life afresh. I left all the childish, and not so childish, animosity behind. The unpleasantness of my past was from a different time and place and weighed less upon me. I was still me; the oddly shaped, slightly awkward individual, but I was unencumbered by my history. I was more excited than scared as I approached university life. I felt like a proper grown-up. While the terms of the trust dictated that I would not have access to the greater part of the fund until I reached the age of twenty-five, I was, nevertheless, quite comfortable in the meantime. I benefited from an allowance that meant I would exist as neither the deprived nor the depraved.

I had my own place to live, although I was technically a tenant, the property being owned by the trust. Doctor Jeffries assured me the arrangement was apposite and legal. I was more comfortable having my own place rather than occupying the halls of residence with other students. I needed my space. I had two forms of transport available;

my bicycle had also graduated to university. Vandalised was no longer an apt moniker for the van but it retained its name with a sense of irony. It had been thoroughly renovated, inside and out, but could not be retrofitted with the more up-to-date features, such as airbags. I replaced the old balloons in the glovebox with new models as a nostalgic gesture.

I immersed myself with caution into student life, attempting to balance the academic with the social. I didn't feel overly conspicuous among my fellow *Engineers-To-Be*. Outside their own group, engineering students were not the most outgoing genus of scholar, which suited my temperament. I perhaps differed somewhat in that my social limitations were reflected in my physical appearance whereas the typical engineer first had to open his mouth and speak before his limitations were exposed. However, they seemed determined to prove they were the most devoted dipsomaniacs. I wondered casually if Ruth had once studied engineering.

I attended a few Freshers' functions in the first week that culminated in the big Freshers Ball. By this time I had got to know a few of my fellow ETBs and was integrated to such an extent that I was persuaded to wear the official Engineering Freshers Ball tee-shirt. It consisted of a plain white shirt emblazoned with the logo "Last Week I Couldn't Even Spell "Injuneer", Now I Are One!" I was less concerned with the message and more concerned with finding a shirt to suit my unusual physique. I was relieved to discover that I could squeeze into the largest size and to find I was but one of many to wear the shirt with a questionable level of pride.

The Freshers Ball proved to be a most educating evening. There appeared to be enough students attending to test the capacity of Wembley Stadium. A celebrity DJ was engaged who was so cool that I'd never heard of him. Pimms promoted its alcoholic wares at discounted rates and many of the students took advantage of the liquid bargain. As a novice drinker, I exercised caution and didn't take up the Pimms proposition. Interestingly, I noticed most students didn't start with Pimms, but only resorted to it when well on their way to Drunksville. Having never partaken of the Pimms' experience I cannot comment on its qualities but it seemed that the tipple was avoided while the taste buds were sober enough to appreciate what was passing.

Many of the students appeared to be competing in the equivalent of sprinting an alcoholic marathon. When I visited the toilets, halfway through the evening, it was with immense disgust that I discovered ponds of Pimms-fuelled puke distributed everywhere. Toilets, sinks, urinals, floors and even windows failed to escape the regurgitated cut-price tipple. For this reason, I have never sampled Pimms, nor will I. To be fair to the brand, their product was in a *last-in, first-out* basis and the excess of vomit sorely tested the sobriety-challenged. Even my usually reliable constitution contained a dry heave or two before I retired outside to take care of my toilet. I was one of the few engineers who'd retained a mostly white tee-shirt by the end of the night, the others having carried out unofficial testing of the material's absorbency.

During the mid-morning break on Monday the sole subject of conversation was comparisons of how much was consumed and how little recalled. Acknowledged as one of the least drunk in our group, I was asked for my version of events. I played dumb, recalling a line from a Christy Moore song with absolute understanding about how he couldn't stand such a crooked man sober. I didn't think it would do my modest standing any favours if I told Steve that when I'd gone outside for a piss I'd found him on his back, in a bush, trousers down by his ankles, moaning for his mummy. He wouldn't have objected. The way they talked, his standing could have only improved. Neither did I tell him that I'd kicked him over onto his side so he wouldn't choke on his own "Pimmsy" vomit. *You're welcome, Steve*, I thought but didn't say.

After a fortnight of acclimatising to student life, I felt well-enough adjusted to advertise for a flatmate. My situation was such that I occupied the larger bedroom with an en-suite bathroom and so entertained sharing the remainder of the flat. As the de facto land-lord, the additional rent money would also be welcome. I posted a notice on the faculty bulletin board and within a week I'd acquired myself a cockney. Warren was a second-year engineering student. He was a larger-than-life individual who self-described as either a "rugby-playing engineer" or an "engineering rugby player". Whichever description, he was devoted to these two facets of his life. To be more precise, he was devoted to the incidental activity that was common to both pursuits. He liked a drink or seven. He appeared determined to demonstrate that activities associated with rugby served simply as a prelude to the real purpose of the sport; post-activity drinkies.

I established the non-negotiable rules early. I'd highlighted these conditions during the lunchtime when we first met. In addition to the standard fare relating to who pays for what and when, I was adamant that flatmate privacy be considered sacrosanct. As the official lessee, as well as technical landlord, I'd also ensured that he'd understood the mod cons provided were a privilege and not a right. The communal home entertainment equipment was not to be relocated or abused. Noise was to be kept to a reasonable level and eliminated after a sensible hour. I wanted to ensure there were no misunderstandings from the outset. Warren had agreed without concession to every point and assured me that he was on the same page.

But, as Bruce Wayne had his alter ego, *Batman,* Warren had *Wazza the Cockney Wide-boy.* I learnt a great deal from Wazza. The vast majority of what I learnt fell under "things to not do again". The first time his rent fell into arrears I ended up lending him a tenner after hearing his sad tale of overdue funds and mislaid cheques. He would pay up in the end, but in such a fashion that I felt grateful when he was less than a month in arrears. He was also overcome with amnesia when in the kitchen. He often forgot he hadn't purchased the food he was eating.

It got to the point where I was obliged to take innovative action. I'd developed a taste for cider and there was usually a two-litre bottle in the fridge, coolly waiting to quench my thirst. I'd begun to suspect that Wazza was helping himself, the liquid volume diminishing without my aid. I discreetly marked the liquid level on the label which confirmed my suspicions when the level dropped without subsequent change to the mark. It wasn't simply that he'd helped himself, I was more concerned that he'd contaminated the product. Wazza was a dedicated "straight from the bottle" man. I adopted a subtle approach rather than confront him; I'd just end up lending him a fiver. I labelled the drink with a note saying "I have spat in here", which I considered both humorous and ingenious. The following day when I checked, I discovered he had added a note of his own beneath mine. It said "So have I". It was about this time I began hiding bottles in my room, to satisfy my occasional alcoholic craving.

Other than his parsimonious tendencies, Wazza proved to be an acceptable flatmate. He took to calling me *Taffy*, to honour my Welsh accent. I didn't object; there was a logic to it and the name ranked at the top of my list of bestowed nicknames. He schooled me in the ways of the engineering student, introducing me to concepts such as the "Mexican Rainbow". This was more than a mere drinking game – it was a "drinking event". The Rainbow entailed downing a selection of various colours of alcopop drinks. The Mexican component involved interspersing the alcopops with shots of tequila. Digestive retention of seven alcopops and six shots was required to rightfully claim mastery of the "Mexican Rainbow". We made an attempt one evening. I paid for the drinks, of course, as Wazza pointed out that he wasn't charging me for the dubious benefit of his tuition. I got to blue before I started feeling a bit green. Wazza gave up on yellow, claiming pre-existing inebriation. As I was less concerned about the colours going in and more concerned with the colour that might come out, I settled for a respectable retirement while ahead.

Wazza was respectful when his rugby chums came to pick him up for training. Even when they dropped off the more intoxicated version later in the night, he retained his civility. Now and again they asked me to join them, but I politely declined. As well as the logistical challenges of meeting up with them after rugby practice, I didn't relish the notion of playing alcohol-content-catch-up with a bunch of lads already on their way to Drunksville.

My social life was not neglected, however. I became friendly with a couple of like-minded, restrained ETBs. We would meet for drinks a few times a week. Unlike other engineering students, we looked upon an evening of drinking as a pleasant stroll through delicately fragranced gardens of alcoholic self-control and not as a riotous drunken blitzkrieg through a boozy battlefield, hacking away at all and sundry.

We would watch on unimpressed in the uni bar as other students gave way to their excessive alcoholic urges. We didn't judge them for their lack of restraint but rather for using their self-inflicted inebriation as an excuse to misbehave. Countless times we observed guys drunkenly approach some unfortunate female patron. Perhaps they believed their charms would prove irresistible, augmented by their state of advanced inebriation. Without exception, they proved to be altogether resistible. On one occasion, a freshly spurned lover took exception at our witnessing his rejection. He looked over to where we sat, talking among ourselves, and said, 'What the fuck are you looking at?' A few patrons turned to see what the disturbance was about. My two companions looked away, and sipped nervously at their beers. I, however, went for a less meek approach. Time to *sit tight*. I put my glass down on the table and sat up straight, giving him my best "Don't make me shit in your bag!" look. Romeo proved unwilling to further engage and walked back towards his laughing comrades.

My companions were so impressed with my performance that I didn't have to buy another round that night. Admittedly, we only had another couple of drinks and I had just got a round in, but I sensed their admiration was genuine. While my prime objective wasn't to watch drunken fuckwits being humiliated, I still took the opportunity to learn from their experiences. Their displays served as an excellent example of "what not to do", but we remained clueless in the ways of "what to do". My associates were as socially awkward as me, borderline Asperger's sufferers that we were. I liked to think that if I was in a similar state to the failed Romeos that my liquid courage wouldn't lead to delusions of social adequacy but I didn't want to test that theory. For matters pertaining to the opposite sex we comprehensively confessed to complete ignorance and inadequacy and moved on.

After six months of student life I was feeling most satisfied with my social progress since arriving at university. I had left Alien and Mutant far behind and Alan, aka Taffy, was now in charge. No,

I had no aspirations relating to interactions with the opposite sex. That was something I might contemplate way in the future. I had achieved enough. I didn't want to taint my progress with unrealistic expectations.

Then I met Juliette.

* * * *

The flat was situated on the edge of a moderate-sized town, close to the university. The town was an ideal size. Too small for a McDonalds but large enough to merit the presence of essential shops. This included a decent supermarket from where I sourced all my groceries and, involuntarily, most of Wazza's. I shopped there every other day, favouring fresh food, both for its nutritional value and as motivation to get to the food before my amnesic flatmate. I'd grown so familiar with the layout that I'd carry out my grocery shopping on auto-pilot, pausing only to confirm the relevance of special offers. One memorable day everything appeared customary. I found myself coming to from my shop-trance in the checkout line, necessitated by the imminent transaction. There were two people before me in the queue as I glanced at the scourge of parents everywhere, the adjacent racks of confectionery, calculated to tempt while you wait.

I deduced from the view of her back that the shopper before me was a young woman. I didn't stare too long, wanting to avoid any potential misunderstanding if she suddenly turned. I figured that anyone behind me would find it considerably more demanding to look away from my abnormal aspect. The thought germinated so that I felt obliged to confirm if anyone was behind me. I turned with care, not wishing to catch anyone in the act, to find no-one behind, so returned to my queuing. It was then I noticed the young woman was growing upset. She had turned out her purse and was in the process of turning out her pockets, in search of money. The checkout chick sat, checking her nails, indifferent to the young woman's desperation. 'You're still three pounds short, Miss. If you haven't got enough you'll have to replace some items.'

'Please, give me a moment. I'm sure I have the money here somewhere.'

'Well, there are other people waiting,' Checkout Chick said.

I turned to see if anyone had joined the queue but it was still only me. It seemed I was the "other people". I considered informing the checkout-chick-of-the-year that I didn't mind waiting. Then I worried it might suggest I was enjoying the spectacle. I did and said what I always did and said: nothing. The girl in front turned to the side and I saw she was on the verge of tears. I felt a little guilty to note she was not unattractive, despite her growing desperation. I found myself overcome with illusions of chivalry and determined to assist this damsel-in-distress. Out of sight, I removed a ten pound note from my pocket and bending down, made as if I was retrieving something from beneath the counter.

'Excuse me, Miss, I think you dropped this,' I said, offering her the note.

She looked at me for a moment, as if confused, but took the note. 'Are you sure? Thank you.'

'No problem,' I said, feeling the blood surge to my face. I was unable to hold her gaze and instead scanned the rows of chocolatey offerings. By the time she had finished paying the sullen checkout girl, I had added a Twix and two Mars bars to my shopping. Well, chocolate is like toilet paper; it's impossible to have too much.

As I left the store, I thought to take advantage of fate and removed a Mars bar, intending to first undress and then despatch it. In my distraction I failed to see the young lady waiting for me outside until I was almost upon her. I thought to move past her, my discomfort growing as I realised she would see my back as I fled. I determined not to prolong the experience for either of us and smiled in simple acknowledgement as I chose my escape route. This plan of action, however, did not meet her approval and, with some skill, she waylaid me, positioning herself on the footpath so I could not pass. My sole options for a quick exit were not attractive. I could either attempt some spectacular acrobatics or choose the much easier option of a quick U-turn and sprint away. Once again, I resorted to my standard approach, standing silent, attempting an innocent look.

'Hi. I wanted to say thanks for what you did.'

'What? I don't know what you mean,' I said, engaging my stupid.

'I think you know exactly what I mean,' she said, her expression composed around a pretty smile. 'I think you're just being chivalrous.'

Wow, she had a nice smile and before I knew what was happening, I spoke. 'Would I do that to you?' I appeared to be taking a leaf out of Wide-Boy Wazza's book, although I was sure I didn't nail his accompanying wide-eyed look. *Shit!* I thought as I felt blood returning to my face. But then she saved me.

'Well, I'll tell you what. Seeing as how I've had a bit of luck, I hope your chivalry will allow me to buy you a coffee.'

'We could all do with a bit of luck now and again,' I said, then blurted out, 'but yes, coffee sounds good,' before she changed her mind.

We proceeded to a small, busy café, close to the supermarket. As we walked I positioned myself to conceal my back. We chatted idly and swapped names as we walked. I was Alan. She was Juliette, ensuring I knew her name was spelled differently to the most famous Capulet. There was an awkward moment as I was forced to shuffle, crab-like, in order to open the door to the café to allow her entry. It was a compromise between dashing ahead, giving her my full, unobstructed posterior view, or spoiling the impression of chivalry by forcing her to open the door herself.

We got the last available table for two, close to the door. I pulled out her chair, maintaining my chivalrous character, and sat down opposite her without exposing too much back. The elderly waitress materialised to take our order. 'Hello, dears. What can I get you?' I hesitated. My preferred café tipple was the cappuccino but this was not without risk. Having sampled the local cappuccino I knew they were liberal with the chocolate powder. It resembled a geological layer rather than a dusting. On one occasion I'd attempted to inhale as I lifted the mug to take a sip. In true Columbian-drug-baron style, I'd snorted a nostril full of powder which resulted in an explosive fit of coughing and spluttering. Before I was able to remove my drink from the path of my violent expectoration, I'd managed to distribute milk froth and chocolate powder across a significant expanse of the café.

'I'll have a tea, please,' I said. Juliette had already ordered a coffee.

'Of course, dear,' the waitress said, approving of my choice. Perhaps she'd witnessed my previous cappuccino-fuelled mishap. She left us chatting as she went to fulfil our order.

As the waitress retreated I took the opportunity to get to know Juliette. Leaning more towards the listener than the talker, I soon discovered Juliette was a recently qualified nurse. She wasn't local to the town but lived nearby in nursing halls of residence, adjacent to the general hospital. She was being picked up later by one of her nursing buddies. She looked about my age, perhaps a little older given she had completed nursing studies. Her shoulder-length, wavy brown hair framed her round face attractively. She wasn't skinny but wasn't overweight. Her figure was rounded and she radiated a strong impression of healthiness. *All the curves in the right places*, I thought with a touch of guilt. Her looks were that of the girl next door, pretty in a real-worldly way. And then she smiled. I had never witnessed such a phenomenon. Her smile transformed her face from pretty to something more wonderful. She glowed with a captivating allure.

Juliette went to lengths to convince me she didn't usually lack the necessary funds when shopping. 'I thought I had enough; obviously! It would be nice for once to find I had *more* than I thought.' When she heard I was an engineering student her interest seemed genuine. 'That sounds interesting. And I do know that doesn't mean you fix cars.' Smart too. I chuckled along with her and tried to affect a sophisticated persona as I poured my unfamiliar tea. I took a sip and recoiled at the unexpected bitterness. *Jesus!* I thought, *it tastes like battery acid.* I added a decent portion of milk and took another taste. Ah, that's better; milky battery acid.

As we chatted pleasantly, I began feeling less uncomfortable. Juliette proved to be agreeable company. At one point she leaned over to me and spoke in a low voice. 'Have you noticed, almost every other table is occupied by couples? Typical!' I leant back from our huddle and risked a quick look around. She was right. Almost all the tables possessed couples in various stages of intimacy. I nodded in agreement and offered a supportive shoulder shrug. 'Are you single?' she asked.

'Yes. There is only one of me,' I said, returning to stupid. *What!!*

'You're funny.' She laughed. *What??*

'Am I? Yes, I *am,* aren't I?' I said, incredulous at my apparent escape. 'And what about you, are you single? Or are you the product of a multiple birth?' *Shit! Don't get cocky, you bloody idiot.*

Juliette laughed again. 'Yes, I'm single. There is only one of me too.'

We chatted for thirty minutes. I sipped at my steadily cooling tea which served to bring me back to Earth with a bitter jolt. It came time for Juliette to leave. 'I have to go, Alan. My friend will be wondering where I've got to. I've enjoyed our chat and I'm glad that you were there to … witness my good fortune. Thanks again for that.'

'I have no idea what you're talking about. You must have mistaken me for someone else,' I said, feigning innocence; badly.

She smiled. 'No, I don't think I have.' She looked set to leave but then hesitated. 'I hope you won't think me too forward but … could I get your phone number? I did offer to buy you a coffee, not tea, so I still owe you.' It took a moment for me to appreciate the implication of her request. Of course, I was delighted to provide my details. I recited the number slowly and clearly for her, plus anyone else in the café that wasn't hard of hearing. We exchanged farewells and I stood to open the door as she left. I sat down as the door closed behind her and contemplated what had just happened. I was so distracted that I took another sip of the cold tea, which served to bring me back to reality.

I processed the data. It's kind of what I do. No-one was injured. No-one suffered any loss or damage to property. I had not offended anyone. I didn't say anything too stupid … might come back to that one. I had not sprayed Juliette with milk froth or chocolate powder. In the end, I'd even felt less uncomfortable than usual around the female of the species. I would talk to the girls in my classes, but that consisted of discussions relating to the coursework. Any recreational discussions were incidental. My most recent encounter, however, had been all about the recreational. It could only be recorded as a massive success for Mr Alan Lavelle. In a nutshell: good memories. Not masturbatory material but memorable nevertheless.

I then considered the parting transaction: the taking of the phone number. I knew, without the slightest doubt, that Juliette was simply being polite, consistent with her pleasant demeanour. It was a gesture I very much appreciated. But I was no fool. She was a female, she was breathing, she was sighted; ergo, she was out of my league. I knew I would never hear from her again.

She called the next afternoon.

* * * *

On Tuesday we concluded that God is dead. Unsurprisingly, there are many subjects that provoke a wide range of opinions for such a small group. Surprisingly, there are a number of subjects upon which the group will agree without fear of dissent; typically pertaining to heavier and more philosophical matters. It's kind of what we do. The existence-of-God debate started with opposing positions but ended in violent agreement. It started with an argument between Voice and Legs. We were on our second spliff of the session, flying nicely at cruising altitude when Legs took exception to Voice's accompaniment of Mr Marley. Legs was upset that while Bob sang the recognised lyrics of "No, woman, no cry", Voice chose to impose his Scottish heritage, singing instead 'Nae girlie, nae greet.'

'That is so annoying, Voice. If you have to sing along, why can't you sing the proper lyrics?' Legs said.

'Ah, away and boil yer heid, ya big poof!' Voice shouted.

'Hey, don't call me a poof! You're the one who said he'd tried cross-dressing!'

'What? I did not say I tried cross-dressing. I said that I got cross *while* dressing. I had trouble doing up my tie, you deaf twat! God, you're a fucking idiot!'

'Oi!' I intervened, exerting my influence as keeper-of-the-peace. 'Careful there, Voice. First you're calling Legs a "poof", then a "deaf twat". Worse still, you called God a "fucking idiot". Stand further away from me when you do that, I don't want to be the victim of friendly fire when you get struck by lightning.'

'Or struck by me!' Legs mumbled.

'What'd you say?' Voice said.

'Nothing.' Legs smiled.

'You don't need to worry about lightning bolts, boys,' Brains said. 'God is dead!'

'And how exactly do you figure that out?' Voice said. And so it began.

'Alright, as you insist. First of all, let's establish some fundamental truths,' Brains said, scanning his audience. Seeing he had our full attention, or lack of inattention, he continued. 'I think we can all agree that Felicity Kendal's Bottom is the embodiment of the most heavenly; a vessel not of this Earth,' he said, dead serious. There was, of course, no dissent; heads were nodded.

'Blessed be!' Voice shouted, raising his hands in supplication.

'"Blessed be" indeed. Therefore, grasping the certainty that FKB is heavenly, it must follow that FKB has been created by God Himself. Do we agree that the enormity of the task would not have been delegated to a lesser deity?' Brains said. We all nodded again, some of us even waved him on, as if to say, 'Yes, no need to state the obvious, move along.'

'Very good. So we all agree that FKB was a direct creation of the Big Guy Himself. I postulate that not only was FKB His creation but that FKB was His *finest* creation. Can anyone think of anything finer?' *Chocolate?* I thought. It's good, but not that good. Heads were shaken this time.

'Okay. Now, try to follow me here. I put it to you fine gentlemen, and Nobby, that the Creator gazed upon His finest and ultimate creation and knew His work was done. He had created that which could not be surpassed. He would have known with absolute certainty that He could never again match the perfection of FKB. As a result of this realisation the Creator would have had no recourse but to de-create Himself. Nothing left to prove, you see. Therefore, I hypothesise that there is no longer a Creator. Or … *God is dead!*' Brains said, far more convincingly than Nietzsche.

'So, let me get this straight,' Voice shouted. 'You're saying that in the 1970s this Creator suddenly realises He's created perfection with FKB. He then thinks, *Well, that's it then* and winks out of existence?'

'That is precisely what I am saying. Although, it may have been as late as 1981, when FKB was recognised as *Rear-of-the-year* but no later.' I sensed little lights igniting in little minds to illuminate the soundness of his logic.

'Wouldn't the Creator still be around though? He would have just retired,' Face said.

'Dead. Retired. It all amounts to the same thing – the absence of an active God. No-one in the driving seat.' I didn't agree. There's a difference between retirement and death. You can retire without dying but when you die, retirement is an unavoidable side effect. I nodded some more, recognising the inescapable truth, nevertheless.

This new knowledge left me with an ethical pickle. If I was to remain faithful in my intent to seek out the Creator on Judgement Day, to compel His final reckoning, would I still be willing to admonish God if He had retired? *Oh yeah, I would!* Even if the Creator chose oblivion over retirement I would nevertheless seek out proof. He wouldn't be the first to fake their death in order to escape justice. Cheating bastard!

Chapter Fifteen

Juliette entered my life with a savage tenderness I had not known could exist. The beginning of our relationship was defined by doubt. I doubted Juliette would contact me; she did. I doubted she would accept my clumsy, embarrassed invitation to dinner; she did. I doubted she would show up; she did. When I picked her up outside her halls of residence, on Saturday at 7.28 pm precisely, I wore my doubt overtly. I'd ensured I wouldn't be late by arriving twenty minutes early and parking, out of sight, on an adjacent street. It was an interminable twenty minutes as I shared my time between watching the clock and feeding my paranoia. I watched the surroundings for signs of police called to investigate the "suspicious-looking geezer in the suspicious-looking van". It's never been the same for van owners since the utilitarian vehicle became known as the conveyance of choice for discerning serial killers everywhere. At least it was good practice should I take up stalking.

I lasted until 7.27 pm, at which time I thought to arrive a few minutes early, preferable to a few minutes late. Juliette was waiting for me by the time I pulled alongside the kerb and disembarked to open the passenger door. 'Hi there. Still the gentleman, I see. Is everything okay?' she said, recognising the surprise in my expression. She had turned up!

'Yes, everything is fine, thanks. Oh, and hello. You look … really nice.' *Really nice? Grow up, Lavelle, you haven't found a bloody conker.* I closed the passenger door, leaving a decent pause after she sat to avoid trapping any body parts. I sat in the driver's seat and closed my door, blushing at my attempted compliment. 'I hope you weren't waiting long for me,' I said, resisting the urge to plead my two-minute margin of innocence.

'No. I was only waiting for twenty minutes,' she said. *What? But I could have been here twenty minutes earlier. Should I tell her? Yes! No! I don't know!* Juliette saved me. 'I'm joking. I'd just walked out of the door when you arrived.'

'Are you serious about joking?' I said, relieved I hadn't revealed my stalker-in-training inclinations.

She laughed. 'Your timing was perfect.'

'Good. It does not do for a gentleman to keep his lady waiting,' I said. *His lady? One minute you're a thirteen year old, the next you're a possessive fop.*

I was thankful when she changed the subject. 'I like your van. Is it new?'

'No, in fact it's close to thirty years old. It's been in the family for a while so I had it restored. Did the engine, bodywork and interior; the full works.'

'Not done *by* an engineer.'

'No. But *for* an engineer.' Not the most sophisticated comeback, but still an improvement on my *fucking idiot-ness* so far.

'Yes, it does look a bit too neat and tidy to belong to a working tradesman.'

'Or a serial killer!' I said, in a prompt return to fucking idiot-ness. *Nice one!* Her laugh sounded a little strained so I continued. 'You know what they say: serial killers always drive vans.'

'Do they now?'

'So it seems. But I inherited the van so I'm not a serial killer,' I said, then blurted 'and neither was my dad!'

'Glad to hear it. I'm sure serial killing would eat into your study time anyway.'

'It certainly would. That's why there are no serial killing courses,' I said, selecting stupid. 'No, there's no masking tape or duct tape or plastic sheeting in this van.'

'Well, I'm glad you've had a tidy-up for me.'

'What? Oh, it's always like this. Most of the time I use my bike; I don't live far from university and it gives me exercise.' I was blathering. 'Hey, take a look in the glovebox.'

'Let me guess. That's where you keep your trophies. Ears, maybe?' I smiled, relaxing a little. 'What's this? Balloons?' She laughed.

'Yep. Well; yes and no. They're the passenger-side airbags.'

I noted the pleasant sound of Juliette's laugh – light and natural. 'Well, I am honoured. It seems I have all the airbags to myself. Tell you what, if it looks like we're going to crash I'll throw one in your direction.'

'Why thank you. But, in the nicest way possible, I hope not to take you up on the offer.'

After much research, I'd chosen a local restaurant with decent reviews, located ten minutes' drive from Juliette's place. I knew exactly how far it was because I'd carried out a dummy run the previous evening. I was leaving nothing to chance, other than my tendency to fucking idiot-ness. I managed to keep my feet out of my mouth for the rest of the trip. By the time we arrived, settled at our table, drinks at hand and ordered our food, I felt more relaxed.

For the first time, I allowed myself to succumb. Juliette proved to be most delightful company. I listened intently to everything she said. My thoughts drifted as I pondered how Juliette was both easy on the eye and on the ear. She was so agreeable that I forgot my usual social awkwardness. I still endeavoured to disguise my physical anomaly but doing so was an unconscious response. I had chosen my apparel with care. Now that I was no longer encumbered by a uniform, I could be selective in what I wore. While it was difficult to find clothes that flattered, I could at least make an effort to wear that which was less unflattering. Given my fortunate financial circumstances, I could even afford to engage a tailor, who fashioned a number of made-to-measure items of the less unflattering variety. The end result was well worth the extreme discomfort I'd endured as I stood in front of the mirrors being measured up.

For dinner with Juliette, I wore a tailor-made shirt and jacket. As she spoke about her nursing work, I grew so relaxed that I thought to take *my funny* out for a spin. 'I couldn't walk for almost a year,' I said.

'Oh my God. What happened?'

'I'd just been born.' My funny proved to be firing on all fours as Juliette laughed.

But then, of course, I spoilt the mood, becoming carried away by the genial atmosphere and I experienced a brief, and unintentional, relapse to fucking idiot-ness. We were despatching our main course when someone started coughing rather loudly. 'Hey, I hope you know the Heimlich manoeuvre,' I said.

'Oh yes. One of the first things we learn in basic first aid.'

'I stopped someone from choking once,' I said.

'Did you?'

'Yes, I took my hands off his throat!' *Oh, nice one; well done! You really want Juliette to think you're an active member of the serial-killer community, don't you?* I put my hands over my face and shook my head. 'Sorry, I seem to be suffering with foot-in-mouth disease tonight. You must think I'm mad.'

She laughed in sympathy. 'No, I still think you're funny. A funny, nice gentleman,' she said, her smile so pretty.

'Thank you for omitting any mention of serial killing ... which I have brought up, yet again! You've been very understanding; better than I deserve. I'm really enjoying tonight. I think you're ... great.'

'That's because I *am* great!' she said, with a look that said, *why wouldn't you?*

That was my last notable faux pas of the evening. Time flew by and before I knew it, it was time to pay the bill. Juliette offered to contribute. 'Please let me pay for my meal; I still owe you a coffee.'

'Certainly not. That would not be chivalrous. Anyway, I found a roll of notes on the floor. It's kind of what I do.'

'Lucky you!' she said and, right then, I did indeed feel lucky.

We wandered back to the van, so comfortable that we walked close enough to bump now and again. I did not, however, possess the nerve to take the giant leap of holding her hand. It was 11 pm exactly when I dropped Juliette back at her digs. We'd spent three hours and thirty-two minutes together and I felt as if I'd just picked her up. I exited the car so I could open the passenger door, as any gentleman would. I opened the door and took Juliette by the hand to assist her egress. I briefly toyed with the notion of attempting *the kiss* but it was quickly rejected, almost as quickly as *the firm handshake*. As it turned out, the parting action was not mine to choose. Juliette put her hand on my shoulder and leant in to kiss me. On the mouth. It took a moment to comprehend what was happening and respond accordingly. I wasn't game to encumber Juliette with my tongue and so I practised restraint. Before disengaging, she touched my lips fleetingly with the tip of her tongue, sending a tingle from my mouth, all the way down south. I resisted the urge to specifically thank her for the kiss but was able to compose myself to the extent that I remembered how to speak. 'I hope we can do this again. That is if you want to, of course.'

'Yes, I'd like that, it would be … *really nice*,' she said, eyes twinkling. 'Call me.'

'I will do exactly that,' I said and watched until she was safely inside.

When she'd kissed me and I'd kissed her back, I'd experienced something of a stirring in the trouser department. A stirring that endured the drive home and that would not be relieved until I could take matters in hand. I now had more and better memories. This time they *were* masturbatory in nature.

* * * *

Lacking comprehensive knowledge of the romantic experiences of life, I had no precedent by which to measure the success of our first date. Thoughts of Juliette filled my world. My mind echoed to the memory of the kiss and I wondered if there could be something more. My distraction was evident so that even my two unperceptive uni buddies took note. 'You alright, Al? You're a bit quieter than usual.'

'No, I'm fine. Had a bit of a tiring weekend is all.' *Go on, ask me what I did. Ask me!*

'What did you get up to then?'

'Well, I didn't get home until late on Saturday. I had a date,' I said, attempting casual.

'What? A *date*, date with a female? Or do you mean the fruit?'

'I do indeed mean a date with a person of the female persuasion.'

'You never said anything. Did you just meet her?'

'No, I met her about a week ago. I must have forgotten about the date.' *My arse, I forgot!* I didn't tell them about the date because I'd thought there was a chance she wouldn't turn up. I'd wanted to avoid awkward questions.

'So did you meet her at uni?'

'No, I met her in town. She's a nurse.'

'Wow, a nurse. You know what they say about nurses, don't you?'

'That they work in hospitals?'

'No. They're supposed to have a healthy disrespect for the human body.'

'I was not aware of that.'

'Yeah, that's what they say. So did you ... you know?'

'What; did we have something to eat? Yes we did.'

'No. Did you ... discover that she had a healthy disrespect for *your* body?'

I chose not to share that I had disrespected myself. 'Excuse me; a gentleman never tells tales!' I said but then reconsidered. In fact, a gentleman would deny the taking place of carnal activity, with due deference to the lady's reputation. 'No, my body was totally respected, as was hers. We went out for a meal and then I dropped her off before going home on my own.'

'Still, a date with a woman; a *nurse* woman!' My buddy was impressed. 'So does she have a name? You going to see her again?'

'Yes, she has a name and it's Juliette and maybe,' I said. *I bloody hope I see her again!*

The guys were awestruck, almost as stunned as I at my progress with a member of the opposite sex. I was unsure what to do with their hero-worship. I never thought I'd be the alpha of any group. Standing up to an aggressive drunk and now dating a bona fide female. Then I looked at the guys; bespectacled and chuckling to themselves. Getting vicarious thrills through my tepid tale of social intercourse. The first flames of pride were extinguished by cold reality; a week ago, I *was* them!

* * * *

On Wednesday we determined that ours was not to be the life of the musical superstar. We'd watched *Platoon* the previous night; a surprising selection by Nobby. Legs had found a Motown album that included Smokey Robinson's "Tracks of my tears". He attempted to recreate a scene from the film where the bare-chested, sweaty "grunts" smoked grass and grooved to the sound of Smokey. While we approved of the soundtrack and their self-medicating pursuits, nobody felt inclined to remove their shirt. The lone exception may have been Brains, the fit bastard. Without exception, however, no-one wished to be on the receiving end of such a display.

Everyone had enjoyed the film, the lack of general chit-chat undeniable evidence of endorsement. It was with some restraint that we declined to commend Nobby on his choice of movie. The closest he got was a cool, 'It was alright, I suppose,' from Voice. However, the next day when in our Happy Places, Voice's resolve weakened. 'Tell you what,' he shouted. 'I liked the soundtrack, even the classical stuff at the end.'

'Yeah, it was good, wasn't it?' Nobby said, taking the lack of complaints as de facto praise, correctly for once. No-one cared to agree.

'I think a good soundtrack makes all the difference to a movie,' Face said. I didn't bother reminding them about *FAFDM* and Ennio Morricone. Philistines!

'Yeah, and I reckon a good soundtrack makes all the difference to a good CD,' Legs said.

'What? *Vaffanculo*, Legs; a CD *is* a soundtrack!' Brains said.

'Oh yeah, I suppose so. What I mean is; music is where the money's at. You need good music for a good film and you need good music … if you want to listen to good music,' he said with twisted logic. 'You know what? We should form a band.'

'That is the most brilliant idea I have ever heard, since you started that last sentence!' Voice shouted from deep within the land of sarcasm.

'Okay then, who can play an instrument?' Brains said. 'And by "instrument" I don't mean your knob,' he illuminated. There was no response. Perhaps, like me, there was reluctance to share stories of tragic trumpet lessons of years past. Brains thought to elicit specific feedback. 'Silent, can you play the guitar?'

'I don't know; I've never tried,' I said from the land of reason.

This approach continued for some time during which a number of minor complications to forming a band were identified. It seemed that no-one knew how to play an instrument, other than their knobs. In the knob department, we were spoilt for choice. After much heated discussion about who had the best singing voice, it became apparent that no-one was considered singer material. In essence, we agreed that we were all various degrees of bad. Also, no-one knew how to compose music or write song lyrics.

Brains summarised. 'So, excluding knobs, we can't play instruments, we can't sing and we can't write music or lyrics. Is that it?'

'That never stopped U2!' Voice shouted.

'No, unfortunately, it didn't,' Brains said.

'Bollocks; so near and yet so far!' Legs said.

'No, Legs. We are not even *close* to being near. You just want to be rich and famous.'

'No, I don't. I just want to have lots of money and be well known.'

I resisted the urge to explain that we had been beaten to the punch in forming a band. There already existed another group of seven geezers who were well-talented in the playing, singing, composing and writing departments. They even played ska; a genre of music which we held in high regard. The group also had a name that would, for us, have been most apt. *Madness*.

* * * *

It didn't take long for Juliette to grip my heart and squeeze. Other organs were also gripped but none as intensely as the heart. Date number one was followed a week later by date number two. A single mention of serial killing in the entire evening, raised by Juliette. 'No dead bodies? Glad to see you've cleaned up,' she said as she sat in the van.

'Of course. Unsecured corpses are *the* major cause of driver distraction.'

Another restaurant, another meal, more kissing. This time two kisses *with* tongue. The first before we'd even made it to the van to drive home. After kissing we'd walked. The restaurant was located in a well-to-do area. We'd strolled past big houses, with big gardens and big flowers; maybe with big burglar alarms to discourage big burglars. We'd tried to guess what the owners did for a living; how they'd earned their big houses. We'd agreed that the area must be inhabited by professionals of one form or another. Doctors, lawyers, drug dealers – the usual fare.

When I dropped Juliette off at her residence, I exited the van to open her door, like a gentleman. For a moment I thought she was leaning over to kiss me but I was conscious of my awkwardness in such an enclosed space. I hoped Juliette understood I wasn't trying to avoid intimacy. She understood. When she got out of the van, we kissed again, for a long time. It was a kiss that left me with a dilemma; what to do with my bulge. With enormous restraint, I resisted the urge to push up against Juliette and demonstrate her influence. Instead, I moved my groin away from her. Once more, I endured the uncomfortable drive home until I could take matters in hand.

Date number three started in much the same manner as former dates. However, the date ended in a very different fashion. I'd chosen a place close to my flat, an upmarket bar where we partook of drinks and snacks. I employed my ready wit to once again impress Juliette. A waiter asked for our drinks order. I asked him, 'Do you serve wine?'

'Yes, sir.'

'White wine?'

'Of course, sir.'

'Do you have Chardonnay?'

'Yes, sir.'

'2002?'

'I believe so, sir. I can check, of course.'

'Excellent. I'll have a pint of cider then.'

'Of course, sir,' he said, without breaking stride and left to fulfil our order.

'You know he's going to spit in your drink, don't you?' Juliette said.

'I'm pretty sure I didn't ask for spit.'

'I think that's exactly what you asked for,' she said, laughing. We decided not to eat heavily, both claiming a lack of appetite. In my case, it was altogether false. After a few drinks I encouraged Juliette to reconsider the menu, in case something took her fancy. She scanned the dessert menu. 'Death by Chocolate? What exactly is that?'

'It's where they beat you unconscious with a jumbo Toblerone and then run you over in a Cadbury truck. It's not fattening but it is *flattening*!' Juliette's sweet laugh caused me to swell with pleasure.

By this stage I had almost cast off my sense of awkwardness. Juliette's company was so captivating that her obvious ease was contagious. I'd been comfortable from the moment I'd picked her up and yet, I remained cautious. We talked, we listened, we drank, we joked and we laughed. We held hands for most of the evening and Juliette rubbed her foot against my leg at one point. I dared not respond in kind, envisioning a clumsy attempt ending in a fractured shin. We spent two fleeting hours at the bar before leaving, hand in hand. I'd parked the van close to my flat, the bar being a short walk away. As we neared the van I ignored my nerves and asked the question that had been on my mind all evening. 'My flat is around the corner. Would you like to see? We could have coffee. I know I need one.' I rambled on, from casual to nervous in seconds.

'Yes, that would be nice. I'd like to see how well you've hidden all the bodies,' she said, nudging me. The solitary body with which I'd needed concern myself was that of Wazza and he was gone for at least another three hours. He'd had an away game that day and by the time he got back to the uni bar and imbibed his usual, comprehensive skinful, he wouldn't stagger home before midnight.

'You're welcome to search thoroughly. I have nothing to hide.'

'How unfortunate for you,' she said, with sympathy.

I opened the front door and we climbed the stairs. I'd tidied up earlier, suppressing the notion of Juliette visiting for fear of jinxing any chance. The flat hadn't been dirty but had needed only a decent tidy, following the path of Cyclone Wazza through the common areas.

'Very nice. No signs of any bodies,' she said.

I can see one, very attractive body from where I'm standing, I thought. *Whoa there*, I cautioned myself as I felt the first stirrings. *Juliette is here for a tour and a coffee; don't get ahead of yourself.*

'So, why don't you make yourself comfy and I'll make the coffee,' I said, leaving Juliette to decide exactly how cosy she wished to get and where. When I returned, two mugs of coffee in trembling hands, Juliette was sitting gracefully on the sofa. She had chosen well, both in terms of comfort and for my subsequent positioning on the seat next to her. I handed her the coffee and sat next to her, close but not touching. I sat awkwardly, in order to face Juliette, wary of showing too much back.

'Mm … this is nice coffee.'

'Yes, it's filter. I'm not a big fan of instant coffee,' I said, going for sophisticated not snobby.

'So, I thought you had a flatmate?'

'Yes, Warren. He's out this evening, he won't be back for hours.' *That's it, Lavelle. Try to sound like there's enough time to get in a quick bout of serial killing.* I felt warm. I could sense my face reddening. I fumbled at the top button of my shirt, needing to improve ventilation.

'What's this? Are you stripping off already?' Juliette said, with a note of playfulness.

'Ah … no,' I said, face flushing. 'Just feeling a little warm, is all.'

'I see. Well, as long as you know that if you're going to start that sort of thing, you'll have to buy a girl a few drinks first. Oh, that's right … you already have.' She leant towards me, mischief in her smile. We kissed and I held Juliette with my right arm, my left being occupied in keeping the mug of hot coffee at arm's length, out of harm's way. By the time we disengaged, the effects of the kiss, combined with my awkward position, had resulted in extreme trouser discomfort. 'So, do you have your own room?'

'Yes, I have my own ... room,' I said, not daring to speak the word "bedroom" for fear of breaking the spell. 'It's the bigger room, has an en-suite.' *What are you doing; trying to sell her the flat?* Juliette smiled, waiting for me to continue. 'Would you like to see it?' I said nervously.

'Sure, but let's check out your bedroom first.'

We put our coffees down and I led Juliette to the bedroom. I was sure that Juliette must have been able to hear the loud thump of my heart. The violent butterflies in my stomach served to calm my arousal. I showed her around the room: the en-suite bathroom, the window, the chest of drawers and, finally, the bed. My ignorant innocence failed to illuminate my subsequent path. I had no experience on which to rely. I was adrift in uncharted waters. Since meeting Juliette I'd often wondered what I would do in this situation but had, without exception, rejected the notion as unrealistic. *Take it slow* was all that came to mind. Not particularly enlightening but it was all I had.

I took Juliette's hand, holding it with care. 'So what do you think? Nice place?'

She thought for a moment. 'Yes, it's a nice place; pretty much what I'd expect from a nice guy.'

'Oh, so I'm all about the *nice*, am I?' I said, not knowing where it came from.

'I don't know, are you?'

Okay, Lavelle; it's now or never. Take your time and be prepared for the "what are you doing?" I leant in, taking my time. Juliette leant in, taking her time. We met halfway. As we kissed, increasingly intense, I lowered my hand from the small of her back. When I got to the point of technical buttock touching I halted, lacking courage to proceed. Juliette held no such reservations and grasped my behind. I followed suit, mirroring her actions, using her movements as my guide. Even when she grabbed at my now hard-again crotch I exercised caution, not knowing how far this would go. It wasn't until we both lay on the bed, completely naked, that I would accept what was happening.

The heat of her sex surprised me. It proved a powerful enticement to hasten. I'd worried about this moment; that it would be over all too soon; that I would have a hair-trigger. My worries were unfounded. Any sense of haste was tempered by fear of the unknown. While my performance had more of the sprint about it than a marathon, there were no false-starts. When we were done, I reflected that she didn't so much take my virginity as I freely gave it up. A willing sacrifice to the Goddess of Sex.

* * * *

And so my sexual and romantic journey began. We became a couple. I saw Juliette every weekend; picking her up after her last shift on Friday and dropping her back on Sunday evening. We spent the intervening period doing "couple" things and not a little "coupling". Our time together flew past, too fleeting, while our time apart dragged out without end. I suffered a physical ache when deprived of her. Her presence alone could pacify the needs that overwhelmed me; a physical imperative that would not be denied, blinding all else.

On Friday afternoon, I'd sit in the van, awaiting Juliette's arrival, heart beating nervously and breath shallow and rapid. I thought that now I understood how Gelert had felt, awaiting my arrival from school; whimpering in excitement and furiously wagging his tail. Of course, my tail was of a different variety and affected more of a salute than a wag. The drive to my flat was protracted by the sexual expectation; an expectation fuelled by Juliette's ministrations to my painful swelling, sorely testing my resolve.

As soon as we arrived we would retreat to my room, hungrily clutching at each other. Our first coupling was quick and frantic, serving the desperate need to satisfy the denied passion of five days. We fell back sated, semi-clothed and pacified for the time being, and regaining our composure. 'And how are you, *Mr Nice Man?*' she said.

I lay back for a moment's thought, heart racing. 'You know what? I'm feeling fine and dandy; *super-nice*, you might say. And how are you today, young Miss?'

'Hmm, fine and dandy too. In fact, I'm hungry now. I seem to have worked up an appetite.'

'Is that so? Let's attend to your hunger then,' I said, eyebrows raised. We repaired our state of dress and proceeded to the kitchen where I prepared sustenance for the battle fought and for those to come. My meals were simple fare. *Pain grillé sous le haricot*, aka toast-under-bean, one of my more popular specialities.

As time passed, I shed some awkwardness and discovered new aspects to myself that I hadn't known I possessed. Through Juliette's patience and subtle guidance I developed a funny, romantic side. Our activities became ritualised: sex first, then food, then family-oriented entertainment. We would splay out on my bed, playing board games; *Guess Who* being a favourite. I didn't allow myself to become encumbered by rules or traditional methods of play. 'Is your person a United supporter?' I said.

'How am I supposed to know that?'

'Well, is he facing the wrong way? Is it a picture of the back of someone's head?'

'No.'

'Right, then he's not a United supporter,' and so on. Rather than focus on obvious facial features, I asked about the individual's mood or preferences. Most of the time this approach did nothing to affect a winning position, but my goals were elsewhere.

After a spell of deep and silly questions I asked, 'Is your person extremely horny?'

'It's you, isn't it?'

'Yes. Well done. You win … me! We should start calling this game what it really is; "Guess Who's Horny?"' I said.

'I think that would be the easiest game in the world.'

'I'm only easy for you,' I said, dead serious, and moved across the bed to pull her close. We flipped the remaining faces down for the sake of modesty. Then we flipped each other. This coupling was slower, more considerate, more exploratory and tender. The passion and need still present but now countered by restraint.

In the after-glow, I held Juliette against me, her head on my chest. 'You know what, we're playing the wrong game,' I said to her once.

'Are you sure? I didn't think you'd want to change games now.'

'No, not that. Maybe instead of *Guess Who* we should play *Connect Four.*'

'Let me guess, would it be *Connect Foreplay*?' She totally got me.

And I held her like that until she drifted off. I always fell asleep after Juliette, spooning her with care so not to wake her. I feared bursting the dream of her; a dream from which I did not wish to awaken. I timed my breathing so that, as she exhaled, I would inhale, breathing her in. I fell asleep to the rhythm of her breathing; feeling content and completed. I was becoming hopelessly lost and I didn't want to be found.

What did she see when she looked at me? Did she see something more than I was? Did she see the potential for something better? I told myself, *Don't expect too much. Take it one day at a time. Immerse yourself in the experience.* I was being gripped with an intensity I didn't appreciate at the time. An intensity I could not hope to appreciate until I had been released.

Chapter Sixteen

There are moments experienced during the pursuit of Casual Therapy that prove to be insightful and profound. These moments are uncommon, occurring only under very specific circumstances. A rarely sighted Sasquatch in our forest of trivial bullshit. Most of the time they expire unrealised due to the general indolence that fuels the gang. Of more common occurrence are those moments that are thoughtless and superficial. These moments endure. Legs was often the originator of "the stupid idea". One of his most memorable suggestions related to developing a rival networking service to Facebook. Mark Zuckerberg need not fret.

'You know Facebook, the social network thingy?' Legs said. We nodded or grunted by way of affirmation. 'Well, I reckon there should be an anti-social network called *Arsebook*.' This provoked a few groans but no-one cared to interrupt more actively. 'No, listen up. It would be for people who don't want anything to do with all that social media bollocks. They could join Arsebook as a protest. Just to let everyone know that they don't give a shit about what people have been up to or what mood they're in. I mean, who cares?'

This explanation was greeted by silence for a few seconds until Brains spoke. 'Let me get this straight. You're proposing to develop a networking site for people who don't want to network?'

'Yes, precisely.'

'*QujmeH moQ*! So, what you're suggesting is that people who don't want anything to do with social networking do the online equivalent of jumping up and down, waving their arms above their heads and shouting "Yoo-hoo everybody; stop looking at me!"'

'Maybe …' Legs sounded less enthusiastic.

'Well, forgive me if I suggest your idea is fundamentally flawed.'

'Yeah well, it's still in the early stages. You know, I'm thinking outside the box.'

'I think you're talking out of your *Arsebook!*'

'I'd back you,' Bomber said. 'It would have to provide a safer alternative to Facebook.'

'What do you mean "safer"?'

'Well, think about when someone is murdered or goes missing, victims of foul-play type situations. They always have pictures of the victim on the news, smiling or drinking or whatever, don't they? Every single picture is from their Facebook profile. It must mean that serial killers use Facebook like a menu, where they trawl for potential victims.'

'I'd be more worried about the early morning dog walkers and joggers,' Brains said. 'It's always them that find the body. You can't tell me that it's pure coincidence.' No-one disagreed. No-one agreed. No-one cared. 'You know what, Legs? You do have something of a knack for coming up with the most useless ideas. What was it last week?'

'That was "sign language for the blind",' I said.

'Yeah, that was a good one,' Legs said, with pride.

'No, Legs, that's my point. It wasn't a good one.'

'Well, you're missing the point. The point being that there *is* no point!' Legs said from the land of confusion. Silence descended. As we so often did at this stage of these types of discussion, there was a collective and comprehensive chorus of inhalation as we deeply imbibed, seeking escape, not enlightenment.

After a spell, the self-medication affecting as it was designed to affect, I gave free rein to my inner philosopher. I considered, *Does everything we do and everything we say* have *to have a point? Does it matter, as long as we are heading in the right direction; we have a desti-nation with purpose? But what if our destination has no purpose; what if it is pointless? Well, then that* would *be* "sign language for the blind".

* * * *

We became *a couple,* and I acquired friends-in-law as a by-product. We were invited to her friends' gatherings together, although I knew it was always a case of *Juliette plus one.* I was not affronted. I was content being the plus one to Juliette. Being with Juliette brought me out of my shell. Our emerging relationship provided me with confidence when socialising more broadly. Nevertheless, I retained an element of shyness, in particular when left to my own devices, unable to feed off Juliette's immediate self-assurance. I didn't mind. My nervousness at Juliette's absence merely served to prove how good she was for me. When together, I enjoyed the company of her friends, her nursing colleagues and their partners. I learnt to function as part of a couple, even if I was the co-star.

We were invited to an engagement party, for the first time as *Juliette and Alan*; acknowledgement of my official status of partner. We attended the get-together that had been organised by one of her nursing friends and her fiancé. We'd even shopped for the engagement present together when I, of course, deferred to Juliette's selection. I still suffered from foot-in-mouth from time to time, most often when carried away by the situation; when I forgot myself. On this occasion, my attempt at wit was *too* witty. I became *the Smartarse.*

Juliette introduced me to her friend's new fiancé, Rob. 'So, you must be the ex-boyfriend then?' I said as my attempted witticism sailed wide of the mark. It met with blank stares all around while I tried to salvage my faux pas. 'I mean, you're the *fiancé* now. You're not the boyfriend anymore.'

'Oh, I see. Right,' he said, not seeing at all.

'And he's not even had a drink yet!' Juliette said, grasping me by the arm. 'Let's do something about that, shall we?' She led me away.

'Sorry; it sounded funny in my head. Not so funny outside it though.'

'Don't worry about it. Rob's a decent enough guy but he's not the brightest. If you see him laughing in a couple of hours, that means he just got it.'

Comforted by her reassurance, but chastened by my indiscretion, I became more circumspect. I was still able to relax and enjoyed the remainder of the night, conversing with less mentally challenged guests. I was companion to Juliette. The night was pleasant. No-one got too drunk and I heard Rob laugh towards the later hours, although I wasn't prepared to take credit for his mirth. Juliette enjoyed the occasion too, or so I thought.

We arrived back at my flat after midnight, both tired. We'd had sex before we left. On the drive home I thought we should simply fall asleep in each other's arms. However, now we were in my bedroom and Juliette, disrobing, revealed her peach-coloured, silk lingerie and, even more important, the promise of what lay beneath. My thoughts turned away from the soporific and towards the carnal. My awakening libido proved a distraction so that I barely heard Juliette's remark. 'Did you see the state of Tracy? What the hell was she trying to wear?'

Did she mean Tracy who wore the short, dark-blue dress, the skirt cut about three inches below her crotch, the dress with colourful tropical flowers all over it, perhaps orchids of some kind, a big red one on her left boob and a big yellow one on her right boob, but they would have to be big to stand a chance of covering *those* boobs, the dress a couple of sizes too small with a plunging neckline and Christ knows how she was able to stay in it? Yeah, I'd seen her. 'No, my sweet. I didn't notice her.'

'Seriously? You didn't notice her boobs trying to escape? She was pushing them in everyone's face!' Juliette sounded annoyed for some reason.

A picture of innocence, I shrugged my shoulders. 'You know I only have eyes for you, my darling,' not wanting to go there. I might have been naïve but I wasn't reckless. Everybody had seen Tracy, or, to be more precise, Tracy's boobs. She had her own *Great Wall of China*-type phenomenon happening. No matter where you were in the room you could see them. In fact, after attending the party I was pretty sure that the Great Wall of China was no longer the only man-made feature that was visible from space.

I recalculated my decreasing chance of coitus and sighed inside as Juliette slipped out of her lingerie and into her glorious nakedness. And yet I smiled, content in the knowledge that she was here with me to hold. My recalculations proved to be over-conservative as Juliette wriggled against me, finding her comfortable place as I spooned her, holding her to me.

'Hello! What do we have here? Has somebody come out to play?' she said, reaching behind her and clutching my erection firmly. 'Well?'

'Can't you feel him answering?' I said. She did. And then, *we* did. Twice, in fact.

* * * *

Months passed during which I felt truly alive for the first time. I was a part of something greater. I was living up to my potential. Juliette became the core of my existence. I lived for our time together. I realised she'd taught me the true meaning of so many things that had been simple words before I'd met her. And not only words like "menstruation". She'd taught me new meanings for old words that I thought I knew. She taught me the meaning of *sex, companionship, purpose, longing* ... But the realisation of what was happening was always tempered by doubt. In my times of uncertainty, I asked myself, *how can someone like her be with someone like me?* I always knew that Juliette was more experienced romantically. How could she not be? I assumed that she had a past; former boyfriends, previous romances. And yet, I allowed myself to be lured away from my doubt. Juliette inspired my sexual confidence, so much so that I determined, at last, to take the initiative.

Saturday evening, the two of us alone in the flat. We'd decided to eat in and had finished a Chinese take-out. We were in the living room, lying opposite each other, playing cards. I stood, saying nothing. 'What are you up to?' Juliette said, eyes twinkling. Still, I did not respond. I moved across to the sound system, selected my acoustic weapon and hit play. As I returned to where Juliette sat, the track began; Terence Trent D'Arby with "Sign your name across my heart". I reached down, offering her my hand. She took it and I lifted her effortlessly, drawing her into my grasp as she stood.

I held her with care, my right hand flat against the small of her back. Her right hand in my left as we moved in time with the music. Juliette smiled, relaxed and beautiful, closed her eyes and leant in to me, head on my chest. We had all the time in the world as we swayed, holding each other close, just us and the music. In her ear, I whispered, in time with the track, 'I'd rather be in Hell with you, baby, than cool Heaven.' She held me closer. I brushed her cheek with my open mouth. I looked down into her face, into her opening eyes, pupils wide, inviting. I kissed her brow with care, then her cheek, then her neck. I felt her shiver. With my right hand, I brushed her hair behind her ear and softly held her face. I kissed her on the mouth. She kissed me more firmly and parted my lips with her tongue. I responded in kind, our tongues entwined. She pulled herself towards me, pushing against my hardening.

Her arms reached around my neck and I lifted her with ease, our mouths locked together. I carried her to the bed and set her down. We sensed each other's arousal. The hardness of my undeniable awakening; the scent of her oestrous, at once most delicate and most powerful. We took our time undressing each other, resisting the compulsion to hasten. I ran my hand along her side, caressing her hips. I cupped the curve of her buttock and, reaching down, ran the tips of my fingers along her sex. She was wet, hot and yielding. Her hand skimmed my stomach, electricity in her touch. She took me in her hand and squeezed – hard. I was inflamed and aching as she guided me into her. I moved inside her as we surrounded each other.

We took our time, negotiating that intimate path between passion and patience. We savoured the coupling, discovering each other. The weight of time inescapable, we shuddered as we climaxed together. Our bodies spent, we held each other. There was no sense of emptiness, only completion. My senses were overwhelmed by her touch, her smell, her taste. I was filled with undeniable love for her.

And so, with lowered voice, I told her. 'Juliette … *I love you.*'

The silence lingered, deafening me. I thought perhaps she hadn't heard. Perhaps I hadn't actually voiced my declaration.

'That's … nice,' she said, it seemed to me intoned with sadness.

And the voice of doubt spoke loud. *You see, that's what happens when you let your guard down. That's what happens when you don't listen. Fucking Idiot!*

* * * *

We always knew when Nurse Debbie was doing the rounds; Brains wore his best, one-size-too-small tee-shirt. Nurse Debbie was young, voluptuous and downright gorgeous by any standard. Other than Brains, the gang reacted with mild discomfort at her presence, threatened by her blatant femaleness. We didn't often discuss things sexual in nature, other than as ammunition to be loosed at the unwary. Nobby leant against the doorway of the gym, scanning the newspaper while scratching at his crotch.

'Oi, Nobby. If you haven't found it yet, you never will. Face it; you have no knob!' Bomber said.

'Highly amusing,' Nobby said, as he continued reading and scratching.

'What's up, Nobby? You got crabs?' Voice shouted.

'How could he get crabs? He's never had a shag!'

'You know how Mary gave birth to Jesus, even though she was a virgin? That was the Immaculate *Conception*. Maybe Nobby got crabs through an Immaculate *Infection?*' Voice said.

'I am not a virgin!' Nobby protested.

'That's true. I heard Nobby lost his virginity last week,' Voice shouted.

'Yeah, his arse is still sore!' Face said.

'*Your* arse!' said Nobby. 'I've got more chance of scoring a shag than you, you ugly bastard.'

'Well, Nobby, at least I can position myself so the girl doesn't have to look at me while we're doing it. Never heard of *doggy position*? No female would ever want to be anywhere near you, never mind shag you. That's even if you could find a prostitute that is blind, deaf, has no sense of smell and has massively low self-esteem. In fact, you'd be hard pushed to keep them in the same fucking room as you even if you paid up-front!'

'Perhaps a kind, ex-prostitute might bequeath Nobby a shag in her will,' Bomber said.

Time to intervene. 'Leave it out guys, you're heading down *Bad-Taste Boulevard*,' I said.

'Yeah, no-one wants to hear about Nobby,' Face said. 'Anyway, for your information, Nobby, I have an *FWB* situation with a girl I was at school with.'

'What, you have a *Friend With Benefits*?'

'What, does FWB stand for *Friends With Benefits*? I thought it stood for *Fairly Wide Bottom*. She has a huge bum; it's lovely.'

Right then, Brains lunged for the remote control, as he had spotted Nurse Debbie approaching. He did what he always did in these circumstances, selecting "Night Nurse" by Gregory Isaacs with impeccable timing. Nurse Debbie materialised at the entrance to the gym. Nobby had beaten a retreat. She was greeted with the lyrics, 'Tell her it's a case of emergency, there's a patient by the name of Gregory'. She flashed Brains a smile. 'Hello, Gregory.' Brains nodded in response. The rest of us squirmed in private at the exchange, maintaining an uncomfortable silence.

Following Nurse Debbie's withdrawal, Nobby resumed his position at the doorway. From time to time Nobby, without encouragement, regaled us with newspaper articles he considered noteworthy. Sometimes, one of the gang rescued the paper to gauge the accuracy of his paraphrasing. It was not uncommon for Nobby to embellish the story somewhat. Some call it *lying*. Today, the noteworthy tale related to an American.

'Listen to this. Some geezer in America was discovered dead in his home. He had a belly full of sleeping pills, had cut his wrists and was found hanging in his exhaust-fume-filled garage. But get this; the official cause of death was a bullet to the brain!'

'Fuck me; that was one serious cry for help!' Voice said, quieter than usual.

'That wasn't a cry for help. That was a cry of "Fuck you all!"' Face said. There followed a protracted silence. Those of us who'd thought our Happy Place was unassailable were proved wrong. The mood plunged as the silence continued. Inhalations were deep and many, searching for reparation. No-one cared to check the article.

'Fuck me; you give *stupid* a bad name!' Brains said, bristling with anger. 'You know what, Nobby? You really are the most insufferable twat there has ever been! You push the boundaries of "twattery" to unimagined limits. You are a true pioneer who deserves to be recognised as such. They should introduce a prize in your honour. *The Nobel Twat Prize!*' Nobby simply shrugged his shoulders and continued reading the newspaper. He seemed unaffected, although the paper quivered a little.

Face lightened the mood, quite unintentionally. 'I don't understand. Why did Alfred Nobel's parents name him after a peace prize?' There followed a great inhalation.

As I endeavoured to find my Happy Place, I considered Brains' proposition. *The Nobel Twat Prize.* I liked the sound of that; it resonated. Of course, if it was ever instituted, Nobby would not prove victorious. The impediment to his nomination would be a lack of global influence. While his contributions to all things *twatty* were numerous and significant within the confines of the hospital, his wider contributions would go unrecognised.

Even so, the *NTP* would be the most vehemently contested prize ever. The nominations would be prolific, coming from all walks of life; an infinite spectrum of candidates. Even discounting Nobby, I could think of more than a few nominees.

* * * *

I had dropped the *'L' bomb* and it had failed to detonate. It had been a spectacular dud. The memory of it overshadowed the remainder of that weekend. Juliette was reticent, lost in her thoughts, unlike her usual outgoing self. It appeared that I had touched a nerve, but

I lacked the courage to confront her for fear of provoking a more extreme reaction. My inner doubt had found its voice and would not be silenced. We were both introspective when I dropped Juliette back at her digs on Sunday. She was pensive. I was apprehensive. When we kissed goodbye I knew her thoughts were elsewhere.

I told myself this was a minor bump in the relationship road, to be expected after several months together. Life wasn't meant to be easy. Surely *I*, of all people, understood that. When I called Juliette later in the week, repressing my anxiety, she reassured me all was fine. She sounded tired but she was at least there. Our conversation lacked the humour that once carried our exchanges. We arranged to spend time together that weekend. After hanging up, my insecurity refused to recede and so I resolved to take action.

The university had a Baking Society, one of the few attractive activities promoted during Fresher's week. The nature of the society had invited my appetite, but the notion of mixing with others had not appealed to me at the time. Now though, I was a different beast, capable of surviving the social vagaries. It was also now less probable that my tamed clumsiness would turn the kitchen into a battlefield. I thought to surprise Juliette with newfound culinary skills. It was a long-term plan.

I arrived at the appointed location to sign up for the single-term course but my inner voice still encouraged doubt. I refused to succumb and my resolve was reflected in an attempt to be droll. A female student handed me a form. 'Hi there. If you could fill out the form and return it to me, we'll get you signed up,' she said. I thanked her and took the form to a nearby desk to complete.

I thought to engage my funny and in that spirit completed the form. When I returned the document, I watched as the girl read through my details. She chose to ignore my comments under "Sex"; I'd written, "Not at the moment, I'm filling out a form". I suspected she would have seen a variety of responses in that particular section, but surely none as witty. She read on. 'When is your birthday?' she said.

'20th of April.'

'Yes, I see that, but what year?'

'Every year,' which was technically correct.

'And what's this you've put under "First Name"?'

'It says "I've only ever had one name".' She didn't raise my response under Last Name. I'd written, "Please refer to First Name".

Unimpressed, she sullenly returned my form. 'I've highlighted the areas you need to redo,' the page a mess of highlighter. And I thought, *Juliette would have laughed. She would have smiled her glorious smile. She would have found it funny. Juliette gets me.* I didn't return the form. I don't think I was missed.

At the time I didn't realise the extent of the alteration to our relationship, despite the assertions of my inner voice. When I next saw Juliette, it seemed she had cast off her sadness, but now there was a barely discernible distance between us, measured by my unrequited declaration. Although my passion was at first seasoned with insecurity, we maintained our rituals. We traversed the obstacle I had planted, setting ourselves back on the path. The voice was not silenced but it was quietened. And yet I was unable to relax. One night I exposed my vulnerability. We had just enjoyed an engaging contest of coitus and lay back on the bed, totally naked. I sat up, preparatory to dressing to prepare a pot of coffee. I paused too long, my back to Juliette.

'What's that?' she said.

'What?' I said, shoulders tense, conscious of my exposed back.

'Wow, you've got a massive pimple right in the middle of your back!' I didn't know what to say. Should I say the impressive pimple matches my impressive back? I almost said that her medical curiosity might be more intrigued by the funny lump on my testicle. A funny lump that subsequently proved to be not funny at all, but quite serious.

'Can I squeeze it?'

'Have I ever denied you anything?' I said, relieved at the apparent misunderstanding. Still, I didn't understand why she was so keen to rid me of my pimply passenger. Perhaps the nurse in her was unable to allow my ailment to go untreated.

By our eight-month anniversary, which I alone acknowledged, I felt reassured to the extent that I suggested to Juliette that we move in together and share my flat. 'Hey, Jules, I've been thinking.'

'Oh dear, that sounds like trouble.'

'What I was thinking was, how about we move in together? You could live here ...' I said, '... with me.'

Juliette was silent for a moment before speaking, her response barely audible. 'I don't think that would work out.'

'Why not?'

'It's too inconvenient. Where I am now is handy for shift work. It's right next to the hospital.'

'I could drop you off and pick you up whenever you needed. It wouldn't be a problem. You could even take the van yourself,' I said.

'You know I can't drive. And anyway, what about Warren?'

'What about him? It's my flat, I can tell him he has to move out.'

'No, it wouldn't work with all the hassle.'

'We could *make* it work; get a place together closer to the hospital. Maybe think it over?'

'No, leave it, Al. It won't work.' She was resolute.

'Okay. I'm sorry. I got carried away. You're right, of course.' I was irresolute. 'Hey, you want to go out for dinner tonight? We could go to the place we had our first date,' I said, trying to change the subject and lift the mood.

'What, the café around the corner?'

'No, not there. Remember the nice restaurant we went to when that guy was choking?'

'Oh, yes. I remember,' she said, it seemed without favour. 'Yeah, fine. We can go there if you want.'

'Okay, great,' I said, not feeling in any way great. I had already booked a table in a wasted romantic gesture. It was then that I began to appreciate the asymmetric commitment to the relationship.

Juliette's mood failed to improve, despite my ever-weakening efforts to inject a sense of romance and playfulness. That night, our rituals neglected, fuelled by anxiety, I held on to her as sleep eluded me. As usual, I held her with care but I sensed something new to her. As if she possessed an impenetrable shell. I knew then something vital between us had changed. Something was damaged or lost. My proposal had been the catalyst that marked the beginning of the end.

Juliette cast off her easy-going disposition. She became preoccupied and unsettled. I didn't understand what was happening; what went wrong or how to make amends. She voiced her unhappiness, but seemed unable or unwilling to particularise her grievances. I frequently asked, 'What's wrong?' But she always responded, 'It doesn't matter.' The implication was clear; there *was* something wrong. The "it" that didn't matter. In the end I capitulated, finding no solace in the ensuing silences.

A week after the unromantic anniversary I discovered what I thought could be the reason for the dramatic alteration to Juliette's demeanour. It was Monday morning and I'd finished shaving. I was distracted by concerns of Juliette as I dropped the used razor into the bathroom bin. I did a double take, looking closer to confirm there was something of interest within. Something white and plastic, looking like a bald toothbrush. I removed it from the bin and noticed the ammoniac hint of stale piss. There were no bristles but there was a small window. There were two distinct red lines running across the window, right next to a small hieroglyphic. It confirmed that two lines indicated a positive test result. The pisser was pregnant.

I stared long and hard at the small, plastic bombshell. At first I thought I held the answer to my recent troubles. But then more questions began emerging, prime among them, *why did she not tell me?* I wasn't sure how I felt. This data would require major processing. I was confused, but more than anything, I was scared. Fear of the unknown and with so much unknown the fear was considerable. I had never questioned the use of contraception, my blossoming notions of sex concerned solely with the act and not of the consequences. I tried to recall when I'd last emptied the bin, attempting to date when Juliette was first aware. No more than a week or so. How long would she need before breaking the news? It didn't matter; she hadn't shared, so not time yet.

I had discovered the evidence but not the courage to confront Juliette with my knowledge. Believing that I now knew the reason for Juliette's withdrawal did nothing to lessen my anxiety. Rather it served to replenish my worry with a more potent fuel. I possessed no inclination to test our strained relationship, preferring to resort to my customary approach. I would say and do nothing. I would wait and I would hope that the situation would turn out okay.

* * * *

Juliette spent less and less time with me, claiming shift work as the pretext. The last time I picked Juliette up from her residence we dined at a nearby restaurant. We spent an uncomfortable, uncommunicative evening together before she returned straight to her digs. Juliette exhibited signs of unease. She seemed to find fault in everything. The food, the drink, the service, even my driving were subjected to her vague criticism. I was incapable of coping.

Exactly nine months from the day I first encountered Juliette shopping, she stopped taking my calls. My frequent attempts at contact must have persuaded her that I would persist until she responded and so, I received a text message. "I need a break, it's not working". Not even one word for every month together. Seven words to change my life. Seven words to break my heart. The message merely proved to stimulate my attempts at contact. Within moments of receiving the message, head pounding at the implications, I called her to discover her phone turned off.

I sent increasingly desperate messages. At first protesting. "I don't understand. It's not fair. Tell me what I have done wrong". Then begging and debasing. "I'm so sorry. Tell me what to do. I'll do anything. I want to give us a chance. I need you!" Then feeble and pathetic. "I miss you so much ..." Every word a painful truth. I didn't care about what I became. I didn't sleep, I didn't eat; I cared only about redeeming myself. After a week of silence, I received a second, final and repeated, message. "I need a break, it's not working."

I sought solace in the bottle. I took to the tequila concealed in my room but that didn't suffice. I needed further fuel to escape my plight. I allowed my self-inflicted intoxication to liberate my thoughts, taking them to previously forbidden places. I became angry. *How the hell could she do this to me? How dare she? I deserve answers!* And so, I determined to confront Juliette. A half bottle of tequila in my pocket by way of an alcoholic alibi to excuse inexcusable behaviour, I drove to Juliette's lodgings. I sat in the van, hours passing, while the cold rain fell, the street lights reflecting sharply off the wet pavement. I steadily drank from the bottle, the liquor burning my throat and fuelling my outrage. An outrage that dissipated and was replaced by apprehension and anticipation the moment I saw Juliette materialise from the darkness. I emerged from the van and intercepted Juliette before she reached the entrance to her digs. I put my hand out towards her but fear prevented touch.

'What do you want?' she said, surprised to see me.

'I wanted to talk to you; I needed to see you.'

'There's nothing to say.'

'No, you can't just say that! I want to know what I did. Why won't you tell me?'

'It wasn't working.'

'What does that even mean? That's no answer!' I said, frustration growing.

'I have nothing to say to you,' she said and moved to pass me.

But I would not be placated. I took her by the arm. 'I know you're pregnant.'

At first her expression registered surprise, but then grew tired. 'No, I'm not.'

'But I saw the tester.'

'I am not *now* pregnant. Do you understand?' I understood. I struggled through the numbness.

'What's going on? Are you hiding something?' I said.

Juliette looked at me with an icy expression of which I did not think her capable. 'If you don't let go and leave straightaway, I *will* call the police!' The fire of her words burned and I released her. It took some moments to appreciate the finality of what she'd said. She had rejected me in more than one way. Even the notion of something that was partially me had been too abhorrent for her to accept. Unworthy of contemplation. Unworthy of discussion.

For the last time, I looked at Juliette and in that instant I recognised something in her expression. The realisation was like a blow. I had seen the flared nostrils, set jaw and hard eyes before. The look spoke a little of fear and anger, but possessed also of enjoyment. More than anything though, it was *daring and defiant*. It was the same expression that Kevin had worn as I reached down to remove his remaining hold on me.

I knew then I would never get a straight answer from her. I walked despondently towards the van, not turning back. I was walking away but Juliette had already gone. Somehow, I made my way home, recalling nothing of the drive. I swallowed the remainder of the tequila and made my way to the off-licence to replenish my stocks. As I encouraged the alcohol to take hold, wanting to achieve a state of drunkenness in which memory could not survive, I wallowed in pathetic misery.

We were no longer together and yet, still I learned by Juliette. Again, she taught me the real meaning of words and sensations I thought to know. I discovered the true meaning of *confusion, pain, emptiness, rejection, loss* … Juliette taught me that you cannot experience true loss without first possessing something worth keeping; something without which life is diminished. My emotions were numb. I felt a physical ache that originated from my chest and radiated to the extremities. Never was an ailment more aptly named than *heartache*.

My attempts at positivity were feeble and easily repelled. I told myself she had promised me nothing and she had delivered on that promise. I berated myself for being pathmatic, rejecting my drunkenness as just excuse. I thought back to those moments when I expressed doubt, when I despised myself for my weakness. Now, it seemed those moments of weakness had in fact been moments of lucidity.

I couldn't let go, I had to understand why I'd been discarded. What we'd had was real; we'd been a proper couple. We'd even listened to Sting together, for fuck's sake! And not merely pre-coital Sting; the solitary acceptable form of Sting, and, even then, *just* acceptable. I was inspired to move to the music system, unsteady on my feet, and scattering CDs, found Sting's crime against music. I walked to the kitchen and ceremoniously dropped the disc from a height, into the bin. It took three attempts and my sense of achievement didn't last.

At first I'd tried to avoid recollections of intimacy, refusing to acknowledge they even happened. But now, I allowed the memories to wash over me, to justify the heartache. I was to find that all the pain I had endured up until that point was nothing. The pain I would suffer would become everything.

I had asked myself: *How can someone like her be with someone like me?* Now my inner voice answered, without contradiction … *She can't!*

Chapter Seventeen

Doc Friendly can sometimes be a real lazy bastard. I may not be his most loquacious patient but referring to ancient case notes still smacks of desperation. Or maybe idleness. The fact he has reference-worthy notes undermines one of my therapeutic theories. The doc is always armed with his notebook, in which he maintains a record of our conversations and my progress, or lack thereof. I have never seen what he chronicles. Once the session is underway, the book is always closed, cover up, when not hidden on the doc's lap. I suppose the doc has grown weary of recording such comments as: "Doesn't want to talk. Changed the subject again. Still won't give a straight answer". As such, I couldn't find fault if the doc simply doodled, as he talked and I equivocated. I thought he might constructively use the time, perhaps composing his shopping list. Maybe he does, but there have been times when he documented my feedback, with commendable accuracy.

I saw the doc referring to notes compiled early on in our ongoing engagement, roughly two-thirds of the way back. I was at a disadvantage as much of the proceedings were a vague memory, at best. My drug-induced mental fog proved to be an impediment to recall. Sometimes the doc's narration caused me to smile as I listened to his official record of our discussions. I took delight in the quality and nature of much of the pure bullshit I'd spoken when my faculties had been less encumbered. This day was not such a case, his records being agonisingly accurate.

'We've talked about your relationships in the past, Alan, in particular with regards to your father. I can see in my notes that you were
involved in a romantic relationship with … *Julie?*' I didn't correct
him. I didn't like where this was heading. 'We never touched on what
happened there, Alan. I think perhaps you felt it was all a bit too soon;
you felt uncomfortable going into detail at the time.' *Uncomfortable?*
There's a fucking understatement! Still, I didn't answer; he hadn't
asked a question. He knew the rule.

'Would you like to talk about it now?'

Balls, I would! 'No, I don't think so.'

'You seemed to have expressed some hurt.' *Which is why I don't
want to talk about it!*

'So, you don't feel that "time heals all wounds"?' *Do I arse!* I
refused to dignify the banality of the question and gave the doc my
"Really?" look. He responded with his finest sympathetic expression; smiling, of course, demonstrating empathy at my plight. But he
wouldn't yield just yet.

'Well, Alan, they say "It is better to have loved and lost than to
have never loved at all". There must be some positives that came out
of the relationship. Perhaps some good memories? Most of the time,
when we look back at relationships there were good times and bad
times. To some extent we choose how we wish to remember these
things.'

'Is that so? And what if, hypothetically, subsequent events cause a
need to re-evaluate some of those so-called *good memories?*'

'What do you mean, Alan?'

'What I mean, Doc, is that sometimes you can't see how ugly
someone is on the outside until you find out exactly how ugly they are
on the inside.' *Go on; write* that *down!*

'That's very interesting, Alan. Quite revealing.' *Interesting?
Revealing? Try totally fucking profound!* I upheld my policy of no question, no response. The doc, acknowledging this, continued. 'Well,
Alan, it has been said that to be human is to love, that we are defined
by our capacity to love. Unfortunately, it doesn't always eventuate that
love is everlasting. Circumstances change. Feelings change.' *That's*

where you're taking us? I was hugely disenchanted at the doc's lazy and thoughtless approach. He'd gone from tired clichés directly to downright bullshit. The doc wasn't performing up to his usual standard; a definite off-day. Perhaps he needed to self-medicate.

My disappointment was such that I relinquished my rule and responded. 'Humankind is *not* defined by its capacity to love. Love is merely the best that nature could come up with to promote the human race. It's all about the genetic process. Boy meets girl; they fall in love; they settle down; they have children. Their DNA is passed on to future generations; the biological imperative satisfied; job done. Love your partner then love your children. And how often does love of partner fade once there is love of child? All the time. Do you truly believe love is necessary for humanity to endure? Beasts of the field don't need love. You can observe that same genetic imperative all throughout nature. All the greater mammals display the hard-wired *procreate-nurture-and-protect* instinct. No, love is redundant. Love is fleeting. Love is a myth created by people who want to appear more dignified than animals in heat!' Doc Friendly was astonished at my uncharacteristic monologue. I'd said more in two minutes than I had in the last two months. I noticed he'd stopped writing, his smile minimal.

'If you don't mind me saying, Alan, that sounds quite cynical for such a young man.' I refused to respond, but I thought, *I'm not bloody wrong, am I? Oh, that's right, you can't say that, can you?*

If he considered my views on love as cynical then I would wait for the doc's return to form before hitting him with my views on hate. When my naïve belief in love had been exposed for the simple-minded bullshit that it was, I had considered that which the doc had raised. I'd questioned the relevance of love to the human race. I'd been hurt. I *was* hurt, that was plain, and that hurt fuelled what he called my cynicism. But I recognised that inescapable truth and made allowance for it. Rather than converge on love, I allowed myself to consider the Point of Hate.

Unlike simple love, hate has no place in nature. It is an emotion, exclusive to humans, that serves no apparent purpose. Hate manifests itself in many forms. Violence is merely one indolent manifestation. Violence is only a default expression of hate, requiring no real thought or premeditation. But hate can be a protracted journey. Hate evolves. Hate endures. Hate is more relevant than love. To hate is to be human. Nothing is as genuine as unadulterated hate.

Love can last the duration of a single life at most, but hate can span generations. I do not believe that our capacity to love defines us as a human. I believe that our capacity to hate defines us as humanity.

* * * *

I sank into a deep depression, wallowing without shame, in misery. The pain of the loss was numbed for a time by my attempts at drunken oblivion. I tried to distract myself with study but I was unable to summon the necessary determination. My studies became neglected. Like my father, I chose capitulation. Not knowing what to do, I did nothing. I reached a place where I stopped eating. Then I stopped sleeping. I didn't give up on sleep, rather sleep gave up on me. I spent wakeful hours in a state of indignation, infuriated at the injustice of it all. I continued drinking to excess until one evening when my intentions started down a dangerous path.

During one drunken session, I resolved to uncover the truth, no matter what the cost. She would not escape me. I vowed to hunt Juliette down; follow her to the ends of the Earth if necessary. I would seek her out in the darkest corner of the darkest place, in the darkest hour of the darkest night. And when I found her I would *make her pay*! The violence of my intent appalled me, shocking me out of my drunken ramblings. But what would I actually do? Would I exact my revenge; damage her as I had been damaged? No; all I could do would be to tell her that I never wanted to see her again and not mean it.

Then I stopped caring. It didn't take long for the alcohol to abandon my system. I didn't regain my appetite straightaway. The abuse of my digestive system served to sensitise my constitution. Unable to contemplate solids, I chose to replace alcohol with caffeine. The heartache persisted, although it no longer defined who I was.

Instead it became a reminder of who I once was. Even when I thought my appetite should be restored, still I could not eat. A dull ache in my stomach and groin constantly afflicted me. I lost weight. My clothing loosened. I spent many hours in my bedroom, listening to sentimental music. Much of which I had listened to with Juliette; typically at various stages of coitus. In an endless loop, I listened to "When a man loves a woman" and "The first cut is the deepest", Percy and Rod working overtime.

Since the dissolution of my relationship with Juliette I hadn't seen much of Wazza. Being an infrequent patron of the kitchen since my appetite absconded, I remained in my bedroom for the most part. Wazza maintained his demanding drinking schedule, interrupted by rugby practice and the minimum of study and so we rarely connected. Lacking my constant reminders, Wazza's rent was now months in arrears. I started wondering what he was doing for food. I hadn't been shopping for some time and doubtless, he had deprived the flat of all things edible. I decided to take a walk, then pay a visit to the supermarket. I thought the walk and subsequent browse through the food aisles might inspire my appetite. I freshened up first; shaving for the first time in weeks, then showering.

I selected my apparel with care, choosing a tailor-made jacket. For fear of stimulating unwelcome memories, I'd avoided wearing particular items of clothing, but no longer. I slipped on my best pair of boots – very comfortable and very expensive. I'd purchased them months ago, when shopping with Juliette. She had reproached me for my lack of footwear, driven by her familiarity with my range of expensive clothing. I hadn't bothered to explain that in the shoe department, I was very much typical, which was not the case for clothing. She'd dared me to make the purchase, despite the cost, and I'd accepted the challenge. I laced up the soft, russet-coloured, calf-leather boots, savouring the state of comfort in which my feet now existed. Restored in part by the token display of self-indulgence, I set out, feeling better. Not *fixed*, but *improved*.

The fresh air was invigorating; a welcome boost to my constitution. I walked at a steady pace away from the centre of town. Soon

I found myself on the pastoral fringes, where the concrete footpaths gave way to grass verges. The day was clear and crisp, a gentle breeze at my back. As I returned, making my way towards the supermarket, I was unable to divest myself of the nagging ache that emanated through my stomach into my groin. I thought to pacify my ill-treated digestion and bought an assortment of essential groceries to that end. I returned to the flat, equal parts restored and aching, relieved to drop the two bags of groceries on the kitchen table. As I made to unpack the bags, I noticed my bedroom door was ajar. As I made my way to my room I heard noises. I pushed the door open to be greeted by Wazza rummaging through my drawers.

'Hey, what's the score, Wazza?'

'Oh hey, Taffy. You scared the crap out me! I was wondering if I could borrow some socks, I don't have any clean ones.' I shuddered to think of the state of his hosiery. Wazza's method of checking sock freshness involved throwing them at the wall. Sticking to the wall indicated a failure in which case he went in search of less sticky examples.

'Judging by the fact that you're already holding a couple of pairs of my socks, you seem to have assumed my permission.'

'Oh yeah. Well, you weren't here. I didn't think you'd mind.'

'Alright. Make sure you wash them properly before you return them.'

'Cheers. No sweat, Taffy.'

'There had better not be! And I haven't forgotten that you owe me rent. What's it now; three months?'

'Yeah, sorry about that. I'm still waiting on a big cheque. I should get it later this week. As soon as I have, I'll get you the rent. Next week at the latest.'

'Make sure it's no later, otherwise you'll have to register as an official charity,' I said, not feeling at all charitable.

'Cheers, mate. Oh, by the way, I haven't seen your girl recently. Everything okay?'

'No, that's over,' I said, the ache returning.

'Sorry to hear that. Never mind. Plenty more fish in the sea,' he said, full of cheer. *And plenty more lodgers on the streets*, I thought. I didn't respond though, being ill-prepared to engage the Cockney Wide-boy.

As Wazza left my room, socks acquired, I noticed his covetous expression as he spied the grocery bags. 'And get your eyes off them too,' I said. 'And your hands!'

'Hey, Taffy. Would I do that to you?' Wide-boy Wazza said. I returned to the kitchen and replenished the empty cupboards, putting temptation out of sight, if not out of reach.

The following day, Doctor Jeffries visited. His work brought him to the area every few months. He sat in the living room as I prepared coffee. 'I haven't heard from you for a while, Alan. Is everything okay? Still seeing that charming young lady?'

'Could be better, could be worse, I suppose,' I said. I retrieved the coffees from the kitchen and walked them over to the doctor.

'Are you feeling well, Alan? You seem to be in discomfort. Have you hurt yourself?' *Christ, how much time do you have, Doc?*

'To be honest, things aren't great at the moment. Juliette and I broke up about a month ago and it's taking me a while to sort myself out. I'm moving a bit funny because of some discomfort in my stomach.' It felt good to talk. I realised that being around Juliette had given me an appreciation of verbal interaction.

The doctor put his coffee down. 'I'm sorry to hear about the break-up, but you need to focus on your health. I'm concerned about the discomfort you say you're experiencing. Tell me, where is the discomfort? Is it a sharp pain or a dull ache?'

'It's an ache. Pretty much constant, although it gets worse when I exert myself. It's in my lower stomach and my groin. I haven't been eating well lately; I think my stomach is protesting.' I didn't trouble him with details of my boozing.

'An ache in the lower stomach and groin, you say? Tell me, have you noticed any unusual swelling or lumps, in particular around your groin?'

I ignored the new discomfort of discussing my existing discomfort. 'Well, I do have a lump on my testicle. I first noticed it a couple of months ago.'

'Oh, Alan. You must have that checked out. Chances are it's nothing serious but you need to get that confirmed. I have a colleague, Doctor Keyes, who practises locally. He's a urologist. Let me call him and I'll arrange for you to see him as soon as possible.'

'Okay, Doctor. If you insist.' I wondered why I didn't feel concerned.

'And, Alan, I'd like to prescribe you something to get you through the short term. Forgive me for saying but you don't seem yourself at the moment. I think the medications you were prescribed previously helped, didn't they?'

He referred to the knock-out pills he'd prescribed when Dad died. 'Well, I don't think they did any harm.'

'Okay then. Take one tablet a day, before bed. If you experience any adverse side effects, especially in mood, contact me at once,' he said, handing me the prescription. 'I'll try to get you in to see Doctor Keyes this week. Promise me you'll keep the appointment and that you'll contact me if you need anything – anything at all.'

'Sure thing, Doctor Jeffries. Will do. And thanks.'

'Try to engage with things you enjoy. Remember how we used to enjoy our weekend walks?'

What, with my dead father and murdered dog?

'I'll try, Doctor.'

* * * *

Three days later, I attended the appointment with Doctor Keyes. The urologist proved to be ill-disposed; borderline arrogant. I didn't know what strings Doctor Jeffries had pulled to get me the appointment but whatever eventuated did not appear to be to the liking of Doctor Keyes. After brusquely questioning me and then roughly examining me he was keen to give it to me straight. 'Well, Mr Lavelle. From what you've told me of your symptoms and from my initial examination, I think the best course of action would be to get you into surgery. To be safe, we should remove the testicle.'

Interesting choice of words; "*We* should remove *the* testicle". Shouldn't he have said, "*He* should remove *my* testicle"? Receiving no response he continued. 'You say you noticed the lump a few months ago. You should have sought advice earlier.'

I scanned the room, looking for the time machine he must possess, his advice being helpful only in the past. Still I did not speak. 'Mr Lavelle, do you understand what I've told you?'

'I believe I do. *You* want to remove *my* testicle,' I said. Was I supposed to care? Was I supposed to be reduced to a babbling wreck, wringing my hands and begging the doctor to save my life? Fuck that!

'Mr Lavelle, it's likely the lump is cancerous, therefore the best course of action is to perform an orchiectomy before it spreads. In the long term, it shouldn't affect your fertility or your ability to have an erection.' I didn't bother telling him that the sole thing likely to rise any time soon was my eyebrow.

'Okay,' I said.

'We'll book you in to do the procedure within the next few weeks. Best to get it out of the way. If you speak to my reception-ist she'll provide you with all the details. I'll see you in a few weeks. Good day, Mr Lavelle.'

Dismissed without ceremony, I went to seek out the receptionist of legend. I approached her desk, noting she was on the phone. Before I got close, she raised her finger as if in warning, erroneously assum-ing my wish to speak. I resisted the urge to look at the ceiling towards which her digit indicated and waited, as had always been my intent. She returned the phone to its cradle and looked at me. She waited for me to speak while I waited for permission to address her. She cracked first, her time being more valuable than mine. '*How* may I help you?'

'Doctor Keyes said I need to arrange to have an orchiectomy performed.'

'Yes, well, we'll have to make all the necessary arrangements before the procedure,' she said. *What, I can't simply walk off the street and have a ball chopped off?* Fucking miserable woman! It seemed that urology isn't the most entertaining branch of medicine. Can't say I'd enjoy messing about with people's plumbing all day but she's only the desk jockey; what's it to her? 'There are a number of forms that must be completed,' she said, handing me a clipboard overflowing with paper. 'While you're doing that I'll check the doctor's records and schedule the surgery.' I took the clipboard, thanked her and smiled to see if it might improve her disposition. It didn't.

I sat in a chair that could have only been designed for a doctor's waiting room. The instrument of torture amplified my existing discomfort. It took a while to work my way through the forms. Every detail of my life needed to be declared in order to deprive me of a testicle. I returned the clipboard to the receptionist, timing my delivery for minimum inconvenience. 'Your procedure has been scheduled for the twentieth of this month at the University Hospital.' Ten days' time; soon enough. She examined the paperwork 'Everything appears to be in order. Oh, just a moment, you haven't completed this section.' She handed me back one of the forms. She seemed a little less miserable to discover I had erred.

'The procedure requires an overnight stay in hospital. You need to nominate someone to pick you up the next day. It's an insurance requirement, to ensure you get home safely.'

'Fine, I'll take a taxi home.'

'I'm afraid that isn't allowable. It must be someone known to you; a responsible person.'

'Known to me? I could ask their name before I got in. Anyway, they'd have to be responsible enough to drive a taxi.'

'Mr Lavelle, you cannot take a taxi home from the hospital,' she said, as if speaking to a dim child. Perhaps she assumed I'd had the surgery regularly. But how often could someone have the procedure, after all? Twice at most.

Irritation increasing, I persisted. 'I don't have a personal driver and I don't have anyone who can pick me up. It will have to be a taxi. I can't see the problem. I'll sign a declaration to that effect, if needed.'

'Surely, Mr Lavelle, you have friends or family you can ask.'

'I can assure you, there is no-one I can ask.'

She persisted. 'But there has to be *someone.*'

'Why are you not listening to me? *I have no-one!*' I turned and walked out of the surgery, the beginnings of a migraine mounting. My head throbbed; my skull and brain seeming out of sync, as I made my way to the van. I sat still for some time, savouring the silence, waiting for the pain in my skull to recede to a level where I could drive home.

I took my time driving home, swallowed some aspirin as soon as I arrived and collapsed on my bed. I lay in the darkened room, head supported by a couple of pillows and breathed deeply. As the headache waned, the throb in my lower regions became apparent again. And then I noticed another returning ache, this time in my chest. I remembered the last words I'd said to the receptionist. "I have no-one!" Then I remembered the heartache.

* * * *

The manner in which my visit to the urologist concluded served as a potent reality check. The recent improvement to my mood proved temporary, unable to be sustained under the persistent onslaught of the receptionist and the implications of my response. I retreated to my room to struggle with my insomnia. Until that point I hadn't thought about those that I'd once considered friends-in-law; people I'd believed to be common acquaintances of myself and Juliette. They hadn't contacted me since the split and I'd made no attempt to contact them, convinced of their actual status as friends by association. "Friends-on-loan" at best. *Bollocks to them, I don't need them.* I cast away the sentimental music and replaced Percy and Rod with Korn and Slipknot, seeking sanctuary in my angry place. I basked in the uncontaminated truth of their rage, allowing the dissonance of the music to compress my thoughts. I wanted a freight train to rampage through my head, blurring what were once the distinct edges of my depression. It was temporary relief, but relief, nevertheless.

I didn't follow up with the urologist. I didn't wish to reconnect with the doctor or his receptionist, preferring instead to remain connected to my testicle. The fate of my testicle proved to be dynamic, however. Doctor Jeffries rang two days after my ill-fated appointment. 'Hello, Alan. It's Doctor Jeffries. I've been speaking to Doctor Keyes. He said there were some problems; that you won't agree to the procedure.'

'No, Doctor. That's incorrect. When I tried to sort out getting the procedure done, his receptionist refused to listen to me.'

'Was this concerning who would pick you up from the hospital?'

'Yes. Three times she asked the question and three times I gave the same answer but she didn't want to listen. I'm sorry. I know you went to some trouble to get me the appointment but if she won't listen to the answer then she shouldn't ask the question.'

'Look, Alan, I don't know the details of what happened, but you do need to nominate someone to pick you up from the hospital. They need to sign a form before you can leave with them. It's a strict policy. Doctor Keyes has agreed to keep the original appointment for the twentieth. I can pick you up on the twenty-first. Please, will you let me do that, Alan?' He sounded worried.

'I've already imposed too much.'

'Of course you haven't. I can reorganise my schedule to conduct some business when I'm there, so it won't be an imposition. You'll need to make your own way to the hospital on the twentieth though. Is that okay?'

'Yes, sure. Of course. Thanks, Doctor and I'm sorry. I got frustrated. I'm just ... anyway. I'll be there. I promise.'

'Good, Alan. It's for the best. And don't worry, Doctor Keyes' performance in the operating theatre is far superior to his bedside manner, but don't tell him I said that.'

'I can't promise that, Doctor. It might slip out under anaesthetic.'

The surgery went ahead as scheduled and by the afternoon of the twentieth I found myself dazed, sore and reduced by one testicle. The pre-op consultation with Doctor Keyes wasn't as awkward as I'd anticipated. The urologist's conduct was succinct, if not chummy. He must have preferred to *do* his stuff rather than *talk* about his stuff. When I regained consciousness in the recovery room, I found myself attended by a plump, middle-aged nurse who proved to be in possession of all the friendliness that Doctor Keyes and his receptionist lacked. 'Hello, Alan, do you know where you are?' she asked in a low voice. I tried to speak but could only manage a groan; my throat sore. I nodded with caution. 'Okay, dear, it might take a few minutes to come around. Don't worry.'

Out of sight, a younger voice spoke. 'Who was his surgeon?'

She scanned the clipboard at the foot of my bed. 'Let's see ... ah, Doctor Keyes,' rolling her eyes at the name.

'Yeah, he is lovely, isn't he?' I croaked.

She laughed. 'Well, Alan, dear. I think you're more or less back with us, don't you?'

I managed a smile, appreciating her friendliness. *What is it with me and nurses?* I thought. My smile faded.

I failed to sleep that night. The ache in my groin was replaced by a sharper, more distinct pain. Neither were my thoughts in a healthy place. The surroundings inspired unwelcome thoughts of Juliette. On the morning of my release, I was introduced to the pharmacist who provided me with painkillers to help me through the hardest part of recovery. I accepted the tablets and prescriptions, knowing I was now one step closer to being discharged. With a sense of relief, I met Doctor Jeffries at reception and he drove me home, all forms signed and accounted for.

'So how are you, Alan? I spoke to Doctor Keyes and he said surgery went well. You should have the results of the biopsy in a week or so but he's confident any damage has been contained.'

'Good to hear that,' I said, not caring, only wanting to get home.

'And how is ... everything else?'

'Yeah, okay, I guess. As well as can be expected.'

'Are you sure? You seem a little down. You must take care of your health. I'm not trying to make light of the procedure you went through, but at least it's been sorted. The hard part is over.'

It didn't feel like the hard part was over. It felt like the hard part had never gone away. It felt like the hard part waited with interminable patience, ready to carry me back to reality should I stray. 'I'm just tired.'

'At least you'll be home soon. You can rest then.'

The remainder of the journey was completed in silence, I had nothing to say. How could I tell him that my last thought before the anaesthetic took hold was, *You know, it wouldn't be so bad if I didn't wake up.* Pathmatic!

Doctor Jeffries saw me back to my flat, waiting as I cautiously climbed the stairs, nursing my painful groin. I preferred the sharp pain that had replaced the dull ache. It was cleaner and more predictable. I insisted on making coffee, wishing to demonstrate my independence. It would have been complemented by biscuits but the Cockney Wideboy had struck; it was a biscuit-free environment. We chatted while coffees were finished and it came time for the doctor to leave.

'I'll head off now, Alan, I have another appointment soon. It's good you have the surgery out of the way now.' He shook my hand, grasping mine in both of his. 'You must take care of yourself, Alan, it's so important. After all that has happened … your father would be so proud of you; he really would. Please, if there is anything you need; if you have any problems at all, it doesn't matter what they are, please contact me, Alan. Will you do that?' He looked worried.

'Thanks, Doctor Jeffries. I will.' *No, Doctor, I won't.*

He left me alone. I wandered into my bedroom, closed the curtains and lay on my bed in the dark, not bothering to remove my boots. The familiar pounding of an impending headache resounded through my skull and I reached for the bag of painkillers. Three strengths of medication had been prescribed, to be dispensed to match the level of pain suffered. Most powerful first when the pain is greatest. I opened a drawer and dropped the bag inside, intact, where they sat next to the tablets prescribed by Doctor Jeffries. Needed but not wanted. What I wanted no-one could provide; morphine for the soul. I welcomed the distraction of the pain, focusing on the hurt in my groin as the hurt in my head receded. I tried to sleep, but I could not. I lay awake, watching the dark ceiling, weighed down by irrepressible depression.

I'd thought that enabling the physical pain would lessen the mental anguish, but I'd been wrong. Again. I began to understand that every time I lost someone close to me, I also lost a part of myself. And it was a good part of me. The part of me where decency lived. First Dad, then my canine companion and then my love. Had I retained any capacity to love? Is the best I could hope for simply an absence of hate? Is this what's in store for me; losing myself one piece at a time? The gradual loss of my spirit no longer adequate, now I'm to be steadily reduced physically? The pounding in my head resumed. I determined to return to the bottle and spite the warning on the meds that said, "May increase the effects of alcohol". I remembered a hidden stash, stored deep in a drawer, safe from a scavenging Wazza. I pulled out the bottom drawer, ready to retrieve the long-forgotten bottle of tequila. Fully opened, I noticed a slip of paper, fallen from the back of the drawer above. The drawer Juliette once used. I retrieved the bottle and put it to one side.

I sat on the edge of the bed and unfolded the note, curiosity growing. I found there were two notes; one in Juliette's handwriting and another I didn't recognise.

Inrush of noise.

As I read through the notes, first Juliette's and then the other, my heart slowed. Every heartbeat was like the blow of a sledgehammer to my chest. Blows that reverberated in my skull. It was impossible to focus. The ever-increasing pressure in my head blurred my vision. I had to read each word over and over again. The chaos impeded my comprehension. As my thoughts swirled in the mental maelstrom, the words started to settle; to solidify.

'Don't know how much longer I can put up with this. I miss you. Can't wait to get back to you. I miss when we fuck. Thinking of you always. I love you, Baby, Juliette.'

And then the reply:

'Hey J, don't worry, you'll be free of him soon. I know how hard it is for you. It won't be long. Can't wait to get you in the shower. I will scrub his stink off you; you know how thorough I am. I can't wait to fuck you too. Love you always, Babe, P.'

My head resonated to the thump of my heartbeat; pressure built to an impossible pitch. I had too many thoughts. I could not contain them. I didn't want to believe; I was *unable* to believe. I didn't know what was real. This could not be happening. Everything was out of control. I felt like a passenger on a plane spinning towards the Earth. Except the fall never ended; there was no ground upon which to crash, to provide release. Between massive heartbeats, I saw the bottle of tequila. I grabbed for it, urgently. I flicked the top off and took a long, deep draught. The liquor burned my throat and hit my empty stomach with a jolt. My burning entrails did nothing to lessen the commotion in my brain.

Ah, yes ... that's it.

I stood, on shaking legs, emptying the contents of the drawer onto the bed. I picked up the bag of painkillers and opened them. It took some time. It was hard to focus on twisting and pushing and twisting and pushing and twisting and pushing. At last, I emptied the bottles of their contents. My quivering hands scattered them across the bedspread. *I can.* I retrieved the tequila from the other side of the bed. I grabbed a dirty glass from the chest of drawers. *I must.* I scooped up the tablets from the bedspread into the glass: white, beige, pink. *That's it.* Twice, I spilled the contents of the glass, but in the end I corralled all the tablets; the glass half full, not half empty. *Nearly.* I took a last look at the glass and raised it to my trembling mouth. *Yes.* I tipped the glass and took half the tablets into my mouth. *Yes!* I had the tequila in my other hand. I lifted the bottle to my mouth and took a pull. *Fucking yes!* I held the contents in my mouth for a second. *Now!* I swallowed. It was almost too much to swallow the mixture; the tablets huge in my throat. I had to push down the rising bile. *No, no, fucking no!* Eyes watered with the effort; I kept them down. *Yes.* The second mouthful of tablets was easier, I was practised now. *Oh yes!* I took another big slug of tequila. The burning was less severe. I lay down on the bed, making myself comfortable. One more pull from the bottle.

The swirling in my head started to fade as the drugs took hold. The spinning slowed and was replaced by a sensation of falling.

And then it happened.

Just after the spinning stopped and before the falling started, I experienced an instant of utmost clarity. There was perfect silence. There was perfect stillness. I experienced an ecstasy of perfect equilibrium. I did not breathe for fear of disturbing the balance. Tears froze in my eyes; not ready to be shed. Then I knew. *Life is imbalance. Death is equilibrium.*

I am *here*. I am *now*. I am exactly where I'm *supposed* to be. The euphoria was pure and absolute.

And then the falling started …

Chapter Eighteen

I lie on a vast, deserted beach. The sand is golden. The ocean is clear and azure. The air is white and dazzling. The sun hangs high in the sky — radiant and ancient. The sand is cool where my body rests upon it. The heat grows, burning my skin. I am trapped between the cold sand and the scorching air. The waves advance and my feet begin to sink into the cool, inviting sand. As the waves lap higher up the beach, I sink further. Now my legs and arms are submerged. My frigid limbs intensify the sensation of burning to my face and torso; all that remains exposed. The waves climb higher, reaching my neck, leaving only my face uncovered. The sand freezes my body as the sun burns my face. Panic touches me as the water laps over my face. Then I welcome the immersion, as my head sinks into the sand. I do not need breath. The cold sand numbs me; erases me. I still my thoughts; craving oblivion. But then I feel a vicious tug. With relentless violence, my entire body is pulled from the sand. My sanctuary is violated. The heat of the sun is unbearable …

I awake, terrified and confused. As realisation dawns, I am utterly devastated.

* * * *

I noticed the beeping first. The sharp sound penetrated the fog in which I found myself. As I struggled to converge on the noise, other sounds emerged. I discerned low, incoherent voices and the sound of metal upon metal. Then clicks. Sounds of machinery doing its job. I resisted the lure of the fog and tried to open my eyes. My eyelids were impossibly heavy. An age passed before I opened them; my vision blurred. It took a few seconds to focus as my surroundings materialised. I lay on a bed, incapable of counting the tubes emerging from me. The beeping came from behind, to my left. The monitor echoed my heartbeat. The room was large, white and austere. Other than a single nurse, I was the sole occupant. I realised with discomfort that I was naked. My upper body was exposed above the bedclothes. I tried to move my hand to lift the bedding, but my arms didn't belong to me. I tried to speak but my throat burned. I tried to marshal my thoughts, but I didn't know what was wrong with my head. It felt hollow and disconnected. I concentrated on blinking my eyes, as if the return of sight would inspire my other dulled senses.

The nurse saw I was awake. 'Mr Lavelle, can you hear me? Do you know where you are?' she said. I tried to speak but only managed a rough croak. Keeping my fragile head motionless, I closed my eyes. My vision improved when I reopened them. 'Mr Lavelle? I'm going to call for the doctor,' she said, her voice loud. She punched a button on the console next to me, and I heard a corresponding tone outside in the corridor. I tried to swallow but my parched throat protested. I had never needed anything as much as I needed a drink right then.

The doctor arrived, attended by another nurse. He moved to the foot of the bed, where he picked up a clipboard. He read from it, then replaced it. 'Can you hear me, Mr Lavelle? Do you know where you are?' he said in an officious tone. I was unable to respond. I blinked and tried to swallow again, wincing in pain. 'You're in hospital, Mr Lavelle. In ICU. You were brought in several hours ago. Do you remember anything?' I wanted him to go away. I wanted to be left alone.

'Yes, Mr Lavelle. You did something *silly*, didn't you? It was touch and go for a while but we were able to save you.' His voice penetrated like a drill to my skull.

I recalled what I did; what I *tried* to do. Then I understood what *he* did. Hate rose up in me. I wanted to reach into his big, stupid mouth and tear his fucking jaw off. I wanted to rip his fucking tongue out. I wanted to turn him into a gurgling, bloody mess on the floor. I wanted him dead. I tried to grab him but my muscles were lead; immovable. I raised my head from the pillow by just an inch, but it was enough to bring the doctor closer. 'What's that, Mr Lavelle?'

I felt completely spent. There seemed nothing left of me. Somehow, I summoned energy from wasted muscles. After another age, I lifted a hand to grasp him by his wrist. He leant in closer, wanting to hear what I had to say. I struggled to speak, lacking the strength to form words. I strained with the effort. *'Nnn ...'*

'Hmm?' He leant closer.

I found reserves of energy from deep within. *'Uuunnn ...'*

He leant even closer. The tempo of the beeping increased as I shook with a final, desperate effort.

'CUNT!' The word reverberated throughout the room and beyond, sounding like the report of rifle fire, echoing across a tranquil valley. Then the solitary sound was the beeping of the monitor as it slowed. My head dropped back to the pillow. I was drained, barely able to keep my eyes open.

The doctor detached my hand from his wrist with ease. His expression was one of pure contempt. He turned and left, a nurse trailing in his wake. I felt a bone-deep exhaustion and closed my eyes. Noises withdrew into the background as I yielded to the longing to retreat into the fog. Even in my muddled state, the audacity of his words had not escaped me. The doctor had supposed I would be indebted to him, for rescuing me.

He had not done me a kindness by saving my life. He had done me a vile cruelty by depriving me of my death.

* * * *

While it would prove difficult to find a more dedicated band of scientists, we are not unreceptive to trying new things. There are rules that apply, of course. The major pillars of Casual Therapy must remain undisturbed. Therefore, the gang agreed to consider Brains' suggestion as an extracurricular activity. We were assembled in the gym, devoting our time to the application of pillar number two. It would be safe to say that most were residing in their Happy Place when Brains made his announcement.

'Hey, guys, your attention please. And you, Nobby. I have a proposition,' he said. 'Through means which I shall not divulge, I have in my possession some fine examples of psychedelic fungi.'

'Huh?' Legs said.

'I think Brains has some *'shrooms.*' Voice yelled.

'*Bien jouer.* Voice is correct. 'Shrooms, magic mushrooms or even "flesh of the gods" as those right-on cats, the Aztecs, called them. Not only do I have a quantity of this product in my possession but I am willing to share, should demand dictate.'

'What's the catch, how much do you want?'

'Face, your cynicism is unwarranted. I require nothing from anyone, not even Nobby. I am willing to share, to allow the gang to collectively enjoy the experience. Notes may be taken, should you wish to deem the occasion a scientific endeavour.'

'I don't know,' Nobby said. 'What are they supposed to do? Aren't they dangerous?'

'Maybe if you leave them in the plastic bag when you swallow them. They are harmless, in no way addictive and they have none of those nasty side effects from smoking grass you are so worried about. It's all upside, Nobby.'

'I dunno, they're still illegal. Must be some reason for that.' Nobby needed convincing.

'Nobby, legality is such a grey area and the effects of 'shrooms are well documented. Euphoria and altered perception being hints of what to expect. We should all take the plunge together. What say you boys? *One for all and all for one?*'

I found it noteworthy that no-one questioned the possible hazard of mixing two hallucinogens. Still, I didn't in fact make a note and, like the others, indicated my willingness to participate. And so the dedicated band of scientists took yet another bold step for the sake of the greater good. Heroes we …

Brains revealed a plastic bag full of small, light-coloured mushrooms. By the time the contents were distributed, we had four of the special fungi each. We returned to our designated spots and sat looking at each other.

'What's up, boys? Don't know how to eat 'shrooms? I suppose I'd better demonstrate. Down the hatch!' Brains said and swallowed his allotted fungi. This proved ample motivation for the rest of us and we followed suit. At first, I thought to chew before swallowing but when the greasy, cold 'shrooms entered my mouth I wanted to get them as far away from my tastebuds as soon as possible. I swallowed and waited for something to happen. Then I waited some more.

Legs asked the question for all. 'How long do they take to work, Brains?'

'Shouldn't take long. Maybe a few minutes.' I wasn't sure what to expect. Already in my Happy Place, I didn't wish to travel far. The *'shroom* place may well be a place where the grass is greener but I prefer a place where the grass is *stronger.*

After ten minutes some of the lads felt the fungi needed assistance and so lit up. With the exception of Bomber, who claimed his nose had fallen asleep, there was a general lack of any noticeable effect. Perhaps the experiment would have yielded different results had we consumed the 'shrooms before we embarked on pillar number two. The performance of our control group suggested the grass may have triggered a blocking effect.

At first, Nobby had prevaricated, but then consumed his mushrooms once he'd observed their non-fatal properties. At first silent, a preferred state for Nobby, second only to *absent*, Nobby sat down at an unoccupied piece of equipment. A strange look passed over his features. He might have smiled, but it was unpleasant, nevertheless. He discovered he had hands and raised them in order to see them better. An expression of dumb wonder overcame him as he waved his hands near his face. A couple of *oohs* and *aahs* escaped him as he continued his hand-waving endeavours. I watched with disbelief as Nobby then discovered he could achieve the same effect by keeping his hands still and moving his head instead. This extraordinary discovery merited a more protracted response. Nobby remarked, 'Oh my God! That is *awesome!*' However, Nobby's constitution appeared incapable of sustaining the level of awe as he took his face in his hands and leant forward, shaking his head.

I tore my attention from Nobby and looked around to see if anyone else was witnessing this remarkable performance. I entertained the notion that the 'shrooms were indeed quite potent and that I was hallucinating. One look at Brains' huge grin convinced me otherwise. He saw exactly what I saw, despite the disparate level of entertainment derived. The others seemed to not notice or, more likely, not care about what happened to Nobby.

Fifteen minutes on from initial ingestion, my perception remained unmoved. I determined to provide feedback to the instigator of the experiment. I sidled over to Brains, who grinned, ear to ear, at Nobby's condition. 'Brains, Old Man. I think you know me well enough to appreciate I'm not one to complain needlessly. I also like to think I know you well enough to understand you appreciate getting to the point. I have to say that these mushrooms aren't doing it for me. To be blunt; they are shit!'

'Close, Silent. To be accurate, they are in fact *shiitake.*'

'Are you serious?'

'Got them straight from the kitchen. Not even a hint of the magical about them.'

'What? Then what's happening to Nobby? He's off his head!'

'Fucked if I know. Perhaps the power of suggestion proved too much for his tiny mind.'

'Shit, Brains. You can't let him go on like that. The silly sod is crying! Man, you have to put him out of his misery.'

'His misery is my joy. He's been asking for it, Silent. Him and his fucking newspaper articles!'

'But he's *Nobby,* for Christ's sake. That's what he does. You've got to tell him.'

'Okay, I'll tell him, but he won't like it.'

'Yeah, but you will,' I said.

Brains' voice broke the spell. 'I have an announcement. The nature of the experiment was not what you were led to believe. The so-called 'shroom experiment relating to *psychedelic* efficacy in fact relates to *psychosomatic* efficacy.'

'In English, Brains,' Face said.

'You have just eaten ordinary store-bought mushrooms. There is nothing in the slightest magical about them. I wanted to see how effective the power of suggestion could be.'

Nobby, by then sitting up, realised the implications of what Brains had said. 'Bullshit! I felt something, they had to be magic!'

'Well, Nobby, if they were, then you seem to have made a quick recovery. Or would you and Bomber's nose disagree? Go on, wake it up and ask!' Brains said. By now, Nobby was flushed with indignation. He knew, as did we all, that the events that had just transpired would inspire a level of scorn and ridicule even he had yet to endure. I felt an inkling of sympathy for him.

'Where did you get them from then?' Legs said.

'From the kitchen. I asked one of the staff to get them for me. Nurse Debbie was most obliging.'

'Yeah, she usually is with you.'

It was then that Nobby unleashed. 'So, you're all about the truth now, are you, *Gregory*?' Nobby's face was an ugly, angry mask. 'Why not tell everyone the truth about you and Nurse Debbie? Go on. Tell everyone she doesn't actually fancy you. Tell them she's only a family friend.'

Brains stopped smiling then. His expression one of pure menace, he leant forward and said, 'You really want to do this, *Knob*? Are you sure?'

'Yeah, I'm sure. Why shouldn't I? You're not my friend. None of you are, apart from Silent.'

'Whoa, let's not get carried away!' I said, lifting my hands, palms forward, sympathy waning.

But now that Nobby had opened the floodgates, there was no return. 'Good old Brains, the ladies really love you, don't they? But I heard you talking to Nurse Debbie. I heard what you said. All those ladies are wasting their time, aren't they? Because you don't like the ladies, do you, Brains? You're fucking *gay!*' The last word echoed throughout the hushed room. Nobby had crossed a line that could not be uncrossed. Not only had he eavesdropped on a private conversation but he had revealed details to the lads. That's not what we did. Ever. Then Brains compounded Nobby's transgression with one of his own.

In one fluid motion, Brains stood and moved across the room towards Nobby. Nobby remained motionless, transfixed by the force of Brains' menace. Brains' long stride took him to Nobby in the blink of an eye. One moment he sat on the far side of the gym, the next Nobby was trapped in his clutches. At this point Face resolved to set the mood, selecting what he considered a fitting soundtrack. "Someone's gonna get their head kicked in tonight" by the Rezillos. By the time the track kicked in, Brains had Nobby against the wall, his forearm across Nobby's throat and his free hand a fist, hovering near Nobby's face; a promise of things to come. Brains had crossed his own line by putting hands on Nobby. Most of us had been there. Some of us even possessed instruments of torture. But it was only ever in thought. This was plainly wrong for so many reasons. There was never any physical confrontation within the group, or not genuine in any case. The boundaries were established, the tacit physical dominance accepted. We simply didn't do that; it was an unwritten law.

I was hugely torn; plagued by ambivalence. I knew I should do the right thing but I struggled figuring out what the right thing was. I walked to where Nobby was being restrained by Brains, taking my time, of course. I could see Brains applying some serious pressure to Nobby's throat. Nobby's eyes bulged and his face was an unhealthy shade of red. The promise of Brains' retribution remained close to Nobby's nose, not yet released. 'You're going to wish you were never born!' Brains said.

'I already wish *you* were never born! Will that do?' Nobby spluttered through compressed vocal chords.

'C'mon, lads, that's enough!' I scolded as I reached the happy couple. While my conscience didn't approve of the spectacle continuing, it did allow me a little leeway, recognising the grievance of Nobby's erroneous accusation of friendship. I grabbed an uncaring Brains by the shoulders but rather than pull him away, at first I leant forward, contributing to the pressure on Nobby's throat. I noticed with satisfaction that Nobby's eyes bulged a little more and his face took on a purplish hue. After a few seconds, I deferred to my conscience and pulled Brains off Nobby. I put myself between them. Nobby clutched his throat, head down, attempting to regain his breath as Brains glared at him. I shrugged my shoulders at Brains, signalling *that's enough* and he took the hint. Brains returned to his seat and, removing a spliff, lit up and inhaled big. He appeared to have regained his composure although his hand trembled somewhat. I turned to check on Nobby who stood upright now, one hand clutching his abused throat. He looked around the room, ensuring his gaze took in all occupants and staggered towards the door. On the verge of tears, he reached the threshold. Turning to take one last look, he exclaimed, '*Wankers!*' I was relieved to find that I hadn't been excluded from his final insult, presumably the accusation of friendship withdrawn.

I resumed my seat and scanned the room. The others took Brains' lighting up as their cue and chose to join him, as did I. The last of the Rezillos' track petered out and we sat in unfamiliar silence, inhaling deeply and reflecting deeply. Then Legs leant forward, a puzzled expression on his face, and I realised what was about to happen. I tried to get Legs' attention; shaking my head, eyes wide, signalling, *don't do it!* But it was to no avail.

'So … you're gay then are you?' Legs said.

'Not sure, haven't made my mind up yet.' Legs still looked puzzled and then the penny dropped. 'Christ! Don't worry, you're all extremely safe!' Brains added. I didn't know whether to be relieved or insulted. I went with relieved.

Thinking back, Brains never called anyone *gay* or *queer* or a *poof* or anything of that nature. In any case, when used, the insult was intended as something other than a statement on someone's sexuality.

As it transpired, Brains' preferences were of little concern. Sexuality was a topic we avoided, being pretty much a sexless bunch anyhow.

Once Brains' indiscretion had been put to one side, Face decided to tackle a far more serious matter. 'So, Silent. What's this about you being Nobby's friend?'

'Fuck off, Face!' I said.

'Fair enough,' he said.

And we never saw Nobby again.

* * * *

When I'd first regained consciousness in the ICU I hadn't known if I was dead or alive. I still didn't know. I knew that I'd not come back whole. There was a hollowness within me. I didn't know what had been taken, or left behind. The hate I'd felt for my self-proclaimed saviour receded as soon as it had arisen and I fell into a dreamless sleep. I awoke in the early hours of the morning, or so I assumed, the beep of the monitor the solitary sound. I saw there were fewer tubes now, but three remained: one in the crook of each arm and one in the back of my hand. I couldn't tell if they were giving or taking. My head felt disconnected and out of sync with my body and its surroundings. I was too exhausted to feel the full weight of despair at my failed attempt to end my life. This time I was able to grasp the top of the sheet and unfold it to cover my naked torso. The effort required would have rivalled the most strenuous of Hercules' labours. A different nurse appeared from behind me. 'Are you awake, Mr Lavelle? Can I get you something?' she said, her voice soft and kind.

I swallowed hard, my throat raw. 'Water, please,' I managed to say.

'Let me get that for you,' she said and disappeared for a second before returning with a small plastic cup of water. She used a control to raise the head of the bed; a movement that served to emphasise the feeling of disconnection between my head and body. When my head caught up, I took the proffered straw in my mouth and drank. The first water to hit my throat shocked with a harsh sting, but with each subsequent swallow the pain abated and I finished the cupful without pause. 'There we go, dear. Let's see how that sits with you, and we can try some more later if you want.' I nodded, closing my eyes. 'The doctor will be here later to see you, but it won't be for a few hours. You should try and rest.' She lowered the bed.

I lay awake, eyes closed, the water restoring my reason. I wondered if the doctor would be my saviour returning. I no longer felt the hate that had arisen in me. I couldn't even muster anger against the doctor. The hate had collapsed in on me, unable to be sustained. I couldn't deflect my hate, and so I absorbed it, bringing it back inside of me, where it belonged.

It was a different and indifferent doctor that came to see me. He checked my charts, he checked my vitals and he checked me out of Intensive Care. My estimated chemical balance permitted my relocation. Before transferring to a public ward, I was allowed to attend to my ablutions, all under the watchful eye of an ICU nurse. Perhaps they worried I would drown myself by sticking my head in the toilet and flushing. When she watched me shower, I lacked inhibition and turned my back as I rid myself of the dregs of the last two days. Once dried and dressed in a fresh hospital gown I was directed to a wheelchair and taken to what would be my home for the longest six days of my life.

I was taken to the psych ward. It was a long room containing a dozen beds, all occupied once I'd arrived. As I was wheeled to my bed, the other patients watched me, and I watched them. All male, consisting of two disparate age groups. Half appeared to be around my age. The other half appeared to be elderly, about their seventies. The middle-aged were conspicuous by their absence. It didn't take long to figure out the reasoning behind the unusual demographic. The younger contingent possessed similar characteristics that identified them as methamphetamine addicts. Their lack of facial fat gave them a gaunt appearance; the dried-up skin around their mouths pulled into a rictus grin. They either lay sleeping on their beds, in a comatose-like state, or when awake moved constantly, forever scratching and twitching. I didn't share their restlessness. In that, I was more akin to the others.

The elderly were mostly occupied with rest, spending their days and nights in bed. They existed in their own Alzheimer-inspired worlds, disconnected from reality. I envied them. Other than an occasional stroll to the smoking room, preferring second-hand smoke to first-hand crazy, I sat in bed reading. I sought escape in the pages of any crappy book I could get hold of. Not yet dismissed as a risk to myself, I remained under the watchful gaze of nursing staff at all times. Whether senile, addict or me, we were all mentally ill-equipped. That is what brought us all together to this place: *fucked in the head.* The days were long and dull. The surroundings and my companions served to prolong the hours without end. The nights were worse still.

On my first night in the ward, I lay dozing, the sleeping noises of the others a distraction, when I realised I had a visitor at my bedside. The dark figure stooped at the chest of drawers by my bed, trying to open them. 'Hey, what are you doing?' I said, surprised. The figure turned to face me and it took a second in the gloom to see it was one of the elderly patients. I supposed he had lost his way to his bed. 'This isn't your bed, you're in the wrong place,' I said.

'Yeah, I know. You're new, aren't you?' he said, his voice soft. 'I was wondering if you had any ice. I'm dying here, man. I'm desperate for a hit. Anything will do. I won't say anything, I promise.'

'I haven't got any ice or anything like that. You've made a mistake,' I said, my words harsh.

'Come on, please. I'll take anything, it doesn't matter how small. I'm fucking gagging here!'

'I told you, I haven't got any. Now bugger off before I call the nurse!' With a dirty look, he returned to his own bed. I didn't take my gaze off him. Either the meth had prematurely aged him or he was a late starter. The incident ruined any chance I'd had of getting rest. All night I'd lie in a state of constant tension, waiting for interlopers. I became exhausted, dozing now and again during the day.

Doctor Jeffries had to come to my rescue again. On my second day in the ward, he arrived looking as worried as I'd ever seen him. I raised my hand, signalling him to wait at the end of the ward. I stood up on feeble legs and walked towards him, not wanting to talk within earshot of the patients and staff. He looked tired and anxious as I approached. 'Alan, I … I don't know what to say. How are you?' His voice was thick with emotion.

'Now, *I* don't know what to say. I'm here, I guess.'

'I've been calling every day. They wouldn't let me see you in ICU and they just told me you were in a public ward. I got a call on Sunday night, saying your flatmate found you unconscious and you were rushed to ICU. I didn't know what to think,' he said, voice unsteady. I couldn't answer. Even if I'd known what to say, I could not answer. 'My God, Alan. What happened?'

My self-hatred erupted. '*What happened?* I fucking *failed*, that's what happened!'

'Oh, please, Alan, don't say that. Your … You mustn't say that.' Then remorse overwhelmed me. Doctor Jeffries hadn't simply been Dad's best friend. He was the uncle I'd never had. The best uncle anyone could wish for. And me? I was the nephew from Hell. I knew Doctor Jeffries would reproach himself, despite his blamelessness.

'I'm sorry, Doctor Jeffries. I don't know what to say. I don't think there's anything I *can* say that's going to make any difference.'

'I'm so worried about you, Alan. It's all been rather shocking. But let's focus now on getting you better. First thing to do is to get you nearer home.'

'Christ, yes, Doctor. I need to get out of this place. There's nothing to do and I can't sleep. All they want to do is keep an eye on me. They won't tell me how long I'm going to be here. It's doing my head in!'

'Well, because of what happened, you need to be under observation for a while. It's not simply a matter of a few days, I'm afraid. What I've done, though, is contacted Glyndwr Hospital, where you stayed before. We have to wait for a vacancy which might not be for a week or so, but I've been promised you'll be next,' he said, regaining control of his voice.

'Thanks, Doctor. The sooner I get out of here, the better. I appreciate what you've done, yet again.'

'Please, Alan. You know I'm always here for you. Now that I know which ward you're in I'll call to let you know what's happening with Glyndwr. I'll keep pestering them, but I'm not sure there's much else they can do. Is there anything I can do for you while I'm here?'

'You wouldn't have a few books hidden away, would you?' I said. *Or a Taser to fend off my fellow fuck-heads!*

'No, afraid not. With any luck, next time I see you will be when I take you to Glyndwr, which I hope won't be too long. I suspect their library may be more extensive than anything here.' He looked less apprehensive now. He grabbed me and hugged me. 'Please take care, Alan. Your health is the most important thing now.'

I returned the hug. 'I'll try, Doctor. And, again, I'm sorry for everything. I know what a pain I am.'

He held me at arm's length. There were tears in his eyes. 'You are not a pain, Alan. I have known you your entire life. You are family to me and I care about you.'

I couldn't bear to look him in the eye; I felt myself tearing up. 'I appreciate that, Doctor, I really do. That means more to me than you could know.'

When Doctor Jeffries had said that I was family to him, I'd been touched. But the remorse would not be pacified. I wouldn't permit that. The hollowness remained, like a vacuum between my stomach and chest. I had to fill it. I wouldn't allow the doctor's caring words to alleviate my guilt. I would gather my self-hatred and my self-loathing and I would take it all inside of me. I would welcome all the emotional filth and use it to feed the emptiness. I would not release myself from the pain I deserved.

* * * *

The day after the fake mushroom experiment, the gang gathered in the rec room to make important decisions about the unimportant. Tonight, the choice of movie was *Silence of the Lambs* or *Forrest Gump*. For me, the choice was clear when faced with either a well-crafted, horror-filled thriller or nearly two and a half hours of insipid sentimentality that sends the viewer into a diabetic coma. I summarised. 'C'mon, guys. It's got to be *Lambs*. *Forrest Gump* is shite!'

'Yeah, but it's got good music,' Legs said.

'So, listen to the soundtrack. This is about the viewing experience,' Voice shouted. I had a supporter. The vote ended as two each with a single dissenter, aka the "I don't give a shit" vote. Most of the time a tie led to the threat of a third movie at which point compromise resulted. Tonight, however, we awaited the potential deciding vote. Bomber had yet to arrive and he was no fence-sitter.

'Has anyone seen Bomber?' Brains said, having again demonstrated his questionable taste in movies.

'I talked to him at lunch. He said he'd be here,' Legs said. Nobby was also absent but no-one wanted to jinx our good fortune. 'Let's give him another five minutes,' Legs said. So we did. Four minutes later, Bomber arrived, one minute to spare.

'Hey, Bomber, just the man. We need you to settle a tie. *Forrest Gump* or *Silence of the Lambs?*' Brains said.

Bomber walked into the room, obviously preoccupied, gazing at his feet as if looking up would force him to acknowledge his thoughts. Sometimes, Bomber would be shadowed by an incautious Nobby, following within the danger zone of Bomber's slipstream. But not today. Bomber was alone. His silence inspired the more perceptive among us to wonder if something had happened. I looked across at Brains; his expression was uneasy.

Bomber looked up and saw the unasked question on our faces. Bomber shook his head, as if troubled. 'He's gone.' No-one spoke; wanting to know and yet not wanting to know the details.

Brains broke the silence. 'What? Nobby, *gone*? Do you mean …' unable to complete the question.

Bomber looked at Brains, realisation dawning. 'What? No, he discharged himself this morning. What did you think he'd done?'

Brains, overcome with relief, spluttered. 'I thought he'd done … *something drastic!*'

'What, you think that self-centred bastard would do the world a big favour like that? No, he's gone to spread his pestilence to a wider audience. You know what they say: when the world ends the only survivors will be cockroaches and Nobby!'

'I pity the poor fucking cockroaches!' Face said.

'Then why the fuck are you moping, Bomber?' Brains said.

'Hey? Oh that. I think the thieving bastard took one of my shirts. I was trying to remember the last time I saw it.'

Brains exploded. 'You stupid bastard!'

Bomber never did find that shirt. He put it down to wastage in the end. If Nobby had worn it he didn't want it back anyway. Bomber did end up doing the right thing though: three votes for *Lambs*.

As we sat, watching the unfolding thrills and making inappropriate comments, I allowed my thoughts to drift. Of all the times I'd wished Nobby would disappear, I'd never thought that I would miss him. It's not often that I am so completely right about something.

Chapter Nineteen

I was defined by fatigue by the time Doctor Jeffries collected me for transferral to Glyndwr Hospital. Although the move was a technical relocation from one facility to another, I felt to have escaped Hell. The sense of relief at fleeing the underworld of the psych ward of dead-eyed, senile meth addicts suppressed the reality of where I found myself. At first, I had to share a room with one other, but they were quiet and kept to themselves. Neither were they senile nor addicted to meth. The more relaxing surroundings enabled me to work on reducing my sleep deficit. More than anything, I was determined to portray the model patient. I was prepared to do whatever necessary to make my stay as short as possible.

My previous visit had been three years earlier, following Kevin's death. During that stay, as a youth, I was resident in a different part of the facility. Now, being admitted as an adult, I had access to the greater part of the hospital facilities. My elevation also afforded me the attentions of Doc Friendly. Indeed, the doc gathered most of his meaningful notes during the time of my first adult residency. In addition to my one-time willingness to cooperate, the doc subjected me to an aggressive drug regime. The drug-inflicted fog led me to share more than the minimum necessary to facilitate early release. I didn't fret too long over the unintentional over-sharing at the time, my focus being on short-term release, not long-term consequences. Towards the fourth week, my acclimatisation to the drugs enabled me to share with more caution.

But I knew that no matter where I was or under what chemical state my constitution found itself, I couldn't escape the fact that I was a failed suicide. I wasn't ashamed of my failure although I was not proud. I suffered from the affliction of rejection. It seemed that not only had I been rejected by life but I had been rejected by death. I had thrown myself into the jaws of death but had been spewed back out, undigested and unwanted. This utter rejection weighed upon me to the extent that I collapsed into myself. But my thoughts cleared as I struggled through the mental haze. I had to learn to disguise my agitation, clasping my hands together to prevent the more obvious signs. I presented Doc Friendly with my most pensive expression.

Everything I said was thoughtful and genuine. I acknowledged what I had *tried* to do. I *owned* my actions. I blamed no-one else. I had been distressed. I had been a victim of circumstance. I had taken to the bottle, ignoring the clear warning on the medication. I was unable to recall the details of my attempt. I was remorseful. I now knew I had the support of Doctor Jeffries. The facts had not changed but things were different. I wanted to be able to cope. I was ready to try. If I had not yet learnt my lesson, I was well on the way to learning my lesson. I made these statements in serious and reflective tones, as if the revelations could have only been revealed through the expert ministrations of Doc Friendly. He was pleased with the outcome of our time together. However, my progress, while commendable, didn't persuade him to let me fly the nest before he felt I was able to function outside his direct influence.

By the fifth week, I thought I was being so clever. I'd drop Doctor Jeffries' name into the conversation from time to time, when notions of support on the outside appeared pertinent. I'd been most careful to refrain from directly requesting release from the hospital, wishing to avoid exposing my strategy. Doc Friendly proved he was at least as smart. He read between the lines.

'Well, Alan. I think we're making some real progress here. I'm very pleased with how you're responding to treatment. However, while we shouldn't dwell on what brought you here, it would be remiss to disregard the unfortunate incident. A most traumatic event, such as you experienced, is not easily resolved. I think we should continue with our good work and review our options next week. What do you think?' he said, his smile sympathetic.

I nodded, reflecting deeply. 'Yes, of course. I understand. Whatever you think Doctor. I want to get better,' while inside I screamed, *Let me go, I shouldn't be here; I don't belong!*

And why not share the truth? Because, the truth would keep me hospitalised. The truth was that I persisted to draw all the self-loathing I could muster into myself and still it did not begin to fill the void. I had time to reflect; to realise that I had never genuinely hated anyone other than myself. No, I was stupid and deserving of all the shit that had happened to me. I deserved all the hate and loathing I had for myself. I couldn't avoid it but I could use it. And so I repressed the truth and I waited, always patient, for an opportunity. It arrived at the end of the seventh week.

Doc Friendly consented to a trial release. I was allowed to spend the weekend away from the facility, subject to certain conditions. He discussed my progress with Doctor Jeffries, having first gained my approval to do so. Once again, I was to avail myself of Doctor Jeffries' stewardship, spending the weekend at his home.

Doctor Jeffries was a regular visitor to the hospital and always asked Doc Friendly after my progress. In fact, the previous week when Doctor Jeffries had asked how I was coping, I had confirmed how crucial Doctor Fenty was proving to the goal of restoring my mental health. But I'd felt it was time to try it on the outside. I was concerned that I would end up institutionalised. I might become over-reliant on all the facility provided. Making the stay so easy would just make the eventual departure so much harder.

So on Friday evening, Doctor Jeffries signed me out from Glyndwr Mental Health Facility. He then drove me to my flat where I was supposed to pack some belongings, pick up my van and travel to the doctor's home. The doctor didn't have time to stay long and so we spoke as I exited his car. 'Okay, Alan. Here we are. Will you be okay now?'

'Sure, Doctor Jeffries. Thanks again. I can take it from here.'

'Okay. Well, I'll see you back at my place.'

'Actually, I was thinking I'd spend the weekend here. I have some stuff to sort out and I think I'd get more rest here. Plus it's less driving for me altogether; only one hour from here to the hospital but two hours by the time I drive to your place and then backtrack to Glyndwr on Monday.'

The doctor was unconvinced. 'Are you sure, Alan? Doctor Fenty released you on the understanding that you would stay at my home.'

'I know, but I was thinking about that during the drive. I can't run away from what I did. Now that we're here, I need to face up to what happened and I know I can do it. Anyway, Warren will be around for company.'

'Well ... if you're certain. Perhaps I should come inside with you, to make sure that you'll be okay?'

'No, Doctor. It's something I have to face by myself and I know you have things to do this evening. I'll be fine and I promise I won't be touching alcohol.'

'Okay ... if you're sure. Pease call me if you change your mind or if you start finding things ... difficult.' He was uncertain.

'I will. Thanks again, Doctor. I'll see you soon,' I said and walked into my flat. The place where I would continue with my life, and come to terms with my failed death.

Concerns for my initial reaction at returning to the scene of the crime proved unfounded. When I opened my bedroom door and walked inside, my first thoughts were that it was inexplicably untidy. Drawers had been opened and contents disturbed, and not just those I'd removed to retrieve the pills and alcohol. It looked more like the aftermath of a burglary than the site of a suicide attempt. I felt no shame, no anger and no apprehension. In fact, I felt ... nothing. Only the heavy emptiness sitting between my chest and stomach that would not be sated. Even when I inspected the squalid living area and kitchen I remained unmoved. Perhaps I was a little amazed at the level of neglect that Warren was able to inflict in eight weeks, but nothing more. Pots, pans, crockery and cutlery, all of which were filmed with grime, littered the kitchen surfaces. The solitary clear spot was the table in the living area where the music system was supposed to live – three clean rectangles conspicuous in the otherwise dusty surface. I shook my head and returned to my bedroom, determining to clean my personal space first before moving to the common areas.

It didn't take long to rearrange my room. I stood at the doorway, when finished, and everything was back to how it had been eight weeks ago. I heard the sound of the front door opening and moved out to the top of the entry stairs.

Warren moved up the stairs, oblivious to my presence. It took him to the top of the stairs before he realised he wasn't alone. 'Whoa, Alan! You scared the crap out of me!'

'Looking at all the crap around here, I'll have to assume you've spent most of the last eight weeks being startled! It's a fucking mess, Warren!'

'Oh yeah, sorry about that, Taffy. I was going to have a bit of a clean in the morning. I wasn't expecting you back so soon,' the Cockney Wide-boy said.

'And where's the music system? You know the rule; it's not to be moved!'

'Oh yeah, that. One of my mates borrowed it. Just recently, though. I'll get it back tomorrow,' he said.

'Sounds like tomorrow is going to be a big day for you.'

'Hey, don't worry about it, Taff. It's all good. You're back now. I was going to visit but I didn't think you'd want any fuss,' he said as he moved past me to the kitchen. A dull throb started in my head. I couldn't be bothered to marshal the energy to be pissed off. I let my shoulders slump and my gaze dropped to the floor.

And then I saw them. A flash of russet. A tiny, focusing point of pressure grew in my head.

'Give me your key. Now!'

'Hey? You want my key? What's up?'

'Give me the key and fuck off. *Now!*'

'What's wrong? What's wrong with you?' He looked nervous.

'Key! Fuck off! Now!'

'Jesus, okay. Keep your hair on.' He dropped the key onto the kitchen table. 'I'll come back tomorrow. Maybe you'll feel better by then.'

'No. You're not coming back!'

'Hey? What about my stuff?'

'Fuck you and fuck your stuff! Consider it settlement for unpaid rent and stolen food and the music system.'

'You're fucking mad!' he said. He went to pass me to leave.

Before he got to the top of the stairs I put my hand on his chest. 'Boots!'

'What?'

'Boots! Now!'

It was then that Warren understood his situation. It took him a while to unknot the laces, fumbling with shaking hands but he managed to untie them. I stood between him and the exit, unmoving until my demand had been met. Warren tossed the boots at me but I made no attempt to catch them, letting them fall to the floor. Only then did I move aside, letting him pass.

As Warren moved by me he muttered, 'I could have let you fucking die.'

'Well, you fucking didn't, did you?' I shouted the accusation at his retreating back. He moved down the stairs and out of the flat, leaving the door open in a final act of petty defiance. I followed him down the stairs and closed the door behind him.

Well, he fucking didn't, did he?

* * * *

Unwittingly, Warren had provided me a great service. Not by calling for an ambulance, but through the simple act of removing and taking my boots as I'd lain insensible. He'd shown me the utter futility of my attempts to integrate with humankind. I must be alone, unencumbered by the need for social interaction. The anger I felt for Warren wasn't the same hatred for the saviour-doctor that had risen up in me. The anger for Warren was controlled and galvanising. It cleared a space in my thoughts, allowing me to understand my place. This time I would take that last small step at the end of my long journey into isolation. That final pace would be my choice. At least I would have that. And so I determined to rid myself, as far as I could, of all traces of others.

I started in what had been Warren's bedroom. I hadn't inspected his room in months, preferring not to know in what condition it might be kept. On opening the door, I was greeted by the stench of stale body odour and unwashed clothing that hit me like a wet, stinking slap to the face. I made for the other side of the room with haste and threw the window open to provide an escape path for Warren's stench.

I returned when I'd finished cleaning the kitchen and living areas, allowing the room to air. It proved impossible to fully rid the room of his stink, but it was much reduced and I was better prepared. I took in the scene that met me. Socks stuck to the wall, clothing strewn across the floor and the unmade bed. It looked like an explosion of filthy clothing. My first decision was straightforward. I made my way to the kitchen to retrieve bin bags and kitchen gloves. Inhaling only when to do otherwise would have led to unconsciousness, I scooped the cloth-ing into the bin bags. My initial thought to separate the clean from the dirty was brief and summarily rejected. All would be bagged and all would be discarded. I felt no compulsion to clean and donate his clothing to charity, although the notion of Warren spotting a needy stranger in his clothing was not unappealing. After bundling the visible clothing into the bags I moved to the chest of drawers. I pulled them open and emptied their contents onto the bed, easier to scoop them into the bag. I placed the two bags full of Warren's detritus outside the room and inspected the modified scene. Happier, but not yet happy. I removed the bedding and that, too, found its way into a bin bag. Three bags full. Nearly done.

I moved back to my ordered bedroom and stood at the doorway, looking upon it with fresh, opened eyes. I'd already washed and changed the bedding since Juliette had left. It hadn't been an act of defiance to the memory of Juliette but rather a sign of moving on. I let my gaze sweep the room, taking in what it now was. A single man's bedroom. And then I saw it. An anomaly. It was pushed into a corner, on top of the large chest of drawers, where I had chosen to overlook its existence. It was a small photograph in a brass frame of Juliette and me, sitting together at dinner. We had been dating for two months at the time, at the pinnacle of our relationship, now that I had the benefit of hindsight. Juliette smiled her unforgettable smile and I sat near her, turned so my back was concealed. I looked happy. I quailed at the artifice of the scene, picked it up and put it with the other waste.

Ignoring the growing throb in my head, I picked up the bags and took them downstairs to the dumpster at the side of the building. As I tossed the last bag into the dumpster, the brass-framed photograph fell from the bag, landing at my feet. I retrieved the photograph, the picture now obscured by shattered glass. But I didn't need to see the picture to recall every single detail; every line and curve, every colour and shade. I dropped the photograph without ceremony into the dumpster. I turned to leave but then hesitated. I bent down, removed the boots and dropped them too into the bin. I returned to the flat, massive gravity resisting my walk up the stairs. Again, I stood at the doorway to my bedroom, looking upon what remained. I moved to the chest of drawers and ran my finger through the accumulated dust, stopping at the clear space where the photograph had once stood. I turned and looked towards the bed, where Juliette used to lie next to me; at the space where she used to be. And I was overwhelmed by the lack of evidence.

I'd thought I could ignore the memory of her, but her absence created a subtle vacuum from which I could not escape. I may as well have tried to escape my own shadow. I could turn my back on the light of the past, but the shadow of what I am was clear and inescapable. And then I sensed a trace of her scent, wondering if it was real. I inhaled with care, tracking the scent to the bed. I uncovered the source and picked up the pillow. The pillow had retained the delicate mixture of the distinctive scent of her skin and the citrus suggestion of her perfume. I held the pillow to my face, closed my eyes and inhaled. Hours later I exhaled, realising I'd fallen into my thoughts. I'd thought I could forget about her, that it was simply a case of mental discipline. I knew then that it wouldn't work. It could never work. I could never forget. When I looked up it was dark. Ages had passed as I'd stood alone in my bedroom, trying to escape my thoughts.

And then, an inescapable revelation: *I don't belong here. I don't belong anywhere.* So I resolved not to *be* anywhere. I would live an existence of perpetual motion. I would walk and never stop. I would not *arrive* anywhere but I would *leave* everywhere. I would outpace the unbearable weight of my existence. I walked out of the room, down the hall and out of the house, barefoot. I walked on, feeling history pull at me, trying to impede me. In time to the pounding in my head, I maintained a pace that kept it out of reach.

Nothing seemed real. I didn't want to believe anything I saw, or anything I heard. I stopped believing I was there, forcing myself to accept I was dreaming. But as I walked, a small, stupid, stubborn part of me that refused to disbelieve, still detected sights and smells and noises. So I acknowledged the sense of cold, dark streets and the damp pavement. I acknowledged the illusion of others walking by me, bumping them as I passed, ignoring their remonstrations.

I ignored the sharp pain in the soles of my feet as I passed from concrete pavement to gravel verge. The part of me that couldn't doubt saw the headlights and heard the horns of the cars, swerving by me in the country lanes. I acknowledged my senses, but I wouldn't trust them. Even when the police car, lights flashing, blocked my way and I was shepherded into the back of the vehicle, I still refused to believe. Hours later, a captive of the police, feet bandaged and a cold, untouched mug of coffee on the table in front of me, I would not believe.

And then I looked up to see Doctor Jeffries enter the room; once again called to rescue me. I stared at his worried expression. I saw a tear run down his face. Then I believed.

* * * *

The consequences of the experimentation with what proved to be magic-deficient mushrooms were never formally addressed. We all subscribed without exception to the *let sleeping dogs lie* school. So much so that when Voice shouted that he was able to source another perception-altering substance worthy of our consideration, he remained un-insulted. We listened quietly, allowing him to speak loudly. 'Lads, I have been advised, by a trustworthy source, that there is a limited supply of world-famous Scrumpy available at reasonable cost for the discerning cider lover. Do I have any takers for this one-time offer?'

'And where is this world-famous Scrumpy from?' Legs asked.

'Well, "world-famous" might be an overstatement. "Nationally-famous" is more accurate. In fact, "Worcestershire-famous" is most precise. That's not what matters. What matters is that this stuff hasn't been made for nearly twenty years since the cider-house closed. It's considered the real deal by all who've tried it, so much so that my contact kept hold of a few crates of the stuff,' Voice shouted.

'So, it was good enough to hoard but not good enough to drink? How come the pub closed; did they poison the drinkers?'

'Look, I don't know how much he started out with. All I know is he has eighteen bottles left and he wants sixty quid for them. As far as poisoning is concerned, the drinkers were poisoned to the extent that any knowledgeable Scrumpy-drinker expects. So, sales pitch done. For a tenner each, *in or out?*'

My interest was piqued. It was Wazza's wandering lips that had deferred my burgeoning cider appreciation. Being more familiar territory than mushrooms, it would be simpler to determine the product potency. 'I'm in,' I said, which led to general capitulation, which in turn led to group consent.

Later on, money exchanged hands at which point arrangements were entered into. The upcoming Saturday evening was the time and the pseudo-gymnasium was the place. Dai was happy to be enlisted as unofficial-official who would ensure our privacy for the duration. To reduce potential contamination of scientific data that might be gathered over the course of the evening, we agreed the session would be all about the Scrumpy. Weed didn't make the guest list. Of course, there was nothing to prevent the gang partaking of a personal spliff, prior to the session. This possibility was not discussed, likely considered yet more material to be deposited in the heavily populated *let sleeping dogs lie* file.

It was a warm and muggy Saturday evening that saw the intrepid band of scientists yet again embark on heroic endeavours. Endeavours that might prove invaluable to the plight of millions. Of course, there was a not insignificant possibility that our endeavours might just lead to the complete incapacitation of six brave pioneers. But we wouldn't prejudge the outcome, dedicated scientists that we were. Legs alone exhibited any sign of wariness. 'Are you sure this stuff is drinkable after, what, twenty years?'

'It's fine. It's not a dairy product, Legs. It doesn't go off.'

'I'm not supposed to mix alcohol with my meds.'

'We all have the same label on our meds, Legs. It says that they "may increase the effects of alcohol", not that you can't drink alcohol. More bang for your buck. It's all win-win!' Voice yelled.

'But how do you know it hasn't gone toxic?'

'Tell you what, I'll take the first drink. If I live, will you then accept it is not poisonous?'

'Okay, that'll do,' Legs said, brightening at the offer.

'C'mon, Legs. It's the least you can do. You've already paid and turned up. I'm game and I have to be careful when I drink because of my medical condition,' Face said.

'Why, what could happen?'

'Well, I get sort of light-headed and my coordination goes to buggery. If it gets bad enough I can even forget what happens.'

'So, you get pissed, then?'

'Yep.'

Fuck this, I thought. I need to have a drink if this is how we are before the session is even underway. In addition to provision of surveillance services, Dai had provided a large container, half-filled with ice to keep the produce cold. The warm conditions had already turned much of the ice to water by the time we reached in to retrieve our first drink. Proper pint glasses had been provided for the occasion.

On opening, a sniff at the neck of the bottle presented an agreeable bouquet – apple and alcohol with nothing of the toxic. I emptied the bottle into the glass and waited for it to settle. Then I waited some more. Then I looked around to see that all possessed a glassful of the same yellowish, cloudy liquid. It was almost opaque, the fine, cloudy sediment swirling in a most mesmerising fashion.

Time to dive in. I took a tentative sip, not waiting for Voice to declare that he wasn't dead. I took the liquid into my mouth and kept it against my palate, holding it until I had a good sense of its scent and taste. Then I swallowed. Then I gagged, grasping my throat with my free hand and doubling over. I started spluttering. On seeing my reaction, the others held their drinks away from them.

'Jesus, Silent! Are you okay? What's wrong with it?' Brains said.

I straightened up, took another, longer draught and gave a big grin. 'Nothing wrong, it's very good.'

'You stupid bastard, Silent! I thought you were choking.'

I grinned some more and drank some more. The others joined me, with caution at first. We settled into an unhurried pace, wishing to savour our allocated three pints. Compliments were made and not a single complaint. Not about the drink, at least. Voice basked in the glory of his success and the alcohol didn't harm our resistance to his loud self-praise. After the first pint, I felt loosened but not yet headed towards incapacitation. So I permitted myself to surrender to the second pint, now convinced that any effects would likely be beneficial and gradual. However, the notion that the sole effects would be positive was being tested by the subject matter of our discussion. It started off harmlessly enough. Face picked up on recent news coverage relating to the illegal use of drugs in sports.

'I reckon it's unfair on the athletes that get banned for testing positive to recreational drugs. They're not performance enhancing. If anything, those sorts of drugs would be performance *reducing!*'

Bomber had been quiet, but no more. 'I think the Olympics is too boring. They should organise it so everyone *has* to take drugs. Make it compulsory for everyone to compete while they're stoned.'

'Yeah that would definitely make the *high* jump more interesting,' Brains said. Face, unappreciative of Brains' wit, decided it was time to lower the tone of the discussion.

'They could change the 4 x 400 metre relay so that instead of each runner passing on a baton they have to share a needle before running their leg. Right? But, at the start of the race, only the first runner has HIV. Then at the end of the race, the last runner is tested to confirm he has HIV too, otherwise the team is disqualified. See? That's one blood test that has to be positive in order to win!'

'Leave it out, Face. That's extremely bad taste, even for you!' I reprimanded him, assuming my position as moral barometer. I suspected Face was using the alcohol as an alibi for his poor judgement. Not on my watch.

The first indication of notable alcoholic influence occurred when Voice requested musical accompaniment to our endeavours. He was trying to request "Night Boat to Cairo". His actual request was, 'Waddabout "Kite Note to Biro"?'

And then we heard an ominous rumbling in the distance, heralding the approach of a storm. The sky was dark and heavy through the glass walls of the gym. Encouraged by nature, I resolved to finish off pint number two and go in pursuit of pint number three. At that stage, my assessment of the potency of the Scrumpy was that it was nothing special. A tasty tipple indeed, but not as potent as Voice had insinuated. At least, that was my view until I sculled the last of the second pint and stood to retrieve my final drink. Rather, I had every intention of standing. My head and body, even my arms, were committed to the act of standing. My legs, however, dissented with extreme prejudice, as I found myself heading floor-wards. Thankful that I hadn't been holding the pint glass in my feet, my cooperative hand held the glass outwards while I bore the brunt of the impact on my side.

Before I attempted to rise, I dedicated a few moments to rubbing my incapacitated legs back to life. My intention was to distribute the alcohol, which had settled in my lower regions, to other alcohol-free parts. *Spread the load* was the plan. While I worked on draining some of the alluvial alcohol from my disobliging legs, Brains felt it apt to question my actions. 'What th'fuck are ya doing, Silent?'

The alcohol hadn't yet reached my upper regions and so I possessed a semblance of control over brain and mouth. 'I think you'll find I was doing that which is known as "falling in the general direction of down."'

'And wha' possessed you to "fall in the general direction of down"?' Brains slurred.

'It would be the fact that I have yet to master the more difficult art of "falling in the general direction of *up*"!'

'I see ...' Brains said. No, he didn't.

'That's okay, lads. Don't worry about me, I'm fine,' I said as I regained my feet. 'And by the way, please don't thank me all at once. You're all very welcome to learn from my demonstration of the hidden effects of this most potent brew,' my opinion somewhat changed from my pre-attempt-to-stand opinion. As I wandered over to the container to rescue my final drink, I sensed my strategy succeeding, as my alcoholic content dispersed itself to places other than my legs. The return trip to my seat was completed without further accident, in a somewhat dignified manner.

I wasn't alone in succumbing to the effects of our alcoholic endeavours. Even Legs, with his extra special lower-limbs, found the settling behaviour of the alcohol to be unsettling. His trip to the container to retrieve his drink was circuitous. He bounced off the gym equipment, straight-line walking proving beyond his ability. 'Whoa, Legs. Where th'fuck are you goin'?' Bomber slurred. 'You's like a bandy-legged pinball!' At least I hadn't taken the scenic route to the floor. My fall had been both straight and down.

Legs braced himself against the wall and turned to look at the source of the affront, taking a long moment to focus on Bomber. He looked upwards, as if searching for a fitting and cutting response. After a few seconds of silence, Legs looked to Bomber once more, lethal reply locked-and-loaded. And then he spoke. '*Ffuuggoff!*' His eloquent rejoinder caused a general breakdown in sensibilities, with the exception of Dai, who remained unmoved. Our laughter was raucous and prolonged, ebbing after a few minutes. It resurrected as Legs meandered back to his seat only to miss on final descent, landing on the floor, arse-first. Somehow, he retained most of his drink despite the heavy landing. However, spillage did occur as he joined our subsequent hysterics at his failure to sit.

By now, my sides ached and tears streamed down my face as I laughed without inhibition. I hadn't let go like this for years. It verged on a novel sensation, and I wondered if I had at long last discovered the ideal formula for balance. Two pints of Scrumpy plus the lingering after-effects of weed and sanctioned medication delivered me to a new destination. Was this the point at which I could cast off my complex inhibitions? But my musings were disrupted by the crashing thunder of the approaching storm. The loud peal startled me, which in turn transformed to anger. I railed against the sobering effects of the heralding of the storm, despising the interruption. And so, I stood up and resolved to remonstrate with nature. I moved to the doorway of the gym with absolute purpose, focused and determined, suffering no suggestion of intoxication.

As I stepped outside, I felt electricity in the air. My hair stood on end. The temperature dropped as the storm approached. A flash of lightning warned of the impending thunderclap, much louder now, as the storm advanced. The alcohol and drugs in my system, along with the charged atmosphere, energised me. Powerful enough to face anything that nature could pit against me. The rumbling deepened as the storm gathered force. I challenged the universe, shouting, '*C'mon*! Here I am!' The flash of lightning preceded the impossibly loud crash of thunder by a mere fraction, signalling the storm's immediacy. I clenched my fists and howled into the storm, matching it rage for rage. 'C'mon, *Fucker*! Do your worst!' The blinding light and deafening boom exploded as one; the smell of hot metal and detonating ozone as lightning struck the metal fencing of the hospital grounds. 'You missed, *Fucker*!' I screamed, throwing my arms out wide, offering the universe a bigger target. I waited for the strike but the storm moved on, unmet and unable to meet my fury.

Then I noticed something at the edge of my vision, a shadow within the lit doorway of the main building. Seconds later, there was another flash of lightning, and I saw Doc Friendly standing in the shelter of the entranceway, looking right at me. The rumble of thunder sounded then, less loud, signalling the storm's departure. I turned to face where the sky had lit up and said, 'Yeah, didn't fucking think so!' When I turned back to the doorway, it was empty. Doc Friendly had retreated. The atmosphere was refreshed by the effects of the storm. I stood for a few moments, dropping my arms to my sides. I walked back into the gym, sober and victorious. The lads stood, blank-faced witnesses to my rage, tracking me as I returned to my seat.

Brains sounded cautious when he spoke. 'You okay, Silent?' I nodded and retrieved my glass to finish off the brew, throat raw from yelling. 'What was that all about?'

I took a moment to look at him, considering the question. I shrugged my shoulders. 'How the fuck should I know? I am a mental patient, you know.'

* * * *

Botanical debris littered the hospital grounds the morning after the storm. Dai had disposed of all evidence of the gang's alcoholic activities, with one exception. That was altogether on me. Doc Friendly had witnessed my incautious display during the height of the storm. It seemed, a display that the doc felt obliged to analyse. When I arrived at our scheduled appointment later that day, it was apparent I was not the first to be questioned about the previous night's events. His usual bonhomie notable by its absence, this was not Doc Friendly. His smile was minimal and cast in determination. This was *Doc Resolute*, determined to get answers from a patient disinclined to provide them.

He was straight down to business. 'Alan, I'm sure you won't be surprised to know there's something rather worrying that I would like to discuss with you.'

'And good afternoon to you too, Doctor,' I said, acting hurt.

'Well, yes. Good afternoon, Alan. I want to discuss what I observed last night, during the storm.'

'Hold on, Doc. Aren't you supposed to ask how I'm eating and sleeping first?'

'Really, Alan. Unless there's something relating to your appetite or sleeping patterns that you must raise, I'd rather we explore your behaviour outside the gymnasium last night.'

'Okay. Well, for the record, I'm sleeping and eating fine. And to what behaviour do you refer?'

'I observed you in the garden during the storm. You appeared agitated. You were screaming.'

'Doctor, you weren't spying on me, were you?' Shocked, I was.

'Of course not, Alan. You were standing in the middle of the garden for all to see. What on Earth were you thinking?'

'"For all to see"? I didn't realise I had an audience, I would have done an encore if I'd known.'

'Now, Alan, this is very serious. There was no good reason for you to have exposed yourself as you did. It was reckless!'

'Whoa, Doc. You're not expressing an opinion, are you? You're not allowed to do that!' *Ha! Caught you!*

'I beg your pardon? When I see a patient acting in a manner that puts them in harm's way then I am obliged to comment. That was an electrical storm, Alan. You could have been struck by lightning. You could have been killed! Did you not realise that?'

'Yeah, well, I wasn't, was I? I was testing a theory,' I said.

'A theory? What theory was this?'

'I theorised that I would be unharmed by the storm. That I was, in fact, impervious to its effects.'

'And what if your "theory" had proved unfounded? Hmm?'

'Well, we wouldn't be having this conversation then, would we?'

'Alan, you need to take this seriously. You displayed reckless behaviour of which I did not believe you were capable. This is a matter of grave concern that needs to be addressed.' I remained silent. He might be breaking all the rules but I would adhere to *no question, no response.* 'I'm flabbergasted, Alan! What on Earth were you doing?'

'What do *you* think I was doing?' *Have some rule number two, Doc!*

'What do *I* think? I don't know *what* to think, that is the whole purpose of this discussion, to find that out.'

'Look, I got pissed off and squared up to the storm. It's no big deal!'

'Well, I think it is a big deal, Alan. A very big deal, indeed.'

'Well, *I* don't!' I said, wanting to end this line of discussion.

Acknowledging the apparent end-move in my argument, he tried a different tack. 'I'm aware that you and some of the other patients are regular patrons of the gymnasium. I've asked around and I have heard troubling reports of what seems to transpire while you are there.'

'I have no idea what you might have heard, but I deny it, nevertheless!' *I'm no grass.*

'I will be making further enquiries but that isn't what's important here. We still need to address your behaviour last night.' He wouldn't relent. *Still no question, Doc.* 'I'm afraid that some of our good work may have come undone.'

'Is that the way you're going to take this?' I said. I stood up to the storm, I can stand up to the doc.

'What do you mean, Alan?'

'I mean, is this your tactic? I'm going backwards now? I'm failing therapy? And then what? More drugs? Different drugs? Do I need more sessions with you, Doc? Is that it?'

'Alan, this is not helpful. You need ... '

'What do I *need*? Do I need to stay here for the rest of my life? I thought the whole point of all the therapy and all the drugs was for me to feel able to stand on my own two feet. Isn't that the object? The entire reason I am here is to enable me to *leave* here!'

'Now, Alan. I think you're getting a little agitated. You need ...'

'There you go with "need" again! I am not agitated, Doc. At long last I'm starting to see the light. There's only one thing I need. I need to get away from here and get on with my life. My life has been on hold since I've been here. Don't you see that what I'm doing here is pointless? It's just *sign language for the blind.*'

'What? Alan, you n ... you should consider what you're saying. It's not a decision to be taken lightly.' The doc sensed he was losing control of the session.

'No, it's time for me to say, "So long and thanks for everything". Cheers, Doc, you've given me the push I needed. I'll head off to my room to pack while you sort out the paperwork.' I stood up, grabbed the doc's hand and shook it with vigour before he realised what was happening. Smiling, I left the room.

I thought to visit Brains before I checked out. I would do him the courtesy of letting him know I was leaving and he could tell the others. I also needed to warn him that the activities in the gym were in the spotlight. I was pretty sure Dai would pass that message on; assuming he hadn't been given the boot. I felt bad that my actions had led to unwanted attention. I was confident Brains would work something out, dedicated scientist that he was. Perhaps it was time to take pillar number two into the great outdoors.

Hounded by ambivalence, I made my way to my room to pack. I was eager to leave but also anxious about what would meet me at my destination. Leaving wasn't the challenge; arriving was. Then, I thought, *Christ, even Nobby had the balls to leave.* At least I wouldn't be taking anyone's clothing with me. But of course, there wouldn't have been much point. Things in this place didn't fit my unique measurements anymore.

Chapter Twenty

And so I bid farewell to Glyndwr Mental Health Facility. After meeting with Brains, and wishing him luck, I decided that I would bid a more personal farewell to the rest of the gang. Hands were shaken but no tears were shed, as was proper. I even had enough time to do the rounds. Doc Friendly couldn't stop me leaving but he could slow the process, and he did. The doc wanted to conduct what he termed an "exit interview". But I remained firm in my resolve to leave, assuring the doc that our earlier session should be considered the exit interview he craved. Once again, he petitioned me to reconsider my decision, wanting me to take more time to understand the implications of my actions. I was not impolite, the doc had earned my respect, but I wouldn't be swayed. I had crossed a line that could not be uncrossed. I had acknowledged rules that should never have been acknowledged and in doing so I had rendered our contest unplayable.

Doc Friendly argued the case for my continued medication, reasoning that interruption could affect my treatment. I assured the doc that I would continue taking the meds, and I meant it. At last, grudgingly accepting my intention to depart, the doc advised that he was always available for consultation should I ever feel the need. He asked that I contact him if I felt that my ability to cope was being tested. I told the doc I would indeed contact him if I started feeling overwhelmed, but I did *not* mean that.

* * * *

There I was; back outside. This time, I was better prepared. Not yet ready to pick up the pieces but at least prepared to accept the consequences of ignoring those pieces. Nor was I yet willing to try to understand some of those pieces. Perhaps one day I'll try to figure out what I don't know. That may be easier. I'll identify the gaps in my knowledge to approximate where I should fear to tread. I'll be a spectator rather than a participant in a game that I'm ill-equipped to play.

I realised that much of what had happened to me had not been forced upon me. To a certain extent, I'd chosen to let it happen. It was time to accept responsibility. I stopped asking myself, *how could she have done this to me?* and asked instead, *how could I have let her do this to me?* I knew that my path was not set. I didn't have to let the memory of Juliette overwhelm me. This possibility provided a distant point towards which I could aim. I'd allowed Juliette to afford me a glimpse of a life that I hadn't known existed. Had Juliette led me on a journey, or had I followed irrespective of whether I had been invited as her companion? I was unable to gauge my level of culpability with accuracy. I thought: *C'mon, Lavelle, think of a fitting metaphor.*

How about this? I'd lived in a land of social simplicity, interacting from time to time with fellow students. Less casual with my cronies and with a flatmate of questionable worth. Nevertheless, I'd possessed the bare essentials for survival. I'd had a not uncomfortable existence, when considered holistically. I'd then met Juliette who had pointed to the shoreline of a different land. A land of hitherto unknown possibilities, where the physical and emotional topography spoke of the promise of happiness and belonging. I'd joined her in a vessel that I'd thought we had commissioned together; a two-seater relation-ship to take me from the land I knew, to the land I wanted. Halfway between the shores of *know* and *want*, she had cast me overboard. Had our relation-ship struck a relation-iceberg that I was incapable of perceiving? No rough seas; no leaking vessel, and yet I'd been consigned to the waters as jetsam. I'd watched as Juliette had abandoned me, navigating alone to the shore I was never destined to reach. It had been my decision to enter the vessel; to aspire to the greener land. It had *not* been my decision to abandon ship. That had been all on Juliette.

I'd turned back to the land in which I'd once been resident. The next decision had been mine alone. I had looked on familiar territory through new eyes. The land where I had once been content now appeared pale and barren compared to the glimpse of the unreachable, verdant foreign shore. I could have made my way back to the land that I'd known. It would have been easy; the current pushing me towards my home port. I could have chosen to tread water, allowing me to inevitably reach the familiar shore. But instead, as always, I'd chosen to do nothing. So I'd sunk, or at least I'd tried. Somehow I'd found myself – dishevelled and nearly drowned – back where I'd begun. *So, how could I use this?* Well, I could acknowledge that there is another land occupied by Juliette and other fortunates. I could also acknowledge that this land is a place I could never visit. But I could choose not to gaze upon it with envy. I would not look towards that other place. I would look inland to the familiar and if my eyes protested, I would close them.

How's that? Meh, laboured and more than a little pathmatic. Still, it was adequate for my purposes. So, could I forgive myself? *Perhaps; in time.* I'd been inexperienced and naïve. I shouldn't blame myself for being unable to foresee the unforeseeable. My self-hatred had proved to be self-serving and impotent; achieving nothing. Of greater importance, could I live with myself? *Yes, I was pretty sure I could.* It was living with others that I found challenging. Well then, I would live a secluded existence without completely isolating myself. I would resume my studies; mixing when I was obliged to mix. I would live alone. Without flatmates to regale me with tales of personal misfortune and to deprive me of consumables.

One of my first acts on returning to the flat was to contact the university administration, to advise of my current status. There were three letters from the university awaiting my return. I'd read them in chronological order, wanting to get the full story. The first had been questioning, the gist being, "Where are you?" The second had been cautionary: "You're running out of time, you need to do something." The third, and last, had been informative and dismissive; "We told you what would happen. You are now an ex-student." Reinstatement to the engineering faculty was not guaranteed, although my decent grades during the first year worked in my favour. A compulsory, but brief, interview with the faculty head was one requirement to further my application.

My grades had established proof of my capability but a discussion was needed to establish my disposition. I shared what I considered the minimum necessary to explain the reasons for my absence. Reasons that, I assured them, would never be inflicted upon me again. The interview concluded with success. Nevertheless, I was required to sit an examination to confirm I had retained knowledge of the first year syllabus. I was afforded three weeks in which to reacquaint myself with the subject matter. I sat the examination, quietly confident. I passed with decent margin, quietly pleased.

I returned as a second-year student. I had to negotiate a new set of classmates. My previous contemporaries were now starting their third-year studies. While I lost a year of study, my tardiness enabled me to avoid one particular awkwardness. Wazza the Cockney Wideboy was now a third-year student, having advanced just once in two attempts. We would see each other now and again, but would never speak. Nothing to say, nothing to hear. I contacted Doctor Jeffries to advise him of my intentions; it was the least I could have done. He was concerned at first that I'd left the controlled environment of the hospital in such a dramatic fashion. He was less concerned when I'd told him of my plans; placated in knowing I had not merely run away. I had a destination towards which I would travel.

So I found myself back in the familiar. I had rewound to a point in my life when I was once settled. I needed to ensure that I didn't repeat the same mistakes. Of course, there were always brand-new mistakes to be made.

* * * *

Two months into the first semester of the second year and I was satisfied with my progress. I caught up regularly with my old cohorts, sometimes to watch drunken students make their unsuccessful alcoholic forays into the world of romance. They never asked the awkward questions that the more socially confident might have asked. "Where have you been? What happened to you?" I was, of course, grateful for this concession. I had no answers to give. The course work was more challenging than the first year, but not overwhelming. I had ample time to devote to my studies and so I was comfortable. The emptiness remained within me. I was unable to escape my past unscathed. But I acknowledged the occasional sense of loss. I coped and I moved on. I maintained Doc Friendly's medication regime. He does know his meds, after all. They didn't appear to be harmful, so it was simpler to keep on keeping on.

I remained a loyal patron of the local supermarket, welcoming the auto-pilot shopping mode of old, lessening the chance of recalling things I didn't want to recall. As I returned to my flat, a bag of groceries in each hand, my thoughts turned to satisfying the needs of the beast in my belly. The needs of the beast in my head were not so pressing. Buying food always stimulated my appetite; hunger being a frequent but easily managed companion.

As I walked to the flat, I heard a noise behind me. The sound of someone clearing their throat. It was dark and when I turned I saw nothing. Then someone emerged from the shadows, someone big. He was tall and powerfully built; the sort of physique won through hard work in the gym. I didn't recognise him. I wondered if he was one of Warren's rugby buddies.

He moved closer, into the light. 'You must be Alan.' I didn't respond. He knew my name, was all I knew. He couldn't endure the silence. 'Don't you want to know who I am?'

Was this the time for *fight* or *flight*? I went with option three – *sit tight*. 'One of Warren's cronies?'

'Who? No. I'm Peter, with a *P* …'

'You're P?' Was this the writer and receiver of notes?

'So you saw the notes then? We wondered if you did.' *We?* He read my thoughts. '*We*, as in me and Juliette.' He waited for me to speak but I couldn't. I was processing. 'She never loved you. She never cared about you. We were fucking the whole time you were together.'

'Tell me something I don't know,' I said, suddenly weary.

'She sent me here. Bet you didn't know that, *Smartarse!*' I was unable to form words. 'This was her idea, you know? You think it was an accident, bumping into her at the supermarket? She knew you couldn't stop yourself. That you'd have to help her. She figured you out right from the start, like the chump you are.'

The question emerged unprompted. I couldn't restrain it. 'Why?'

'Why what?'

'Why … everything?'

'You are such a fucking idiot! Did you think someone like Juliette could ever be interested in someone like *you*? It was a scam; it was all for your money. You're worth a few quid, you know!' His words tumbled in my head. I could hear, but understanding took time.

'Fuck me; am I going to have to start from the beginning? Your dad was worth eight million when he died. You were his main beneficiary. Ruth wasn't happy. She reckoned she deserved more than the allowance he'd left her. When her son died she lost the only way she had to dispute the will. She told her friend Louise. Remember Louise – Ruth's best friend? Louise said she'd help. She even said her daughter could help. Guess who Louise's daughter is?'

'Juliette,' I said, barely audible. I thought I'd never say that name again.

'Well done!' He clapped, mocking me. 'Juliette came up with the whole plan. She worked out how to get rid of you. She's smart like that, but I guess you're seeing that now. Juliette found out everything she could about you, you pathetic fuck! She said it was so easy getting you totally dependent on her; to get you to fall in love with her.' At last it was starting to make sense. Gaps were being filled.

'Juliette said you're *mentally fragile*. She planted three testers before you found the one in the bathroom. She was never pregnant; she got them from hospital patients. Did you really think she'd chance falling pregnant to *you*? She knew you'd fall apart when she dumped you.' Of course, she'd been right. Juliette had lifted my physical and emotional being up to lofty heights so that the subsequent fall would be so much worse; the landing fatal. And she had been so very close to achieving her goal.

'Juliette has it all figured out with Ruth. Once you're out of the way and Ruth gets hold of the money, Juliette will get her cut. She'll never have to work again.' There was so much to take in, to process.

'She knew you'd try and top yourself; it runs in the family, after all. She didn't think you'd fail though, she didn't realise what a loser you are!'

'Runs in the family? What are you talking about? My dad died of a heart attack. He didn't kill himself.'

'Who's talking about your dad? Fuck! You don't know anything, do you? Your *mother* topped herself when she found out that your dad did the dirty on her with Ruth!'

The knowledge that my mother killed herself because of Dad's infidelity touched something inside me. A connection was made or broken; I couldn't tell. I heard a *plink* in my head, like the element of a light bulb yielding after one, final, desperate burst of light. But the light that went out was not a light that illuminated; it was a light that blinded. Then I saw. I had carried the guilt of my mother's death with me my entire life when it should have been my father's burden. But it wasn't over yet; Peter was still sharing.

'Juliette didn't send me here to educate you.' His hand disappeared behind his back and when it re-emerged he held a large hunting knife. 'She sent me here to *kill* you! Poor Alan. What a sad fuck. So much tragedy in his life and then he ends up the victim of a random mugging.'

Was this it? The shootout scene in the Western of my life? My final showdown? My moment of truth? He had me at a disadvantage. He was armed, whereas I was unprepared. Cheating bastard! I didn't react in the way he expected.

'Well; are you fucking deaf as well as fucking stupid?'

I finished processing.

Focus.

I resolved to reveal myself. I dropped the grocery bags and unbuttoned my shirt before also dropping it to the ground. Peter looked confused by this act. Uncertainty built as the situation evolved into something he could not anticipate. I lifted my hands waist-high as if to show Peter I was unarmed. But I wanted to show him that I *was* armed. I took my time to turn, standing up straight and tall, rolling my shoulders down and forward. I flexed and clenched the musculature of my back. I felt blood flow into dormant muscles as I allowed them to engorge, unhindered.

I exposed the monster on my back. I wasn't like others who carried their monster on the inside. They coated themselves in untruth; veneers of deceit. Like chocolate-covered turds. I carried my monster on the outside, exposed to all but myself. I allowed Peter time to absorb my magnificent, powerful, terrible aspect. I flexed wings of flesh. 'What do you see when you look at me?' I said.

When I faced him again, his expression had changed. I asked again, louder. 'What do you see when you look at me?'

'What? What the fuck are you talking about?' His cocky façade faded.

'*Do you see me?*' I screamed. He didn't answer. I allowed myself to feel something akin to pride as I noticed his arrogance was now absent. A look of doubt, perhaps tempered by fear, took over his expression.

Peter struggled to reconcile these unforeseen happenings. I resolved to assist him no further. I kept still. He saw me for who I was then, irrespective of whether I was recognised. In exposing myself, I'd made my move. The next step was his. The change in his expression spoke of a decision made; determination replaced confusion. He swapped the knife from right hand to left and back to right, gripping it with purpose. He took a step closer to me. Then another. Still, I didn't move.

He was quick on the draw. The speed at which he moved was deceptive for someone so big. But I too was quick. He expected me to recoil; to move away from the lunging knife, but I didn't. Instead I moved towards him. He was surprised but was still able to swing the knife towards me, stabbing me deep in my lower back. I felt flesh give way to the sharp steel; skin and tendon parted to admit the blade. It was a cold sensation; no pain yet, I wouldn't permit it.

It was the sole strike he made with the weapon. I wrapped my arms around him, trapping his arms against his sides. I grasped my hands together in the middle of his back. I held him motionless, offering a sense of the unyielding place in which he found himself. He struggled to move; dropping the knife, the sound of metal hitting concrete was as sharp as the blade itself. He struck my eyebrow with his head, bursting the flesh. I felt blood run down my face. But it was already over. I took his weight in my arms, restraining further movement.

Then ... I ... squeezed.

The monster engaged. Pistons pumped, cables thickened and strained. I closed my eyes and opened valves. I allowed all the humiliation and self-loathing, all the artifice and lies, every cheek turned, every tongue bitten, every name called, all the hatred and rejection and pain, all the emotional filth of my life to fuel my act. Too late, Peter realised the hopelessness of his condition, understanding the impossible strength of my embrace. 'What ... no ... no ...' He squealed as I crushed the life from him. His desperate keening turned into an inhuman gurgle as the air was forced from his lungs, never to return. I felt bones resist and then *snap* as they gave way; broken end grated against broken end. I heard joints *pop* as they yielded. As he fell silent, I heard another sound and I realised this sound was of my making. I would not be silenced. I *could not* be silenced. I howled, shaking with desperate rage.

I relinquished my hold. His lifeless body collapsed to the ground. The body that once consisted of flesh and bone, and something more, was now a skin-sack of offal and broken glass. His corporeal remains lay inert on the pavement, so obviously ruined and corrupted. I wondered if his spirit had finished its descent yet; surely on its way down. Perhaps I'd find out soon enough. I felt heavy. I couldn't stand. I sat down hard and lay back. I was cold and light-headed. The sharp pain of the wounds made itself known, now that I had time to acknowledge such things. As I lay on the path, life escaping from me, I thought: *All these years I asked* how *these things happened to me when I should have asked* why? I succumbed to the longing to close my eyes. I was so very tired.

It was inevitable that I'd ended up in this place. It had been too late for Peter when he'd confronted me. Too late when he'd revealed the devastating truth of my family; of my life. The final tableau was inescapable from the moment Juliette had snared me in her trap. I had been a dull moth to her bright flame. Everything that had led up to this point, this point in which I *belonged*, was irrelevant. Live a lifetime to experience just one moment and then live a lifetime *in* that one moment.

The one thing that mattered was that I lay there, darkness leaking into the gutter, slowing as the unrestrained pressure of release dropped. My final thought: *Huh, what do you know? No-one gets to ride off into the sunset in my Western!*

Cold, then. Black …

Chapter Twenty-One

Sergeant Perkins knew he'd done something to upset the chief. Every time a non-job cropped up, he was pulled from the roster to meet the need. *Need someone in the early hours of the morning to sit around waiting at the local hospital? Perkins is your man!* Christ, he was bored. He knew he was a token presence at best. Procedures required a police presence at the hospital when a coronial inquest was on the cards. *Chain of Custody issues.* Bloody waste of time! A young nurse wandered by, the corridor so quiet he could hear the rustling of her starched uniform as she walked. He even got a smile. *Not bad*, he thought. At least a seven and the uniform doesn't do any harm. He watched her all the way to the end of the corridor until she passed through the door. Sgt. Perkins wished he was a doctor. Even though they work longer hours than a copper, they get paid heaps better. Plus they have perks; all the nurses they can eat.

The distraction passed; his thoughts returned to the chief. Why was he pissed with him? Maybe he heard about the joke he told the lads about the chief leg-humping the new female constable. Everyone could see he was gagging to get into her. He was like a horny little puppy every time he saw her. He fawned all over her, doing everything to get in there bar climbing into her pants. No, it must be something else. It wasn't only him; everyone talked about that at the station. Did the chief think Perkins was responsible for the scratch on his new Jag? Of course, Perkins *was* responsible, but he was pretty sure he'd covered his tracks. That area of the carpark wasn't covered by CCTV. Or was it? It wasn't his fault. Well, not altogether. The chief didn't know how to park. He should get a smaller car. Or a bike.

He heard the swing doors open and turned, hoping to see the nurse returning. *Maybe I'll chat her up this time. Nothing better to do.* He was greeted by the far less attractive sight of his nemesis, Chief Inspector Dixon, bearing down. Perkins should have expected that. At three in the morning, the only thing that gets the chief out of bed was death or the prospect of promotion. Of course, the chief was in a foul mood. *Try sitting here for the last six hours,* Perkins thought. Perkins stood to attention as the chief approached. 'Morning, Chief.'

'Yes, yes. Perkins, isn't it?' he said. His expression was drawn and tired, failing to hide his displeasure at being called out at such an unpleasant hour.

'Yes, sir.'

'Well?' the chief said.

'Sir?'

'What news is there? You must have something to share with me, Perkins, or am I wasting my time?' he said.

'Well, sir. I have the preliminary coroner's report,' Perkins said as he reached for a folder from the chair. *You arrogant arsehole!*

'And? What does it say?'

Perkins opened the folder and skipped to the summary. 'Deceased's name is Peter Wilson. The coroner found evidence of multiple fractures to both arms and collar bones. Both shoulders dislocated. Four crushed vertebrae. Eight fractured ribs. A punctured lung and penetrative wound to the heart. Initial cause of death thought to be cardiac arrest. He's pretty confident of the findings, sir.'

'And how did the deceased die? What hit him?'

'Well, sir. The coroner did say the injuries sustained were consistent with a victim of an industrial accident. However, initial investigations suggest that the deceased was involved in an altercation with the second party. It appears that the second party, well … crushed him to death, sir.'

'Are you telling me someone fatally *hugged* him?' the chief asked.

'The coroner believes so, sir, and the evidence supports that estimation.'

'And where is the second party?'

'Name of Alan Lavelle. He got out of surgery a few hours ago. He sustained some injuries. Fourteen stitches to a head wound and surgery to repair penetrative trauma sustained to his side and back. They think they've saved his kidney, but they'll need to keep an eye on it. He needed a major transfusion; he'd lost a lot of blood.' Perkins didn't need to refer to his notes. He remembered what had happened to Lavelle.

'And how did Mr Lavelle sustain his injuries?'

'The evidence suggests Lavelle and the deceased were involved in an altercation. It appears that the deceased stabbed and struck Lavelle. We dusted the knife found at the scene that confirmed the deceased alone had handled the weapon. The blood on the blade matches Lavelle. It appears that after Lavelle was attacked, he crushed the deceased with his bare hands.'

'*With his bare hands?* Have you got a statement from him yet? What has he got to say? Is he claiming self-defence?'

'No, sir. He refuses to make a statement. In fact, he refuses to talk. All he said was that he'll only speak to a Doctor Fenty, out of Glyndwr Hospital.' Perkins recalled talking to Lavelle. His recovery from the anaesthetic had been abnormal. He'd come around almost at once, no sign of grogginess or not knowing where he was. That was usually the best time to get them talking, when they might let something slip. But this guy; he'd been instantly aware. He'd just said he wanted to speak to this doctor, repeated it once and then fell silent. Then he'd stared at the wall, like he was somewhere else.

'Has anyone contacted this doctor?'

'Yes, sir. I made contact about an hour ago. He lives in North Wales. He's an hour and a half away. He should be here in about thirty minutes.'

'Yes, I can work that out myself. I'm not stupid!' *You fucking are!*

'Wait here and when this doctor arrives, see if you can convince him to get some answers to this mess. Think you can do that?'

'Of course, sir.' *Fuck you, sir!*

'Right, well there's nothing more I can do here, so I'll be off. We'll catch up later when, I hope, you have something to tell me.'

'Right you are, sir.' *Don't crash your Jag on the way home to your warm bed, you ignorant fuck!*

Perkins watched the chief retreat through the swing doors, glaring at him all the way. He was happy to see the back of him but not looking forward to the inevitable follow-up discussion. He was also thankful he didn't have to interview Lavelle. There was something not quite right about him; something he couldn't put his finger on. It wasn't simply his odd physique; a physique that suggested hidden capabilities. Perkins had seen the body of the other guy. It was all bent out of shape. It looked *wrong*. The dead guy was big and his insides were totally shredded. Whoever did that to him was something more than simply dodgy.

But it was the expression on Lavelle's face that gave Perkins the jitters. He'd seen both victims and perpetrators of violent crimes. Often they had this strange expression that suggested an absence of consciousness; of dissociation from the incident. Lavelle was different. There was something odd happening in his head. There was activity behind those eyes that troubled Perkins. No, let this Doctor Fenty character speak to him.

Now, where's that nurse?

* * * *

I found myself in yet another fucking hospital! I wondered if there was such a scheme as "Frequent Patient Points". I must have accumulated enough points to own a really expensive piece of equipment. Perhaps an MRI scanner. Christ, I might even have enough to merit my own hospital wing. Indeed, I seemed to be the solitary patient in this part of the hospital. I had a big room all to myself and I even had personal security. The policeman that had spoken to me in the recovery room was posted outside. I could see him through the glass panel in the door when he got up now and again. He didn't look happy. I hoped he hadn't been too offended when I told him I'd only speak to Doc Friendly. I'd needed time to gather my thoughts and I hadn't trusted myself to be adequately equipped to speak to a police official. Plus, I hadn't felt inclined to *trust* the police official. Couldn't be too cautious, given my circumstances.

I knew he was dead. I'd overheard the policeman discussing *the deceased*. Even if I hadn't overheard him, the image of Peter lying on the pavement was behind my eyelids, revealed every time I closed them. It was obvious from the way his body looked there was a complete absence of life. I wasn't sure how I felt about that. I didn't want to analyse what the consequences might be right then. That's why I'd asked for Doc Friendly. One more session, to play a different game. No rulebook this time. It would be the session that defined our relationship, professional and otherwise.

Think of the devil! I could see Doc Friendly talking to Sergeant Happy outside the door. The doc was doing most of the listening at first. He nodded his head, his smile the picture of approachability, as the policeman talked. When the doc responded I could see his hands moving about at the bottom of the glass panel. He was a lot more animated than the copper. I knew their discussion was over when I saw the doc raise both hands before him, palms forward. That was his signature move when he considered the conversation terminated. Sure enough, the door opened and the doc walked in, looking concerned; his most sympathetic smile was in place.

'My goodness, Alan! I was told you'd been involved in some sort of altercation. How are you?'

'Hi, Doctor Fenty. Thanks for coming. Yeah, I'm doing okay ... considering.'

The doc grabbed a chair from against the wall and carried it to the side of the bed. He sat. 'The sergeant told me you wanted to speak to me. In fact, he told me you wouldn't speak to anyone *but* me.'

'That's right. Look, Doc, it wasn't my fault this time. I didn't want any of this. I tried, Doc. I really tried!' I was shocked by the sudden emotion that constricted my throat.

'It's okay, Alan. I'm here for you. We can speak about whatever you want. The police asked me to gather information about the incident, but I told them I'm here for *you*, not for *them*. And I mean that, Alan. You can say as much or as little as you want. It's up to you.' He took my hand in his. I squeezed his hand with care, letting him know that I appreciated the contact.

And then … I talked.

I told him *everything*. I held nothing back; no detail too small. I talked like I had never talked before. I talked as if I would never talk again. I told him about my school days; the hostility and ostracism. I told him all about my father; his life, his transgression, his guilt, his capitulation … his love. I told him of my anger, my disappointment; my crushing remorse. I told him all about Ruth and Kevin. How they inflicted themselves on our once idyllic life. I told him of their duplicity; their insidious malevolence. I told him everything about my part in Kevin's death. I told him about Juliette; the pleasure and the pain, the rejection … the loss, the loss, the loss. I told him about the confrontation with Peter; about the revelations that shattered my perspective forever. I told him about the pact, the deception and my unknowing part in it all. I even told him about Gelert.

I don't know how long I talked for but it must have been hours. When I looked up, a different policeman was at the door and light streamed through the window. Throughout my discourse, I had sipped at my glass of water, to counter the dryness in my throat. The water jug was empty by the time I'd finished.

The doc made a few encouraging comments when I began but he soon fell silent, his role solely that of the listener. By the time I was done, he'd removed his glasses. He wasn't smiling. He hadn't smiled for some time. The silence drew out. I had nothing more to say. Doc Friendly didn't know *what* to say.

Then I thought, *How about that? The act of unburdening has had an unexpected consequence. The emptiness that filled me for so long … has gone.*

Epilogue

Report Extracts

This report has been prepared at the request of David Hughes, Senior Partner of Hughes and Hughes, the Representative of Alan John Lavelle.

I have prepared this report on the understanding that it may be used in consideration of mounting a defence against criminal proceedings (decision pending) that may be initiated against Alan John Lavelle.

In preparation of this report I have relied upon the following information:

- Documents
  - Patient records from the files of Doctor Graham Fenty, Chief of Psychiatry, Glyndwr Mental Health Facility.
- Interviews and Observations
  - On 3rd of the inst., I interviewed Mr Alan John Lavelle at Leicester General Hospital.
  - On 15th of the inst., I interviewed Mr Alan John Lavelle at Glyndwr Mental Health Facility.
  - On 16th of the inst., I interviewed Dr Barry Jeffries, MD, at Glyndwr Mental Health Facility.

Clinical Assessment

Alan presents with low levels of neuroticism, which is confirmed by the results of his personality testing (refer Appendix 3 for full personality testing results). He presents as private and introspective.

It is clear that he is a sensitive individual who has been impacted by a number of adverse events in his life. In particular, the death of his father was a defining incident. It is to Alan's credit that he has endured this event and has expressed a determination to make his father proud.

Alan is introverted. While he does not actively seek out the company of others he is nevertheless comfortable mixing in social settings. Alan advised that since the first year of his university studies he has a number of classmates with whom he regularly socialises.

Alan is currently coming to terms with the events of the night of the 2nd. His recollection of the events, and his advice relating to the background leading up to the events, appear to be complex. While it is not within my brief to comment on the legal implications of the events, it is apt that I provide commentary relating to how these events have affected Alan. The events are in part connected to the breakup of a romantic relationship that resulted in significant impacts to Alan, to such an extent that Alan attempted suicide. Following this attempt, Alan was admitted to Glyndwr Mental Health Facility as an in-patient. Alan responded well to treatment, but it should be stressed that the treatment consists of long-term measures, including ongoing therapy.

Alan has spoken freely about the events of the night of the 2nd, which is encouraging. In addition to the physical impact of injuries he sustained, Alan was subjected to mental trauma, brought about by the disclosure of a number of facts previously unknown to him. These facts relate to the failed romantic relationship and to circumstances relating to the death of his mother (she died when Alan was eleven months old). Alan is still coming to terms with both the physical and mental impacts of that night.

Conclusion and Recommendations

Alan enjoys good physical health and is recovering well from the injuries he sustained on the night of the 2nd.

Alan does not have a history of substance abuse. He advised that he enjoys an occasional alcoholic drink when socialising with his university colleagues.

Alan is financially secure. He is the beneficiary of a significant trust fund, founded by his father and administered by Doctor Barry Jeffries.

Alan has a history of mental health issues, suffered intermittently over the last four years. Until two months ago, he had been an in-patient of the Glyndwr Mental Health Facility for a period of approximately ten months, before discharging himself to resume his engineering studies. Alan had made satisfactory progress relating to the issues that he had at the time of admission (attempted suicide).

Alan has regular contact with Doctor Barry Jeffries who is a family friend. Doctor Jeffries remains close to Alan. He has stated his willingness and ability to continue supporting him, both in his capacity as fund administrator and as family friend. Alan understands the importance of this relationship and has expressed his intention to maintain his connection to Doctor Jeffries.

In my opinion, at this time, Alan is not a risk to himself, or others. There remain, however, outstanding issues relating to the impacts of the night of the 2nd on Alan's mental health. In order to ensure Alan's successful rehabilitation, it is essential that he lives in a secure and structured environment, close to supportive resources. In the immediate term, I recommend that Alan be admitted as an in-patient to the Glyndwr Mental Health Facility. His previous admissions have demonstrated his ability to react positively to the support provided.

I believe that the outlook for Alan's future is positive. He is physically healthy and financially secure. He is determined and capable of excelling at his studies and his results to date suggest he is on target to achieve a high-level Engineering Honours degree. He has demonstrated success in responding positively to therapy and I have no reason to doubt that this will also be the case for his most recent issues, relating to the events of the 2nd.

Doctor Graham Fenty
MB, ChB, DPM (Eng), FRCP, FRC (Psych)

* * * *

Things seem … different now. My surroundings are familiar, but I have changed. When I walk, I sense a subtle alteration to my perspective. My view is not quite the same. I have cast off some of my self-consciousness. I stand taller and straighter. I am more accepting of my bearing. I feel changed in other ways too; changes that are harder to define.

Some say that people can't change but I don't believe that. I believe people can't help *but* change; that in fact people cannot persist. I'm starting to believe that a life is made up of living through many versions of ourselves. Versions that are being modified, over and over again, by our experiences. Conscious life is not described by "birth, then life, then death". I believe that *Big Life* is enclosed between *Initial Birth* and *Final Death* and that our lives are composed of a series of unceasing smaller deaths and births. We live a series of *Little Lives*.

Most external changes happen over a long period, discernible if you refrain from constantly studying your outer self. Others will weigh your exterior, as they have mine. Internal changes that alter the spirit can be much quicker. Sometimes they are instantaneous. The act of discovery can be like giving birth to new sensations or convictions. It can also be akin to death, when the discovery destroys a previously held belief or understanding. Sometimes birth is savage and death is tender.

Consider those who go to war. Some come back as someone less. Some come back as someone more. All come back as someone changed.

* * * *

I sit on my bed, reading. I hear a knock and look up to see the doc standing in the doorway. He taps his watch. 'Don't forget our appointment in ten minutes, Alan,' he says. I look at him, studying his expression. His smile is genuine; it's genial and I find it reassuring. I nod my head by way of acknowledging his comment, but I say nothing.

I am Silent.

Mick Gallogly is a product of Ireland, assembled in England, shipped to Wales before being imported to Australia where he currently lives. The middle-aged refugee of the mining industry started his working life at fifteen when he was employed shifting gear between stalls at a market. It's all been downhill since then. *Outside-in* is his first novel.

www.ingramcontent.com/pod-product-compliance
Lightning Source LLC
Chambersburg PA
CBHW071247170626
46809CB00001B/116